RESOUNDING PRAISE FOR
*NEW YORK TIMES* BESTSELLING AUTHOR

# J.A. JANCE

"J.A. Jance is among the best—
if not the best."
*Chattanooga Times*

"In the elite company of Sue Grafton
and Patricia Cornwell."
*Flint Journal*

"J.A. Jance does not disappoint."
*Washington Times*

"Crime and characters are the lifeblood
of Jance's books."
*Portland Oregonian*

"Jance's [novels] show up on bestseller lists . . .
One can see why."
*Milwaukee Journal Sentinel*

"[Readers] are enthralled by Jance's ability
to infuse life (and death) into her books . . .
Evidence shows that J.A. Jance is a hit."
*The Columbian (WA)*

## Books by J. A. Jance

*Joanna Brady Mysteries*

DESERT HEAT • TOMBSTONE COURAGE
SHOOT/DON'T SHOOT • DEAD TO RIGHTS
SKELETON CANYON • RATTLESNAKE CROSSING
OUTLAW MOUNTAIN • DEVIL'S CLAW
PARADISE LOST • PARTNER IN CRIME
EXIT WOUNDS

*J.P. Beaumont Mysteries*

UNTIL PROVEN GUILTY • INJUSTICE FOR ALL
TRIAL BY FURY • TAKING THE FIFTH
IMPROBABLE CAUSE • A MORE PERFECT UNION
DISMISSED WITH PREJUDICE • MINOR IN POSSESSION
PAYMENT IN KIND • WITHOUT DUE PROCESS
FAILURE TO APPEAR • LYING IN WAIT
NAME WITHHELD • BREACH OF DUTY
BIRDS OF PREY • PARTNER IN CRIME
LONG TIME GONE

*and*

HOUR OF THE HUNTER • KISS OF THE BEES
DAY OF THE DEAD

# J.A. JANCE
# NAME WITHHELD

## AVON BOOKS
*An Imprint of HarperCollinsPublishers*

AVON BOOKS
*An Imprint of* HarperCollins*Publishers*
10 East 53rd Street
New York, New York 10022-5299

Copyright © 1996 by J. A. Jance
ISBN: 0-380-71842-1
www.avonbooks.com

First Avon Books paperback printing: March 1997
First Avon Books hardcover printing: January 1996

Avon Trademark Reg. U.S. Pat. Off. and in Other Countries, Marca Registrada, Hecho en U.S.A.
HarperCollins® is a registered trademark of HarperCollins Publishers Inc.

Printed in the U.S.A.

20 19 18 17

To Cessa, and also in memory of Linda Howard

# Prologue

With Seattle's New Year's fireworks display due to begin soon, the Peters girls—nine-year-old Heather and ten-year-old Tracy—and I shut down our Uno game at twenty minutes before midnight. While Tracy put away the cards, Heather and I retreated to my penthouse condo's kitchen to prepare our celebratory New Year's drink—Thomas Kemper root beer floats.

This was a first for me. Back in my boozing days, if I had still been standing by the time New Year's toasts rolled around, you can bet I wouldn't have been swilling down root beer or champagne, either. MacNaughton's and water would have been far more like it. Even sober, root beer wasn't my first choice, but the girls had overruled me on that score.

Their dad, Ron Peters, is an ex-partner of mine, although we've been friends now for far longer

than we were ever partners on the homicide
squad down at Seattle P.D. He and Amy, his second wife and the girls' stepmother, had splurged
on one of those hotel sleep-over New Year's din-
ner/dance affairs. With Ron in his wheelchair
and Amy six and a half months pregnant, I'm
sure the romance end was far more important
than either the drinking or the dancing. I suppose
they saw their New Year's night on the town as
one last prebaby fling.

For my part, I was glad to step in and play
uncle for the evening, letting the girls spend the
night in the spare bedroom of my condo in downtown Seattle. We had ordered pizza, watched a
couple of videos (why someone doesn't strangle
that little brat in *Home Alone* I and II I'll never
know!) and played several hands of killer Uno,
all of which Tracy won without even trying.

Out in the kitchen, I ladled scoops of ice cream
into partially filled glasses while Heather, frowning in concentration, carefully added enough root
beer to fill the three glasses with foam without
ever overflowing any of them.

"Did you know my mom's coming back from
Nicaragua?" she asked pensively.

Actually, I did. Women are forever complaining about how men never talk about anything important. Loosely translated, that means anything
personal. Generally, they're right. We don't—not
to women and usually not to each other, either.

There is, however, one major exception to that
rule. In the not so exclusive fraternity of divorced-

wounded men, when it comes to comparing notes on the unreasonableness or capriciousness of ex-wives, man-to-man discussions can and do take place. They tend to turn into impromptu contests—sort of "My ex-wife did this and can you top it" kinds of competitions.

With what was going on down in California, where my ex-wife, Karen, was battling cancer, I wasn't really playing that game anymore. That fact hadn't kept Ron from crying on my shoulder when his ex-wife, Roslyn, had resurfaced after a two-year hitch with some far-out "Holy Roller" commune down in Central America.

Earlier that week, minutes after opening a letter from his ex-wife, an agitated, grim-faced Ron Peters had wheeled his chair into my office on the fifth floor of the Public Safety Building.

"Damn it!" he had grumbled, waving the paper in the air. "Roz is coming back."

"So?" I had returned. It's easy to be unconcerned when the ex-wife in question bears no relation to you whatsoever.

Actually, that isn't true. I did have a remote connection to Roslyn Peters—as a benefactor. Years earlier, I had stepped in to provide a large chunk of the initial seed money that had shipped her and some of her New Dawn associates off on a mission. They had left Broken Springs, Oregon, and headed down to Nicaragua to establish an outpost for their particular brand of religion among the urban poor in the city of Managua. I provided fully deductible mission "grant money." At least that's what my tax return said.

Realistically, my "grant" was nothing more or less than a bribe. In return for a sizable check to the charity of her choice, Roz Peters had relinquished custody of the girls to Ron, their father. Ralph Ames, my Mr. Fix-It attorney, had brokered the deal with the attorney from New Dawn. On the face of it, that sounds pretty heartless—as though the kids went up for grabs, as though they were wrested from a caring, loving mother and auctioned off to the highest bidder. The reality was a little different from that.

New Dawn isn't the worst cult there's ever been. As far as I know, nobody's died in it, or because of it, so far. And when I came up with the idea of getting the girls back and asked Ralph to see what he could do, he set off for Broken Springs, muttering a string of weasel words and saying the whole scheme didn't stand a chance in hell. But once he got there and saw how things were—the primitive housing and sleeping arrangements as well as what passed for hygiene, food, and medical care—he turned into a regular legal tiger. He raised so much hell that the New Dawn attorney couldn't get him out of town fast enough. When Ralph came back to Seattle from Oregon, the girls came with him.

"Well," I had said to Peters the previous week, "I suppose it was bound to happen eventually. You didn't expect her to stay down there forever, did you?"

"I had hoped," Ron said, his black look telling me that he had much preferred having the better part of a continent between himself and his ex-wife.

"According to her, New Dawn is planning to start a mission down in Tacoma," he continued. "They're taking over a derelict old church down in Hilltop."

In recent years, Hilltop has turned into a volatile multiracial neighborhood, the kind every American city seems to have these days. Similar in racial and socioeconomic makeup to Seattle's Rainier Valley, Hilltop has been plagued with more than its fair share of violence and gang warfare. It shows up in newspaper articles and on television news broadcasts, usually in conjunction with stories recounting the sad aftermath of yet another drive-by shooting or drug deal gone bad. It's the kind of place where armed kids insist on using other kids—preferably unarmed ones—for target practice.

"Roz is a grown-up," I had counseled. "If she wants to be an urban missionary, let her do her thing. Besides, some of those shooters and drug addicts down there might actually benefit from a close encounter with a missionary."

"By the way, you're not allowed to call her Roz anymore," Peters said. "Her name is Constance now—Sister Constance. And being a good and loving Christian, she's coming home to take me to court. She's going to sue for joint custody."

"Don't tell me she's planning to take the girls

along with her to Hilltop!" I echoed, my own dismay now mirroring Ron's.

"That's the general idea," Peters said. "When is Ralph Ames due back in town?"

"On the third. He and Mary are off on a Caribbean cruise. As soon as I hear from him, I'll clue him in on what's happening."

Now, though, standing in my midnight kitchen and faced with Heather's calm pronouncement, I searched for a way to sound relatively noncommittal. "Really," I said.

Heather nodded. "And she wants Tracy and me to come live with her."

"Down in Tacoma? Is that something you want to do?" I asked.

"Well," Heather replied pointedly. "She *is* our mother, you know."

Her answer didn't leave me much of a comeback. "Hurry up, you guys," Tracy called from the living room balcony. "It's almost time for the fireworks to start."

I carried the tray of foaming drinks outdoors and set it on the table on the chilly lanai. Without having to be told, the girls both bundled themselves into coats. After my recent bout with pneumonia, I did the same. I stepped outside just as the radio countdown ended and the first pyrotechnic blasts boomed off the top of the Space Needle, sending bursts of red and blue sparks cascading over the city. With the barrage of fireworks lighting the sky overhead, the girls and

I clinked glasses and wished one another a Happy New Year.

Heather and Tracy turned back to the display, their eyes alive with excitement. Watching my little charges, I felt a sudden surge of regret rather than joy that left me unable to share their childish wonder. For them, the start of a new year still meant beginnings. For me, this coming new year threatened the very likely possibility of yet another whole series of wrenching endings, not the least of which was the likelihood of losing track of the girls themselves.

Much as that would hurt, I could still see that it was really none of my affair.

*Stop being such a meddlesome, selfish dolt*, I told myself firmly. *Knock it off, and stay out of other people's business.*

Then, as yet another huge bouquet of fiery orange and yellow mums rose in the air and filled the nighttime sky with light and smoke, I realized that my focus on losing Heather and Tracy's sunny day-to-day presence was a way of avoiding what else was going on in my life right then— another countdown in far-off Rancho Cucamonga, California, where Karen, my first wife, was suffering through the final stages of cancer. That painful realization hurt so much that, for the first time in weeks, I wanted a drink. A real drink. Fortunately, I didn't have any booze in the house, and taking care of the girls precluded my setting off in search of some.

With the fireworks' mortars still booming

through the night, I took my glass, went back inside, and sank down into my recliner. The girls bounded into the room a few minutes later, their eyes alight with glee, their cheeks glowing pink from the frosty outside air.

"What's the matter, Uncle Beau?" Heather asked. "Didn't you like the fireworks?"

"They were fine," I said. "I came inside because I got cold."

I didn't try to explain that the chill I was feeling was one that came from the inside out, rather than the other way around.

# One

I was showered, dressed, and had rousted the girls out of bed for breakfast when the telephone rang at eight-ten the next morning. We had planned a New Year's Day outing to the Woodland Park Zoo, but a call from Seattle P.D. immediately put that plan in jeopardy.

"Happy New Year," Sergeant Chuck Grayson said jovially. "Hope I didn't wake you."

Murder doesn't necessarily observe holidays, so even on New Year's Day, Homicide Squad shifts had to be covered. As a single man with no local family obligations and a take-it-or-leave-it attitude toward football, I had volunteered to be on call the first of January. That was long before I had accepted an overnight baby-sitting assignment with Heather and Tracy.

"Happy New Year to you, too," I answered. "I

may be up, but I'm not necessarily at 'em. What's going on?"

"We've got a floater right there in your neighborhood. Just off Pier Seventy," Grayson answered. "Since it's just down the hill from Belltown Terrace, I thought it might save time if you went there directly, rather than coming down here first."

"Sure thing," I said. "No problem."

I put down the phone and turned back to the girls, who were happily shoveling their way through bowls of Frosted Flakes. Under Amy's diplomatic influence, Ron Peters has somewhat modified his stringent health food stance, but from the ecstatic greeting the girls had given my box of sugar-coated cereal, I had to assume that for them, Frosted Flakes were a rare and welcome treat.

"You have to go to work, right?" Tracy asked, sighing in disappointment.

"Yes." I drained the last slurp of coffee out of the bottom of my cup.

"Does that mean we won't be going to the zoo?"

"At least not this morning," I said. "We'll have to see about this afternoon. In the meantime, you can watch the Rose Bowl Parade on television. That should be fun."

Heather made a face. "Parades on TV are *boring*. They're lots more fun in person."

Influenced by the two recently viewed *Home Alone* nightmare videos, visions of my pristine condo destroyed by child-produced mayhem danced through my head.

"I'm sorry to leave you by yourselves like this. Your folks have a late checkout, so they probably won't be home before four or five. You won't get in any trouble, now, will you?"

"We'll be fine," Tracy said.

"You know how to run the TV. I want you both to stay right here in the apartment until I get back. There's microwave popcorn in the cupboard, bread, peanut butter and jelly . . ."

"And lots more root beer," Heather added.

I knew the girls to be relatively self-sufficient. For one thing, this is a secure building, and when both their parents are at work (Amy is a physical therapist at Harborview Hospital), the girls do spend some time alone. I knew, for instance, that in the event of an emergency, they had been told to notify the doorman. Even so, I felt that by leaving them on their own I was being somewhat derelict in my baby-sitting duty. "With any luck, maybe we'll still be able to go to the zoo later this afternoon."

The girls exchanged eye-rolling glances that said they didn't consider that a very likely possibility. Battling a certain amount of lingering guilt, I finished strapping on my semiautomatic and headed out the door.

From Belltown Terrace, my condo building at the corner of Second Avenue and Broad, to the murder scene at Pier 70 on Elliott Bay is a straight shot of only four blocks. Some people might scoff at the idea of my getting the 928 out of the underground garage and driving there, but in Seattle distances can be deceiving. Taking the glacial ridges into consideration, four downhill blocks going down are a whole lot shorter than the uphill ones coming back.

The few minutes in the car gave me a chance to shift gears, to go from a cozy holiday-type atmosphere into a work mind-set, where man's inhumanity to man is the order of the day.

I found the entrance to the pier itself was blocked by a phalanx of official vehicles. Some were from the department, some were emergency fire and Medic One vans, but a fairly large number were of the ever-present and ever-circling news media variety. Dodging through the crush as best I could, I met up with Audrey Cummings, the assistant medical examiner, on the far side of the yellow crime-scene tape. The two of us walked down the thick, creosote-impregnated wooden planks together.

The assistant M.E. was in a foul mood. "Dragging some drowned New Year's Eve reveler out of the drink isn't exactly how I had planned to spend my day," she groused.

Dr. Audrey Cummings is short, stout, somewhere above the half-century mark, and not to be trifled with. She usually shows up at crime scenes looking far more like a lady accountant than she does a medical examiner. This time, however, instead of her trademark crisp blouse, wrinkle-free blazer and skirt, and sensible heels, she wore a pair of plaid wool slacks, loafers, and a leather jacket. For her to appear at a crime scene dressed that casually, it was clear she really had intended to take the day off.

A little knot of officers was gathered along the edge of the pier. We made our way through them just in time to see a dripping, fully clothed corpse be lifted from the Harbor Patrol police boat and deposited faceup on the dock. The victim, clad in a sodden wool suit, appeared to me to be a late-thirties Caucasian male.

"What did I tell you?" Audrey said, in a supposedly private aside to me. "That's one drowned rat if I ever saw one."

One of the Harbor Patrol officers, Rich Carlson, clambered up on the pier. He nodded in my direction. "Wouldn't count on that if I were you, Doc," he said to Audrey. "Most drowning victims I've seen don't turn up with bullet holes in the backs of their heads."

"A bullet hole?" Audrey repeated.

Carlson nodded. "It's small enough that it can't have been a very high caliber weapon, but at close range, it doesn't take much."

Stepping up to the corpse, Audrey Cummings squatted beside the sodden body, gazing at the dead man respectfully but curiously, with the watchful, no-nonsense demeanor that, in the gruesome world of medical examiners, must pass for bedside manner.

"How long ago was he spotted?" Audrey asked.

"Not very long," Rich answered. "A female jogger noticed him in the water just after sunrise. Her name's Johnny something-or-other. You should be able to get her name and address from dispatch. We found him wedged against one of the pilings under the pier. It took a while for us to drag him back out into the open."

While Audrey did her thing, I, along with several uniformed officers, searched the pier and areas of nearby Myrtle Edwards Park. As far as I was concerned, the possibility of finding any relevant evidence seemed remote. Considering the impact of currents out in the bay, the victim could have been murdered miles from where he'd been found. Still, we went through the motions of treating the whole area as an official "crime scene."

The other officers were still combing the area when Audrey finished with her preliminary examination. I hurried back over to where she stood, stripping off a pair of latex gloves. "Any I.D.?" I asked.

She shook her head. "Our Mr. John Doe has no I.D., no wallet, no money, and no rings on him, although he's worn two rings recently. One is missing from his left ring finger, and one from the right. His watch is gone, too."

"So we may be talking robbery here, or else that's what we're supposed to think. And chances are, our victim was a married man."

"Chances are," Audrey agreed.

"Rich was right about the bullet hole?"

Audrey shuddered and nodded. "Unfortunately, yes."

I looked at her warily. Crime scenes don't usually affect her that way. "What's the matter?" I asked.

"Remember back a few months ago when I took that leave of absence?"

"Yes."

"I worked for two weeks as a volunteer in Bosnia, trying to identify the bodies that were found outside a Muslim enclave that had been overrun by the Serbs. Those two weeks gave me a whole new understanding of the words *execution-style slaying.*"

"And that's what this is?"

"Looks like it to me."

I could see that the murder had affected Audrey in a way she hadn't expected. "Any sign of a struggle?" I asked, hoping that answering routine questions might help Dr. Cummings regain her composure.

She shrugged. "The body's been in the water for some time—several hours, anyway. The abrasions we're seeing could be from a struggle of some kind, or they could be from being washed around on rocks and/or pilings."

At the street end of the pier, a slate-gray van, part of the medical examiner's fleet, edged around the barrier and started down the dock. A television-camera truck tried to follow but was headed off by a uniformed patrol officer. Sighting the van, Audrey pulled herself together. "We'll get him loaded up and out of here, then."

"Anything else you can tell me that might help us hook him up with a missing person's report?"

"Blue eyes, blond hair, six one or so. Tattoo on the inside of his right wrist. It says MOTHER."

"Not very original," I said.

"They never are."

I waited until the body was loaded in the van. When they left, so did I. It crossed my mind that it had to be a slow news day in Seattle with nothing much to fill up the allotted airtime, since a flock of television cameras stood waiting on the sidewalk when I made it back to Alaskan Way. One of the reporters, a woman, came tripping behind me like a puppy nipping at my heels as I headed back to the car.

"Detective Beaumont," she called after me. "Can you tell us whether or not this shooting is gang related?"

*Who told you it was a shooting?* I wanted to ask her. *And, who said anything about gangs?* "No comment," I said. If she was out looking for a "lead story" for the evening news, she was going to have to find it without any help from me.

Holiday traffic was almost nonexistent as I drove down to the Public Safety Building. I found on-street parking in a loading zone a mere half block from the front door. Up on the fifth floor, in my cubicle in Homicide, I used my handy-dandy laptop to fill out the necessary paper in jig time. There wasn't much to report. I called down to 911 for the name and number of the early-morning jogger who had called in the report from a cellular phone. The 298 prefix on Johnny Bickford's home number meant her phone listing was a relatively new one on Queen Anne Hill.

I dialed the number, but there was no answer. I declined to leave a message on voice mail. Cops dumb enough to leave voice mail messages with potential witnesses are almost as likely to get calls back as encyclopedia salesmen.

Two and a half hours after I left home, I drove back down Third Avenue toward my building through the wide, flat streets of the Denny Regrade. Because of the one-way grids, I had to go as far as Broad before turning over to Second. My heart fell when I rounded the corner at Second and spotted a fire truck parked directly in front of the entryway awning to Belltown Terrace. A KIRO television crew from Third and Broad was hustling across the street in front of me.

*The girls!* I thought at once. Worried that something awful had happened to them, I slammed the Porsche's tires up against the nearest sidewalk, sprinted across the street, and made for Belltown Terrace's canopied entrance. In order to reach the door, I had to push past the news-film crew, including the same lady shark of a reporter I had last seen down on the street at the end of Pier 70. A momentary spark of recognition passed between us as she realized that for the second time that day, I wasn't going to answer her damned questions.

Kevin, one of Belltown Terrace's more recent

doormen *du jour*, hustled to let me in.

"Where's the fire?" I demanded.

"No fire," Kevin replied.

"Why the fire truck, then? What's wrong?"

"The party room is full of soapsuds. The suds finally stopped flowing, but not before they set off the alarms. Now the fire department is trying to clean up the mess and figure out where it all came from."

"Soapsuds?"

Kevin nodded. "Scads of them. Mountains of them."

Kids, soapsuds, and hot tubs can be a real pain in the neck. Some time when you have nothing to do for the next six hours or so, try putting half a bottle or so of dishwashing liquid in a Jacuzzi and turning on the jets. Within minutes, you'll have a hell of a mess. I know, because Heather and Tracy pulled that stunt once before, or at least one of their friends did when she was invited over for Tracy's eighth-birthday slumber party.

Ron and Amy lived on one of the higher floors then, in a unit with a Jacuzzi tub in the master bath. As a result of that little escapade, we had discovered a flaw in the building's plumbing design. The drainpipes for that side of the building go straight down to the garage, where there's a sharp elbow. The suds had backed up at the elbow and had come bubbling out the drainpipe and vent in the party-room kitchen.

I had assumed that having lived through the

aftermath of that crisis, Heather and Tracy would have learned their lesson. But faced with a repetition of that earlier offense, I immediately assumed that the girls had once again staved off high-rise boredom by running some of my Palmolive liquid dishwashing soap through the Jacuzzi.

Bent on wringing their scrawny little necks, I bounded into the nearest elevator and pressed the button labeled PH. For *Penthouse*. Nothing happened.

"Sorry, Mr. Beaumont," Kevin explained. "The elevator's off right now. You see, as soon as the alarm goes off, the elevators return to the ground floor and . . ."

I didn't hang around long enough to listen to any more of peach-fuzzed Kevin's useless explanation. He was still going on about it as I dashed into the stairwell and started pounding my way up one flight of stairs after another.

Twenty-fifth-floor penthouses are swell. The views are spectacular, as long as you don't have to walk all the way up. I was upset when I left the lobby. By the time I staggered up to my door and stuck the key in the lock, I was winded and furious. As the door swung open, I could hear the drone of the television set coming from the den. The air was thick with the smell of freshly popped microwave popcorn.

I charged into the den to find the two innocent-looking wretches sitting side by side and cross-legged on the floor. A stainless-steel bowl of popcorn nestled between them.

"All right, young ladies. What exactly have you two been up to?"

Tracy's eyes grew wide. "What do you mean? We popped some popcorn," she murmured. "Just like you said we could."

"I'm not talking about popcorn. Which one of you has been fooling around with soap in the Jacuzzi?" I demanded, forgetting completely that we live in a country where people—even kids—are presumably innocent until proven guilty.

Heather flounced to her feet and stood there glaring back at me, both hands planted on her hips. "Don't you yell at my sister!" she commanded, looking irate enough to tear me apart. If I hadn't been so bent out of shape, her pint-size fury might have been comical. But her outraged reprimand was enough to make me realize I *was* yelling.

I took a deep breath. They were both there; they were safe. Why the hell was I so upset?

"All right, all right," I said. "I'll calm down. Just tell me the truth. Which one of you put soap in the Jacuzzi?"

"We didn't, Uncle Beau," Tracy answered. "We were both right here watching TV the whole time. Honest."

"But somebody ran soap through a hot tub," I said. "The fire department's downstairs—on your floor, by the way—trying to clean it up."

"Come on, Tracy," Heather said, her voice stiff

with disgust. "Let's get our stuff and go."

"You're not going anywhere," I objected. "Your parents still aren't home."

Heather glared at me. "Why should we stay here?" she demanded. "You're mad at us for something we didn't do."

As Heather hurtled out of the den with Tracy on her heels, I followed them. While they turned in to the spare bedroom to retrieve their stuff, I continued down the hall to the master suite and bath. The glass shower stall was flecked with drops of water from my morning shower, but the Jacuzzi itself was bone dry. Unused. The only wet thing in the bathroom was my own still-damp towel.

Flushing with embarrassment and contrite as hell, I hurried back down the hall to the spare bedroom, where they were gathering their overnight stuff into a pair of shopping bags.

"Wait a minute," I said. "Hold up. I'm sorry. I can see now that you didn't do it."

Heather wasn't in a mood for accepting apologies. "But you *thought* we did," she stormed. "I'm leaving anyway."

"Heather, please," I begged, "I made a mistake."

But she wouldn't let up. "You made Tracy cry."

"I didn't mean to. It's just that—"

"Something was wrong, so you thought we did it. Because we're kids."

"Yes, but I don't think so anymore. Really. I'm sorry. I apologize."

I'm convinced Heather Peters will be a heartbreaker when she grows up. She relented, but not all at once. She glanced coyly up at my face through eyes veiled by long blond lashes. "Cross your heart?"

"And hope to die," I returned. "Sorry enough to take you both to lunch, anywhere you want to go."

"Even McDonald's?"

"Even McDonald's, but only if you promise not to tell your dad that I took you there."

The shameless little imp grinned in triumph. "Well, all right then," she conceded.

When we left the apartment, the elevators still weren't working. We had to walk down twenty-four flights of stairs, but going down was a whole lot easier than climbing up. When we stepped outside the lobby, the news crew was still there. The reporter was busy interviewing Dick Mathers. Dick and his wife, Francine, are Belltown Terrace's resident managers.

Dick is one of those people who is incapable of talking without waving his hands in the air. He gave me what felt like an especially baleful glare as the girls and I walked past him, but I disregarded it. Some days I seem to feel more paranoid than others. And seeing the news crew gathering info about a flood of soapsuds, I knew for sure it really was a slow news day in Seattle.

In fact, I never gave the incident another

thought, not during lunch at McDonald's, and not during the afternoon the girls and I spent—along with hundreds of other people—at the sunny but cold Woodland Park Zoo.

When we came back to the condo, everything seemed to be under control. The fire truck and news cameras were gone. The elevator was working properly. When I dropped Heather and Tracy off at their unit on the seventh floor, Ron and Amy were back from their big night out. They both said they'd had a great time. As I closed the door to their apartment and headed for my own, I breathed a sigh of relief. The girls were home, safe and sound. No problem.

My false sense of well-being lasted well into the evening—almost to bedtime. Ron Peters called upstairs at a quarter to ten.

"We've got trouble," he said. "Can I come up?"

"Sure."

He was there within minutes, looking distraught. "Ron, what's the matter?"

"It's Roz," he said. "She's back in town. She's staying at her mother's place down in Tukwila."

"So?"

"Did you leave the girls alone today?" he asked.

"Only for a little while," I told him. "I was on call. A body floated up under Pier Seventy, and I—"

"Roz called me about something on the evening news. She said the reporter was interviewing Dick Mathers, the manager, over something about soapsuds when you and the girls came out of the building. He blamed the 'two little girls who live in the building' for the problem. He said he believed they'd been left without adequate supervision. Roz—I mean Sister Constance—wanted to know if there were any other girls who live here besides Heather and Tracy. I told her no, they're the only ones, but that anybody who said they'd been left alone was lying because they'd been with you the whole time. But if you were out . . ."

"Look, Ron, the girls were fine while I was gone. And believe me, they had nothing whatever to do with all that soap."

"You should have heard her on the phone. There's going to be trouble over this."

Again, since Roz Peters wasn't *my* ex-wife, it was easy for me to wax philosophical. "Come on, Ron, don't hit the panic buttons. It's no big deal. After all, what could Roz possibly do with a bunch of soapsuds?"

The answer, of course, was a whole lot different from what I thought. Roz Peters, otherwise known as Sister Constance, had every intention of turning a little molehill of soapsuds into a mountain of trouble. It pains me to say that I never saw it coming.

But then, I never do.

# Two

I was pretty much feeling on top of things when I headed to the department the next morning. A yellow Post-it note was plastered on the wall next to the entrance to my cubicle by the time I got there. "See me," it said. It was signed, "L.P."

The *L.P.* in question, Captain Larry Powell, is even more of a troglodyte than I am. I've gradually moved into the modern era enough so that I can tolerate voice mail. I've gradually learned to hunt and peck my way around a computer keyboard. There are even times when I've found a fax machine downright useful. Larry, on the other hand, has come only as far as Post-it notes. That far and no further.

"What gives?" I asked, sauntering up to the open door of the captain's fishbowl office.

"I hear you took on yesterday's floater. Any

progress on that one so far?"

"Not yet. It's still early. That's what I'll be working on this morning."

"Is it something you'd mind handling alone?"

Did Br'er Rabbit mind being thrown in the briar patch?

"No problem," I said, trying not to let Larry see the grin that threatened to leak out through the corners of my mouth. "Why? What's happened to Sue? Aren't she and I partners anymore?"

Detective Sue Danielson has been my partner for several months now. She's young and fairly new to Homicide—a transfer in from Sex Crimes—but she's also a capable investigator. I knew she had taken her two boys and gone to visit her folks in Ohio over the holidays, but I also knew that her sons were due back in school that morning.

"She's stuck in Cincinnati with chicken pox."

"Traveling with kids is always so much fun," I said sympathetically.

"It's not the *kids* who are sick," Larry Powell told me. "It's Sue."

"Chicken pox? At *her* age?"

"Evidently," Larry observed dryly.

When Jared Danielson had come down with chicken pox early in December, Sue had said she remembered being sick with the same thing back when she was a child. I mentioned that to Larry.

"Evidently, she was mistaken," he replied. "And from what I hear, right this minute she's one sick little lady. It'll be several days before she stops being contagious and can get on an airplane to come back home."

"Tough break," I said, "but don't worry about me and Mr. John Doe. The two of us will get along fine without her."

The captain nodded. "I figured as much, but if you need help, let me know."

"Sure thing," I told him.

Larry's phone rang just then. He waved me out of his office, dismissing me. Before heading back to my cubicle, I took a little detour down to Missing Persons. There I found Detective Chip Raymond moving stacks of paper back and forth across his desk.

"Looks like a giant game of solitaire," I said.

Chip glanced up at me balefully and shook his head. "Don't I just wish. Where the hell do all these people go?"

"Away?" I offered.

Detective Raymond didn't appreciate my helpful suggestion. "Cut the cute, Beaumont," he said. "Whaddya want?"

"Any of those MPs got a tattoo saying MOTHER on a right wrist?"

Chip Raymond left off sorting papers and turned to a computer. He typed a series of commands on the keyboard, and then sat frowning at the display, waiting for an answer. When it came, he shook his head. "Not so far," he said. "One of yours?"

"Is now," I nodded. "He's a New Year's Day floater."

"I'll keep a sharp lookout and let you know right away if anybody matching that description turns up. What else can you tell me about him?"

I gave him the same information Audrey Cummings had given me, then Detective Raymond went back to sorting his morass of paper. I stood in the doorway of his cubicle for a moment, watching. "I seem to remember someone saying that the age of computers was the beginning of the end of paper; that we'd all be living in a paperless society by now."

Raymond nodded. "I remember people saying that, too," he said, morosely surveying the stacks of paper littering his desk. "I think I want my money back."

Laughing, I went back to my own office. The amount of paper I had to contend with was downright modest compared to Chip's.

That day, the fifth floor where the Homicide Squad resides was in a state of relative bedlam if not downright siege. Everybody was milling around, trying to get organized as to how best to deal with the caseload generated by a flurry of year-end violence: two alcohol-related vehicular homicides; an apparently fatal domestic violence case; and two Rainier Valley drive-by shootings that, although not fatal, still fell into Homicide's jurisdiction. No wonder Captain Powell had asked me if I'd mind working the case alone.

The first order of business was to track down the lady jogger who had reported finding the floater's body to 911. I've learned that more often than not, the "innocent" people who "discover" the bodies aren't nearly as innocent as they ought to be. It's as though they get so antsy waiting for their crime to be discovered that they go ahead and report it themselves, just to get it over with. So I was somewhat skeptical when I tried calling Johnny Bickford's number a little later that morning.

When a man answered, I asked to speak to Johnny Bickford. He coughed, cleared his throat, and said, in a clearer and higher-pitched voice, "Yes."

"Are you Johnny Bickford?" I asked.

"I was last time I checked," the voice returned. "Who's this?"

Johnny Bickford had to be a die-hard smoker. "Detective J. P. Beaumont, with the Seattle P.D.," I answered.

"Oh, hi there," she returned in an almost welcoming croon. "This has to be about the man in the water. I expected a call yesterday."

"I tried," I said. "Nobody was home. In my business, there's not much point in leaving messages."

"I don't see why not," Johnny said. "I would have called you back right away."

"Well," I said, "would it be possible for me to drop by today, maybe later this morning?"

"Certainly. How soon?"

"Say fifteen minutes?"

"That barely gives me time to get decent, but that'll be fine. Do you drink coffee, Detective—?"

"Beaumont," I supplied. "And yes, I do. A cup of coffee would be great."

Johnny Bickford's address on West Mercer led me to the bottom floor of a small eight-unit condominium complex on the view side of Queen Anne Hill. In this case, the view wasn't all that great, unless you happen to be a fan of grain terminals, which I'm not.

I rang the bell. The blonde who answered the door was almost as tall as I am. She wore a white, long-sleeved robe edged with something soft and furry, along with a matching pair of high-heeled, backless slippers. The outfit looked as though it had been copied from a 1930s Bette Davis movie. So did the foot-long cigarette holder.

"You must be Detective Beaumont."

I nodded, handing her one of my cards. After giving me a coy look, she immediately tucked the card into her bra. "Won't you come in?"

I stepped into a black-and-white room: white leather couch, chair, and carpet; black lacquered furniture. Huge black-and-white oils of nothing recognizable covered the walls. A silver tray laden with a french-press coffeepot, coffee cups, saucers, and spoons as well as cream and sugar was waiting on the coffee table.

"Won't you sit down?" Johnny offered. "And how do you take your coffee, black or with cream and sugar?"

"Black will be fine," I said.

Johnny motioned me onto the couch and then took a seat on a nearby straight-backed chair. She sat primly erect, shoulders not touching the chair, knees close together, legs demurely crossed at the ankle. And that was part of what gave her away. Modern-day ordinary women seldom pay that much attention to the finer points of posture and deportment. Not only that, the hand that passed me my cup and saucer wasn't exactly fragile and feminine.

Robe and slippers be damned, Johnny Bickford wasn't a woman at all, or rather, wasn't all woman.

"I meant to go jogging first thing this morning," he/she was saying. "Here it is, only the second of January and I'm already breaking one of my New Year's resolutions, but I just couldn't bear to go back down the waterfront after what happened there yesterday. The problem is, I'm not in good enough shape to run up and down the hills in this neighborhood. Besides, I barely slept last night. Nightmares, you know. That poor man. Do you have any idea who he is?"

"Not yet. We're working on it. Tell me, Johnny, where were you when you first saw the body?"

"I had just come up through Myrtle Edwards Park, and I was more than a little winded." Johnny laughed, the sound more of a donkey's bray than anything else. "That's not entirely true. I'm fairly new to this jogging thing, and I went out on Pier Seventy to watch the water traffic and to catch my breath. I was coming back down the pier to head home when we saw him. He wasn't floating, really. He was sort of pushed up against one of those old dead-head logs down along the edge of the water. Then a tugboat or something came by, fairly close to shore. The wake was enough to jar him loose. He disappeared under the dock."

"You said *we*. Was someone there with you?"

"There was a lady in a wheelchair on the dock with me. I mean, we were on the dock at the same time, although we weren't actually together, you see. She was the one who spotted the body first, although I was the one who called it in because I was the one with a phone in my pocket."

"This other lady, did you get her name?"

"No."

"And you called from your cell phone?"

Johnny nodded. "I carry my trusty little cellular phone with me at all times. I used to live up on Capital Hill, you see," he/she said. "Up there, I worried about gay bashing, especially late at night. Downtown here, it's mostly ordinary muggers and homeless lowlife panhandlers. They don't give a damn if you're gay or straight. I'd have to call them equal-opportunity criminals," Johnny said with another raucous hoot of laughter.

"I guess you would," I agreed, although I didn't find the joke particularly funny.

There was a momentary lull in the conversation. Johnny Bickford looked thoughtful. "I suppose the poor man committed suicide, didn't he? Jumped off a bridge or something? You have to be feeling terribly low to just go ahead and end it all that way."

It was interesting to me that one of the first people on the scene still thought John Doe had jumped off a bridge, while that television reporter there at the scene had specifically asked and had already somehow known that the victim had been shot. How did she know that? I wondered in passing before turning my attention back to Johnny. It didn't seem all that out of line to let the star witness know a little more about what was really going on.

"It doesn't appear to be suicide," I said. "We're investigating the case as a homicide."

"Oh, my goodness!" Johnny Bickford exclaimed, clutching his/her throat. "How awful!"

I'm surprised he/she didn't simply faint dead away at the news. I'm glad it didn't happen, however, because I'm not sure what my response should have been if he/she had.

I had been asking questions and filling in the contact report as I went. At the top of the form officers are expected to circle the appropriate title—*Mr., Mrs., Ms.,* or *Miss.* Stumped, I left that one blank while I went on taking the information.

I asked all the usual questions, but other than having found the body, there didn't seem to be that much more Johnny Bickford could add to what I already knew. When we finished and I handed the paper over to Johnny for a signature, his/her eyes went directly to the top of the form and stayed there for some time. Finally, taking the pen I offered, he/she signed the paper with an overstated flourish and handed it back.

Looking at the top of the form I saw that the word *Ms.* had been circled in a bold, heavy-duty line. While I surveyed the form, Johnny Bickford observed me with a defiant stare.

"Even though I've never been married, *Miss* doesn't really apply to someone in my situation," Johnny Bickford said. "I couldn't choose 'None of the Above' since that one wasn't listed. *Ms.* will be far more suitable after the first of February. That's when I'm scheduled for the next step in my sex change."

"I see," I said awkwardly, since the pause in the conversation made it necessary for me to say something.

Johnny Bickford simpered at me over the brim of his/her coffee cup, and then took another dainty sip of coffee. "*Do* you?" he asked. "My doctor doesn't believe in doing it all at once. He says Rome wasn't built in a day."

"No," I agreed, wishing I sounded less stupid than I felt. "It certainly wasn't."

Carefully, I set down my own cup and saucer on the table and gathered up my paperwork. "I'd best be going," I said.

"Can't I talk you into staying for another cup of coffee?" Johnny Bickford asked with a flirtatious smile. The look alone was enough to make me want to bolt for the door.

"No," I stammered uncomfortably, getting to my feet. "No, thank you."

"Too bad." Johnny said. "I think you're awfully cute."

I was already on my feet when Johnny reached into the pocket of his white robe and pulled out a tiny, four-inch-long scrap of newspaper article and handed it over to me. Quickly, I scanned through it:

### BODY FOUND AT PIER 70

The body of an unidentified man was found floating in the water near Pier 70 New Year's Day, spotted by an early-morning jogger.

Dr. Audrey Cummings, King County Assistant Medical Examiner, stated that the man had died as a result of undetermined causes.

Seattle police are investigating.

When I finished reading the brief article, I started to hand it back to Johnny Bickford. "Would you sign it, please?" he asked.

"Sign it?" I repeated, not quite comprehending. "You mean autograph it like it was a baseball card or something?"

Johnny beamed and nodded. "Exactly. I want to send it to my folks back in Wichita. I'm not mentioned by name, of course, but they'll be thrilled to know that I was the jogger in question. And having a real detective's signature on it will make it that much better. My mother is a big fan of true crime."

*What the hell?* I thought. "Where do you want me to sign?"

"Anywhere."

Doing my best to mimic a doctor's prescription handwriting, I scrawled my signature across the body of the article and then handed it back.

"Thanks," Johnny said gratefully. "If you don't mind, I'll send your card along with the article. You have no idea how much this will please my mother. She would have liked me to be a policeman, you see. I've never quite had the courage to explain to her why that wouldn't work."

I made for the door and Johnny followed. As I started down the steps, he was standing in the doorway, carefully holding the front of his robe to keep it from yawning open. I have no idea how one goes about staging a series of sex-change operations, but I have to admit, Johnny Bickford did have a figure.

He must have understood my questioning glance. He smiled. "They don't call them WonderBras for nothing," he said.

I was still blushing when I closed the car door and shoved the key into the ignition. I kicked up a spray of wintertime, road-sanding grit as I backed out of the driveway and headed downtown.

I was just starting south on Fifth Avenue when a call came in for me on the radio. "Sergeant Watkins wants to know what's wrong with your pager," the dispatcher said. "He's been trying to reach you for the past fifteen minutes."

In recent years, pagers, along with laptop computers and Kevlar vests, have all been added to the ordinary police detective's tools of the trade. There are circumstances in which all of them offer some advantage. As far as I'm concerned, when it comes to pagers, though, the bad far outweighs the good. It's a real annoyance, especially when I'm in the middle of a complicated witness interview, to have a pager buzzing away in my pocket, telling me that I really need to be talking to someone else. A pager can be almost as obnoxious as the phone company's little custom-calling gimmick—"Call Waiting." Call *Interrupting* is more like it.

Having been issued a brand-new pager, I do buckle under and wear it, but that doesn't mean I always keep the infernal thing turned on, especially not in interview situations. I try to be conscientious about turning it back on once I'm through talking to witnesses. In my hurry to leave Johnny Bickford's place, however, I had completely forgotten to do so.

"What's he want?" I asked.

"Something about Chip Raymond needing to get in touch with you. He says it's important. Want me to patch you through to Watty?"

*Not particularly*, I thought. Besides, if Chip was trying to reach me, that probably meant someone had turned up who looked like a possible match with Mr. Floater John Doe. "Can you put me through to Detective Raymond?"

"No can do. Watty, yes. Detective Raymond, no."

"Put me through to Sergeant Watkins, then," I said. "I might as well get it over with."

But when Watty's voice came through the radio, he didn't say a word about the pager, not at first. "Detective Raymond wants you to meet him at thirty-three hundred Western ASAP. The name of the company is D.G.I., 'Designer Genes International.'"

"Do you have a suite number?"

"No, it's a brand-new building. According to Chip, the same outfit evidently owns the whole thing."

"Did you say *D.G.I.*? I'm assuming that's not jeans, as in Levi's?" I asked.

"Right," Watty replied. "The other kind: G-E-N-E-S, as in DNA. It's one of those new bioengineering companies. Some kind of cancer research."

"Did Chip give you a name of the man he thinks is my guy?"

"Yeah. Wolf. Don Wolf. He's the operations manager there. Newly transferred up from California."

"Okay," I told Watty. "If you can raise Chip, either by phone or radio, tell him I'm on my way."

"That shouldn't be too difficult," Watty told me. "Unlike some people who shall remain nameless, Detective Raymond actually uses his pager. On a regular basis.''

I didn't miss the sarcasm in Watty's voice. As official reprimands go, it was relatively harmless. If he had actually ordered me to keep my pager on at all times, I probably would have done so, but it would have been compliance under duress. Sergeant Watkins is smart enough to know that he gets the best work out of his people when he lets them use their own judgment in non-life-threatening situations.

Riding herd on a bunch of homicide detectives has to be a whole lot like being a parent and, no doubt, almost as thankless. Watty Watkins is a past master at doing both—raising kids and running detectives. His hand on the reins is sometimes light, sometimes firm. He gets what he wants by alternately ordering and cajoling. Nobody in the department has ever accused the man of not giving a damn.

I reached down and switched on my pager. "All right, all right," I muttered. "It's on."

"Good."

"And I'm sorry."

"That's okay, Beau," Watty said. "These things happen."

That was all there was to it. Clearly, I was in the wrong. Watty and I both knew that, but once I had apologized, he didn't waste both his time and mine by rubbing my nose in it. If I had been in his shoes, I doubt I would have exercised the same kind of restraint.

It all goes to show why Watty's the sergeant, and I'm not. It might also explain why after all these years, he's still married to his first wife.

That's not luck at all. It's because he's one hell of a nice guy.

# Three

These days the traffic lights on Seattle's Fifth Avenue are supposedly timed to benefit drivers who actually observe the speed limit. Theoretically, a driver ought to be able to go from the upper end of the Denny Regrade to the International District at the far end of the downtown area with only one or two stops along the way.

While I'd been on the radio, I had come south, sailing along with traffic. Beyond University, however, just about the time I realized I needed to go someplace other than back to the Public Safety Building, forward progress ground to a halt. For the next two interminable blocks, Fifth Avenue was coned down to a single left-hand lane. The numbskull directing traffic wouldn't allow a right-hand turn on Seneca, not even for a homicide cop who had slapped a portable blue flasher on top of his vehicle.

I finally managed to turn west on Madison. Once out of the southbound gridlock, I made it back north with no further hassle. The Denny Regrade is a flat area north of Seattle's downtown proper that has been carved from where Denny Hill used to be. It ends at the bottom of Queen Anne Hill. Denny Avenue runs on a diagonal across the northern end of the Regrade, providing a logical boundary. Logic disappears, however, in a sudden curve where, for no apparent reason other than to bedevil newcomers, Denny transforms itself briefly into a street called Western.

With three lanes of traffic roaring past, I ducked into a passenger load zone outside the building marked 3300 Western and tried to get my bearings. When I first moved back into the city, that block had been the site of a once-fine steak house. In its later years, the place degenerated into a singles-scene joint before shutting down altogether. For years, a fading billboard had promised that a hotel would soon be built on the property. Obviously, that plan had come adrift, because a spankingly new six-story glass-fronted office building sat there now.

The six-foot-tall brass letters that said D.G.I. were easy to spot. So was the fountain, closed down for the winter, that graced a front-door plaza. What wasn't easy to find was parking. Just then, Chip Raymond sauntered out through the door, waving me around to the north end of the building, where I found a discreetly camouflaged entrance to an underground garage. Chip beat me

back inside and waved me into a slot marked VIS-
ITOR.

"Have you been waiting long?"

Chip shook his head. "As soon as the report
came in by phone, I figured the guy was probably
your floater. I didn't want to go charging in here
to check it out without having you along. When
Watty couldn't find you right off, I grabbed some
lunch on the way—a hamburger from Dick's. I
bought two. You want one?"

"No, thanks. I'm fine. What have you got?"

Chip unfolded a computer-generated piece of
paper and read off the information. "Name's Don
Wolf. Donald R. Moved up here from La Jolla,
California, a couple of months ago to assume the
position of operations manager at Designer Genes
International. Thirty-eight years old. Six feet one
inch tall. Weighs about one eighty-five, one
ninety. Blond hair. Blue eyes. Tattoo on right
wrist that says MOTHER."

"Way to go, Chip. It sounds like my guy, all
right."

"According to the man who called in the report—"

"Who was that?" I asked.

"Somebody named Bill Whitten," Chip answered. "He's the CEO of D.G.I. He said he and
this Wolf character were supposed to have a
meeting yesterday afternoon, and Wolf didn't
show."

"For good reason," I said.

Chip nodded. "There was supposed to be another meeting this morning—at seven. When Wolf didn't show for that one either, Whitten started trying to track the guy down. The call was put through to my desk at ten o'clock, just a little while after you left the department."

"Wait a minute," I said. "Doesn't that strike you as soon? Family members would report it in less than twenty-four hours. But that seems early for people at work."

Chip nodded. "The same thought crossed my mind, but that's before I learned about his car. Wolf is nowhere to be found, but his car is right here in the garage. It's that white Intrepid over in the corner. I took a quick look at it and couldn't see anything wrong. Anyway, the situation seemed thorny enough that I didn't want to go upstairs to see Whitten without having somebody from Homicide along with me."

"Good call, Chip," I told him. "Let's do it."

We stepped into the elevator and rode up one floor to the lobby, where a sweet young thing was "womaning" a reception desk and switchboard. By mutual if unspoken agreement, Detective Raymond was the one who presented his credentials. There was no need to bring up the word *homicide* until we had a positive identification.

"We need to see Bill Whitten, please," Chip said. "I believe he's expecting us."

Moments later, we were back in the elevator riding up to the sixth floor. The interior walls of the elevator were covered with some kind of upholstered material that still reeked of new dye.

Because of my involvement with the syndicate that bought Belltown Terrace, I know a little about the development and relative cost of downtown Seattle real estate. This particular six-story building—underground parking garage, upholstered elevator, and all—hadn't come cheap. An operation like this represented a big chunk of investment capital, especially considering that Designer Genes International was the building's sole occupant.

Chip Raymond was evidently having much the same thought. He ran one finger across the plush material that covered the walls. "No wonder cancer research is so expensive," he said.

I nodded. "Whatever kind of genes we're talking about, they must be solid-gold plated."

Just then, the elevator door opened and we stepped off into another lobby with a desk occupied by a vividly made up, middle-aged lady who greeted us with a gracious smile when Chip presented his card. "Mr. Whitten's on the phone right now," she said. "I'm his assistant, Deanna Compton. He asked that I show you into the conference room. Would either of you care for coffee?"

If I had encountered Deanna Compton and her unruly mane of red hair on the street, I would have taken her for either a real estate maven or a well-to-do matron. She was dressed in a flawless, navy-colored, double-breasted pantsuit. She wore spike heels that barely peeked out from beneath the hem of her pants. With all the gold on her body—rings on nearly every finger, earrings, and several gold chains—I'm surprised she didn't clank like a knight in armor.

"Is your coffee genetically engineered?" I asked.

Deanna smiled again, this time with somewhat strained tolerance, as though mine was an old and not entirely welcome joke.

"I wouldn't know about that," she said. "We use Starbucks. You'll have to ask them."

Chip passed on the offer of coffee; I accepted. While she went to fetch same, I examined our surroundings. The mostly glass-walled conference room was sumptuously appointed. The windowed wall to the west looked out almost eyeball to eyeball with the huge globe that sits atop the *Seattle Post-Intelligencer* building on Elliott. Beyond that was the slate expanse of Elliott Bay edged by Bainbridge Island in the distance.

The furnishings in the conference room—oblong table, ten chairs, and an enormous credenza—were made of some kind of light-colored wood, polished to a high gloss. Like everything else in the D.G.I. building, the furniture spoke of quality, of designers working for someone with both an eye for class and a bottomless checkbook.

Chip and I both took chairs along the far side of the table. When Deanna Compton returned, bearing a cup of coffee, she opened a drawer in the credenza and pulled out a brass, felt-bottomed coaster. Examination of the coaster re-vealed an engraved version of the Designer Genes International company logo—the letters *D*, *G*, and *I* artfully entwined to mimic a credible modern rendering of an ancient coat of arms.

"First class all the way," I muttered to Detective Raymond, passing him the coaster.

He glanced down at it with an "I'll say," and handed it back.

"Sorry to keep you waiting," a portly, balding man announced from the open doorway of the conference room. Compared to the way the secretary was dressed, this guy looked like your basic rumpled bed. His khaki-colored double-breasted suit could have used a good pressing. "I see Deanna brought you coffee," he said.

Chip and I both rose in greeting. "Mr. Whitten?" Chip asked.

"Yes."

"I'm Detective Raymond with Missing Persons. I talked to you on the phone earlier. This is Detective Beaumont."

Whitten moved briskly into the room and shook our hands with a broad-handed, surprisingly strong grip. Then he took a seat at the end of the table. "I don't know why you guys are bothering to hang around here," he grumbled irritably. "If Don Wolf had shown up for work this morning, I wouldn't have called you, now would I?"

"It's possible we may have already found him," I suggested quietly.

Whitten looked at me sharply. "Really. Where?"

Without a word, I extracted one of my business cards from my wallet and slid it down the table where it stopped directly in front of him. Whitten picked it up, held it out at the far end of his arm, and squinted at it.

"This says *Homicide*," he objected, looking questioningly from the card back to me. "I thought you were from Missing Persons."

"Chip here is from Missing Persons," I said. "I'm Homicide."

There was a long pause during which Bill Whitten's eyes sought mine. It's a moment that happens in every investigation when the people closest to the victim first become aware that the unthinkable has happened. Homicide cops are trained to observe the survivor's reactions, to gauge whether or not the response is typical, and if not, why not.

Whitten leaned back in his chair and steepled his thick fingers under his chin. "I see," he said. "You're saying you think Don Wolf is dead? When did this happen?"

His was a measured, emotionless reaction, the response of someone to expected, rather than unexpected, news, and one that fully justified Chip Raymond's reluctance to approach the D.G.I. interview without having someone from Homicide along for the ride.

"At this juncture, we're not one-hundred-percent sure," I told him. "An unidentified body washed up in the water off Pier Seventy early yesterday morning. As you know, that's only a matter of a few blocks from here. From the sound of the description you gave Detective Raymond, I'd have to say the dead man could very well be your missing Don Wolf. We'll need someone to come over to the morgue at Harborview to verify our tentative identification.''

"He was in the water? What happened, did he drown?''

I shook my head. "It's too soon to say. There'll have to be an autopsy report. That'll take a few days, and a toxicology report will take a few weeks beyond that. My suspicion, however, is that death came instantly in the form of a wound from a single bullet.''

Bill Whitten blanched visibly. "Don was murdered then?''

"We're investigating the case as a homicide," I corrected. "Whether or not the victim turns out to be Don Wolf remains to be seen. That's why we're here. We need someone who knew Don Wolf to come along down to the morgue and try to give us a positive I.D.''

"You want me to do that?" Whitten asked.

I nodded. "That would be the first step. Actually, the third. Before we leave the building, I'd like to take a look at Mr. Wolf's office for a moment, and also at his car, if I may. I understand it's still parked in the garage.''

"Certainly, but—''

"Furthermore, until we have ascertained

whether or not the dead man is Mr. Wolf, it would probably be better if you didn't mention any of this to anybody, just in case the victim turns out to be someone else."

"Not even to Deanna . . . to Mrs. Compton, my secretary?" he asked.

"No," I responded. "Not even to her."

Whitten led us out of the conference room and diagonally across the reception area to an office located in the southeast corner of the building. The door was closed, but unlocked. "Here it is," he said, opening the door into an airy, windowed room.

Don Wolf's office was as compulsively clean and carefully organized as the furniture in a model home. Nothing at all appeared to have been disturbed. A bank of carefully framed diplomas graced one of the two nonwindowed walls. The other was covered with bookshelves. On the credenza behind the desk was a framed, eight-by-ten photo—a head shot of a smiling, glasses-wearing brunette.

"That's his wife," Whitten told me when he saw me looking at the picture. "Her name's Lizbeth. She's still down in La Jolla, waiting for the house to sell."

"That's enough for now," I said. "We can come back here later. Please ask that no one go in or out of this room until we do, would you?"

Whitten nodded. "Mrs. Compton will see to it," he said. As we left Don Wolf's office, we stopped in front of his assistant's desk. "Please cancel my appointments for this morning, Deanna, and for lunch as well. This may take some time. Also, please lock up Don's office and don't allow anyone in it until further notice."

"Certainly," Deanna Compton said, frowning up at him. "Is anything wrong?"

"I don't know," he returned. "It's too soon to tell."

Detective Raymond and I had arrived at the building in separate cars. If this was going to be a homicide investigation, there was no further reason for Raymond to stay involved. Down in the parking garage, he took his vehicle and headed back to the Public Safety Building while I drove Bill Whitten to the medical examiner's office in the basement of Harborview Hospital.

Those kinds of victim identification trips, often made in the company of a grieving relative or a close personal friend of the deceased, can be emotionally devastating at times. Some survivors chatter incessantly as a device to hold back the looming reality as well as the pain. Others endure the awful ordeal in stoic silence. Moments into the ride I realized Bill Whitten was no close personal friend.

We had just turned into traffic on Western when he leaned back in his seat, loosening the seat belt around his considerable girth, and heaved a gloomy sigh. "I might just as well tell you this right up front," he said.

"Tell me what?"

"Don Wolf and I didn't get along. In fact, I

hated the son of a bitch. I'll probably end up being what you cops call the prime suspect."

"You hated him?" I asked. "How come?"

"Because he was out to get me," he said. "He came here two months ago. According to his résumé, he was some kind of hotshot financial guru. His résumé said he was a real genius, a Harvard-educated, MBA-wielding, money-raising fiend in the world of genetic engineering. I even sold the board of directors on him. The problem is, Don Wolf may have looked great on paper, but in person he was something else. He was one of those smart-assed guys who won't take direction from anybody. A total jerk, in other words, but it's hard to tell that from a résumé and a couple of interviews."

I stole a glance in Bill Whitten's direction. He sat with his arms folded staunchly across his chest, with his eyes staring out the front windshield. "Detective Raymond told me you and he had a meeting scheduled for yesterday. What was that all about?"

Whitten considered for some time before he answered. "He was going to take me to the board of directors and ask them to force me out," he said finally. "Me, the guy who started D.G.I. and built it from the ground up!"

"Why?"

There was another long pause while Whitten's face reddened with suppressed fury. "He claimed he'd found evidence of wrongdoing on my part, that I'd been illegally skimming money and diverting it to my own use."

"Had you?" I asked.

"No, goddamn it! I hadn't. Don Wolf brought in some money, I'll give him that. He said he could deliver investors, and he did. The problem is, those investor dollars came with all kinds of strings. He was undermining me and bad-mouthing me every chance he could get. He made so much trouble that some members of the board of directors have actually started questioning my every move, including Saturday-morning quarterbacking my decision to build this building. I keep trying to tell them that you can't attract the best people if you don't have a world-class research facility. D.G.I. is that, and I'm the one who made it happen. Little old me—Billy Whitten from Seattle, Washington."

"Would it have worked?" I asked.

Whitten glowered at me. "Would *what* have worked?"

"Would Don Wolf have been able to force you out?"

He shrugged. "I guess we'll never know now, will we."

"Maybe not," I agreed, but what I had already heard was enough to spell the beginning of motive. From that point of view, everything Bill Whitten said would bear careful scrutiny.

Because of a massive ongoing construction project at Harborview Hospital, we had to park two blocks away, but the walk turned out to be pleasant enough. Pale midday sun was beginning to burn through the overcast, turning the day almost balmy. It felt more like spring than early January.

Once inside the M.E.'s dingy basement lobby, I asked for Dr. Cummings. Within moments, Audrey emerged from her own private office dressed in her usual crisply sensible costume. I started to introduce her to Bill Whitten, but that proved unnecessary.

"Why, Bill," she said, smiling a friendly greeting and holding out her hand. "How good to see you again. What in the world are you doing here?"

Whitten jerked his head in my direction. "I'm with him," he said. "Detective Beaumont here seems to think the unidentified body that was found off Pier Seventy yesterday belongs to someone who works for D.G.I." He stopped and then added a slight modification, "Someone who *used* to work for D.G.I."

Frowning, Audrey turned to me. "Really?"

I nodded in confirmation. "There's a good possibility," I said.

Audrey Cummings shook her head sympathetically. "One of your people? That's too bad, Bill. I certainly hope not."

"Don Wolf never was what you could call one of *my* people," Whitten replied with a grim smile. "In fact, as far as I'm concerned, if the dead man turns out to be him, I'll be the first to say it couldn't have happened to a nicer guy."

Coming from a self-admitted prime suspect, that blurted comment came as a surprising admission. He said it right there in public, in front of God and everybody. Usually, good manners dictate that people—even suspects—not speak ill of the dead, certainly not that soon after somebody kicks off. But with regard to Donald R. Wolf, although Bill Whitten was the first to express that derogatory sentiment, he certainly wasn't the last.

The body tagged with a John Doe label around his toe did indeed turn out to be Don Wolf's. A departed Don Wolf's. But as I was to learn over the next few days, the man was hardly anybody's *dearly* departed Don Wolf.

He was dead, and it turned out that, with one notable exception, no one in the world seemed to be the least bit sorry.

# Four

Every homicide case is different, and yet there are always similarities. One of the most difficult aspects of beginning an investigation involves notification of the next of kin. I didn't know it then, but in the case of Don Wolf, it was going to be far more difficult than usual.

Once Bill Whitten had provided the positive identification we needed, I continued to ask questions while giving him a lift back to D.G.I. headquarters. "You told me earlier that Don Wolf was married, and that the woman in the picture in his office is his wife."

"Some people are more married than others," Whitten replied.

I let that pass for the moment. "What did you say his wife's name is? Elizabeth?"

"No, *Lizbeth*. No *E*; no *a*."

"And she's still down in California?"

"As far as I know."

"You have phone numbers, addresses, that sort of thing?"

"In his personnel file. I'll have Deanna locate them for you as soon as we get back to the office."

"Were they having marital difficulties of some kind?"

Whitten seemed to consider before he answered. "From what I could gather, she wasn't exactly overjoyed at the prospect of moving to Seattle."

"Did he have any children?"

"None that I know of. He and Lizbeth haven't been married that long—only a matter of months. There could be kids somewhere from a previous marriage, but I wouldn't know about that. Again, that might be in a personnel file as well, especially if the children were listed as beneficiaries under the group insurance policy."

"How much insurance?"

"Two and a half times his annual salary. A quarter of a million, less some change."

"You paid him a hundred thousand a year, then?"

Whitten nodded. "Salary plus."

"Plus what?"

"A finder's fee on the new investment dollars he brought in."

"If he was making that kind of money, there shouldn't have been any financial difficulties. Were there any other problems?"

Whitten gave me a sidelong glance. "You mean

problems with anyone other than me?"

"Look, Mr. Whitten, let's don't make this difficult. At this point, I don't regard you as any more of a suspect than I do anyone else. If you'd like me to Mirandize you and let you have a lawyer present when we talk, I'd be happy to oblige. For right now, I'm just gathering general information."

By then, we had arrived back at the D.G.I. garage and pulled into a parking place. I opened the door to get out. When Bill Whitten made no move to exit the car, I settled back in my seat, closed the door, and waited. For almost a full minute, neither one of us moved or spoke. Whitten seemed to be pondering something important, and I didn't want to rush him. Finally, he made up his mind.

"I believe I already told you Don Wolf wasn't a nice man," he said.

"You did mention something about it."

"Well, I wasn't just blowing smoke," Whitten said defensively. "I have proof."

"What kind of proof?"

"My father was a pioneer in the in-store security business. He started his company—the company I started out with—back in the mid-forties, right after the war. In the economic boom that followed, shoplifting became a rising phenomenon. Stores that were large enough to pay the freight hired their own in-house detectives and security, but lots of companies were far too small to handle that kind of expense on a full-time basis. My dad's company provided roving bands of detectives for hire who went from store to store on a needs-only basis.

"In the sixties, as soon as the technology became available, Dad became a pioneer in installing in-ceiling or wall-mounted security systems. Later on, we branched out into scanners as well."

"Video cameras, you mean?" I asked.

"Yes, among other things. My dad died of cancer a number of years ago. When I sold the whole thing off a couple of years ago, I made out like a bandit. So did my mother."

"Where's all this family history lesson going, Mr. Whitten?"

"D.G.I. is my baby," he said. "I'm the one who started it. I'm the one who brought in the scientific expertise to do the research and who raised most of the money that built this building yet Don Wolf thought he could walk in here and take it away. Instead of just letting him have it, I decided to fight him with all the tools at my disposal."

"So?" I asked, although I had a reasonably good idea of where Bill's seemingly rambling tale would end up. "Are we talking employee surveillance here?"

Whitten nodded. "It's the same kind of system we had in our old corporate headquarters before we sold it off. This one is newer, of course. More bells and whistles. There's a hidden camera and microphone in every office," he explained. "I don't necessarily use all of them all the time.

Some of them, the ones at the front of the building and in the garage and elevators, are on twenty-four hours a day. Others I only activate from time to time."

"On a needs-only basis?" I suggested. "Sort of like your father's traveling detectives?"

Bill Whitten grinned for the first time all day. "There is a certain similarity," he said. "Within a week of Don Wolf's showing up here, I had already figured out his game and turned on the camera in his office. I figured that sooner or later I'd come up with something that would make it possible for me to nail that bastard's ass."

Compared to the worlds of commerce and science, Seattle P.D.'s little interdepartmental rivalries seemed almost commonplace.

"In the old days at our old company, my dad went over the tapes personally," Whitten continued. "Here at D.G.I., so did I. Lately, though, I've been so overbooked that Deanna sometimes comes in on weekends and goes over the tapes for me. If there's something she thinks I need to know about, she brings it to my attention."

I must have looked slightly askance at that arrangement. "Deanna Compton is a trusted employee," Bill Whitten assured me. "She's one of the handful who made the switch to D.G.I. from my father's old security company. Deanna is like me. She's been an employee here since almost before there was a *here*, since before D.G.I. was a gleam in my eye."

"You're telling me that when Mrs. Compton

scanned through the tapes she found something then? Something incriminating?"

Bill Whitten paused for so long before he answered that I was afraid he was going to stop talking altogether.

"Yes," he said quietly.

At that point, I knew better than to push. Again, I shut up and waited him out. "She usually does that on weekends," he continued finally. "This week, she came in on Saturday afternoon. She called me as soon as she saw it. I came down and took a look right away. In view of what's happened, I can't help thinking that I should have done something differently, but at the time, I was only thinking of my own hide. I had already found out that he was going to make his move on me this week, at the board-of-directors' meeting on Wednesday afternoon.

"Once I saw the tape, I thought I could get him to back down. That's when I called him and set a private get-together for yesterday, to see if I couldn't get him to listen to reason."

"It sounds to me a little like blackmail," I said.

Whitten eyed me shrewdly. "I'd rather say I found a solution that I thought would work out best for all concerned. He wouldn't get me axed, and I wouldn't turn him in to the cops. That way, D.G.I. wouldn't end up being taken to the cleaners by all kinds of bad publicity."

"So what's on the tape?" I asked.

"Don Wolf brought a girl here, Detective Beaumont," Whitten said.

"A girl?" I asked. "What girl? When?"

"I don't know what girl. And it was earlier last week. Wednesday night and Thursday morning, according to the time stamp on the tape."

Lots of people bring friends and relations into their offices during nonworking hours. They do it to show off, I suppose. To let their families and loved ones know a little more about what their work environment is like. The fact that Wolf was with another woman when he still had a wife down in California was another issue, but not all that unusual. What I couldn't quite understand was why Bill Whitten found the idea of an in-office assignation so disturbing.

"That doesn't sound like such a big deal to me," I said. "It reminds me of that day last spring when people all over the country were supposed to bring their daughters along to work. For that one day, Seattle P.D. was crawling with little girls, all of whom want to be detectives when they grow up."

"Believe me, Detective Beaumont, it wasn't anything at all like that," Bill Whitten said.

"What was it, then? And what does all this have to do with the price of peanuts? You saw the girl?"

"Yes," Whitten answered. "But not in person. Only on tape."

"Is she anyone you recognize?" I asked. "One of your employees?"

Whitten shook his head. "No. Relationships between employees are officially discouraged."

"You said you'd never met Lizbeth Wolf. Is it possible it was her? After all, it was a holiday. Maybe she came up from California for a visit."

Bill Whitten shook his head. "Come on," he said, opening the door. "I'll show you."

He heaved his heavy frame off the car seat. Then, walking briskly, he led me to the elevator. In the sixth-floor reception area, he stopped directly in front of Deanna Compton's desk.

"Don Wolf is dead," he announced brusquely. "Detective Beaumont here is handling the investigation. You're to give him access to whatever he needs—personnel records, carbons of phone messages, anything at all."

Deanna Compton did a sharp intake of breath. Under a heavy layer of blush, her cheeks paled, but she never lost control. "Of course, Mr. Whitten," she said without any other crack appearing in her coolly competent exterior.

"And we'll need to see those tapes from the other night, both the one from Don's office and the other one from the front entrance. Let's do the elevator tape as well. Bring them to my office right away. We'll watch them in there. Hold all my calls, and tell people I may not be able to get back to them before tomorrow."

Nodding, Deanna stood up and started away from her desk. Then she stopped. "What about his wife, Mr. Whitten? Does she know? Do you want me to call her?"

Bill Whitten looked questioningly at me.

I shook my head. "No," I said. "This kind of

news shouldn't be delivered by a disembodied voice over the telephone. It's always better to have someone do it in person. I'll contact someone in law enforcement down in La Jolla. They'll dispatch an officer to speak to her and give her the news."

"Oh," Deanna Compton said, "I see."

"And in the meantime," I added, "it would probably be better if you didn't tell anyone else. Otherwise, we'll end up with dozens of people calling up the wife before anyone has time to deliver the news officially."

"I understand perfectly," Deanna Compton said. "I won't tell a soul until you give me permission. And I'll go get those tapes. It'll take a few minutes because I locked them in the vault downstairs for safekeeping."

Bill Whitten showed me into an office that was outfitted with the same kind of blond wood furnishings that had been in the conference room. Whitten's private office was located on the same side of the building as the conference room. As befitted the boss, his window boasted an unobscured view of the snowcapped Olympics.

Offering me a chair by the window, Whitten busied himself with a computer keyboard and mouse located on the credenza behind his desk. When it came to electronics wizardry, he was no slouch. Using a series of computer-generated commands, he closed the blinds, turned off the lights, and brought a twenty-seven-inch television console rolling out from behind the sliding doors on a wall-mounted media cabinet. Once Deanna Compton delivered the tapes and left the room, he used another command to click shut the lock on his office door.

In the old days, that kind of technical display would have provoked me to astonishment, but Ralph Ames, my attorney, has seen to it that my apartment is equipped with the latest in exotic home security and control systems. Mine not only tells me the usual stuff about whether or not the place is on fire or if someone has broken in, it can also do other homey little tasks like opening and closing the blinds at set times and under set conditions. In the mornings, it automatically grinds and starts my first cup of coffee. As long as I remember to load in the beans and water the night before, my morning shot of SBC java can be waiting for me as soon as I open my eyes and crawl out of bed. It's an efficient system, as long as I remember to turn the damned thing on.

After studying the labels, Whitten selected one of the three tapes Deanna Compton had delivered, and inserted it into the VCR. Then, for several long seconds, the man's expert fingers flew over the keyboard and mouse, turning on the VCR, fast-forwarding the tape to the exact place he wanted.

My first view of what turned out to be Don Wolf's office was one that remained static and shrouded in darkness for some time. It looked more like a still photo as opposed to television's usual moving images. Careful examination re-vealed the shadowy interior of an unoccupied office. In the lower left-hand corner of the screen, a digital readout relayed the word PAUSE.

"All the offices and labs are equipped with sound and motion detectors," Whitten was explaining. "They deliver a combination of time-lapse and video images. The lights come on automatically when someone enters any room in the building, and they go off two minutes after the room is vacated. The video scanners, when activated, work much the same way. As you can imagine, with a building this size, trying to watch everything would be a physical impossibility. That's why we do spot checks here and there."

"Sort of the way the IRS does audits."

Whitten nodded then continued with his guided tour. "The video equipment is very compact—about the size of a pack of cigarettes. There's an individual unit concealed in every room's thermostat panel. The images captured by the various cameras are transported via fiber optics to a panel of video recorders."

Just as Whitten stopped speaking, the image of Don Wolf's office, visible on the television monitor, came to life. Overhead lights flashed on, bathing the office in fluorescent illumination. The constant PAUSE sign in the lower left-hand corner of the screen changed abruptly to reflect a date and time: DECEMBER 27, 11:47:34 P.M.

For the first second or two, no one was visible, but I heard a hoot of girlish laughter.

"Still, I feel funny about this," the voice of a

young-sounding woman said as the giggle subsided. "Like we shouldn't be here. You're sure
alarms aren't sounding somewhere?"

"I'm sure," a man answered who was, presumably, Don Wolf. "After all, Latty, this is *my* office.
Who's going to object?"

*Latty. What kind of name is that?* I wondered.

"Besides, if I weren't allowed to be here during
off hours, I wouldn't have the security code, now
would I?" Wolf continued. He was in full view
now, and I could see that Don Wolf and my dead
floater were indeed one and the same.

"It'll only take a few minutes," he was saying.
"I just want to show you how the downtown skyline looks from the desk in my office. It's very
romantic. Want some more champagne?"

There was another—slightly tipsy—giggle. "I
shouldn't. And, Donnie, you shouldn't either. Remember, you still have to drive me home."

"Other than Mrs. Compton, do any of your
other employees know about this camera system
of yours?" I asked, while the man I assumed to
be Don Wolf made a big production of putting
down his own champagne glass and taking the
young woman's. Smiling up at him, she watched
while he filled it. Observing the whole thing on
tape, I revised my original "slightly" tipsy up to
*very*.

"Mrs. Compton and I are the only ones who
need to know," Bill Whitten answered. As he
spoke, his voice took on such a peculiar huskiness
that I couldn't help looking at him. He was lean-

ing forward in his chair, watching the screen with such all-consuming intensity that I pretty well guessed what was coming.

I've been a cop for a long time. As I turned back to the screen, I more than half expected the woman Whitten had referred to as a "girl" to be some pint-size, preteen hooker plying a traveling, desktop version of the world's oldest profession.

What I saw on the screen instead was an eye-catching blonde, probably in her early twenties. A shapely Marilyn Monroe look-alike, Latty dressed the part in a low-cut, tight-fitting white dress and improbably high heels. As Don Wolf filled her champagne glass, she suddenly yelped and jumped back when a drop of carelessly poured bubbly spilled from the rim of the bottle, landed on bare skin, and then dribbled down the curve of her ample cleavage.

"Oops," Don Wolf said, noticing the spill. "Let me get that for you."

He leaned close to her. With a quick flick of his tongue, he licked away the errant drop and then nuzzled his face in her bosom. The girl giggled and moved back farther away from him, waggling a reproving finger.

"Come on now, Donnie," she said. "Don't start. You know that's not nice."

"How can you say such a thing?" he grinned. "It seems very nice to me."

While she smiled and sipped her champagne, a still-grinning Don Wolf stripped off his jacket and tie and dropped them on the desk. Then he picked up his own glass and filled that one as well. Once both glasses were brimming, he took Latty's free hand in his and pulled her toward him.

"A toast," he said, "to my lovely Latty. You make me feel like the luckiest guy in the whole world."

After a brief sip, he drew her along with him toward the window. "Allow me to show you my million-dollar view."

She giggled. "You've already shown me your view. We were here last Sunday afternoon, remember?"

"Maybe so," he replied, "but it's so much better at night. Come on."

The move toward the window took them off at an angle and outside camera range. For a moment, the tape was quiet while neither Don Wolf nor the girl made a sound.

"Notice anything different about the room?" Bill Whitten asked.

With people out of the picture, the view of the room was essentially the same as I had seen earlier from the doorway of Don Wolf's office—a shot showing the backs of the two captain's chairs facing the desk, the desk itself, and the credenza beyond it.

"Well?" Bill Whitten asked me impatiently. "Do you see it or not?"

As I tried to see what he meant, Latty was murmuring, "I see what you mean—it is very beautiful, especially with all the lights on in the buildings. It looks . . ."

Her voice faded away, muffled by what sounded like a kiss. An interval of impassioned necking followed. Trying to ignore the panting and the breathless moans, I continued to study the room, trying to find whatever it was that Bill Whitten's question implied was out of place. It took a while, but finally I spotted it.

"His wife's picture is missing."

"That's right," Whitten returned. "I have that on film, too, by the way. Don put it away in the top drawer of his credenza on Wednesday afternoon, just before he left work. That proves he must have been planning to bring her here all along."

"It doesn't prove anything," I corrected, "although it may suggest that he was planning to bring *someone* here with him."

By now, the necking had escalated into a series of sexually aroused groans and whispers. I'm no Peeping Tom. Listening to or even watching somebody else make out isn't my idea of a good time.

"Look," I said impatiently. "Is there any point to all this?"

"Just wait," Bill Whitten replied. "You'll see."

Latty suddenly reappeared on the screen. Her lipstick was smeared, her hair in disarray. "Donnie, we've got to stop now while we still can," she said breathlessly.

"But I want you."

"I know you do. And I want you, too. But not like this. I already told you that, and we agreed. Let's quit now, please," she begged. "Take me home before we end up doing something we'll both regret."

Don Wolf followed Latty into camera range, his arms outstretched. "Oh, baby, don't do this to me. Don't tell me to stop, not now. Please. Just let me hold you."

Trying to pat her hair back in place, she slipped away from him and headed for the door. Don Wolf caught her by one arm and yanked her back to him.

"Ouch!" she cried out in surprise. "Donnie, that hurt. Let me go!"

But he gave no sign of having heard. "Please, baby," he murmured again, clasping her in his arms and pressing her against his chest. "Please don't leave me like this. I want you so much it hurts—so much that it's driving me crazy. I want—"

"No!" she said firmly, placing both hands on his shoulders and bodily prying herself away from him. "Let's don't get carried away. I don't—"

A demanding kiss cut off Latty's objection in midsentence. Don's encircling arms tightened around her once more, pinioning her against him. When she struggled to get loose, the two of them weaved back and forth, swaying jerkily like a pair of awkward dancers.

"Please, Don, don't," she said again, once she

finally succeeded in freeing her lips from his. "That's enough now. No more."

There was a clear note of annoyance in her objection, but no alarm, no panic. Not yet, although there certainly should have been.

"Don!" This objection was firmer than the previous one, but she still wasn't actually fighting him. "Donnie, what are you doing? Stop it!"

But he didn't stop. Catching her off balance, Wolf effortlessly shoved Latty backward between the two captain's chairs in front of the desk. Latty's backward movement stopped abruptly when her hip slammed into the edge of the desk behind her. Yelping in pain, she sank back against the desk, trying to steady herself while at the same time attempting to separate herself from Don Wolf's overpowering embrace.

For a moment, it almost worked. In fact, he seemed to back off. He thrust her away from him. Further unbalanced by this unexpected shove, Latty fell back on the surface of the desk with a head-cracking thump. As she fell, he reached out and caught the bodice of her dress in one knotty fist. What followed was a terrible rip as the fragile material tore down the middle.

"Don!" she shrieked. "What have you done to my dress?"

I found myself gripping the arms of my chair. I felt like I did when I was a terrified little kid, sitting in a darkened theater next to my mother, watching Snow White about to take a bite of that terrible poisoned apple.

*Don't take it, don't take it!* I had willed silently
to the lovely cartoon figure on the screen, while
my tiny fingers had clutched the sticky armrests
in helpless desperation. But no amount of little-
boy urging had saved Snow White from her fate
back then. And now, my adult gut-wrenching
horror did nothing to save Latty from what was
coming.

Don Wolf fell on her like an enraged beast,
slapping her into submission, tearing off her
panty hose and panties, prying her flailing legs
apart with his body. Crying out, she squirmed
and fought beneath him, but the smooth, polished wood of the desk worked against her. She
could gain no purchase. There was no escape.
Don Wolf was stronger than she was.

When it was all over, when Latty lay nearly
naked and sobbing on the desk, the indifferent
caption on the screen said 12:01. The entire incident, from beginning to end, had taken less than
fifteen minutes.

It seemed much longer.

# Five

My collar was too tight. There wasn't enough air to breathe in Bill Whitten's darkened office. "Damn!" I said. "What a good-for-nothing shit!"

"Pretty rough, isn't it," Whitten said.

I had seen worse, but still... "Is that it?" I asked.

Whitten shook his head. "No, wait."

"You mean there's more?"

Back on the screen, Latty was sobbing and struggling to sit up. "I'm going to leave now," she gasped. Her lower lip was bleeding and starting to swell.

"Oh, my God, Latty," Don Wolf said, as though waking from a stupor at the sight of the blood. "What have I done?"

He reached out one hand as if to help her. She

cringed away from him. "Don't *touch* me," she screeched. "Get away."

"But, baby," he whined. "Please. I never meant to hurt you, I swear. I just got carried away and—"

"Shut up!" she hissed furiously. "I'm going to walk out of here and you're not going to stop me."

"Latty, I can't believe I did this to you. I'm sorry, so sorry. Please don't go. Please say you'll forgive me."

"I'm going to walk out," Latty continued, as if he hadn't said a word. She stumbled to her feet. When she did so, her torn dress fell away from her body. She grabbed the frayed edges of material and tried to hold them together. Swaying unsteadily on her feet, she finally located her shoes and slipped them on. Then she reached out, snagged Don Wolf's jacket off the desk, and wrapped it around her shoulders. I could see the reflexive chattering of her teeth, but somehow, she wasn't crying any longer. In fact, considering what had just happened, she seemed astoundingly calm. And cold sober.

By then, Don Wolf had moved across the room so he was standing between her and the door; between her and the lens of the camera as well. He was tucking in his shirt, zipping his pants.

"Don't go, Latty. Not like this."

"Call me a cab," she returned doggedly.

"I'll take you home, Latty. I promise I won't touch you again. Honest."

He moved toward her, but she recoiled, stopping only when the desk was safely interposed between them.

"I told you, don't touch me! Don't you ever come near me again!" she commanded. "Call a cab."

Shrugging, he picked up the phone and punched out a number from memory. "My name's Don Wolf," he said. "I need a cab at thirty-three hundred Western." He waited for a moment, listening. "That's right," he said. "It's an office building, not an apartment. Just pull up by the front door. We'll be waiting in the lobby."

He put down the phone. "The cab should be here within fifteen minutes."

"*I'll* be waiting in the lobby," Latty corrected, struggling to keep her voice under control. "You stay right here until after I've gone."

"But Latty," he objected, "I—"

"Just shut up!" she seethed. "Don't you say another word. I never want to hear your voice again, not ever!"

"But I have to ride downstairs with you," Don wheedled, sounding both apologetic and conciliatory. "The elevator is locked. You need me to run the keypad."

Sometimes, in situations like that, in the minutes after something awful happens, anger is the only force capable of holding hysterics at bay. Or maybe anger is just another form of hysterics—one that allows people to function for a time before they fall apart. I wondered how long Latty's anger would carry her.

Wolf stepped aside, clearing a path to the office door. Latty stood leaning against the desk, seeming to gather strength even as she clutched Don Wolf's oversized jacket closed around her. Finally, she straightened and lurched toward the door. I know it was only an illusion of camera placement, but for a disconcerting second as she moved forward, she seemed to be looking directly into my eyes. The girl on the screen was a pale ghost of the one who had entered laughing minutes before. In the course of those few brutal minutes, something in Latty's carefree spirit had been shattered, possibly forever. Her face was frozen into a hollow mask; her eyes, empty. The desolation written there almost broke my heart.

Just inside the door she paused and moved to one side. "If you have to run the elevator, you go first. But if you touch me again, I swear to God I'll kill you."

"I won't," Don Wolf agreed instantly. "Not ever. I promise."

He moved toward the door as well, buckling his belt as he walked. He stopped just within camera range and turned to look around the room. Maybe he was checking to see if anything was out of place. Nothing was. When he turned back to the doorway, there was the damnedest smirk on his face. The son of a bitch looked as though he was proud of himself.

That single passing glimpse, captured for all time on Bill Whitten's hidden camera, made me want to puke. As a homicide cop, I'm haunted by murder victims. Finding the killers and bringing them to justice becomes a holy crusade. Right then, however, with Don Wolf's smirk still lingering in the air, I had the sense that justice had already been served. Someone had taken care of Don Wolf. In the process, his killer had saved the state of Washington a considerable amount of time, trouble, and expense.

"I told you he wasn't a nice guy," Bill Whitten said.

Bill Whitten was obviously a master in the art of understatement. The security system on screen switched off the light. Shadowy darkness returned to the screen, everywhere but in the caption box in the bottom left-hand corner. There the stark white letters read: DECEMBER 28, 12:04:20 A.M.

Whitten switched off the VCR. "So do you want a copy or not?" he asked.

Unaware that I had been holding my breath, I let it out. I may have been short on motivation for finding Wolf's killer, but my duty was nonetheless clear. "Yes," I said.

From an evidence standpoint, the tape meant nothing. In order for a recording to stand up in a court of law, at least one of the people being recorded must have given permission. Otherwise, the recording constitutes an illegal wiretap, information from which is generally inadmissible. I was relatively sure neither Don Wolf nor Latty had any knowledge as to the camera's existence, so neither of them could be deemed to have given consent.

Right at that moment, however, I was looking for probable cause rather than a conviction. In showing probable cause, the rules are a little less stringent.

"You'll most likely want to see these other two tapes as well," Whitten added, jerking his head in the direction of the other two plastic holders Deanna Compton had placed on his desk. "I'll have those copied at the same time."

"What are they? Don't tell me he did it again," I said.

Bill Whitten shook his head. "I figured you'd want to see them just for the sake of completeness," he replied. "One is from the ride down in the elevator. The other is from the cameras stationed outside the front entrance of the building. He sent her home in a Yellow Cab, by the way."

"What about New Year's Eve? Was he working that night?"

"He was for a while, up until around eleven."

"Doing what?" I asked.

"Who knows?" Whitten shrugged. "Getting ready to chop me off at the knees, I imagine."

In response to Bill Whitten's keyboard commands, the TV monitor slid back into the cabinet, the doors in front of it closed, and the blinds opened, filling the room with the unexpected light of watery, midwinter sunshine. Watching this process I remembered what Whitten had said to me earlier, in the car, about him being a prime suspect.

"Is there any truth in Don Wolf's charges?" I asked. "That you were diverting funds?"

Whitten's somber gaze met mine across a vast expanse of polished desk. "There are diversions and then there are diversions," he said.

"In the event of an independent audit of the company books, do you think you'd be exonerated?"

"That depends on the CPA," Whitten answered casually, but not quite casually enough. Something in the way he looked at me—the tiniest flicker of an eyelid perhaps, put me on edge and on point. Before I could say anything further, however, he reached out and tapped the keyboard once more, unlocking the door to his office. He immediately pushed a button on his phone.

"Yes, Mr. Whitten?"

"Deanna, I need you to make copies of these three tapes for Detective Beaumont. He'll need them as soon as possible."

"I may not be able to do that until after lunch," she said.

Whitten glanced at me. "Do you want to wait?" he asked. "Or would you rather have them delivered later on today?"

I checked my watch. The morning was already almost gone, and I had barely made a start. "It might be better to have them delivered."

Whitten spoke back into the intercom. "Whenever you get around to it will be fine," he said. Then he turned his attention on me. "I suppose you'll need to see both his apartment and his car, won't you?"

"Yes, but—"

He punched the intercom again. "Deanna, you'll also need to call the manager over at Lake View. Even though you can't tell Jack Braman what's happening, you can let him know that Detective Beaumont will be stopping by. Jack should let him into the apartment. We'll fax written permission if he needs it. And call the dealer on the car lease and see if he can make arrangements for a duplicate key on Don's Intrepid."

"Right away," Deanna answered.

"Why is it you have access to Don Wolf's apartment?" I asked.

"D.G.I. owns it," Whitten replied. "Don leased it from the company temporarily in order to facilitate his move up from California. Lake View is on Lake Union, just south of the Fremont Bridge. Do you know where that is?"

"I can find it. Now about these tapes . . ."

"Yes?"

"If the taping was done without consent, and if word about them gets out, you could end up having an invasion-of-privacy problem on your hands."

"With the girl?"

"Possibly."

Whitten shrugged. "I guess we'll just have to cross that bridge when we come to it. I look at it this way: With Don Wolf dead, sooner or later you'd come looking for me because of what was going on between the two of us. If nothing else, the tape shows that I'm not the only one who had a problem with good ol' Mr. Don Wolf. I may be a good solid suspect, but at least I'm not the only one."

I did my job then—the job I'm paid to do. Even though my motivation was lacking, even though Don Wolf wasn't a prince among men, I was still obligated to investigate his murder. As I pulled out my low-tech notebook and pencil, I glanced back over my shoulder toward what I was sure was a dummy thermostat near the door.

"Are *we* being taped?" I asked.

Whitten grinned. "We could be if you want to be."

"No, thanks," I said. "I'll pass."

I spent the next hour asking Bill Whitten all the customary questions: about where Don Wolf had come from prior to joining D.G.I.; about how long he had been there; and about exactly what were his duties and responsibilities. As Whitten and I talked, there was one thing I couldn't quite understand, one thing that didn't really add up. Bill Whitten was the founder of D.G.I. Everything I had seen and heard led me to think he was the brains behind the whole operation. Why, then, would he have been so spooked by the arrival of Don Wolf, a Johnny-come-lately?

The only thing I could figure was that there must have been some merit to Don Wolf's

charges of fiscal irresponsibility. *Diversions*, as
Whitten had called them. And if a company-
owned condo on Lake Union was part of D.G.I.'s
"research" holdings, then the late and unlamented Don Wolf may have had a point. But
rather than bearding the lion in his den, I made
up my mind to check with Audrey Cummings.
Since she had obviously known the man on sight,
she might also know some of the side issues that
would help me make sense of what was going on
with D.G.I.

When I had dredged everything I could out of
Bill Whitten, I left his office and stopped by
Deanna Compton's desk, where she had evi-
dently handled everything.

"The tapes still aren't ready," she said. "The
car dealer is sending a messenger over with a key,
and the manager at Lake View is expecting you
to drop by a little later. Just buzz the manager's
number, and he'll let you in. Now, is there anything else?"

"The wife's address and phone numbers?"

"Oh, of course. Here they are. You'll let us
know when you reach her? If she's coming up to
Seattle, she may need help with hotel or travel
arrangements, that kind of thing."

"Yes, Mrs. Compton. As soon as I reach her, I'll
let you know."

"And when the tapes are ready, they should be
sent where?"

I handed her one of my cards. "The Public

Safety Building," I said. "Homicide's on the fifth floor."

As I rode down in the plushly upholstered elevator, I remembered what Bill Whitten had said: "There are diversions, and there are diversions." What had he meant by that? Did this building qualify? In order to do cutting-edge cancer research, was it really necessary to have a padded elevator? Or a condo on Lake Union? Don Wolf may have been a first-class bastard, but I wondered if perhaps he had been right when it came to Bill Whitten's financial management of Designer Genes International.

Down in the garage, I peered in the windows of Don Wolf's compulsively clean Intrepid. Not a piece of paper, not a single latte cup littered the spotless interior, nor was there a single fleck of mud on the outside. Over the years, I've learned to distrust people who keep either their vehicles or their desks too pristinely clean. Don Wolf was dead, but he was clearly just another case in point.

Wanting to learn more about Bill Whitten, I called the M.E.'s office at Harborview and asked to speak to Audrey Cummings. "Come on, Beau," she objected when I told her what I wanted. "Can't this wait? I was just running out to catch some lunch. I have to be in court by two."

"Where are you going to lunch? Maybe I can meet you there."

"Sure," she said. "Meet me at the Gravity Bar.

It's probably not your kind of place. Do you know where it is?"

Audrey Cummings is a strict vegetarian. In the course of communications between someone like her and a devoted junk food junkie like me, the word *lunch* inevitably suffers in translation. The Gravity Bar is a juice bar located between First and Second on Virginia. I've been there once or twice with Ron Peters, and Audrey was absolutely right. It's not my kind of joint. Carrots may be fine for rabbits, but when it comes to drinking the damned things, I draw the line.

"I know where it is," I said.

"Good. Meet me there in fifteen minutes."

I did. Perched on futuristic metal furniture that looked as if it had been liberated from the set of *Blade Runner*, I sipped a chewy glass of pulpy, freshly squeezed orange juice while Audrey ate her avocado, sprouts, and tomato croissant and downed two huge glasses of carrot juice.

"So tell me about Bill Whitten," I said as she munched away.

"What about him?"

"Whatever you can tell me."

"Smart man," Audrey replied without hesitation. "Dedicated. Overbearing. Egotistical. Well connected. Long on drive, but short on science. I guess that about covers it."

"He's not a trained biotech researcher?" I asked.

"No, but enough money can rent a whole lot of talent."

"And Whitten has that much money?"

Audrey frowned before she answered. "Earlier this year I heard a rumor that D.G.I. might be in trouble, but nothing really solid."

"Where do you know him from?"

Audrey laughed. "Mostly from cancer charity functions, the auction circuit, that kind of thing. I'm sure you know the drill." The laughter died and her brow furrowed. "You're not thinking Bill Whitten had anything to do with Don Wolf's murder, are you?"

"He told me so himself," I answered. "Said he might just as well because I was sure to figure it out myself eventually. I believe the term he·used was *prime suspect*. What do you think?"

Long before I finished asking the question, Audrey Cummings was already shaking her head in an emphatic *no*. "I don't think so," she said.

"Why not?"

"Did he tell you about his father?"

"He said something about him dying of cancer, I believe. Something about that leading him to what he's doing now, to being involved in cancer research."

"Gordon Whitten had cancer," Audrey told me. "But he didn't die of it."

"What did he die of then?" I asked.

"He committed suicide," she said. "He went down to Mexico for some kind of oddball alternative treatment. When that didn't work, he killed himself. Blew his brains out. Believe me, if Bill Whitten was going to knock off Don Wolf, he wouldn't have done it with a bullet to the back of the head. Never. Not in a million years."

And put that way, I have to admit, Audrey Cummings' theory made a lot of sense. What it sure as hell didn't do was make my job any easier.

A few minutes later, when she had to rush off to her court appearance, I headed north to the Fremont district to take a look at Don Wolf's condo. A message taped to the security phone at the Lake View Condos announced that the manager had been called away and would return in a few minutes.

Retreating to my car, I pulled out my laptop and made a start at translating my notepad notes into a form the brass at Seattle P.D. deem acceptable. I still don't know what I did wrong, but smack in the middle of writing a paragraph, the damn cursor quit. It got stuck halfway through the words *Designer Genes* and wouldn't budge. A little box appeared in the middle of the screen. GENERAL PROTECTION FAULT, I think it said, or words to that effect. YOU MUST SAVE YOUR WORK OR YOU WILL LOSE IT.

Which, of course, was a lie. The cursor was stuck. I couldn't have saved my work if my life had depended on it.

In over twenty years of being a cop, the words GENERAL PROTECTION FAULT have never once popped up in the pages of my never-ending series of dog-eared little notebooks. They never have, and they never will. Which is why, slick though they may be, computers will never altogether replace pencil and paper.

And they won't replace detectives, either.

# Six

Jack Braman, the Lake View Condo's surprisingly youthful manager, returned eventually. He was short, round, and effusively helpful. When I clued him in as to what was going on, he was suitably distressed. With keys jangling nervously on a heavy key ring, he led me to the elevator of the five-story complex.

"I've been managing condos for three years now," he said, shaking his head. "Never had one of my residents get murdered before, although I guess Don Wolf was a likely enough candidate."

To look at him, Jack Braman didn't appear old enough to be out of high school for three years, to say nothing of managing condos.

"What do you mean by that?" I asked.

Braman shrugged. "From what I understand, he had a wife down in California somewhere, but being married sure as hell didn't seem to slow him down none. If you catch my drift," he added.

"You mean Don Wolf had female visitors?"

"Constantly."

"The same one or different ones?"

Jack Braman shook his head. "Different ones, although there was one who was here so much I was starting to think maybe she was his wife. But there were younger ones as well. Girls who were closer to my age than his."

"Hookers?" I asked.

"I wouldn't know about that," he said. "Not for sure, but I guess they could have been."

Flushing furiously, Jack Braman turned the key in the lock and pushed open the door to Don Wolf's apartment. As soon as he did so, the appallingly unmistakable odor of death gushed out into the hallway.

Braman's eyes widened. He gagged and choked and almost fell. "My God. What's that awful smell?" he demanded.

Had Jack Braman ever been a homicide cop, he wouldn't have had to ask. I reached out a hand to steady him and to keep him from stepping forward into the apartment and possibly destroying evidence.

"Go call nine one one," I said. "Tell the dispatcher to send a patrol car and a crime scene investigation team. Tell the operator to notify the medical examiner's office."

Braman looked at me through watering eyes. "Medical examiner?" he repeated. "That means somebody's dead here. I thought you said Don

Wolf died somewhere else. Out on the water or something."

"I did."

"But what's this, then?" Braman asked weakly. His color had gone so bad I was afraid he was going to pitch forward flat on his face. "If somebody's dead in here, who is it?"

"That's what we have to find out," I said. "Go make the call. Hurry now."

Shaking his head, Jack Braman shambled away. Meanwhile, I sidestepped around the door, avoiding the usual traffic pattern, and eased my way into the overheated room.

If this was Don Wolf's apartment, the place was totally in character. It was neat as a pin. Nothing in the elegantly appointed living room appeared to be out of place. The door had been locked when Jack Braman opened it, and there was no sign of forced entry.

Trying not to disturb any footprints, I skirted the edge of the fine white carpet as I headed for the hallway. There the reek of decaying flesh seemed far worse than in the living room. Breathing through my mouth and using a handkerchief to grip the knob, I opened a closed bedroom door. Even though I'd had ample warning, the overpowering stench inside left me gagging.

Because the blinds were closed, the room was enveloped in a dusky gloom. Even so, it was still possible to see the grim spatter pattern of blood and gore that had been sprayed across the headboard and the wall over the bed where a lump of pathetically still humanity lay concealed beneath a brightly colored comforter.

Obviously, the person on the bed was dead. Once upon a time, I would have rushed forward just to make sure there was nothing I could do. Once, but not now. This isn't the good old days. When it comes to murder cases, investigating officers find themselves on trial right along with the defendants. Under the minute glare of the media, even the slightest misstep in procedure can be damning. As a consequence, we've all learned to avoid doing anything that might jeopardize the chain of evidence.

In other words, standing in the doorway of that foul-smelling room, I couldn't afford to do a damn thing, not without other cops to witness my actions and to back up my assertions of whatever was found there. And from that position, although I could see the form on the bed, the mound of covers made it impossible to see whether the victim was man or woman, adult or child. That didn't keep me from drawing my own possible conclusions.

*Is it Latty?* I wondered. That would make sense. She had threatened Wolf on the videotape. Had she made good on that threat, only to be stricken by overwhelming guilt afterward?

The very possibility filled me with an ineffable sadness. The blonde I had seen on the video had been so young and vital and beautiful. It offended me to think of her taking her own life. Given society's deplorable track record for apprehending and prosecuting rapists, it isn't too surprising that some victims resort to vigilante justice. But why commit suicide? In this case, it seemed to me that even the dumbest court-appointed attorney in town could have gotten her off.

Outside the building, the distinctive wailing of separate sirens announced the arrival of several emergency vehicles in the street below—as a fire truck, a Medic-One van, and at least one blue-and-white converged on the Lake View Condominiums. Hurriedly, I made my way back to the entrance to the apartment. The person in the bed had been dead for days. With no hope of a life-saving rescue, I wanted to intercept the crush of well-intentioned, fully booted EMTs and firemen who were no doubt on their way.

Out in the hallway, I almost collided with the first person who burst out of the elevator—a pasty-faced Jack Braman. Right on his heels was a grizzled Seattle Fire Department captain, a man I'd seen on occasion over the years. Nostrils distended, he stopped in midstride. Like me, he knew as soon as he smelled the odor that there was no point in going any farther.

"Too late?" he asked. I nodded. The captain turned back to his milling crew. "Okay, guys. Nothing to be done. If we hang around here, we'll only be in the way. Somebody grab that elevator before it gets away."

Herding his squad like a brood of unruly chicks, the captain corralled them back into the elevator door. Jack Braman, too, hovered uncertainly in the hallway. He seemed undecided about whether to go or stay.

"I guess I'd better head back downstairs," he said, swallowing hard, and leaping into the elevator just as the door closed. "That way, I can let people in if they need to be."

"Good idea," I said. "You go ahead."

With the elevator gone, I glanced around at the rest of the fifth floor. There were evidently four apartments and a locked utility door of some kind. The room behind it might have been a garbage chute or maybe a laundry room. Early on this weekday afternoon, none of the other fifth-floor residents were home. If they had been, they certainly would have been in the hallway by now.

I had heard the elevator open and shut downstairs. Now it was once again creeping upward. I hurried back to the elevator lobby in order to be there when the door opened once again.

This time, the first person off the elevator was Audrey Cummings. "I thought you were stuck in court," I said.

She shook her head. "My case was continued. I was already in my car on my way back to the office when the call came through. I should get the prize for being here before anybody else."

Right behind Audrey, almost treading on the backs of her high-heeled shoes, was my own personal nemesis from Seattle P.D., none other than Detective Paul Kramer. He was accompanied by his most recently acquired partner, a novice detective named Sam Arnold.

Kramer looked at me. I looked at him. "What are *you* doing here?" we both said at the same time. It sounded almost like one of those responsive readings at church, but believe me, neither one of us asked the question with joyous, worshipful, or love-filled hearts.

Detective Kramer and I don't get along. We haven't from the first day we laid eyes on each other. He's one of those ambitious, ass-kissing sons of bitches who's out to make a reputation for himself, no matter what. If somebody gets in his way, too bad. He'll walk over or through them to get where he's going. I've pretty much made up my mind that if the day ever comes when Paul Kramer gets promoted to a supervisory position in Homicide, that's the day I turn in my badge.

We're not talking one-sided here. The feeling is clearly mutual. Paul Kramer seems to resent the hell out of everything about me. He's forever griping about my money, about where I live, about the clothes I wear, and the car I drive. For some reason, my penthouse unit at Belltown Terrace really chaps his butt. He never fails to razz me about me and my high-roller neighbors. Maybe it was funny the first ten or fifteen times he mentioned it, but it isn't funny anymore.

"I'm working," I said. "What about you?"

"And how'd you get here before we did?" Kramer demanded, squaring off in front of me there in the hallway "Watty assigned the call to us. Besides, I thought you were supposed to be chasing after the New Year's floater."

"I am," I answered, making an effort to keep my voice even. "This happens to be the floater's apartment. I'm the one who found the body in there."

The attempt to keep the strain out of my voice must not have been too successful, at least not as far as Audrey Cummings was concerned.

"Now boys," she said, slipping between us. "Be nice. What do you have here, Beau?"

"This way," I said, leading them to the door to Don Wolf's apartment. "The body's on a bed in the bedroom. I didn't go all the way into the room for fear of disturbing something important. It may be a suicide."

"Suicide?" Kramer sneered. "You haven't been in the room, but already you've figured out that it's suicide? Beaumont here must have inherited some of Superman's X-ray vision," he added over his shoulder to his young partner. Sam Arnold had just come to Homicide after a two-year tour of duty in Property Crimes. This couldn't have been more than his second or third case.

"Yes, sir," Kramer continued. "Detective Beaumont here is the latest version of the Man of Steel."

Ignoring him, Audrey pulled out a notebook and began scribbling preliminary notes. "Can you give me any background?"

"It turns out my floater raped a woman in his office several nights ago. On the twenty-seventh.

The victim threatened to kill him afterward. I'm thinking she may have made good on the threat and then killed herself afterward."

"Name?" Audrey asked.

"Of the rape victim? Latty. That's all I have on her so far."

"Wait a minute," Kramer objected. "Wait just a damn minute. You're telling me the floater is a rapist? How do you know that?"

"Because I saw it," I snapped. "On tape."

"He did it at D.G.I.?" Audrey asked.

"That's right."

"What's a *D.G.I.?*" Kramer demanded. "Sounds like the two of you are talking in code."

"Designer Genes International. That's the bio-tech company down on Western where Don Wolf worked. When he brought the girl into his office, a hidden security camera recorded the whole thing."

"The rape you mean." Kramer grinned. "That sounds pretty kinky. Where can I get a copy of this tape, or are you putting it out on a pay-per-view basis?"

Pocketing her notebook, Audrey proceeded to the apartment door. "We could just as well get started," Audrey said. "You've called for a crime scene team?"

"They were summoned the same time you were. They should be here any minute."

Without entering the room, she turned on Sam Arnold and fixed him with a reproving stare. "When we go on in, stick close to the wall and well away from any footprints or spatters. You got that, Detective Arnold?"

Kramer's hapless new partner cringed under her gaze. Something told me this wasn't the first time he had dealt with the lady.

"Got it!" he repeated quickly. "Yes, ma'am."

Out in the hallway, the awful stench had dissipated a little, but once inside the apartment, the odor was again overpowering. We headed toward the bedroom, following the same circuitous path I had used earlier. Sam Arnold made it around the perimeter of the room all right, but as he neared the bedroom door in the hallway, the smell proved too much. He began making a small gurgling noise in his throat.

"Oh, for God's sake, you useless little wimp," Kramer growled. "Get the hell out of here before you barf all over our shoes."

Retching, and trying to cover his mouth with his hand, Arnold bolted for the door to the apartment. He made it to the outside hallway, but just barely.

Audrey sighed and watched him go. If there had been footprints to be found in the carpeting of the doorway, they were gone now, mashed flat by Detective Arnold's pell-mell retreat. "Damned kids!" she muttered, shaking her head.

Rank has its dubious privileges. In a world of parallel bureaucracies, an assistant medical examiner outranks mere detectives. Kramer and I followed Audrey into the gore-spattered bedroom. Seattle isn't known for having flies in the dead of winter, but I heard an unmistakable buzzing of flies as we made our way into the room.

"Am I having a hot flash or is it hotter than hell in here?" Audrey demanded.

"It's hot," I said. "I checked the thermostat as I came by. It's set at eighty."

"Eighty? Christ!"

"You want me to turn it down?"

Audrey shook her head. "We'd better leave it where it is, at least until the crime scene techs show up. Of course, by then, we'll all be baked to a crisp."

Taking the lead, Audrey approached the bed from the left-hand side. "Yikes," she said. "The whole back of her head is gone."

"After you," Kramer said, motioning me forward with an exaggerated bow.

Following the same path Audrey had taken, I, too, approached the bed. Because I had been watching my feet, I was right beside the bed when I finally looked up. The first thing I saw was the woman's lifeless left hand dangling over the side of the bed—a left hand with a wedding ring. I didn't recall that the girl on the tape had worn a ring of any kind. And looking further, at the terrible carnage of the bed itself, I realized at once that my initial theory was wrong. The exiting bullet had destroyed the back of her head, but the face was pretty much intact.

"It isn't her," I said. "It isn't who I thought."

"First it is and then it isn't," Phil Kramer said

tauntingly from over my shoulder. "Make up your mind, Beaumont. So who is it now?"

"Don Wolf's wife," I answered.

"Are you sure?" Audrey asked.

"I think so, although I've only seen her picture. Her name's Lizbeth. She's from La Jolla, California. Bill Whitten told me that when Don Wolf moved to Seattle a couple of months ago, she stayed put in California waiting for the house to sell."

"So maybe some of your guesswork isn't so far off the mark after all," Kramer said. "And maybe it's still murder and/or suicide. Supposing the wife found out her husband was up here screwing around. She probably came looking for him with blood in her eye and then did herself in afterward. Closing these two cases should be duck soup."

"Nobody's closing anything until I know for sure who she is," Audrey Cummings snapped. "I want positive I.D. Comparison with a picture isn't good enough. I'll want fingerprints and dental records or both."

"This must be the place," Janice Morraine said from the doorway, announcing the arrival of the crime scene investigators. "It's hot as blue blazes in here. You don't expect us to work in this much heat, do you?"

Janice, a criminalist by trade, is the lead crime scene investigator for the Washington State Patrol Crime Lab. Those who make the mistake of calling her a *criminologist* do so at their own risk.

Smart ones never make the same mistake twice.

"It's hot all right," Audrey replied, "but don't touch that thermostat until one of your guys dusts it for prints."

Behind me, Kramer heaved an impatient sigh. "Dust it for prints? How come? The woman blew her brains out. Don't tell me we're going to squander the next three days jumping through hoops and treating the scene like it's from a multiple—"

"There's a weapon here on the bed. Looks like a three fifty-seven. That may be what killed her. For right now, I'm calling it homicidal violence. It was obviously close range. It may turn out to be suicide, but I doubt it."

Kramer groaned. When you're on a fast track, cases cleared in a hurry look better than those that take longer. A call of homicidal violence meant our job was just starting.

"What makes you say that?" he asked.

"The wall," Audrey Cummings answered confidently. "Women don't usually go out in ways that leave that kind of mess for somebody else to clean up."

"Mess?" Kramer echoed.

"Mess," Audrey Cummings repeated firmly.

"Okay," Janice Morraine said, taking charge. "You'd best move out of the way and let us get started."

While Janice Morraine and Audrey Cummings conferred near the bed, Kramer led the way out of the room. "I've never heard anything so dumb," he grumbled under his breath.

"I think I'd shut up about that if I were you, Detective Kramer," I told him. "At least as long as Audrey Cummings is within earshot."

"But the *mess*? What kind of fruitcake reason is that?"

I shrugged, enjoying Detective Kramer's annoyance. "When it comes to women," I told him, "like it or not, there are some things you just have to accept on faith."

# Seven

I followed Kramer out of Don Wolf's apartment, directly into the arms of Captain Lawrence Powell, who saw me and did a double take. "Watty said Detectives Kramer and Arnold were here. I thought you were supposed to be working on the floater?" he said.

It seemed to me I'd already been down that path. "I *am* working the floater," I said. "This is his apartment. Our initial and still tentative I.D. would indicate that the dead woman found here is his wife."

Larry sniffed the air. "She's been dead for a while."

"A day or two," I agreed. "With the thermostat turned up to eighty degrees, it doesn't take long for a body to go bad."

"You're thinking it's maybe a double, then?" he asked.

Kramer shook his head and horned his way into the conversation. "For my money, I'm thinking it's maybe a homicide and/or suicide."

"Audrey Cummings from the M.E.'s office doesn't necessarily agree with that theory," I mentioned while Kramer shot me a withering look.

"What does she say?" Captain Powell asked.

"She's calling it a double," Kramer grumbled. "And she's going for a full-court press."

"And I'm sure you three are going to give her your full cooperation," Powell said with an encouraging smile.

"Absolutely," Detective Kramer replied at once, deftly executing a judicious U-turn. It amazed me that he could pull it off without so much as missing a beat. And without Captain Powell catching on to his game, either. "No question about that," Kramer continued. "We were just about to start dividing up responsibilities."

"How?" Powell asked.

No one had previously discussed the division of labor, but once again Kramer covered himself. "Since Beaumont here was already tracking down the floater's background and next-of-kin notification, we thought he should go on with that while Detective Arnold and I go to work on the neighborhood here."

The captain nodded. "Sounds reasonable," he said. "Let's not stand around here jawing about it, either. Get busy. I was in a meeting with Chief Rankin when the call came in. Do you realize that, counting this one, the city of Seattle now has a total of four homicides in just over two days? And if the one critical-condition drive-by victim at Harborview kicks off, that'll make five? Believe me, that doesn't bode well for the year, and it doesn't bode well for the chief, either. I'm putting you both on notice that he's going to be wanting progress. Immediate progress!"

"So what else is new?" I asked with a shrug. I couldn't resist the jibe. When the brass starts jumping up and down and demanding results yesterday, when they lose track of the fact that instant results often breed long-term disaster, that's when I have a hard time keeping a civil tongue in my mouth. In those situations, faced with all that bureaucratic huffing and puffing, I think a little healthy disrespect is good for all concerned. Kramer's exasperated answering glower warned me that he disagreed.

No doubt he wanted to distance himself from my moderately disrespectful jibe. Maybe he was worried that some of my reputation as Homicide's smart-ass-in-residence might rub off on him. And, although my comment may have irked Detective Kramer, it seemed to have very little effect on Captain Powell, who was more than capable of taking recalcitrant homicide cops in stride.

"Where do you stand on your end of it, Detective Beaumont?"

"I'd best be making some phone calls," I told him. "If Lizbeth Wolf turns out to be alive and well down in San Diego, then our tentative identification is wrong and we've got a Jane Doe dead in that apartment and two sets of next-of-kin notifications to handle."

"Get with the program, then," Powell told me. He turned to Kramer and Arnold. "And you two guys are canvassing the neighborhood?"

Kramer nodded. "And talking to the people in the building? All we're waiting on is an approximate time of death so we have some idea what to ask."

About that time, the elevator door opened. A police photographer stepped into the hallway. Captain Powell waved her into the apartment just as Audrey Cummings emerged, peeling off a pair of latex gloves. She must have heard the tail end of Kramer's answer.

"I'd say she's been dead for days. My guess, pending the autopsy, is two or three, but it could be less. The extreme heat in the apartment may have distorted the condition of the body. Who's going to be working on the identification?"

"I am," I answered. "I.D. and next of kin both."

Audrey nodded. "Good. Let me know what you find out. And remember, Beaumont. Positive I.D. None of this secondhand crap."

"Sure thing," I said. "I'll get on it right away."

I pushed the down button. When the elevator came, Jack Braman was inside and running the controls with a key. "That way, I can keep track of who comes and goes," he told me apologetically. "There's a whole bunch of reporters downstairs. I was afraid some of them would sneak into the garage and then go on upstairs without anyone knowing."

"Good thinking," I told him.

He stood there looking at me. The elevator key was in the lock, but since he hadn't pushed any buttons as yet, we still weren't moving.

"Is something wrong?" I asked.

He shrugged. "I was just wondering if . . . well, you know . . ."

"Know what?"

"Who it is? The person who's dead, I mean?"

"We don't know for sure. It may be his wife. We're checking."

"That would sure be better for me," he said.

His comment mystified me. "Better for you? What would?"

"If it turned out to be his wife," Braman replied. The elevator stopped, but he switched off the key, and the door didn't open. "Husbands and wives knock each other off all the time," he said. "That kind of thing happens. But if a hooker or even just a girlfriend were to turn up dead in the building, people might think I wasn't doing such a good job of managing the building. You understand that, don't you?"

"You're telling me that from a PR standpoint, it's more respectable for the building and better for your job performance if the victim turns out to be a resident's wife instead of a girlfriend or a prostitute?"

Braman nodded. "Don't you think so?" he asked, turning the key and opening the door.

"Actually," I told him, "I've never given the matter a whole lot of thought."

Just as Braman had warned me, a miniconvocation of local representatives of the Fourth Estate was taking place in the entry courtyard of the Lake View Condominiums. Phil Grimes, the guy who'd been tapped to replace Ron Peters in Media Relations, was standing in the middle of the crowd and being bombarded by the roving pack of reporters. It seemed obvious to me that since he'd just arrived on the scene, he probably wouldn't have much of anything to report. That didn't keep the newsies from peppering him with questions.

Using Grimes as a diversion, I headed for my car. I was almost there and thinking I had made a clean getaway when I heard someone calling me. "Detective Beaumont."

I stopped and looked back. Behind me, missing her cameraman, was the same television reporter I'd encountered twice the previous day, both at Pier 70 and out in front of Belltown Terrace during the soapsuds debacle. High heels clicking on the cement, she came hurrying after me. She was surprisingly old for a female television reporter—forty at least—but her makeup and clothing certainly made the most of what was there.

"Maribeth George," she said, holding out her hand. "Could I talk to you for a minute?"

Knowing who she was and what she did, I didn't exactly fall all over myself in my eagerness for a private chat. Years of being a cop have bred in me an instinctive distrust for the media—any kind of media. Even good-looking women in nice clothing. Maybe especially good-looking women.

"Miss George," I said coolly. "No doubt you've been in the news game long enough to know that detectives aren't supposed to talk to reporters."

My rebuff didn't seem to faze her. "Not even off the record?" she asked. "I left Stan and his camera over there," she added, jerking her head back toward the noisy group of reporters still eddying around Phil Grimes. "It's just the two of us. No recording devices of any kind."

"What do you want to talk about?" I asked.

Maribeth George had short brunette hair with a vivid streak of white that started just over her left eyebrow. Her dark-gray eyes, fringed by long, thick lashes, were made darker still by the carefully applied makeup that surrounded them.

"Somebody's dead in there, right?"

I nodded. With Audrey's van emblazoned with a KING COUNTY MEDICAL EXAMINER logo parked in the driveway, there wasn't much point in denying the obvious.

"Is this victim related to . . ." Maribeth George paused, "to yesterday's shooting victim down by Pier Seventy?"

I crossed my arms. The response was absolutely instinctive. So far, all that should have been internal law enforcement information only, including the fact that Don Wolf had died of a gunshot wound rather than drowning. As soon as I made the defensive, giveaway gesture, I could have kicked myself for it. Instead, I tried to cover up the instinctive *faux pas*.

"Shooting victim?" I asked, feigning innocence.

The reporter's somber gray eyes grew troubled and darker still. "The man they fished out of the water yesterday. Is that case related to this one? And if so, who are these people?"

"With regard to the second question, we're withholding names pending notification of next of kin. As for the first one, now that you mention it, maybe you'd like to explain to me exactly what makes you think that the man in the water was shot."

"A woman in a wheelchair told me," Maribeth George answered at once.

"What woman in what wheelchair?"

"The one down at Pier Seventy yesterday morning. She wasn't actually on the pier when I got there, but she said she had been. She claimed she was one of the people who found the body, but she didn't give me her name. In fact, she *refused* to give me her name. And now . . ." Maribeth's voice trailed off into nothing.

"Now what?" I prodded.

"I know you were working on that other case yesterday. I saw you there. And I know that homicide cases get passed around in rotation, so you most likely wouldn't be working on a new one unless it was somehow related to the one you were already working on. Right?"

I suppose one of the reasons detectives and journalists are always at one another's throats is that we're so much alike. We're all in the business of finding out what happened and who did what to whom, and we all want to be first in nailing down that information. An observant Maribeth George had put two and two together. Reporters, especially good-looking ones who are smart enough to come up with the correct answer of four, are definitely bad company for the likes of me.

"I trust you'll forgive me if right this minute I can't say yes or no," I said, reaching into my pocket and pulling out a card. "But I would most definitely be interested in whether or not this wheelchair lady of yours calls again."

Maribeth studied my face for a moment before she took the card. "I see," she said. "So that's how it is."

I nodded. She shrugged and stuffed my card into the pocket of her blazer. "I doubt I'll hear from her again," Maribeth said.

"But if you do, you can reach me at any one of those numbers," I said helpfully.

Maribeth George smiled. "Or I could just come across the street from the station and buzz you on your security phone. By the way, whatever happened with that soapsuds thing? The manager told me he thought little girls who live in the building were responsible for making the mess."

Talking to women can be mind-boggling at times. Maribeth George skipped effortlessly from murder to soapsuds in less than a heartbeat. "The girls didn't have anything to do with it," I answered shortly.

"You know them then?" Maribeth asked. "The little girls, I mean."

"Yes." I didn't add that I had supposedly been in charge of the girls at the time in question. Had I been doing my child-care job properly, the finger of suspicion never would have been pointed in their direction in the first place.

"The girls aren't yours, are they?"

"No. They're the daughters of a friend of mine."

"Well," she said, giving me one of her cards in exchange for mine. "Whoever did it," she said, "it doesn't seem like that big a deal."

"Right," I said. "It isn't. Now back to your wheelchair lady. You aren't planning to write anything about her, are you?"

Our conversation was like a fast-moving game of Ping-Pong with first one player on the offensive and then the other. It was my turn to spike the ball over the net. That comment immediately put Maribeth George on the defensive.

"I was," Maribeth said after a pause.

"Please don't," I said. "Not right away. If you run it prematurely, there's a chance it could jeopardize the investigation."

"Which one?" she asked.

I shook my head and didn't answer. "Maybe both?" she asked. The woman was downright dangerous. "What about after you make an arrest?"

"At that point," I said, "you're welcome to broadcast anything you want. You'll wait then?"

She nodded. "I suppose," she said.

I started to walk away, then turned back to her with one last question. "There were a lot of people down at Pier Seventy yesterday morning. Why do you think the wheelchair lady picked you out of the crowd as the person to talk to—or did she talk to lots of people and you're the only one who's bothered to come forward?"

Maribeth shrugged and laughed a surprisingly self-deprecating laugh. "You know how it is when you're a media babe," she said with a grin. "Lots of people feel like they know you even though you don't know them. I've been a frequent and almost daily guest in thousands of homes since I came back to Seattle last summer. She probably thinks of me as a friend of the family."

"Media babe?" I repeated, not quite believing my ears. "I would have thought . . ."

Maribeth laughed aloud. When she did, I noticed that her teeth were white and straight. "That the words *media babe* aren't exactly politically correct," I added.

"You're right," she agreed. "They aren't, and I'd strongly recommend against you using them in public, especially if there are female reporters anywhere within hearing distance. It's like African Americans and the *N* word. When blacks use it on other blacks, they usually do so with impunity. If you or I were to use it, all hell would break loose."

"What would happen if I called you a media babe?"

She grinned again. "You know about hell, fury, and women, don't you?"

I'm not used to joking around with reporters, but I laughed in spite of myself. "I feel the same way about outsiders who call detectives *dicks*," I told her.

"See there?" she said.

Phil Grimes disappeared into the building. We could both see that the group that had surrounded him was starting to break up. "Hey, Maribeth," the cameraman called. "Where'd you run off to?"

"Gotta go," she said to me. "See you around."

She trotted off to rejoin her cameraman, and I climbed into my car. Glancing at my watch, I was surprised to see that the afternoon was half shot. It was already after three. Other than finding a second body, I had accomplished very little. I still had done nothing at all about contacting Don Wolf's next of kin or about finding some kind of foolproof verification for Lizbeth Wolf's I.D. Bearing all that in mind, I headed straight for the office.

On my way to my cubicle in the Public Safety Building, I had to walk directly past Sergeant Watkins' desk.

"Wait a minute," Watty said. "Don't go down there without taking this with you."

He handed me a large white envelope with D.G.I.'s return address printed in the upper right-hand corner. The words HANDLE WITH CARE—CONTAINS VIDEOTAPES had been handwritten in huge block letters across the top of the envelope. No doubt these were the tapes Deanna Compton was going to copy and send me.

Watty looked up at me and grinned. "What is it?" he asked. "One of those Blockbuster evenings?"

"Not exactly," I told him. "I don't think any of these will be quite that good."

As I continued down the hallway I ripped open the envelope and shook out the contents. A typed memo fell into my hand along with the three tapes.

To: Detective J. P. Beaumont
From: Deanna Compton

Enclosed please find copies of the tapes you requested. I have cued them all to what I believe are the pertinent spots so you won't have to go scrolling through the whole thing.

If I can be of any further assistance, please be sure to let me know.

Deanna Compton,
for Bill Whitten

For a moment, I considered calling Designer Genes International and letting Bill Whitten know what was going on, that Don Wolf's wife was most likely dead right along with her husband. But I decided against it. Just because Audrey Cummings didn't think Bill Whitten was capable of shooting someone didn't mean I had to agree. As far as I was concerned, Whitten was still a suspect.

With the tapes and note still in hand, I bypassed my own office in favor of one of the small conference rooms at the end of the hall. There, I plugged the first tape into the slot of the VCR. I had a one-in-three chance of picking the right tape first time up to bat, and I won big.

True to her word, Deanna Compton had cued the tape to the right place. When the tape came on the screen, Latty and Don Wolf were standing in the elevator. Wolf was standing next to the controls, and Latty was pressed into the far corner, with as much distance between the two of them as was humanly possible in that confined space.

I watched the whole sequence. The whole time they were in the elevator they maintained an absolute silence. "One down, two to go," I said, pulling the useless tape out of the VCR and inserting another.

The second tape was the one with the rape on it. There was no need to watch that one again. I ejected it, and inserted the third. This time, the screen held two separate, side-by-side images.

Both cameras were mounted from much the same position over the front entryway door of D.G.I., but they were aimed in opposite directions. One looked out on the driveway and the busy street beyond. The other focused on the front door of the building. The readout in the corner of the screen said: DECEMBER 28, 12:06:32 A.M. That meant this was from Thursday morning, less than ten minutes after Don Wolf's assault on the girl named Latty.

Seconds later, the elevator door opened. Latty and Don Wolf came across the lighted lobby toward the door. Wolf was still dressed in his shirt sleeves; Latty still clutched his oversized jacket around her ruined clothing.

As they came toward the lobby door, a sudden movement from the other part of the screen caught my eye. Glancing there, I expected to see the arrival of a cab. Instead, the driveway area where the cab would naturally have stopped was empty. Puzzled about the unidentified movement, I flipped the remote control to rewind.

Because I don't watch television all that much, I'm not nearly as handy with what Heather calls *clickers* as Ron's two girls are. Naturally, I overshot the mark and came to a stop with the readout showing DECEMBER 27, 11:45:50 P.M. I had rewound beyond the place where I wanted to stop by almost twenty-five minutes.

"Damn!" I muttered aloud. "Too far."

I was about to fast-forward the tape when a car slid into the camera's viewfinder and stopped in front of the building. The headlights went off, but no one got out. From everything Bill Whitten had said, I had assumed Don Wolf and Latty had been alone in the building, but here, only a few minutes before the two of them had appeared on the screen in Don Wolf's office, someone else had made a midnight call on the headquarters of Designer Genes International.

Because the screen was separated into two simultaneous images, the picture on the department's twenty-one-inch viewing screen was very small. I leaned closer, trying to ascertain what I was seeing. And when I did, I could barely believe my eyes.

The car was an older-model Crown Victoria, vintage 1988 or so. In the distorted mercury vapor lighting, the vehicle appeared to be lavender. A car that old—what used-car salesmen always call "reliable transportation"—is the kind of vehicle that blends. It's old enough not to be out of place in some neighborhoods and new enough to fit into others. What set this one apart, however, was the distinctive, clam-shaped attachment that had been fitted to the vehicle's roof. I recognized it at once, because, except for the color, it was almost a carbon copy of the one on Ron Peters' Buick.

If it weren't for Ron, I wouldn't have known anything at all about Braun Chair Toppers. These units, resembling old-fashioned, top-of-car luggage carriers, are specially designed for carrying wheelchairs. They come complete with motorized lifts that raise or lower chairs as needed.

I know for a fact there aren't all that many
Brauns around Seattle these days, because people
who need wheelchair capability tend to go after
one of those newer-model minivans—ones that
come with either lifts or ramps. Ron Peters had
bought the Braun after a single look at prices on
the vans had thrown him into an almost terminal
case of sticker shock. The Chair Topper had provided him with a relatively inexpensive way of
converting his old sedan into a wheelchair-
carrying mode of transportation. It had worked
so well, in fact, that when his Reliant died an awful death as a result of a car chase through the
Sea-Tac Airport parking garage, he was able to
move the Chair Topper from the dead Reliant to
its secondhand Buick replacement within a matter of days.

Seconds and minutes ticked away in real time
while I continued to watch the video of the
Crown Victoria parked in front of D.G.I. I des-
perately wanted to catch a glimpse of the person
driving the wheelchair-equipped car. After all,
Maribeth George had just told me that a woman
in a wheelchair seemed to know a good deal
about this case.

*Get out*, I found myself silently urging the unseen driver. *Get out of the car and let me take a look
at you.*

But no such luck. Nobody moved. Occasionally, cars and headlights slid past on Western, but
the parked car didn't move, the doors didn't
open. Then, at exactly 12:07:00, and with no dis-

cernible warning, the headlights flashed on. The
Crown Victoria pulled away from the curb,
paused for several seconds, and disappeared onto
Western. On the other half of the screen, Don
Wolf and Latty were just emerging from the elevator. So the movement that had caught my eye
had been the Crown Victoria leaving, not a cab
arriving.

Moments later, two people came out through
the building's front door. They stepped out to the
edge of the driveway, almost to the same spot
where the Crown Victoria had been parked earlier. Latty was crying again, but as far as I could
tell, no words were exchanged during the next
eight minutes while they waited for the cab. They
were both underdressed for the weather. Looking
at the shivering, weeping girl pictured on the
screen, the father part of me couldn't help wondering where the hell she had left her damn coat.

Finally, a Yellow Cab pulled up to the curb.
Naturally, Wolf darted out and opened the door.
Ignoring him, Latty walked around to the other
side of the cab and let herself into the car.

As I switched the tape to rewind, I felt a surge
of relief. Latty had gotten into a cab that had
taken her somewhere—to an address. And with
an address and a description, I'd be able to learn
Latty's last name.

*Now we're getting somewhere,* I told myself glee-
fully. *Now we're finally getting somewhere.*

# Eight

For several minutes after I clicked off the VCR, I sat without moving in the darkened fifth-floor conference room. I had replayed the front-entrance sequence several times. I had even played the beginning of the rape tape to double-check the exact time Don Wolf and Latty had arrived at his office.

There was no doubt in my mind that those several occurrences were somehow interrelated. The Crown Victoria had parked in front of the building about two minutes prior to Don Wolf and Latty's appearance in his office. Assuming they had parked in the garage under the building and maybe necked a little on the way inside, then it was conceivable that whoever was at the wheel of the Victoria had followed them to the building. And the fact that the unseen driver had gunned away from the curb just as the elevator door opened meant that whoever it was hadn't wanted to be spotted.

Now, after switching on the light, I pulled out my notebook and began to assemble a TO DO list.

1. Locate and notify Wolf next of kin.
2. Locate proper I.D. on Lizbeth Wolf.
3. Find Latty.
4. Find Wheelchair Lady.
5. Watch the ten o'clock news.
6. Rewatch the tapes on a big screen; license #???
7. Work on report.

*Making* TO DO lists is always far easier than *doing* TO DO lists, but I left the conference room and headed back to my cubicle to get started. My first call was to D.G.I. Bill Whitten wasn't in, so I asked to speak to Deanna Compton.

"Detective Beaumont," she said when I identified myself, "did you get the packet I messengered over to you?"

"Yes, thanks so much. I've taken a cursory look at the tapes, and I have a couple of questions for you. Does D.G.I. have any wheelchair-bound employees?"

"Wheelchair? No, none that I can think of. Why?"

"There was a car with a wheelchair rack parked in front of the building on the night Don Wolf took the girl up to his office. I was wondering if you had any idea who the vehicle might belong to and whether or not there was a legitimate reason for it to be here. For instance, could it belong to someone working on the janitorial crew?"

"If it does, I don't know anything about it."

"Let me ask you something else, then. On your personnel records, do you ask employees to list people who should be contacted in case of emergency?"

"Yes."

"Could you check and see if Don Wolf listed anyone other than his wife?"

"You can't find her?"

Time to duck and run. Right that minute I didn't want to reveal to anyone even the most general details of the grisly remains we'd found waiting for us in Don Wolf's condo. "Not at the moment," I said. "I was hoping you could help me locate someone else."

"Just a minute, please," Deanna said. "I have his file right here."

There was a long pause. I could hear paper shuffling on the other end while she looked through the file. "No," she said eventually. "Lizbeth is the only one listed here."

"I see."

"Does it list a place of birth?"

"Tulsa, Oklahoma."

I thought about that for a moment. Birth records generally stay put, but people don't necessarily do the same. Trying to track down someone that way can be a time-consuming, tedious process. What I needed was a shortcut.

They say the only things in life that are certain are death and taxes. But right up there on the list, running a close third, are calls from college and university alumni associations. I think it's virtually impossible to permanently dodge the armies of telephone-wielding fund-raisers who track their potential victims to the ends of the earth.

"Where did Don Wolf go to school?" I asked.

"His bachelor's is from Stanford. MBA is from Harvard."

With Deanna reading me the information, I jotted down the degrees Don Wolf had earned, his majors and minors, and the years in which the degrees were conferred. Obviously, at four o'clock in the afternoon, it was far too late to talk to anyone at Harvard. But there was a chance I could still reach someone down at Stanford.

In the past, I would have played it straight— called in, identified myself properly as a police officer, and then worked my way up the chain of command. Recently, though, my months spent in a tempestuous off-again/on-again relationship with a lady named Alexis Downey, a development officer who raises funds for the Seattle Repertory Theatre, has given me another perspective.

Alexis is an enticing handful, but she's one of those women who, although she has a strong career track going, also has an audibly ticking biological time clock. We broke up completely when I finally convinced her that, at my stage of advancing middle age, I would never be willing to take a second crack at fatherhood. Being with Alexis has taught me a thing or two, not only about women, but also about how devious-minded and cagey development officers can be.

Bearing that in mind, I approached the Stanford alumni office with what I knew would be irresistible bait. Once I had a likely candidate on the phone, I identified myself as Roger Philpott, an attorney with Bates, Philpott, and Orange. (I figured if I was going to try my hand at lying I could just as well have some fun with it.) I told the young woman on the phone that one of the university's alums had died suddenly and there was a chance, if no other heirs could be located, that his entire estate would be left to the university.

"Is it a very big estate?" the young woman asked. The audible catch of excitement in her voice made me feel like a regular heel.

"It's the biggest one I've ever handled," I told her. That, at least, wasn't a lie.

"Do you have his matriculation number?" she asked, and I knew I had her. I couldn't provide a matric number, but I gave her everything else—the year Don Wolf graduated and the degree he'd received, and then I waited. And waited. And waited some more, listening to Muzak all the while. Finally, she came back on the phone sounding puzzled and disappointed.

"There must be some mistake," she said. "I can't find a Donald R. Wolf registered that year.

In fact, the closest Donald Wolf I've found is a Donald B. who graduated in electrical engineering, but that was five years later than the date you gave me."

"That's strange," I said. "Let me do some more checking and get back to you."

I put down the phone and sat looking at it. If one statement on a job application isn't true, chances are other things are false as well. I picked up the phone once more and redialed D.G.I.

"Do you have Don Wolf's previous employment records?"

"I suppose," Deanna said, sounding slightly impatient. "Just a minute."

Again there was a period of paper shuffling before Deanna came back on the line. "Do you need complete addresses?"

"Please," I said.

Deanna ended up giving me three names, addresses, and phone numbers: Downlink, San Diego, California; Bio-Dart Technologies, Pasadena, California; Holman-Smith Industries, City of Industry, California. It was almost five o'clock by then, but I figured even if the switchboards were closed, I'd probably still connect with someone.

I dialed the first number. After two rings, the distinctive disconnect sound came through the receiver, followed by a recorded message. "The number you have reached is no longer in service. Please check the number and dial again. If you feel you have reached this number in error, please hang up and dial the operator."

My first thought was that maybe the company had just moved, but a check with the operator came up empty. Mentally, I crossed Downlink off the list. I tried the number listed for Bio-Dart. This time, a little kid answered. Figuring I had somehow misdialed and rather than trying to explain, I hung up and redialed with the same result. This time, though, the phone was wrested away from the child by a woman.

"Who is this?" she demanded.

"I'm looking for a company named Bio-Dart," I told her, and then read off the number Deanna Compton had given me. "They probably do some kind of bioengineering."

"That's my number, mister," the woman responded. "But there's nobody here but my son and me. The only kind of bioengineering we do here is an occasional batch of chocolate chip cookies."

"There must be some mistake," I said. "Please excuse the ring."

The number for Holman-Smith turned out to be a disconnect as well. In other words, as near as I could tell, not one of those three companies existed at the moment. I was beginning to wonder if they ever had. Most likely, the Harvard MBA would turn out to be equally bogus, but checking on that would have to wait until morning.

When an investigation runs into an unexpected blank wall, that's the time for partners. Sometimes, all it takes is a brainstorming session over a cup or two of coffee to figure out a way to get back on track, but Sue Danielson was stuck in Cincinnati with a bad case of chicken pox. That meant brainstorming with her was out, and I sure as hell wasn't going to try mulling things over with Paul Kramer. When it comes to the free-flowing exchange of ideas, Detective Kramer is definitely not my type.

What I did do finally was pick up the phone and call Audrey Cummings at the medical examiner's office up in Harborview Hospital. "Make this quick, Beaumont," she said. "I was supposed to start Don Wolf's autopsy half an hour ago."

"Did you print him?"

"No. We could, but don't usually do that unless there's a question of identification."

"There might be in this case."

"Are you trying to tell me that Bill Whitten misidentified the body?" Audrey asked. "It would be nice to know exactly who's dead and who isn't."

"What I'm saying is that the person Bill Whitten thinks of as Don Wolf may have been someone else all along." As briefly as possible, I went on to explain the difficulties I'd encountered in trying to locate possible next of kin. Then I enumerated the phony employment and educational references I had blundered into along the way. I must have made a fairly good case of it. When I finished, Audrey capitulated.

"All right, all right," she agreed. "We'll print

him, then. But you won't have either prints or autopsy results before noon tomorrow at the earliest. If you have something for me on the woman by then, maybe we can make a trade—prints on him in exchange for a positive I.D. on her?"

"It's a deal," I told her, although it didn't seem very likely that I would meet that noontime deadline, not at the rate I was going.

It was long after five when I finally gave up on the first item of my TO DO list and took an initial crack at number two. If you believe what passes for homicide cops on television, this job entails nothing more than car chases and pitched gun battles. On a day-to-day basis, I spend far more time with a telephone glued to my ear than with a weapon in my hand.

My first call on that score was to Alpha-Cyte, the La Jolla biotechnology company Deanna Compton had told me had employed Lizbeth Wolf. And because I was calling so late in the afternoon, my efforts met with exactly what they deserved—an unguided trip through a voice-mail jungle.

"Alpha-Cyte's office hours are nine to five, Monday through Friday," the recorded voice told me. "If you know the extension of the person to whom you wish to speak, please dial that number now; otherwise, stay on the line for more options."

Voice-mail options never include quite what you want, especially if you don't know exactly who it is you need to speak to or what his or her extension number might be. The last choice was to leave a message and someone would get back to me.

"I don't think so," I said, and hung up. "It's time to send out for reinforcements."

With the help of a directory assistance operator, thirty seconds later I was on the phone with Captain Wayne Kilpatrick, a homicide supervisor down in La Jolla, California.

"What can I do for you, Detective Beaumont?" he asked, once I had identified myself.

"I'm working on a case up here in Seattle," I told him. "Two of them, actually. It's possible both victims may be former residents of La Jolla. I'm trying to verify I.D.s and do next-of-kin notifications, and I'm running into walls."

"Maybe you'd better fill me in on the details."

That didn't take long, because it turned out I didn't know much. "I'll get someone on it right away," Kilpatrick said when I finished. "I'll check with Dispatch to see if there's an emergency number on record for Alpha-Cyte. And we'll check out that home address you gave me as well. I'll have one of my officers get back to you ASAP. Give me your number."

Instead of one number, I gave him the full set— home, office, and cell phone. "Thanks for the help," I said.

"Whaddya expect?" Captain Kilpatrick returned. "It's our job."

"One more thing," I added. "Do you have access to any old telephone books?"

"How old?" he asked.

"Last year's," I said. "Maybe even the year prior to that. I'm looking for the last place Don Wolf listed as a place of employment before taking the job in Seattle."

"You're in luck there," Kilpatrick told me. "Last year's phone book is the only one I have. Somebody stole my new one."

"Look up a company called Downlink," I told him.

"It's not here," Kilpatrick said a few moments later. "How could he give it as a place of employment if it doesn't exist? Sort of makes you wonder what he was up to, doesn't it."

"It does," I muttered, putting down the phone. "Indeed it does."

Returning to my TO DO list, I placed a check mark beside number two before turning my attention to number three: Find Latty.

In that regard, the greatest possibility of success lay with the cab driver. In the best of all possible worlds, Don Wolf would have called Farwest Cab instead of Yellow. Years ago, I was involved in a case where a Farwest cabby was murdered. What initially looked like a straightforward robbery gone awry actually turned out to be a complicated insurance plot staged by the man's estranged wife and her boyfriend. I was the one who cracked the case and sent both the wife and boyfriend to the slammer. Whenever I need Farwest info, I can always get it—fast and without any hassle.

Back in my Fuller Brush days when I was working my way through school, I learned the value of third-party referrals. It was always easier to sell brushes to someone if a neighbor up the street called ahead to say I was coming. Naturally, I called Farwest first.

"Hey, J.P.," said Wally, one of Farwest's old-hand dispatchers. "Long time no see, especially now that you don't need your butt hauled out of bars on a regular basis. How long you been off the sauce?"

"Two years and a little bit."

"Good for you. I just passed five. Still going to meetings?"

"Some," I said, although the correct answer probably should have been "hardly any."

"What can I do you for?" Wally asked.

"I need some help with a Yellow."

"Either you need your vision checked or you're screwing up the alphabet. Farwest is in the *F's*, not the *Y's*," Wally told me. "And our cabs are green, not yellow."

After I explained the situation, there was a pause during which Wally sent out several cabs. "You know, J.P.," he said a little testily, "there are ways to get at those customer logs through official channels."

"I'm aware of that," I returned, "but all those channels take time. And mountains of paperwork."

"You can say that again," Wally sighed. "So all right. I'll see what I can do, but I'm not making any promises. Some of those Yellow guys are jerks. How can I get back in touch with you?"

I gave him my numbers. Then, smiling to myself, I replaced the receiver in its cradle and put a check mark beside number three. I was definitely making progress. For number four, I called upstairs. Ron Peters answered his own phone.

"Are you still here?"

"No," he answered. "I've mastered the art of being in two places at once. What do you want?"

"To talk to you. Are you on your way out the door right this minute?"

"I should be, but I'm not. Come on up. I need to talk to you, too."

One would think that in the natural order of police hierarchy, the chief's office would be the undisputed departmental sanctum sanctorum. But at Seattle P.D., the chief's office has an open door compared to the Internal Investigations Section. I.I.S., on the eleventh floor, is ruled by the iron hand and unwavering Eagle Scout mentality of one Captain Anthony Freeman. In the world of I.I.S., security is paramount. Even after hours, just to drop by and visit with Ron Peters for a couple of minutes, I had to sign in and out at the reception desk.

Somehow, despite perennial budget tightening, Captain Freeman manages to keep I.I.S. looking more like reasonably well appointed corporate offices than the jumbled mishmash of aging office furnishings that exists in every other department of Seattle P.D. Ron Peters' office didn't measure

up in grandeur or view to Captain Freeman's, but
it was a damn sight better than my crowded cubicle on the fifth floor.

"What's up?" Ron asked, wheeling back to his
desk after letting me into the room.

"Tell me where you got your Chair Topper," I
said.

Ron grinned at me. "What's the matter," he
quipped. "Are your heel spurs acting up so much
that you're headed for a chair? Amy tells me surgery can do wonders for those these days."

"It's not for me," I said. "It's the case I'm working on—two related cases, as a matter of fact.
Each one comes complete with a mysterious
wheelchair-bound female witness who drives
around in an elderly Crown Victoria with a Chair
Topper on it that looks a whole lot like yours."

"Cool," Ron said. "No telling what people in
chairs are up to these days. If the lady in question
bought her Chair Topper locally, you can pretty
well figure it came from Rich's Northwest Mobility. It's up in Snohomish County, on Maltby
Road."

To people who live in the Denny Regrade,
words like *Snohomish* or *Maltby Road* are enough
to give you heartburn. Those hard-to-place place
names denote exurbs, not suburbs. Foolhardy city
dwellers who venture out in search of them
would be wise to arm themselves with a current
copy of *The Thomas Guide*.

"I assume Rich is the owner, then?" I asked,
making a quick notation in my notebook.

Ron shook his head. "Rich is long gone. He started the place as a customizing joint for hot rods. A young couple named Eddie and Amanda bought Rich out years ago. After a while, they ended up going straight, as they put it. They're out of hot rods completely. They still do customizing, all right, but now it's strictly to create handicapped-accessible vehicles."

"Would they talk to me?" I asked.

"Who, Eddie and Amanda? Of course they would. I'll call ahead and let them know you'll be stopping by. When?"

"Tomorrow sometime," I said. "I'm sure as hell not going to fight my way over there now in the middle of rush-hour traffic."

"Wise decision," Ron agreed. "I'll call them first thing in the morning. Anything else?"

"Not right now." I stood up to leave, but Ron motioned me back into my chair. His face grew suddenly somber.

"Have you heard from Roz yet . . . from Sister Constance, I mean?" he asked.

"Sister Constance!" I said. "Why would I be hearing from your ex-wife?"

"You probably won't hear from her directly," Ron said, "but you'll be hearing from someone. She's coming after us demanding full custody. She's charging Amy and me with willful child neglect."

"Child neglect!" I exclaimed. "You and Amy? You've got to be kidding."

Ron shook his head sadly. "I'm not kidding, Beau. I only wish I were."

# Nine

**H**alf an hour later, I skulked back down to my fifth-floor cubicle. I had been feeling pretty cocky when I checked off *Find Latty*. I wasn't nearly as chipper when I put the little check mark next to number four, *Find Wheelchair Lady*. Somehow, the possibility that Ron and Amy Peters might lose permanent custody of Heather and Tracy had taken the blush right off my little investigatory rose.

I studied the remaining items on my list. There wasn't anything on it that I couldn't do at home. The big-screened TV—useful for reviewing the tapes and also for watching the news if I managed to make it all the way to ten o'clock—was right there in my den. And as for working on reports, including the almost completed ones the computer had eaten, that could be done on my laptop—assuming I could get the damned thing

136

running again—while sitting in my very own recliner.

Gathering things into a wad, I was about to switch off the overhead light when Detective Kramer stuck his head in the doorway. "There you are," he said, "I thought you were still here."

*Caught*, I thought.

"With any luck, I wouldn't have been," I told him cheerfully. "What's up? If you're going to brief me on what you and Arnold found out this afternoon, couldn't it wait until morning? I'm beat."

"One of your star witnesses just stopped by to pay a visit," Kramer said. "I told her to wait in my office while I tried to track you down."

Kramer's cat-eating-shit grin as he spoke warned me that something wasn't quite right. "What star witness?" I asked.

"Her name's Johnny," he said. "Johnny Bickford. And she particularly asked for Detective Beaumont. She wasn't the least bit interested in talking to anyone else, even though I tried to assure her that we were working the same case."

Groaning inwardly and wondering how long Johnny Bickford had been traipsing around the fifth floor, I followed Kramer down the hall to his cubicle, which happens to be two doors away from Captain Powell's fishbowl. Parked next to Kramer's desk sat Johnny Bickford in 100-percent full-dress drag, complete with frosted wig, impossibly high heels, dark-colored panty hose, and a tightly belted trench coat which emphasized that Johnny's Wonder-Bra was still performing its figure-producing magic. A massive leather purse sat on the floor next to his feet, which were demurely crossed—at the ankle.

Looking at him made me think of that old 1950s classic *Some Like It Hot* with Marilyn Monroe, Tony Curtis, and Jack Lemmon. I remember seeing the movie back then and being pretty much mystified by all those men running around in women's clothing. And although I'm supposedly older and wiser than I was in Ballard back in 1959, I have to admit that I *still* don't understand it. Nor, would I venture to say, do most of my Homicide colleagues on the fifth floor of the Public Safety Building.

"Hello, Johnny," I said without enthusiasm. "You wanted to see me?"

Chirping with glee, Johnny leaped to his/her feet the moment I appeared in the doorway. "Why, there you are, Detective Beaumont. I was about to give up hope that this nice Detective Kramer would ever be able to find you. He's been *so* helpful."

"I'll just bet he has," I said. "Come on, we'll go down to my office to talk."

"You're more than welcome to talk here if you like," Detective Kramer offered genially.

"No," I said, giving Kramer a black look. "I don't think so."

"Detective Beaumont is right," Johnny added. "I've already taken too much of your time, but I do appreciate your visiting with me. Detective

Kramer and I were just sitting here chatting. You police officers do lead such interesting lives."

"Yes," I agreed grimly. "We certainly do."

While Johnny groped for his purse, Kramer planted himself in the doorway, blocking our exit. "Johnny here seems to have a very high opinion of your skill as an investigator," Paul Kramer said with a deceptively bland smile. "She dropped by the department to ask you to sign an autograph for her mother back in Wichita."

"Another one?" I asked.

"Another one?" Kramer repeated. "You mean you've signed autographs before? Sounds more like a major-league baseball player than a cop. You don't charge for it, do you?"

"No," I said. "No charge."

Kramer shook his head. "I don't understand it," he said. "Nobody's ever asked me for my autograph."

Now it was my turn to smile. "I'm sure Johnny here could remedy that. As far as your mother is concerned, one detective's signature should do just as well as any other's, shouldn't it?"

"I suppose," Johnny agreed dubiously, "but the truth is—no offense, Detective Kramer—I really did have my heart set on Detective Beaumont's. You don't mind, do you?"

"Oh, no," Kramer said. "Not at all!"

That's what he *said*, but it wasn't what he *meant*. On the face of it, the whole idea of someone wanting a detective's autograph was more than slightly ridiculous. Still, I knew enough about Kramer to understand that he was feeling slighted. And jealous. I could see that for myself in the involuntary twitch that was tweaking the corners of his thin mouth. The twitch, combined with the humorless glower in Kramer's eyes, warned me that both Johnny Bickford's request for an autograph, along with his outrageous appearance, would be a hot topic around Homicide for months to come. Detective Kramer would see to it.

"Let's go, Johnny," I repeated. "I'm sure Detective Kramer has work to do."

Hoping we wouldn't meet too many of my fellow detectives along the way, I herded Johnny down the hall and into my cubicle. Once seated at the chair next to my disaster of a desk, my visitor began fumbling in the purse. What he finally excavated was an envelope containing a carefully folded newspaper article.

"A reporter called me this morning from *The Seattle Times*," Johnny said. "She interviewed me about finding the body. The article came out in this afternoon's edition. Since my name actually appears in this one, I thought I'd rather send it home to Mother instead of the first one where I'm only the nameless jogger."

JOGGING INTO HEALTH AND HOMICIDE

Johnny handed me the article, and I scanned the first several lines:

When Johnny Bickford went jogging down along Alaskan Way on New Year's morning, she was only keeping a New Year's resolution to take better care of herself. Trying to get into better shape has now embroiled the lower Queen Anne resident in a homicide investigation. She has spoken to police detectives in regard to one of the two violent deaths and several assaults that marred Seattle's New Year's celebration.

As Ms. Bickford rested on Pier 70, catching her breath, she spotted a body floating facedown in the waters of Elliot Bay. Seattle police investigators have since stated that the victim, a white male in his late thirties, died as a result of a gunshot wound. The victim has been tentatively identified, but his name is being withheld pending notification of next of kin.

I looked up at Johnny Bickford, who was watching me with rapt attention. "Where do you want me to sign this thing?" I asked.

"Right under the headline, I suppose," Johnny said. Shaking my head, I started to comply. "You didn't tell me he died of a gunshot wound," Johnny continued reproachfully.

"It wasn't something you needed to know," I returned. "As a matter of fact, the newspapers weren't supposed to know it, either."

Johnny Bickford mulled that last statement while I finished signing the article and passed it back to him. "I suppose you think it's morbid, my wanting you to sign the articles," he said.

"It's none of my business one way or the other," I answered.

"You see," Johnny went on, "I've always secretly wondered what it would be like to be involved in a murder investigation, and now I am."

"Excuse me," I returned. "You discovered a body, but that doesn't mean you're involved."

"But couldn't Seattle P.D. use someone like me?" Johnny asked. "As an informant or something? Believe me, I could get into places a regular cop could never dream of going."

"I'm sure that's true, but I don't think the department is in the market for that particular kind of information."

"But Detective Kramer said..." Bickford stopped.

"What exactly did Detective Kramer say?"

"That each detective develops his own network of informants. I thought maybe I could work for you. On a voluntary basis, of course. I wouldn't expect to be paid anything. I just think it would be utterly fascinating."

The phone rang at my elbow. In order to answer it, I had to unearth it from beneath a mound of loose paperwork. "Detective Beaumont, here."

A brisk female voice came on the line. "This is Sally Redding, with Yellow Cab. I understand you were looking for some information?"

"Just a sec," I said into the phone. Then I

turned to Johnny. "This is private," I told him. "You'll have to go."

Nodding, Johnny picked up the purse and started toward the door. "But, if you change your mind . . ."

"If I do," I said, "I'll be in touch." Johnny left my cubicle, and I turned my attention back to the phone. "Sorry," I said, "someone was here in my office, and yes, I did need some information."

"The owner of the company has authorized me to tell you what you need to know," Sally Redding said. "The car you were asking about is number eleven forty-eight. On that particular night, the twenty-eighth, it was driven by Norm Otis. He picked up a fare from thirty-three hundred Western at approximately twelve-twenty A.M. and drove her to a building on Main Street in Bellevue. The number there is one zero two eight five Main."

"Is that a house or an apartment?" I asked, jotting the information in my notebook.

"I can't tell that from the record," Sally Redding answered. "We have building information for pickups, but not for dropoffs."

"When can I talk to Norm Otis?"

"He came on duty at six tonight, but he's off on a call right now. Do you want me to have him get back to you when he's available?"

"Please," I said. "The sooner the better." I gave her my collection of possible phone numbers.

"I'll see what I can do," Sally returned, but she didn't sound exactly overjoyed at the prospect.

"I appreciate your help, Ms. Redding" I said. "I really do."

"Right," she said, sounding unconvinced.

"And be sure to have him try the home number first. I'm leaving the office as soon as I finish gathering things up. I should be there in just a matter of minutes."

I parked the 928 on the P-4 level of the Belltown Terrace garage and took the elevator as far as the lobby, where I stopped off to pick up my mail. As I headed back toward the elevator, the lobby door opened and in came Gail Richardson and her Afghan hound, Charlie.

A renter of one of the larger upper units, Gail is some kind of bigwig on a Seattle-based sitcom that had just been renewed for a second season. She's a tall, good-looking woman in her late forties. Her hair is snow white, without, as she tells it, the benefit of any chemical enhancements. She is one of the few people I know who can manage the difficult feat of appearing totally dignified while holding a leashed dog in one hand and a plastic bag of still-warm dog crap in the other.

When I stepped aside to allow her and the dog aboard the elevator first, however, she looked decidedly harried. And knowing that some of her holiday company had been staying with her for the better part of three weeks, I guessed at the problem.

"When do you finally get your life back?" I asked.

She flashed me a woebegone smile. "Maybe

never. I'm sure you heard all about it."

"All about what?"

"My mother took Charlie for a walk today and forgot how to get back to the building. Luckily, one of the Denny Regrade security officers spotted them and knew where they belonged. I hate to think what would have happened if he hadn't come to the rescue."

I had been introduced to Gail's mother, Nina Hopper, at a Belltown Terrace pre-Christmas party. Nina, a birdlike woman in her mid-to-late eighties, had seemed bright enough when I talked with her, but we had spoken for only a matter of minutes.

"She forgot where the building was?" I asked.

Gail nodded. "My sister had mentioned her growing forgetfulness and that it was becoming more and more worrisome. She had talked about getting one of those bracelets for her, so other people could help her find her way home if need be. Here in a strange city, her getting lost like that could have been disastrous. And then after that mess with the hot tub . . ."

"What mess with the hot tub?" I asked.

"Don't tell me you didn't hear about that. It even made the news. Mother thought she would help me out by cleaning the bathroom. She must have put half a bottle of liquid soap in the tub. Then she turned on the water and the jets and shut the bathroom door. By the time I realized what was happening, the bathroom was floor-to-ceiling bubbles. I guess it made a terrible mess in the party room." The door opened and Gail and Charlie stepped off.

"You mean your *mother* did that?" I asked, holding the door open.

"Yes."

"Did you know that Dick and Francine blamed Heather and Tracy?"

Gail nodded. "It's an understandable mistake, I suppose. I didn't have a chance to tell them about it until late last night, after I finished cleaning up the mess in my own apartment."

I tried not to let my face betray the smug relief I felt now that the girls had been totally exonerated. "I'm sorry things are so bad with your mother, Gail," I said sympathetically. "Is there anything I can do?"

She looked at me and smiled. "You already did it," she said. "You gave me a way of letting off steam *before* I walk back into the apartment. Believe me, that's a big help. Good night."

I rode on up to my own floor. It struck me that Dick Mathers, Belltown's resident manager, ought to go on TV and make a public apology for accusing Heather and Tracy of the hot tub bubble caper, but that didn't seem likely. Dick Mathers isn't the apologizing type.

Once in the den, I pored over the tapes on my big-screen TV. Unfortunately, it didn't make any difference. No matter how hard I tried, I couldn't make out the license number on the back of the Crown Victoria. I'm enough of an expert to know that enhancing a video image is possible, but I didn't have either the technical skill or the equipment to do so, not there in my apartment at nine o'clock at night.

The phone rang about then, offering a welcome interruption. "Detective Beaumont?" a man's voice asked uncertainly.

"Yes."

"This here's Norm Otis with Yellow Cab. I know I was supposed to call you earlier this evening, but it's been real busy tonight. This is the first chance I've had."

"That's all right, Mr. Otis. Did Sally Redding tell you what I wanted?"

"She sure did. About that poor girl from last week. I'm glad to hear someone's doing something about it. I felt really sorry for her, just as sorry as I could be. I don't think I've ever heard anybody cry as hard as that. Like her heart was broken. But she didn't hire me for my advice—only to drive the car—so all's I could do was take her where she wanted to go."

"Where was that?"

"Main Street in Bellevue, number one zero two eight five Main Street."

"Sally Redding already gave me that," I told him.

"If you already knew where I dropped her, why do you need to talk to me?" Norm asked.

"Is that a house? An apartment?"

"Neither. A business," Norm answered. "Looked to me like a china shop. It worried me that she was getting out at such a strange place in the middle of the night, so I made sure she was safely inside before I drove away."

"Do you remember the shop's name?"

"A woman's name, but I don't remember any more than that."

"It wasn't open, was it?"

"Are you kidding? This was the middle of the night. Sometime after midnight. No, but she had a key. She let herself in, and I saw her monkeying with a keypad right by the door, so she must have been turning off an alarm."

"It's probably where she works," I surmised.

"I'd say," Norm Otis agreed.

"Did she mention anything at all about what had gone on before you picked her up?"

"No, but you could sort of figure it out. I mean her clothes were torn half off. She had a cut on her lip. And the asshole who did it had nerve enough to walk her out to the curb. Had to be him, because he was in his shirtsleeves, and she was wearing a man's jacket. He tried to open the door for her like a gentleman, just as nice as can be. As if nothing in the world had happened. But she wouldn't have nothin' to do with him."

"And she didn't say a word about what had put her in that state?"

"Nope. Not a word. Like I told you. She gave me the address and then cried her eyes out the rest of the trip, from downtown Seattle right on across the I-Ninety bridge." Norm paused a moment and then added, "Are you going to get that guy, Detective Beaumont?"

"I don't have to," I told him.

"Why not?" Norm asked.

"Because somebody else already has. He's dead."

"Dead?" Norm repeated.

"Murdered," I said.

"Hot damn!" Norm replied. There was another pause. "Who did it?"

"I don't know. I'm the detective assigned to the case. I'm working on it."

"It wasn't her, was it?"

All too clearly I remembered what Latty had said to Don Wolf on the tape and in the heat of absolutely understandable anger: *If you touch me again, I swear to God I'll kill you.*

"It could have been," I said carefully.

"Jesus," Norm Otis whispered. "I hope not. She was a real pretty little girl. Looked just like a young Marilyn Monroe. Isn't there such a thing as justifiable homicide in cases like that?"

"There is," I said, "but it's hard to prove. Besides, I'm just a cop. All that legal crap is up to the prosecutor's office and the defense lawyers."

"Maybe she'll find herself one of those smart lawyers who'll get her off," Norm Otis said wistfully. "But let me give you my home number just in case somebody needs it. I mean if it would help for someone to know what kind of shape that poor girl was in that night, I'll be glad to go to bat for her."

"We'll see," I said. "Go ahead and give me your number. We'll need to get a statement from you anyway. Just in case."

# Ten

I fell asleep some time before the news came on, and slept like a log. One phone call at a time, I was making progress, and my evening's worth of phone calls made me feel as though I was on track. I woke up early, rewrote the several reports the computer had eaten the day before, and then headed for the office. I was sitting in my cubicle using the Ethernet card on my computer to send files to the printer on our local area network when Watty poked his head in at the doorway.

"The captain wants to see you," he said. "He's looking for your paper."

"He can have my reports," I said, "just as soon as I finish printing them."

I never should have said it aloud. The words were no more than out of my mouth when a message decorated with a tasteful stop sign flashed on the screen. PRINTER IS OFF LINE OR OUT OF PA-

PER it said. PLEASE CHECK YOUR PRINTER AND TRY
AGAIN.

"Damn!" I exclaimed, heading down the hallway toward Captain Powell's office. "If Henry
Ford's Model T's had been this undependable,
we'd still be using the horse and buggy."

"Aren't you going to try to fix it?" Watty asked
after me.

"No," I told him. "That's not my job. I'm a detective, not a nerd."

Captain Powell was waiting in his fishbowl office. A brass plaque on his desk gave his name
and rank. On the front of it, someone had attached a Post-it that announced, "This is a com-
puter-free zone." *My sentiments, exactly,* I thought,
as I dropped into a chair in front of the cluttered
desk.

"Any reports for me this morning, Detective
Beaumont?" Captain Powell asked. "Or are you
too busy handing out autographs these days to
bother doing mundane things like actually writing reports?"

Even though I had figured Kramer would try
to make the most of Johnny Bickford's visit, I
guess it still surprised me to have the first derogatory comment come back to me from Captain
Larry Powell. Gritting my teeth, and trying not to
let on how much that bugged me, I went into my
lame 1990s version of "My dog ate my home-
work. Twice."

Powell listened impassively to my sad story.
Because he doesn't actually *use* computers, I think

he considers himself above the fray. "I want those reports," he said, when I finished. "I want them on my desk ASAP. You realize, of course, that this is turning into a very sensitive case."

*Double homicides are always sensitive,* I thought, but I didn't say it aloud. Powell's glower as he sailed a piece of paper toward me was enough of a warning that this was no time for one of my typically smart-mouthed comments.

I caught the paper in midair. On it was a list of four names—names and nothing else: Carrol Walsh, Crystal Barron, Martin Rutherford, and DeVar Lester.

I read through the list. None of the names belonged to people I knew personally, but they were nonetheless names I recognized. These were all high-profile people. You couldn't live in Seattle without knowing something about them.

Carrol Walsh was a newly made software multimillionaire who had created a media splash by donating a mountain of money to Fred Hutch cancer research. Crystal Barron, an heiress from back East, had taken up life on a Lake Union houseboat after divorcing her fourth hubby, an aging Hollywood star. Martin Rutherford was a corporate free spirit who had been cut loose in an acrimonious buyout by one of Seattle's premier family-owned and -operated coffee roasting companies. DeVar Lester was an ex-football player who had made a bundle on an outrageously overpriced rookie contract with the Seahawks only to end up blowing his knee in a preseason workout without ever playing a single pro game.

I dropped the paper back on Captain Powell's desk. "What about them?" I asked.

"Those are the people Detectives Kramer and Arnold are off to interview this morning."

I picked up the list and studied it again. "Interview them?" I asked. "How come?"

Powell leaned forward in his chair. "Because these people are recent major investors in D.G.I., or did you already know that?"

"No," I admitted. "I had no idea."

"And you probably also have no idea that Martin Rutherford, the ex-coffee-bean guy, is dating the mayor."

Seattle's mayor, Natalie Farraday, is a divorced single mother who, since her election, has gone through several boyfriends at the rate of about one a year.

"I guess I had heard that," I said, now understanding the implications and how this had suddenly become such a sensitive case. "I'd heard it, but I think maybe I'd forgotten."

"So what exactly are you doing to solve it?" Powell asked.

Hurriedly, I gave Captain Powell a shorthand version of what I had learned so far. He seemed even less impressed with that than he had been with my tale of computer woes. When I finished, Powell sat looking at me, drumming on the surface of his desk with a pencil eraser.

"I spoke to Detective Kramer at some length before he and Detective Arnold hit the bricks,"

Powell said thoughtfully. "Based on this new information," he said as he gave the list of names a meaningful tap, "I was going to assign another pair of detectives to the case, but Kramer asked me not to. He said that pulling in more people at this point would probably do more harm than good. He says he thinks the three of you will be able to pull it out of the fire. What do you think?"

The public seems to like the "task force" approach to major crimes. Unfortunately, from my point of view, when it comes to effective investigations, *less* is usually *more*.

"Kramer's probably right, Captain Powell. I think we're making progress."

"And you don't think you need any more troops?"

"Not at this time."

Captain Powell glanced at his watch. "All right, then," he said. "I'm giving the three of you twenty-four hours to bring this case to some kind of order. If I don't have really solid progress by tomorrow morning at this time, the head count goes up. Understood?"

Nodding, I rose to my feet. "Is that all?" I asked.

"Not quite," Powell answered. "There's one more thing."

"What's that?" I asked.

"Let me remind you, Detective Beaumont, complacency can be a dangerous thing." While he spoke, the captain's steady gaze held mine. "When cops lose their edge—when they stop be-

ing hungry—that's about the time they get careless. The next thing you know, somebody gets
hurt."

I paused in the doorway. "What's that supposed to mean?"

"Do yourself a favor," Captain Powell returned. "You're a cop, not a professional ball
player, Beau. Until further notice, no more autographs. Is that clear?"

"Perfectly!" I said.

I stormed back to my office, grabbed my jacket,
and headed for the great outdoors. "Hey, Beau,"
Watty said as I charged past his desk. "Where are
you going? You forgot to sign out."

Initially, I headed for the motor pool. I think if
I had run into Paul Kramer along the way, I
would have punched his lights out. Halfway to
the motor pool, I changed my mind—not about
cleaning Kramer's clock but about taking a company car.

"Hell with it," I muttered under my breath,
startling a sweet young thing clerk headed downstairs with a cartload of file folders. Kramer could
be pissed off about where and how I lived, and
Captain Powell could order me to not sign autographs, but if I wanted to drive my Guards Red
Porsche on my trip to Bellevue, then I would, and
nobody—including Captain Lawrence Powell—
was going to stop me.

The 928 didn't exactly observe the speed limits
as I crossed Lake Washington on the I-90 bridge.
Fortunately, the state patrol didn't spot me or

pull me over. That would have been tough to explain. By the time I turned off on Bellevue Way, I had cooled down a little.

For someone who has lived downtown for years and who often walks from home to work, the problem of going from Seattle to Bellevue isn't so much a matter of geography as it is one of mind-set. Seattle has a city feel and smell and look to it. Office workers and tourists, drunks and bums mingle on sidewalks on multilane one-way streets filled with traffic.

Bellevue, on the other hand, a city one quarter the size of Seattle proper, is an alien kind of place where, although high-rise buildings dot the skyline, Main Street is still a narrow, two-lane cow path. For some strange reason, North East Eighth, the real main drag, is several blocks to the north.

Downtown Seattle seems intent on banking and commerce while downtown Bellevue is more inclined toward serious shopping. It's a place where Mercedes-wielding, Nordstrom-bound matrons have been known to run down any fellow shoppers who have nerve enough to try to reserve a parking place without benefit of a four-wheeled vehicle. Seattle's largely liberal, pro-Democrat citizenry see Bellevue as a suburban hotbed of rich, recalcitrant Republicans—a questionable place to visit and one where you certainly wouldn't want to live.

I arrived on Main Street in what is quaintly called Old Bellevue, with all my Denny Regrade, dyed-in-the-wool Seattleite prejudices still firmly intact.

It turned out to be easy to find the address I'd obtained from Yellow Cab. Dorene's Fine China and Gifts—complete with a woman's name—was right where Norm Otis had said. Finding the place was simple. Getting in wasn't. Dorene's was closed. A sign on the door said they supposedly opened at nine-thirty. My watch read nine-fifteen.

Like Seattle, Bellevue seems to have an espresso cart stationed on every corner. The one outside Dorene's was no exception. I figured the price of a *latte* and *biscotti* would give me the right to ask the cart's long-haired proprietor what, if anything, he knew about Dorene and company.

He shrugged his grunge-clad shoulders and shook his purple-tinged locks. "I think Latty goes to school in the morning. She usually doesn't come to the shop until after noon," he said. "The old lady usually opens up, but she more or less gets here when she gets here, earlier or later, depending."

It was an answer, although not a very definite one. I hung around for a few more fruitless minutes. Finally, it made sense for me to try seeing Eddie at Northwest Mobility first and come back to Bellevue about the time Latty herself was due to show up for work.

I headed off toward Snohomish, threading my way through the maze of suburbs with the help of my faithful companion, *The Thomas Guide.*

Since Ron had told me that Eddie and his wife had started out as hot-rodders, I headed for Rich's Northwest Mobility with a whole headful of preconceptions. I expected a run-down garage with derelict vehicles scattered behind it, maybe an aging, marooned motor home of an office, and a motley collection of worker-bees whose grease-covered clothing went far too many overhauls between washings.

Turning left off Maltby Road onto a narrow paved track that ran through a thicket of towering trees, I was sure my worst suspicions would be confirmed, especially when I saw the ominous sign that warned, in no uncertain terms: STAY ON PAVED ROAD. That generally means if you wander off, you'll be caught in mud up to your hubcaps before you can say *Triple-A Towing*.

My first inkling that I was mistaken came when I saw the second Rich's sign, the one sitting in the middle of an ornate bricked entryway. I rounded a corner and found myself looking at a collection of several neat, low-built buildings, all painted an inviting pale yellow, nestled at the base of a grass-covered hill. I counted three separate garages on either side of a central paved area. At the far end of that central courtyard was a well-maintained house and yard. Taken together, the garages and house formed a U-shaped outline, the interior of which was parked full of wheelchair-accessible vans. Some of them looked brand new. Others were obviously older and waiting for service at one of the stalls in the various garages, all of which seemed to be fully occupied at the moment.

I parked my 928 out of the way as best I could. At the near end of the U was a sign that must have been a holdover from the old hot-rod days: STREET ROD ALLEY. Unnoticed, I walked toward a group of people gathered around one of the shiny new vans where a heavyset man in a wheelchair was laughingly rolling himself up a gentle ramp into the vehicle. Once inside, he turned around and gave his audience a triumphant thumbs-up. While they responded with a rousing burst of applause, the man headed, chair and all, toward the driver's side of the car, where he seemed to clamp his chair in place.

Looking down at the ground clearance of the Aerostar van, I noticed that it was no more than three or four inches off the ground. *That might be fine for getting the wheelchair in and out*, I thought to myself, *but how the hell is he going to get over the major speed bump between here and Maltby Road?*

As if in answer to my question, the man switched on the engine. Without the slightest hitch, the ramp retracted and the outside door closed. Then, with a pneumatic sigh, the van's fender began to rise. When it quit moving, the van sat on ordinary tires, with the floor level and frame the exact same level as any other minivan. Meanwhile, the guy in the chair put the van in gear and began backing out of the lot. I stepped out of the way to let him pass. When he drove by me, he was grinning from ear to ear and wav-

ing in every direction, like the marshal of a
Fourth of July parade.

"Sorta gets to you, doesn't it?" a tall, green-
eyed man said, stepping over to where I was
standing. "Watching 'em drive off the lot on their
own that first time always puts a lump in my
throat."

He paused for a moment, watching the van disappear from view. Then he turned to me, holding
out his hand. "By the way, I'm Eddie Riveira,"
he added. "Is there something I can do to help
you?"

"Yes," I answered, pulling out a card and
handing it over. "My name's Detective J. P. Beaumont with the Seattle Police Department. I'm
looking for some information."

Eddie smiled. "Most people are," he said.

"A friend of mine owns one of your units, one
of those Braun Chair Toppers."

"Really, who's your friend?" Eddie asked.

"Ron Peters."

"Oh, that's right. The young cop from Seattle
P.D., the one who wiped himself out by going off
one of those unfinished freeway interchanges that
used to be down by the Kingdome?"

"That's the one," I said.

"I had a message from him a little while ago,
but I haven't had time enough to return the call.
How's he doing?"

"Fine," I answered. "He and his wife are expecting a baby. In April sometime."

"He already has kids, doesn't he?"

"Two," I told him.

Obviously, Eddie Riveira took a very personal interest in the people who were his clients, because he clearly remembered Ron Peters. "Last time I saw him he had wrecked his car. We moved that old Topper of his from one vehicle to another—to a Buick, I think—and modified the brakes and accelerator. With two kids already and a baby on the way, he's going to have to break down and get himself one of my vans. He'll love it. Is that what you came to talk to me about?"

"Actually, it isn't. I'm working a case that may involve somebody with a Chair Topper a lot like Ron's. Only this one is on a 1988 lavender Crown Victoria."

Eddie frowned. "Lavender?" he said. "I only know of one eighty-eight Crown Victoria, but that one's powder blue."

I shrugged. "I saw it at night. I could be mistaken about the color."

"Virginia, then," Eddie said. "It belongs to Virginia Marks."

"Do you know where she lives or how I could get in touch with her?" I asked.

"Sure. If you'll come into the office for a minute, I can probably give you her number."

We started toward the office—a real one, not a makeshift motor home. Along the way, where once converted hot rods must have sat, now at least a dozen spanking new vans were parked, side by side, showroom style. Eddie Riveira must have been reading my mind.

"It's the same technology we used to utilize raising and lowering hot rods. We just put it to a little higher use, that's all."

Once in the office, Eddie called up Virginia Marks' name on a computer screen. "Here it is," he said. "This may be an old address. She used to live in a little complex over in Kirkland. I don't know if she's still there or not. At one time, she had talked about moving to downtown Bellevue. From what I can tell, she probably spends more time working out of that car of hers than she does at home."

"You say she works out of her car? What does she do, run a vending machine route? Work as a sales rep?"

"She's a detective," Eddie Riveira told me. "Same as you."

Except Virginia Marks wasn't just like me. I'm a cop. Virginia was a freelancer, a private eye. Eddie fumbled through a plastic holder and ended up showing me Virginia Marks' business card. AIM RESEARCH, it said. Those few words and two phone numbers were the only things printed on the card.

"The bottom number is a cell phone," Eddie said. "That's the one where you're most likely to catch her."

"What can you tell me about her?" I asked.

Eddie shrugged. "A little rough around the edges. Personally, I don't have that many dealings with her. Usually, Nancy or Amanda handles her. Virginia doesn't like men, and she doesn't make any bones about it. We're in business to service the customer. If she doesn't want to talk to me, that's fine with us."

"What's wrong with her?" I asked.

"Wrong?" Eddie repeated.

"How did she end up in a chair?"

"Pulled out in front of a Suburban right here on State Route Five Twenty-two. The car she was driving back then was a little one, a Honda, I believe. The accident barely dented the Suburban, but it creamed Virginia's car and sent her to the hospital for six months and rehab for six months after that. She came out a paraplegic at age forty-eight. According to Amanda—that's my wife, by the way—one of the reasons Virginia Marks likes that old Crown Victoria of hers so much is that it's big. Maybe sitting inside all that sheet metal helps make her feel safe."

A worker, a young man in startlingly clean coveralls, hurried up to where Eddie and I were standing. "Sorry to interrupt, Eddie, but could you come look at something for a minute?"

Eddie excused himself and went away. I stood looking around. Behind the house and the one garage was a minipark with broad sidewalks that ran through a carefully manicured grassy area to two separate gazebos. In the middle of the plot of grass was a complex, fortresslike jungle gym built over a bed of freshly spread bark. On the sidewalk next to the play area, a woman bundled in coat and gloves sat in a wheelchair, watching while two little girls whooped and shrieked from the top of the jungle gym's slide.

Eddie came back. "Sorry. Is there anything else?"

"Just one other thing. How much does one of these vans set a guy back?"

"About forty thou," Eddie answered. "About the same as one of your basic luxury cars.

"Okay," I said. "Thanks for the help. By the way, where's the nearest cup of coffee?"

He pointed east. "Coffee you can have here, but if you want something to go with it, I recommend the Maltby Café," he said. "Go to the end of the road and turn left. It's not far."

"And the food?" I asked.

"Their breakfasts are great."

I treated myself to French toast and tried calling Virginia Marks of AIM Research at both numbers listed on her card. I tried several times. Each time I hung up just as the voice mail recording came on. I wanted to talk to Virginia in person. I had no interest in leaving a message at the sound of the tone.

Voice mail is fine, but only up to a point.

# Eleven

No longer famished and in a somewhat more agreeable frame of mind than I had been earlier, I headed back to Bellevue. It was eleven-thirty by then. The sign on the door of Dorene's Fine China and Gifts had been flipped over from CLOSED to OPEN.

When I stepped inside, a bell over the door tinkled merrily, announcing my presence. The guy at the espresso cart had said that Latty was usually in the store by now, but the person behind the counter was a white-haired woman. I guessed her to be somewhere beyond her mid-seventies.

"May I help you?" she inquired, looking at me over a pair of rectangular half-size glasses that perched on the very tip of a beakish nose.

"I'm looking for Latty," I said.

"Is that so?" the woman said in a brisk, businesslike fashion. "Well, as you can see, she's not here. Is there something I could help you with?"

"I came to talk to her about a friend of hers," I said.

The woman was barely five foot three, but she puffed herself up and straightened her shoulders so she looked an inch or two taller. She spoke firmly, reminding me of a teacher offering guidance to a recalcitrant schoolboy. "I already told you. Latty isn't in yet. She won't be until much later this afternoon."

"Do you have any idea where I could find her between now and then?" I asked, pulling out one of my cards and placing it on the countertop between us. The woman picked up the card. After peering at it for a moment, she shot me a questioning look, then she returned the card to the counter. Bird-boned but nonetheless formidable, she was one of those much-facelifted women—one who wasn't giving in to the aging process without putting up one hell of a fight.

"She'll be in when she's in and not a moment before. I'm Latty's aunt Grace. Her great aunt, really," she added with a disdainful sniff. "I'm Latty's grandmother's sister, but let's don't split hairs. I don't go in for all that *great* stuff. Plain *Aunt Grace* will do just fine."

"Ma'am, I'm afraid I'm not making myself sufficiently clear. This isn't a social call. If you have any idea where Latty is at the moment, I must insist that you put me in touch with her. This is a serious matter. I need to ask her a few questions."

"Such as?"

"As you can see by my card, Mrs.—"

*"Miss,"* Aunt Grace supplied, placing clear emphasis on the word. "Highsmith. Miss Grace Highsmith. You see, unlike my sister Florence— Latty's grandmother, that is—I never married."

The first time I heard Grace Highsmith's name, it seemed oddly familiar somehow, but I dismissed that momentary impression and forged ahead. "As you can see from my card, Miss Highsmith," I continued, "I'm with the Seattle P.D. The Homicide Squad. We're currently investigating the death of an individual who died sometime New Year's Eve. We have reason to believe that your grandniece may have been acquainted with that person."

"I see," Miss Highsmith said. Behind me, the bell chimed over the door once more. I turned to see a bent woman, leaning over a metal walker, come tottering into the room.

"Morning, Grace," the woman said. "Did my order come in yet?" she asked, peeking sideways in our direction. "The wedding's this weekend, you know."

"Yes, Maxine," Grace Highsmith replied. "I haven't forgotten. We had a big order come in from UPS this morning, but I'm not sure if your Denby's in there or not. We won't be sorting through the packing slips until Latty comes in later this afternoon. Could we get back to you on this either then or early tomorrow?"

"Either one will be fine," Maxine answered. "I

came down for a manicure and thought I'd check in with you while I was in the neighborhood." Turning her walker in a wide circle, she headed back for the door. I hurried over to hold it open for her. "Why thank you, young man," she said. "That's very kind of you."

When the door closed behind Maxine, I returned to Grace Highsmith. "Where were we now?" she began somewhat vaguely. "Oh, that's right. You wanted to talk to Latty. As I said, she isn't in right now, but that doesn't matter. In the long run, I don't believe talking with her will be all that necessary."

Grace Highsmith wasn't a receptionist, but she had the typical gatekeeper mentality, which is to say, I wasn't to go anywhere near her niece until she was damned good and ready to let me. "Excuse me, Miss Highsmith, I don't believe you understand—"

"Oh, I understand perfectly." Unperturbed, she smiled up at me. "You and I will have a little chat first, Detective Beaumont," she added pleasantly. "After that, you can decide whether or not you need to speak to Latty."

"Miss Highsmith, withholding information in a case like this—"

She waved aside my half-uttered objection. "Oh, I know all about that," she said. "I watch police dramas on television all the time. It's just that there's no reason to upset Latty with any of this. The poor girl's suffered enough already. Excuse me, would you, Detective Beaumont? I'll need to make a phone call and get someone in here to cover the store for the next little while. If you'll just wait here a moment . . ."

Without pausing to hear any possible objection on my part, Grace Highsmith disappeared behind a curtained doorway into a back room. I was tempted to follow her, but I didn't. That seemed rude. Besides, what could a sweet little old lady do—run out some back door and disappear? She remained out of sight for a matter of several minutes, but I did hear her making a phone call at one point. That was followed by a long period of silence. Just as I was beginning to worry that I'd been duped after all, she reappeared, carrying a purse and a ring of keys.

"Have you had lunch, Detective Beaumont?"

"Breakfast," I answered. "Just a little while ago, as a matter of fact, so I'm not very hungry . . ."

"I had my Cream of Wheat at six o'clock this morning, just as I always do, so I'm really quite hungry. Let's go up the street. I'll have a bite of lunch, and we can talk there."

"But what about the store?"

"Oh, that," she said dismissively. "It'll take our part-time clerk a little while to get here from Redmond, but don't worry about the store. We're rather informal here at times. I'll just turn over the sign. My customers know that someone will be back eventually."

Occasionally, it's better to go with the flow than to put up an argument. I would have preferred talking somewhere a little more private than a restaurant, but Grace Highsmith seemed so determined to do things her way, that I didn't object. After all, who am I to refuse a little old lady a bite of lunch?

On my way into the store, I had noticed a couple of restaurants in the immediate area. One—a tearoom-looking place—was almost directly across the street, while a Mexican food joint was about a block away. Instead of going into either one of those establishments, however, we walked past both to the next cross street, headed north for half a block, and turned into something that looked like a little cottage. It turned out to be a restaurant—Azalea's Fountain Court.

One look at the white-clothed tables inside told me this was a fine dining establishment rather than a hole-in-the-wall coffee shop. A petite blonde stepped out from behind a grand piano in the foyer and greeted my companion by name.

"Your usual table today, Grace?" she asked.

The older woman frowned. "No, Shelley, I think we should have a booth today. The far one in the corner if it's available. Someone may be joining us."

I wondered at that. This had seemed like a spur-of-the-moment arrangement. Who could possibly be joining us?

We were led to a green plush banquette in the far corner of the cozy, plant-lined room. After dropping off menus, the blonde named Shelley disappeared, returning almost immediately with a glass of white wine and an extra place setting. No question. Around this place, Aunt Grace was a regular.

"Shelley," Grace Highsmith began, observing the niceties, "this is Detective Beaumont of the Seattle Police Department." She paused, seemingly for effect, letting the words sink in while she took a delicate sip of wine. "And this is Shelley Kuni, Detective Beaumont. She's the owner of this fine establishment."

"I'm happy to meet you," I said.

Shelley smiled. "Would you care for a glass of wine as well? This chardonnay is particularly nice."

"No, thanks. Just coffee for me," I answered. Shelley hurried off to get it.

The room was fairly small—four or five booths and about that many tables. The service bar with both wine and coffee was in the corner of the room, close enough for the conversation to continue while Shelley poured my coffee.

"Detective Beaumont can't have any wine because he's on duty, you see," Aunt Grace announced airily. "He's questioning me about a murder."

I glanced around the room. Fortunately, it was early enough in the lunch hour that we were the only patrons in the place when Grace Highsmith dropped that little bomb.

"No!" Shelley exclaimed. "Really?"

I nodded. The whole idea of wearing plain-clothes is so that everyone you talk to won't necessarily know you're a cop. For everyone within hearing distance in Azalea's Fountain Court, my cover was totally blown.

Shelley set the cup and saucer in front of me. "Cream and sugar?" she asked smoothly as though the words *murder* and *detective* hadn't penetrated her consciousness.

"No, just black."

I suppose restaurant people have to be fairly flexible. Somehow, Shelley Kuni managed to act as though she were totally unperturbed by what Grace Highsmith was saying while at the same time seeming to hang on every word. It reminded me of a circus tightrope walker. "Whose murder?" Shelley asked.

"Don Wolf's," Grace answered at once.

"Not the one who—"

"Don Wolf!" I exclaimed, slopping half my coffee into the saucer. "How did you—?"

"Yes, exactly," Grace replied with a peremptory nod, cutting both Shelley and me off in midsentence. "The very one I told you about last week."

As if the lunch bell had sounded somewhere, several new sets of customers arrived in the entrance lobby all at once. Shelley hurried to meet them. There were at least two other separate dining areas in the restaurant. I don't think it was an accident that Shelley led all the new arrivals off to one of those, leaving our part of the dining room still relatively empty except for Grace and me.

I turned an accusatory stare on Grace Highsmith. "I told you I was investigating a death," I
said. "I didn't mention the word *murder*. Not
once. And I *never* mentioned the victim's name."

Grace smiled sweetly. "The murder part is
strictly a matter of common sense," she told me.
"After all, you are a homicide detective, aren't
you?"

"But how is it you happen to know the victim's
name?"

Over the rim of her wine glass, Grace Highsmith fixed her bright-eyed stare on my face.
"What kind of detective are you? Do you even
have to ask?"

I held her gaze with one of my own. "As far
as I know, the victim's name is being withheld
pending notification of next of kin. It would indicate that you might possibly have inside knowledge—"

"Precisely," Grace interrupted. "I knew you'd
catch on eventually. Statistically speaking, I understand that the perpetrator almost always
knows his or her victim."

With impeccably bad timing, our waiter appeared just then, smiling cordially. "What will
you have today, Miss Highsmith?" he asked.
"Your usual?" She nodded. "Extra cilantro on
that jalapeño grilled cheese on plain whole
wheat?"

"Of course," Grace replied. "What's the soup?"

"Shelley's tomato basil. It's very nice."

"I'm sure it is," Grace said. "Soup then."

"And for you, sir?" the waiter asked, turning to me.

"Nothing," I said. "Just coffee."

"Very well."

He went away, disappearing silently around the corner into the kitchen as more guests showed up in the lobby and filtered into the room, gradually filling the other banquettes as well as some of the freestanding tables. It was an attractive, intimate dining room—totally lacking in privacy, and absolutely wrong for conducting a homicide interview.

Grace took another delicate sip of her wine then set down the glass. She glanced first at her watch and then at the front door as though awaiting someone's arrival. "I suppose we could just as well get started then. What is it you want to ask me?"

When we had first sat down, Grace Highsmith had placed her pocketbook on the table beside her napkin. Now, replacing her chain-held glasses on her nose, she opened the purse and peered inside before turning it at a fifteen-degree angle.

To my absolute astonishment, a small, stainless-steel handgun came spilling out onto the table. The gun was a compact .32 ACP. It's a weapon I know, but up until then, I had seen only one. The new Seecamp autos are so popular that there's a fifteen- to eighteen-month waiting list at the factory for anyone who is interested in buying one. The .32 ACP is a small, readily concealable gun most often used by police officers as a backup weapon.

Fortunately for everyone in the restaurant that day—yours truly included—it is also considered to be a very safe weapon in that it's unlikely to discharge when dropped accidentally. Or even deliberately. It is designed to use only Winchester Western 60-grain Silvertip hollowpoint rounds. Which means that it's not worth a damn for target practice, but it can be deadly at close range.

The surprisingly loud thunk the gun made when it landed on the white linen tablecloth made the hairs on the back of my neck stand on end. I wasn't the only person in the dining room who noticed. At a table just across from us, a tall, fiftyish blond woman had been seated along with a gray-haired, bearded man. When the gun landed, the man rose to his feet. "A gun!" he blurted. "She's got a gun!"

The blonde had just raised her newly filled water glass to her lips. Choking, she dropped the glass, which bounced off the edge of the table and then plunged to the floor, where it splintered into pieces and sent a spray of icy water and glass fragments scattering three feet in all directions.

A concerned service staff converged on the mess from every direction. The unexpected appearance of the weapon had caused a sudden burst of adrenaline to shoot through my system. The gun lay on the cloth and Grace left it there, making no effort to grab it. Realizing from the fact that she wasn't reaching for the weapon that there was no immediate danger, I covered the offending gun with my napkin. Once it was out of sight, I pulled it over to my side of the table.

"This thing isn't loaded, is it?" I demanded.

Grace Highsmith shrugged. "Probably," she said. "It usually is. That's how we keep it."

"It's yours then?"

She nodded.

"Do you have a license to carry?"

"Not exactly."

"As far as I'm concerned, *not exactly* means no license," I told her. "No doubt you realize that's a violation." I lifted the napkin and looked down at the little .32 automatic. "Loaded or not, what are you doing with a gun in your purse?"

"I assumed you'd want to have it," she said. "According to the shows I see on television, that's one of the first things the detectives go looking for—the murder weapon."

"You're saying this is a murder weapon? As in Don Wolf's murder?"

"Of course," Grace Highsmith replied. "What other murder would I possibly be talking about?"

That's when I signaled for Shelley. She came to the table looking slightly pale. "Is everything all right?" she asked. I noticed then that the blonde and her companion had been discreetly moved to another table—one nearer the door.

"You wouldn't happen to have a doggy bag, would you?"

"Certainly." Shelley disappeared into the kitchen and returned moments later with two pieces of foil. I scooted the .32 onto one piece and covered it with the other. After twisting the ends together, I slipped the foil-wrapped package into my pocket.

Clearly happy to have the gun out of sight, Shelley nodded approvingly. "Could I interest either one of you in a complimentary glass of champagne?" she asked.

The appearance of the gun and the shattered water glass had caused enough of a stir among her lunchtime diners. People were no longer openly staring, but Shelley seemed determined to regain the lost atmosphere and settle ruffled feathers. To that end, a waiter was passing through the room pouring out free glasses of champagne.

"None for me," I said.

"I'll have some," Grace Highsmith said brightly. "Champagne sounds delightful."

Shelley left our table while Grace smiled at me beatifically. "Well then, Detective Beaumont," she said, "this is really quite civilized, isn't it. I can sip a glass of champagne while you read me my rights. Then we can get on with it."

"Get on with what?"

"My confession, of course, although I do wish Suzanne would hurry up and get here. I know she'll have a fit if I tell you all this while she's not here."

"Your confession to what?"

"To Don Wolf's murder, of course."

I took a moment to assimilate that bit of information. "Who's Suzanne?"

There was a momentary pause while Shelley herself stopped by our table and poured Grace Highsmith a flute of champagne. Grace took her time tasting it before answering my question.

"Suzanne Crenshaw," she said finally. "She's my attorney."

Just then, as if on cue, the front door blew open and a woman rushed inside. Heavyset and flushed, possibly from a combination of both cold and overexertion, she was a thirty-something, dark-haired woman dressed in a navy-blue business suit. She paused in the doorway of the dining room, searching through the diners until she caught sight of Grace at the end banquette.

As soon as their eyes met, a look of intense relief washed over the younger woman's face. She made a beeline for our table. "There you are," she said, leaning down long enough to brush a glancing kiss across Grace's parchment-skinned cheek. "I was afraid I'd be too late."

"Oh, no," Grace reassured her, "you're right on time."

"Is there some kind of problem?" Suzanne asked, eyeing me warily.

"No problem," Grace said. "Detective Beaumont is being the complete gentleman. Speaking of which, here I am, forgetting my manners. Suzanne Crenshaw, this is Detective Beaumont. Detective Beaumont, Suzanne."

Suzanne Crenshaw held out her hand to shake

mine, but the look she turned on me was anything but friendly. "What's this all about, Grace?" Suzanne asked. "What's going on here?"

"Nothing much so far," Grace replied. "We've only just ordered lunch, although I did give him my gun. I didn't like carrying it around in my purse. It could have gone off. Sit down now, Suzanne. As soon as you order your lunch, we'll try to bring you up to speed."

With a single warning glare in my direction, Suzanne Crenshaw sat. "Grace, what gun?" she demanded.

"Don't worry, Suzanne. Everything will be fine. I believe Detective Beaumont was about to read me my rights."

"Read you your rights!" Suzanne Crenshaw exclaimed. Around the restaurant heads once again swiveled in our direction.

"Hush, Suzanne," Grace ordered. "Don't make such a fuss. Before we go into all that, why don't you order lunch. And for goodness sake, have a glass of champagne. They're giving away free samples today. It'll settle your nerves."

While Suzanne Crenshaw stared at her client in what looked to me like thunderstruck amazement, an unruffled Grace motioned at the waiter, who came to our table at once. "My guest here will need to place her order," Grace said. "And could we have another glass of champagne, please?"

She said all this without the slightest hint of awareness that the sensation created by her dumping a gun on the table in the middle of a crowded restaurant was responsible for the presence of "sample" champagne. To his credit, the waiter didn't bat an eyelash, either.

"Of course," he said. "Right away."

I don't believe I've ever met anyone quite like Grace Highsmith. She was a living, breathing personification of the term *noblesse oblige*. In other people, it would have been regarded as bullying or high-handedness, but there was such an air of graciousness about her that people tended to do what she wanted regardless of their own intentions in the matter. That went for me every bit as much as it did for Suzanne Crenshaw.

An uneasy silence existed around the table while the waiter returned with the champagne and took Suzanne's order. As soon as he was gone, the lawyer turned her attention on me. "I suppose coming here was your idea?" she demanded, glaring at me.

"As far as I knew, all we were doing was coming here for lunch."

Suzanne Crenshaw wasn't convinced. "What's all this about 'reading rights' then?" she asked.

"The Fountain Court was my idea, not his," Grace interjected. "I wanted to go somewhere nice so I could feel relaxed while I gave him my confession."

Suzanne Crenshaw's eyes bulged. "Confession to what?"

"Why, to Don Wolf's murder, of course," Grace Highsmith said with a smile. "It was premeditated, you see. I planned it well in advance."

Suzanne Crenshaw's jaw dropped. "Grace!" she exclaimed. "You can't say that."

"I most certainly can," Grace Highsmith replied archly. "Detective Beaumont hasn't read me my rights yet. As long as that's the case, I can say anything I please."

# Twelve

While Suzanne Crenshaw stared daggers in my direction, the waiter, with his continuing knack for perfect timing, returned once again.

"Have something nice, Suzanne," Miss Highsmith advised. "I ordered the grilled cheese because it happens to be my favorite. And since this may be my last meal on the outside, I'm going to have some dessert. You go ahead and have whatever you want. It's my treat."

Suzanne perused the menu and settled on the grilled salmon, a mixed greens salad, and a flute of the free champagne. Once the waiter left with her order, Suzanne stood up. "Come with me, Grace," she said. "I believe we both need to go powder our noses."

Grace started to object, then didn't. The two women went off to the rest room together. When they returned, Grace was as sprightly as ever, while a tight-lipped Suzanne Crenshaw was even more grim.

"You can read me my rights now, Detective Beaumont," she commanded. "Let's get on with it."

Obligingly, I pulled out my handy-dandy pocket cheat sheet and read Grace Highsmith her rights. The lack of privacy in the room disturbed me enough that I flubbed one or two of the familiar lines. That was no problem, however, since Grace knew the whole routine by heart and was able to prompt me with the correct verbiage whenever necessary.

When we finished with that, she gave me another cheery smile while I returned the card to my wallet. "That wasn't so bad now, was it, Detective Beaumont?"

Doggedly self-conscious, I dragged my scruffy notebook and ratty pencil out of my pocket. Miss Highsmith frowned disapprovingly.

"You mean you aren't going to tape-record my confession? I thought all police officers carried those cute little miniature recorders."

"We usually record confessions down at the department, so they can be properly transcribed and signed at a later time. At this point, I merely want to ask a few questions."

"I see," Grace sniffed. "I suppose you'll do that after you take me in. I thought we'd be going straight to the confession right now. Otherwise, I wouldn't have bothered dragging Suzanne away from her office."

Suzanne Crenshaw's mixed greens salad arrived at the table. "Well," Grace Highsmith urged the moment our waiter's back was turned, "let's get on with it."

"Where do you live?" I asked.

"I have a little place up above Juanita, just down the hill from Juanita Drive," she said. "It was our family's summer place when I was a little girl. Now I live there full time."

Over a forkful of salad, Suzanne Crenshaw sent me a withering look. "Miss Highsmith's home is on Holmes Point Drive on the shores of Lake Washington, between Champagne Point and Denny Park," the attorney said.

The way Suzanne made that pronouncement implied that Grace Highsmith's Holmes Point Drive address alone should have commanded considerable respect from a lowlife homicide cop. I didn't really need Suzanne Crenshaw's help in that regard. I had pretty well figured out on my own that the lady seated in the booth next to me was an old-school, old-guard, old-money, and thoroughly remarkable woman.

"And what exactly was your relationship to Don Wolf?"

"Mine?" Grace hooted. "Good gracious! How can you even ask such a dull-witted question, Detective Beaumont. Of course, I had no relationship with that..." She paused, groping for a word. "That... slimeball... is that the proper term, Suzanne?"

Chewing her salad greens, Suzanne Crenshaw simply nodded.

"Slimeball of a man," Grace finished.

"How did you know him then?"

"I didn't *know* him," Grace corrected firmly. "I knew *of* him. I only saw him in person that one time down near Pier Seventy, and that was certainly enough."

"What about his wife?" I asked.

"Once again," Grace Highsmith replied. "I know *about* Lizbeth Wolf, but of course, I've never met her in person."

"Never?"

"Never."

"Let's go back to what you said about seeing Don Wolf."

Grace's unblinking gaze met and held mine. "What about it?"

"When was that exactly?"

"Why, when I killed him, of course," Grace Highsmith snapped. "Don't be coy, Detective Beaumont. It doesn't become you."

Convinced that every ear in the room had to be trained on the conversation at our table and wondering how all this would play in local newspapers, I backed off a little. "Maybe you could tell me what brought Don Wolf to your attention."

"Latty, of course. My niece."

"What's Latty's full name?"

Grace glanced at Suzanne. "Do I have to answer that?"

Suzanne Crenshaw grimaced and then nodded her head. "Look," she said. "As you know, this entire meeting is in direct opposition to my best advice. But since you're obviously determined to go through with it, Grace, you'd better go ahead and answer."

"Sibyl Latona," Grace said. "I think you'll agree that's a perfectly awful name! Her mother—my actual niece, and a disagreeable one at that—was a Greek and Roman mythology major at the University of Washington back in the late sixties before she dropped out of school. She's the one who stuck that poor little baby girl with such a ridiculous handle. *Sibyl* alone would have been bad enough. *Latona* has to do with a goddess who changed men into frogs or some such women's lib nonsense. Latty's grandmother—my sister—and I were the ones who shortened it to *Latty*. That's unusual, too, but at least it's something a person can live with. Life can be very tough on children with unusual names."

Having grown up bearing the onus of an unusual name myself—Jonas Piedmont Beaumont—I felt more sympathy for somebody stuck with a name like Sybil Latona than Grace Highsmith could possibly have realized.

"What's Latty's last name?" I asked.

"Gibson," Grace answered.

"And where does she live?"

"Over the shop," Grace said. "There's a little apartment up there. It's not very posh, but after all those years of living in a bus, Latty is very appreciative of even the most primitive accommodations. At least this has indoor plumbing, which is more than you can say about what she lived in before."

"A bus?" I asked.

"Abigail Gibson, Latty's mother, is something of a free spirit," Suzanne Crenshaw put in helpfully. "Latty's younger years were spent as a vagabond. She grew up being shuttled all over North America in a converted school bus which Abby insisted on driving back and forth from Alaska to Mexico City."

"Where did Latty go to school?" I asked.

"She didn't," Grace answered shortly. "Abby home-schooled the poor child. My niece was a very early advocate of that, although the term *home schooling* would seem to imply having a proper home in which to do it. For my money, a converted school bus doesn't qualify."

"I see," I said.

Grace eyed me speculatively. "Do you, Detective Beaumont?" Then she shook her head. "No, I don't believe you do. You can't possibly. Schooling requires a whole lot more than just learning vocabulary words and rules of punctuation. Real education is far more complicated than that. It's where children hone their communication skills. It's where they learn the rules of socialization. It introduces them to the real world. My niece, Abigail, tripped out early and hasn't touched down on the real world in years."

"Drugs?"

"I'm sure there were drugs early on, of course. Now Abby's just evolved into one of those permanent kooks. She's totally irresponsible. She's never worked a day in her life. She lives off her trust fund, and still has friends with one-word names like *Moonbeam* or *Rainbow*."

Suddenly, reflected in Grace Highsmith's straight-backed disapproval, I caught a glimpse of generations of Highsmith familial warfare in which rebellious daughters were evidently the rule rather than the exception. If Grace and her sister's generation had given rise to permanent hippies, Latty Gibson would turn against her own upbringing and evolve into an ultra-right-wing, conservative, card-carrying Republican.

"As I said," Grace continued, "Latty never attended a regular school. As a consequence, she's grown up lacking the most rudimentary skills for getting along with other people. Not surprisingly, she sees herself as the consummate outsider. Now that she's older, I've been trying, in some small way, to give her the opportunity to see and experience how normal people live. Have you ever met my niece, Detective Beaumont? Latty, I mean."

I shook my head. Seeing Latty Gibson in Bill Whitten's surveillance video didn't count as an official introduction.

"She's a very beautiful young woman," Grace said. "And I'm not just saying that because she's my niece. She's lovely, but I don't think that fact has ever dawned on her. When Abby became pregnant with Latty, back in the early seventies, she absolutely refused to marry the young man who was the baby's father. Why she found him so repugnant, I'll never know. He's done all right for himself. He went on to become a very successful lawyer down in California. Now he's a judge on the California State Court of Appeals. And he paid child support the whole time, although Abby never told Latty any of that. She made him out to be a complete monster which, I suppose, is typical.

"Anyway, growing up in that kind of an atmosphere, with only sporadic influence from sensible people like her grandmother—Florence died several years ago—or me, you can imagine that Latty is quite confused when it comes to members of the opposite sex."

"And that's where Don Wolf comes in?"

"It certainly is," Grace said.

Raising a discreet finger, she signaled for yet another flute of champagne. In all my years of being a cop, I don't think I've ever conducted an interview in quite such elegant surroundings or with quite so much bubbly. Champagne and homicide interrogations don't generally go hand in hand.

"Latty met him at one of those dance clubs downtown someplace just a few weeks ago. Right before Thanksgiving. As soon as she told me about him—you have to understand that Latty tells me things that she'd never dream of telling her mother—as soon as she told me about him, I knew it was serious. There are telltale signs you see, if you just know what to look for. A funny little glow young women get about them when they're falling in love for the first or second time. I noticed it right away—the glow, I mean. The upturned corners of her mouth. And, of course, he was all she could talk about for days on end. She told me that he was as serious about her as she was about him, that he wanted a relationship.

"I understand that word—*relationship*—is very big now," Grace added with a thoughtful frown. "In my day, girls didn't want a relationship; they wanted a wedding band. The really sensible ones still do."

"Let's go back to Don Wolf for a minute," I interjected, but I could just as well have saved my breath. Once Grace Highsmith launched herself into her story, nothing anyone else said could sidetrack her.

"Years ago, I told Abby that I was leaving everything I own to charity—to Children's Hospital. That is no longer true, of course. Since Latty came back to Seattle late last summer, I've reconsidered that position. The poor girl wasn't born with a silver spoon in her mouth, although she certainly could have been. And due to the haphazard way she's been raised, she didn't have the advantage of a real education, either. I've been encouraging her to take courses at Bellevue Community College and that kind of thing. I picked up Dorene's when a friend of mine retired due to ill-health. I've worked there part of the time because it's fun and because I enjoy it. But I'm letting Latty manage it for me to give her a little on-the-job training in the world of business."

"About Don Wolf . . ." I hinted.

"Oh, yes. I do tend to ramble a bit now and then. According to my will as it is currently written, Latty will be my sole beneficiary. That includes paying those ridiculous amounts Suzanne tells me are so-called generation-skipping taxes. That being the case—Latty being my sole heir, I mean—I was interested in learning more about this Don Wolf character. Latty kept hinting that she thought he was wonderful husband material, and I didn't want her marrying some gigolo.

"As far as I could tell, however, there were several bad signs. I knew he was new to town and quite a bit older than she was, so I did the only sensible thing—"

"And hired a private detective," I finished.

This time, Grace Highsmith's smile was nothing short of glowing. "Why, Detective Beaumont, how in the world did you know that?"

"I am a detective, too, remember?"

Grace laughed. "Why, yes, I suppose you are. Well, Virginia Marks comes from a longtime Eastside family. Her grandparents' place was just down the road from ours—from our summer cabin, that is. Back then, the Marks family was fairly well to do, but then they ran into some bad investments and had to sell out far too early to reap the kind of financial benefit that would have been possible only a few years later. Both Virginia's parents died while she was fairly young, and so she and her brother have pretty much had to shift for themselves. That's not all that bad. Working is good for you, don't you think?"

I nodded and then attempted to steer things back to the question at hand. "So you hired Virginia Marks to do a background check on Don Wolf. Then what happened? Did she discover anything important?"

Grace Highsmith didn't answer immediately. While she seemed to struggle with indecision, Suzanne Crenshaw reached out and grasped the older woman's forearm. "Grace, if you've changed your mind . . ."

"No, thank you, Suzanne," Grace managed. "I'll be fine in a minute. It's just terribly difficult, you know. Terribly difficult."

She took a deep breath and looked at me. "Don Wolf raped my niece, Detective Beaumont. It happened last Wednesday night, around midnight, in his office in downtown Seattle."

"How did you find out about it?" I asked.

"Latty told me, but I would have known even if she hadn't. Virginia was following them that night, and she saw them coming out of the building afterward. Latty was crying. Her clothes had been torn to shreds. From the way Latty looked as they came out of the building, Virginia deduced what had happened. She reported the incident to me, and I asked Latty about it the next day. I told you before, my niece is quite incapable of lying. That's another thing Abby never taught her—the art of telling a plausible fib when necessary. So she admitted the whole thing, even though it broke her heart to have to do it."

"What happened next?"

"What do you suppose? I had my detective find out where that low-down worm would be and when I could catch him unawares. Then I went down to the shop, took the gun out of the drawer where we keep it—for protection, you see. And after that, I took care of him."

By then, Suzanne was shaking her head in obvious despair. "Grace, please . . ." she objected, but Grace ignored her completely.

"Where did you find him?"

"I had told Latty not to see him again, but she made arrangements to meet him down in Myrtle Edwards Park at eleven-thirty on New Year's Eve. I followed Latty there, and when she left him alone, I shot him."

"Where?"

"In the park. I already told you."

"Where exactly did you shoot him? In the face? The chest? The back of the neck?"

"Does that matter?" Grace Highsmith asked. For the first time she looked slightly flustered.

"Actually, it does. Especially in a confession."

Grace frowned. "I'm afraid I don't remember exactly. I must have been too upset at the time."

That was the moment when, as far as Grace Highsmith's so-called "confession" was concerned, the whole thing fell apart. In twenty-plus years of being a cop, I've been compelled to use deadly force on occasion. Each and every time, I've been what Miss Highsmith would have termed "upset," but I've never had the good fortune of forgetting even one incident. I remember them all—in vivid, bloody color and in heart-stopping detail.

Instead of mentioning that, I patted the pocket in which I had deposited the Seecamp. "Where did you get the gun, Miss Highsmith? I happen to know this particular weapon is very popular, and there's a minimum of a year-long wait to purchase one of these new from the factory."

"That I simply won't tell you," Grace declared. "A gentleman friend of mine gave it to me, and I'm not about to involve him in this tawdry business. He's a very nice man and doesn't deserve to have his name dragged through the mud."

By then, Suzanne had eaten her way through the grilled salmon. The waiter took her empty plate and then stopped by with a fully loaded dessert tray. It contained the usual things one expects to find in a place like that—fresh mandarin orange sorbet, double chocolate cheese cake with a Bailey's Irish Cream mousse, a coconut mousse tart, and a caramel apple cake.

Suzanne took the chocolate mousse. When the waiter looked at me, I started to shake my head. "Oh, please join us for dessert at least," Grace insisted. "You must have something. It'll do you a world of good. Try the cake. It's my absolute favorite. That's what I'm having, along with a cup of decaf."

I'm a sucker for anything with caramel on it, so I knuckled under. "All right," I said.

When the cake came, it was nothing short of delectable. The single layer of rich, moist cake was covered by a caramel sauce and topped by a dollop of whipped cream. Grace Highsmith broke off a tiny forkful and put it in her mouth. As she did so, her eyes misted over for the first time.

"I don't suppose they'll have desserts like this in the King County Jail," she said wistfully.

"They don't," I agreed. "But who said anything about jail?"

"You are going to arrest me, aren't you?" Grace Highsmith asked pointedly.

"No," I said. "I don't think so."

She looked clearly offended. "Why not?"

"Miss Highsmith, when it comes to murder investigations," I explained, "the process of making arrests is far more complicated than most people think."

"What about the gun?" she asked.

"What about it?"

"Was I or was I not carrying the murder weapon?" she demanded.

"That remains to be seen," I told her.

Her face fell for a moment, then brightened once more. "But I was carrying a concealed weapon."

"Carrying is a misdemeanor," I said. "For simple carrying we usually confiscate the weapon and issue a citation, unless the person is actually brandishing and placing people's lives in danger, which you weren't. Furthermore, since we're outside Seattle city limits, I couldn't arrest you anyway. Bellevue isn't part of my jurisdiction."

For the first time since I met her, Grace Highsmith appeared to be gravely disappointed. "Shoot," she said. "I suppose I should have thought of that. We could just as well have gone there for lunch."

Moments later, the waiter dropped off the check. Grace may have been upset, but she deftly slipped the bill off the tray before I ever had a chance to touch it. As the waiter went away to take care of the credit-card transaction, Shelley stopped by the table one last time.

"How was it?" she asked.

"Perfect," Grace answered "For what I thought was my last meal, it was absolutely wonderful."

Shelley frowned. "What do you mean, *last meal*, Grace? Are you going away?"

"I thought so. I was under the impression Detective Beaumont would be arresting me and I'd be spending the rest of my life in jail. Now it turns out I'm not going to jail after all. I'm disappointed. Very disappointed!"

It turned out that in a lunchtime of bizarre conversational twists and turns, Grace Highsmith had finally managed to say something that momentarily rocked Shelley Kuni's virtually unshakable composure. For a second, the restaurant owner paled, glancing back and forth from Grace to me. Finally, Shelley leaned down and gave the older woman a hug.

"I'm sure everything will work out just fine," she said. "If you do end up in jail and the cooks don't serve caramel apple cake, maybe I could send some in for you special."

"Oh, Shelley," Grace said, her eyes misting once more. "You're one of the most thoughtful people I know."

Being a gentleman, I walked Grace back to her store on Main Street. There was no further conversation. She was obviously quite put out that I had failed to perform as expected. When we arrived at Dorene's, the door was open, but the middle-aged woman I glimpsed through the window couldn't possibly have been Latty Gibson.

"I'm still going to need to talk to Latty in person," I said, pausing outside the door. "Will you give her my number and ask her to call?"

"Oh, all right," Grace agreed.

"And I'll want to speak to Virginia Marks as well. I've already tried calling her, but I only reached her answering machine."

"She's out of town," Grace said. "She's due back sometime later this afternoon. I expect to hear from her as soon as she gets in."

It sounded to me as though Virginia Marks was still working for Grace Highsmith. "Do you know where she's been?"

"Of course. She's been down in California."

"Doing what?"

"Tracking Don Wolf."

"But why? The man's dead."

"As Mark Antony said about Julius Caesar, 'The evil that men do lives after them.' These are the nineties, Detective Beaumont. Just because the man is dead doesn't mean he can no longer hurt her."

There was a short pause before I finally tumbled to what she meant. "You mean AIDS?"

"Of course I mean AIDS. I haven't brought it up with Latty, because I don't want to alarm her unnecessarily. Nonetheless, Virginia is trying to find out if he had any other . . . sexual connections. Besides his wife, I mean."

It crossed my mind that for that kind of information, a trip to California wasn't the least bit necessary. In fact, all Virginia Marks would have needed to do was talk to Jack Braman of the Lake View Condos. But I didn't tell Grace Highsmith that. It wasn't my job.

"I'll need to talk to Virginia Marks as soon as possible, Miss Highsmith," I said. "And to Latty as well. Please give them my phone numbers. Here's another card in case you misplaced the first one. It would be better for all concerned if they contacted me rather than having to be tracked down."

This time Grace Highsmith slipped the card into her pocket. She seemed suddenly subdued and diminished. "You knew right away I was lying, didn't you," she said.

I nodded.

"I was a fair actress once," she said sadly. "I really thought I could pull it off. Now that it's out in public, though, my confession is probably going to cause a good deal of trouble."

"Telling me doesn't mean it's public knowledge. Don't worry about it," I added. "I certainly don't hold it against you. After all, Latty's your niece. You were only trying to protect her."

"Thank you, Detective Beaumont," she said. "You've been most kind."

I opened the door and let Grace back into her shop, then I climbed into the parked Porsche and started the engine. As I glanced in the rearview mirror, I noticed that a van with a television station's logo emblazoned on the front was waiting to pull into my parking place.

At the time, I didn't think a thing about it, although, if I'd been smart, I would have.

# Thirteen

**O**nce I was in the car and headed back into Seattle, I remembered the previous day's hassle with Sergeant Watkins about my not using the beeper. Just to be on the safe side, I checked the display. As soon as I saw the number on the readout—Watty's, of course—I felt like one of those fork-bending psychics.

I called him on my cellular phone. "Detective Beaumont," he grumbled. "Where the devil have you been? I've been looking everywhere. I even checked with motor pool, but they told me you hadn't signed out a car."

"I've been busy," I said. "What's up?"

"I'll tell you what's up. The Media Relations folks have been climbing all over me for the last hour and a half. Phil Grimes is fit to be tied."

"Media Relations? How come?"

"The jail commander is calling every other

200

minute, complaining because the street outside their sally port is blocked almost solid with wall-to-wall television trucks, cameras, and reporters."

"What's going on at the jail?" I asked. "Have I missed something important?"

"Don't try running that phony innocence crap past me, Detective Beaumont," Watty growled into the phone. "This time, I'm not falling for it."

*Phony innocence?* For once, it wasn't a matter of feigning innocence, because I didn't have the foggiest idea of why Watty was so steamed. One thing was painfully clear, however. It had something to do with me.

"What's going *on*?" Watty continued. "I'll tell you what's going on. Right around eleven-thirty, somebody supposedly in the know faxed every damn newspaper and television and radio station in town and told them that early this afternoon, Seattle Homicide Detective J. P. Beaumont would be arresting Grace Highsmith and charging her with the murder of Don Wolf. The accompanying confession to Don Wolf's murder appears to be handwritten on Grace Highsmith's personal stationery and over her signature."

"But I didn't even meet up with her until . . ." Suddenly feeling half sick, I remembered how long it had taken Grace Highsmith to come back out of the back room. She hadn't tried to skip out on me. She had simply outfoxed me at every turn.

"She sent out a signed confession? And an advance announcement of her impending arrest?"

"That's right," Watty returned glumly.

I tried making light of it. "Come on, Watty. You know how this stuff goes. There isn't a major case on the books where we don't end up with at least one or two phony confessions. This one's no different."

"Believe me, Detective Beaumont, it *is* different. Now where is she, Beau? Did you arrest her or not?"

"No, I didn't arrest her. Her confession was so full of holes it was a joke—a put-up deal. The last time I saw Grace Highsmith, she was walking in the door of her gift shop in downtown Bellevue. I don't understand why everybody's so upset. There was never any question of my arresting her."

"Why the confession, then?" Watty asked.

"Grace Highsmith is a nice little old lady who was trying to protect her niece."

"Nice little old lady!" Watty scoffed. "Here she is, confessing to a killing and announcing the victim's name in public when we haven't even released that information to the media. Makes the whole department look like a bunch of jackasses. And if she's so damned nice, Detective Beaumont, how come she knew the victim's name?"

"I already told you, Watty. She was trying to protect her niece."

"So the niece is the killer then?"

"Could be. I don't know," I said. "Not yet anyway, although there's a good possibility. The aunt gave me a gun that may be the murder weapon. She opened up her purse and dumped a thirty-two auto out onto the table right in the middle of lunch."

"Is it the murder weapon or isn't it?" Watty demanded.

"Maybe."

"Look here, Detective Beaumont. I want a lot more than *maybes* on this, and I want it fast. Where is this alleged murder weapon right now?"

"In my pocket."

I didn't add that it was wrapped up in doggy-bag aluminum foil. I don't think Sergeant Watkins would have seen any humor in that.

"You'd by God better find out whether it is or not," he fumed. "I want a definitive yes or no, and the sooner the better. If I were you, I'd take the damn thing straight to the crime lab and check it out. And I'd do it before Captain Powell nails you. He's hot."

"Hot? What's he upset about?"

"About your not keeping us informed about what you're doing, that's what. If one of his officers is investigating a member of the University of Washington Board of Regents with regard to a current homicide case, then it stands to reason that the captain would appreciate having that information come to him directly from the detective involved and not from some lippy television reporter who looks like she just got her high school diploma late last week."

A few words leaped out at me from Watty's latest harangue, and they left me stunned: *Mem-*

*ber of the Board of Regents!* Did that mean Grace
Highsmith? . . . Of course, no wonder her name
had sounded so familiar.

"Now where the hell are you?" Watty continued. "Captain Powell was looking for you a few
minutes ago, and so was Detective Kramer."

Obviously, at that precise moment, they both
wanted to see me a whole lot more than I wanted
to see either one of them.

"Like you suggested, I'm on my way to the
State Patrol Weapons Section in Tacoma," I said
quickly. "If I head down there right away, I may
be able to make the trip before rush hour rather
than being caught in the middle of it."

"I want to hear from you the moment you
know anything," Watty said. "You got that?"

"Got it," I said.

"What about this next-of-kin situation on both
Don Wolf and the I.D. on the second victim? With
his name out over all the media, people are beginning to link the two cases. The captain wants
to know—"

"Tell him I'm on it," I said. "I'll keep you
posted."

"Good," Watty returned. "You do that."

Once I hit I-5, I turned south toward Tacoma.
In the old days, two o'clock in the afternoon
would most likely have been pre-rush hour.
Nowadays, in the Seattle/Tacoma area, rush hour
tends to last twenty-four hours a day. I made
fairly good time until I got to the diamond-lane
construction zone and a three-car injury accident

down by Boeing Field. From then on, it was stop-and-go traffic all the way to the Midway landfill. A drive that should have taken forty-five minutes max took almost two hours.

That's the price of progress, I guess. Used to be, in order to get to the weapons experts, all I would have had to do was walk down a couple of flights of stairs. For years, most of the local functions of the Washington State Patrol crime lab were performed in the Public Safety Building in downtown Seattle. In recent months, however, all that had changed as the crime lab moved into more modern and supposedly more earthquake-proof quarters elsewhere. The firearms section was now working out of a temporary location on the outskirts of Tacoma.

Gabe Rios is a forensic scientist who specializes in weapons, especially firearms. When the receptionist led me into his cluttered office, I was pleased to note that here was a man whose work space was even messier than mine. Sitting with his feet propped up on a paper-strewn desk, Gabe was so deeply engrossed in reading a gun magazine that I wondered if he'd even notice our presence.

"Sorry," he said, when he eventually looked up and caught sight of us. He put down the magazine, made some kind of notation on a computer keyboard, then looked back at me with a lopsided grin as the receptionist dropped me off and then backed out the door.

"Hey, Detective Beaumont. Long time no see. What brings you all the way down here to the wilds of east Tacoma?"

Without a word, I handed over the foil-wrapped package.

"Lunch?" Gabe asked. "Beau, you shouldn't have."

"Don't worry, I didn't," I returned. "It's one of those new Seecamps."

"Pretty little thing, isn't it," Gabe said, once he untwisted the foil and the .32 was exposed to view. "What is this, your new backup weapon? Did you stop by to show off and rub our noses in it? I understand these little babies are real tough to come by."

"It's not mine," I said. "This one fell out of a little old lady's purse, right in the middle of lunch. There's a good possibility it's a murder weapon. Did the medical examiner's office send over the bullet from the New Year's Eve shooting?"

"Which one?" Gabe asked.

"Don Wolf. The floater with the bullet in his head. Has Audrey Cummings sent you anything on him yet?"

"I think so," Gabe said. "Hang on a minute." Frowning in concentration, he rifled through the top layer of debris stacked on his desk. At last, he unearthed a large manila envelope which he waved at me in triumph.

"See there?" he said. "I knew it was here somewhere. It came in just a little while ago. I've taken a preliminary look at it, but that's about all. The bullet's in pretty good shape, considering, so I'd say it mostly went through soft tissue."

I nodded. "That's right. Base of the skull at point-blank range."

Gabe looked down at the .32 auto and clicked his tongue. "They may be little, but oh my."

"How's the rifling?" I asked.

Fortunately, most people never have to look down the barrel of a gun. If they did, they'd see a series of spirals. Those markings, known in the trade as lands and grooves—lands for the raised parts and grooves for the depressions—are what put the spin on a bullet when it comes through the barrel of the gun, leaving behind a series of distinctive marks. These marks are called rifling. For an expert like Gabe, rifling patterns from one gun are distinctly different from those made by any other. To him, they're also as easy to differentiate as two different sets of fingerprints would be to someone who spends all his or her working hours dealing with the details of putting fingerprints into the Automated Fingerprint Identification System.

"Pretty good for a hollowpoint," Gabe answered. "Want me to lift prints off the gun before I test fire it?" he asked.

"You can try, but my guess is it's been wiped clean."

Gabe shrugged. "It can't hurt to try." He got up and headed for the door, taking the .32 with him. "This may take some time, especially if we're lifting prints. Make yourself at home, Beau. You're welcome to use both my phone and my desk if you want, as long as the mess doesn't bother you too much."

"Thanks," I said. "The phone would be a big help, and the mess looks just like home."

Careful not to turn any of the stacks of paper into miniavalanches, I gingerly made my way around Gabe's desk, eased into his leather chair, and picked up his phone.

On the way down in the car, I had tried reaching Captain Kilpatrick down in La Jolla. It hadn't been a particularly satisfying experience. "The captain's in a meeting, and I don't know anything at all about a next-of-kin notification," the young woman on the phone had told me in a tone that implied she didn't much give a damn, either. "I don't know if he'll be back in his office this afternoon or not. He may go straight home after the meeting."

"Would you mind taking a message, just in case?"

"Who did you say was calling?"

"Beaumont," I had answered. "Detective J. P. Beaumont of Seattle P.D."

"Where's that?" she had asked.

"Seattle. All the way up here in Washington State."

"Oh, really?" she had said vaguely. "I always thought Seattle was somewhere in Oregon."

Gritting my teeth, I had gone on to leave a message asking Kilpatrick if there were any new de-

velopments in the Don Wolf case. I had ended
the call and spent the rest of the trip to Tacoma
grousing about the half-witted nim-nulls who
had decided public schools in this country no
longer needed to teach geography.

That exercise in mental curmudgeonliness had
kept me occupied. It had given me an excuse to
gripe at someone else, and had provided enough
intellectual interference to keep me from thinking
about some of my own issues. Like Grace Highsmith's all-too-public confession. Like Captain
Larry Powell's current case of righteous indignation. Like Detective Paul Kramer's whining.

It took time to sort through all the hoops it
takes to make a third-party long distance call
from Gabe's office phone. Call me a Luddite if
you want, but please spare me from all that new-
fangled telecommunications equipment with all
the computerized bells and whistles. There was
something wonderfully simple and straightforward about the old days when you picked up a
telephone receiver and some nice lady said,
"Number, please." Back then, if you wanted to
bill a call to another number, all you had to do
was say so.

In Gabe's office at the crime lab in Tacoma, I
discovered the hard way that it isn't easy to make
the Washington State Patrol's long distance provider coordinate with Seattle P.D.'s long distance
provider. I dialed in access codes until I was blue
in the face before I finally made a telephone ac-

tually ring in far-off La Jolla, California, at ten after five.

Not only did the phone ring, but—miracle of miracles—a live human voice answered, "Homicide Captain Wayne Kilpatrick speaking."

"Detective Beaumont of the Seattle Police Department, Captain," I said.

"Oh, yeah," he returned. "I just found your message asking about whether or not there are any new developments. Unfortunately, I don't have much of anything to report from this end. I turned that situation over to one of my people, Detective Enders. Haven't you heard from her yet?"

"Not so far."

"Hold the phone and let me see if I can track her down."

He put me on hold. I was grateful that, instead of the strains of Muzak, only silence greeted my ear. After what seemed like several minutes, Kilpatrick came back on the line. "Are you still there?"

"So far."

"Hold on and I'll transfer you."

After only one ring, a woman answered. "Detective Lucille Enders," she said.

"Detective Beaumont here," I said. "Seattle P.D."

"Sorry I didn't get back to you earlier—I got called out on another case."

"That's all right. Do you have anything for me?"

"As a matter of fact, I do. I spent a big part of my morning at Alpha-Cyte talking to a guy named Harry Moore who owns the place. I picked up Lizbeth Wolf's mother's name, address, and phone number, but I still haven't been able to locate her. Moore seemed really broken up by the idea that something may have happened to Lizbeth Wolf. He wanted details, and I told him I didn't have any. That he'd have to talk to you or to someone else up there in Seattle to get the whole story. He gave me his direct line at work as well as his home number. He said for you to go ahead and call regardless of how late it is."

She read off the numbers, and I jotted them down. "And the mother?"

I heard the shuffle of pages as Detective Enders thumbed through her own notebook. "Here it is. Her name's Anna Dorn. She lives in Laguna Beach."

"What about finding anyone connected to the other victim, to Don Wolf?" I asked.

"I've run into a brick wall there," Detective Enders told me. "It's as though he never existed. Are you sure you didn't make him up?"

"I'm relatively certain I didn't."

I looked over my notes. "How far is Laguna Beach from where you are?" I asked.

"Ninety minutes or so, depending on traffic. Why?"

"Damn!" I said. "That's too far. I guess I'd better call there and see if someone in the Laguna

Beach police department will go out and track her down."

"Why, what's going on?"

"Don Wolf's name was inadvertently released to the media today, and the connection to Lizbeth can't be far behind," I explained. "I'm afraid the mother will end up seeing it on television or reading it in the newspaper before we have a chance to notify her in person, especially since we still don't know for sure whether or not the second victim is Lizbeth Wolf."

"I'll handle it," Lucille Enders said briskly. "I'm off shift now. I was just completing some paperwork. I'll leave for Laguna Beach as soon as I finish."

"I can't ask you to do that, Detective Enders. I'll—"

"Nobody's asking me," Lucille cut in. "I'm telling you, I'll handle it. And I'll call you and let you know when it's been done."

"Why would you do that?" I asked.

"Because I'm a mother, too," Lucille Enders answered. "And because Lizbeth Wolf is Anna Dorn's only child."

"Thank you," I said. "Thank you very much."

Who says there's no place in the world for women detectives? Maybe I would have said so once, but not anymore. I've learned my lesson.

When I finished that call, at least I already knew all the necessary codes. Compared to the first long distance call, the second one was a snap. And even though it was almost five-thirty by then, Harry Moore answered his direct line at Alpha-Cyte.

"Detective Beaumont," he said. "Ever since Detective Enders left, I've been sitting here hoping you'd call. Tell me, what happened?"

"It's all very sketchy, so far. At this time, we're reasonably sure Don Wolf was murdered. If the victim found in his apartment turns out to be his wife, she may or may not have committed suicide."

Harry Moore's sharp intake of breath was almost a sob. "Oh, my God!" he whimpered. "Suicide? I was afraid that's what you were going to say. If she killed herself, it's my fault. All my fault."

"Why would it be your fault?"

"We had a big argument, a couple of days after Christmas. She left in a huff."

"What was the argument about?"

"What else? That worthless husband of hers."

In Harry Moore I had encountered yet another nonfan of the late, great Donald Wolf.

"Wait a minute, Mr. Moore. Let me ask a question. How well do you know Lizbeth Wolf?"

"Very well. She started working here as an intern while she was still in college. I trained her myself. She's done virtually every job here, from the most intricate research procedures to typing annual reports."

"Can you tell me if she was right- or left-handed?"

"Left, of course. Why do you need to know that?"

I closed my eyes, remembering the scene in Don Wolf's bedroom. I could still see a clear image of the dead woman's lifeless left hand, complete with gold wedding band, hanging down on the left-hand side of the bed. Potentially, that made one more piece of the puzzle slip into place. The gun had been found on the other side of the bed. If Lizbeth Wolf actually turned out to be the victim, Audrey Cummings was right in saying she hadn't committed suicide.

"In that case, Mr. Moore, if it's any consolation, I think I can assure you that the dead woman, whoever she is, was murdered."

"Did Don Wolf kill her?" Harry asked.

Good question. We had all been going on the assumption that Don Wolf had died first, thus leaving him out as a suspect in the death of the woman found in his condo. That possibly erroneous conclusion was largely based on the fact that his body had been found first. I made myself a note to check with Audrey Cummings to see if the autopsy had allowed them to pinpoint time of death for either victim.

"By person or persons unknown," I said.

"Just wait," Harry Moore said. "You'll see. I always knew there was something terribly wrong with that guy. Oh, he looked great. He was a snazzy dresser—a real lady's man. But when he waltzed in here last summer and swept Lizbeth off her feet the way he did, I knew right then

something wasn't right. Lizbeth had been with
me for so long that she seemed more like a member of my family than an employee. Like the
daughter I never had. Maybe I was a little over-
protective, and I think Lizbeth resented it. But
jeez, I could tell from the start that the guy was
bad news. It's hard for someone like me to keep
my mouth shut. Then last week, when the SOB
proved me right, I had to go and open my big
yap and tell her 'I told you so.' After that, all hell
broke loose."

"Maybe you should try telling me the whole
story," I suggested, "from the beginning."

Harry took a deep breath. "Don Wolf showed
up down here midsummer of last year. I forget
now where he and Lizbeth met. Once they did, it
was whirlwind courtship time. Within weeks, she
was wearing a rock for an engagement ring. I
tried to tell her that he was rushing things too
much and pressuring her into getting married before she knew enough about him. These days,
with all the drug dealing and such, when
somebody has plenty of money and no visible
means of support, no regular job, you can't be too
cautious. So anyway, when I tried to talk her into
slowing down and taking some time to get to
know him before jumping into anything, we had
a huge fight. I was afraid she was going to up
and quit on me. In the end, she just told me to
mind my own business. Two weeks after that—
less than a month after they met—they ran off to
Vegas and got married. And two months later, he

tells her, 'By the way, I've got this new job up in Seattle. See you around.' Lizbeth tried to pretend that his taking off like that didn't matter, but it did. It had to hurt like hell.''

''My understanding was that she was down here waiting for the house to sell,'' I said.

''In order to sell a house, you have to list it,'' Harry Moore said. ''That business about staying here to sell it is what she told everybody, just to save face. And who can blame her? There she was, a blushing first-time bride almost forty years old. And what happens? The groom takes off and leaves her high and dry.''

''So what happened last week?''

''Lizbeth called me from home. She had been off on sick leave for several days the week before Christmas, and Alpha-Cyte shuts down completely between Christmas and New Year's. She called me, crying. She asked me to come over because she needed to talk to someone, and she didn't know where else to turn. When I got to the house, she was in pretty bad shape. She had been in bed for two days with a terrible cold. Not only that, she'd just received a letter from Don saying there had been some kind of mistake. That there had been a glitch in the proceedings somewhere along the line. The upshot was that Wolf's divorce from his first wife hadn't been final at the time he and Lizbeth eloped to Vegas. According to him, it turned out they weren't married after all. That sleezeball was a bigamist.''

*Among other things*, I thought. "What then?" I asked.

"First I said, 'I told you so,' which, as my wife pointed out later, was exactly the wrong thing to say. Then I offered to put Lizbeth in touch with my personal attorney so she could get some advice on her legal standing—like, did she need an annulment or could she take the bastard to court and sue his socks off? I don't know why I bothered. It was just like pissing into the wind."

"Why do you say that?"

"Because as soon as I finished, she asked if she could have another week off once the Christmas holidays were over. She said she was going to drive up to Seattle and try to straighten things out with Don. And I said, 'What's to straighten out? Stay the hell away from the slimy bastard.' I probably said some other things, too. I don't remember it all. I'm sure I hurt Lizbeth's feelings. I guess I'm not what you call a sensitive guy when it comes to women. I just wanted to protect her is all. I didn't want her to be hurt."

Harry Moore's voice broke. I could believe that the connection between him and Lizbeth Wolf went beyond the ordinary employer/employee connections, although I couldn't sort out exactly what their relationship might have been.

"When was this conversation, Mr. Moore?"

He cleared his throat. "The twenty-ninth. Maybe even the thirtieth."

"She would have driven?" I asked.

"Yes," he said. "Lizbeth loved to drive. She

had herself a little four-wheel-drive Subaru wagon. Even with snow, she wouldn't have had any trouble getting over the mountains."

"When I first told you about Lizbeth, Mr. Moore, you asked me if her husband had killed her. Was there any particular reason you said that? Do you know anything about him that would make him a possible suspect in your mind?"

Harry thought for a moment before he answered. "I think Don wanted to be rid of her," he said. "I don't think he had any idea that she wouldn't give him up without a fight. I think he just expected her to lie down, play dead, and take his word as gospel about their not being married. But she wouldn't do that. The last thing she ever said to me was that some things were worth fighting for, and marriage was one of them. I couldn't believe it. Sometimes I just don't understand women at all, do you Detective Beaumont?"

"No," I said. "Not at all. But let me ask you one more thing, Mr. Moore. This is about Don Wolf now. How close is the biotech community down there?"

"Did you say *community*?" he returned. "That's not quite the right term, Detective Beaumont. I'd say it's closer to a snake pit. Why?"

"But do you pretty much know what the other guys in your field are doing?"

"Of course. Nobody in his right mind turns his back on another snake. Why?"

"I was told Don Wolf had a considerable reputation as a financial wizard in biotech. His previous places of employment were listed as Downlink of San Diego, California; Bio-Dart Technologies, Pasadena, California; Holman-Smith Industries, City of Industry, California. Ever heard of them?"

"Never," Harry Moore replied. "I can do some checking around, if you like, and see what I come up with."

"You do that, Mr. Moore. And let me know what you find out."

I put down the phone in Gabe Rios's messy office and sat there staring at it. Latty Gibson and Lizbeth Dorn Wolf weren't the only people Don Wolf had lied to. He had also pulled the wool over Bill Whitten's eyes. Of the three, Whitten seemed like the only one who had seen through to the real back-stabbing Don Wolf. And maybe he, more than the others, had been prepared to defend himself.

All of which meant that Bill Whitten was right. He needed to stay on my list of prime suspects, and although it was a very short list, I reminded myself to keep him close to the top. Right under Latty Gibson.

# Fourteen

I had no more than put down the phone after talking to Harry Moore when a proud Gabe Rios appeared in the door to his office. Grinning from ear to ear, he gave me the old thumbs up.

"Congratulations, Detective Beaumont. You've got yourself a Seecamp thirty-two auto murder weapon," he said.

"Gee, thanks," I returned glumly.

Gabe frowned. "What's the matter, Beau? For somebody who just found a critical piece of evidence, you don't sound very happy."

"I'm not," I said. "I may have a murder weapon, but that doesn't mean I have a murderer."

Gabe shrugged and booted me out of his chair. "You have to start somewhere," he said. "For right now, I just eyeballed things. I'll get the official ballistics report put together and sent up to you through regular channels. You should have it by the first of next week."

"That's the soonest I can have it?"

"You know it is."

"What about prints?"

"Wiped clean."

"That figures," I said.

Grace Highsmith obviously watched too many police dramas on television. How could I possibly have expected anything else?

"Okay," Gabe said. "Out of my chair so I can get back to work."

As I vacated the chair, he was already reaching for the magazine he had been reading when I had first entered his office. "Reading magazines?" I asked with more than a trace of sarcasm. "Is that really part of your job description?"

He grinned. "What do you think?" he asked. "How else am I going to stay up-to-date?"

On the way back to Seattle, I puzzled over what I had learned so far. The gun—Grace Highsmith's gun—really was the weapon that had been used to murder Don Wolf. That lent a good deal of credence to the theory that Latty Gibson was the killer, and that Aunt Grace had attempted to confess to the crime in an effort to save her niece from a long prison term.

But if Grace had gone to the trouble of confessing to one murder, why not to both? If a capable defense attorney—and Suzanne Crenshaw seemed plenty cagey—could somehow manage a plea of temporary insanity. If evidence of the rape were somehow admitted into courtroom proceedings, that could possibly prove mitigating circumstance.

But with all the focus on Latty, I couldn't afford to ignore the other possibilities. The other detectives and I had somehow fallen into the trap of thinking that Don Wolf had been the first to die. But that might not be the case. The question raised by Harry Moore about whether or not Don Wolf had murdered Lizbeth was one that merited some serious consideration.

And then, there in the distance, stood Bill Whitten. Another station heard from, as they say, and one I couldn't afford to ignore.

I must have driven another five miles or so before I realized what I had done. Even lacking proper identification, I had given the second victim a name. In my mind, Audrey Cummings notwithstanding, the dead woman found in Don Wolf's apartment was Lizbeth Wolf and nobody else. Harry Moore had told me that Don Wolf had been determined to be rid of his relatively new wife. One way or another, now he was.

The trip back to Seattle from Tacoma took far less time than the drive down. Part of that was due to the fact that I was dreading the inevitable ass-chewing from Captain Powell. But by the time I finally made it back to the fifth floor at ten past seven that evening, I knew I was home free. Powell's a day-shift kind of guy. He might stay late to work a case, but never just to issue a reprimand.

Ducking into my cubicle, I paused long enough to take three messages off my voice mail. One was from someone I didn't know—a lady named Hilda Chisholm. She left two numbers—both for work and home—without giving me even a glimmer of information as to why she was calling. That wasn't particularly disturbing or unusual. In my line of work, I often receive phone calls from witnesses who are reluctant to leave important information of any kind on a recording device. They have to be handled on a person-to-person basis. Consequently, I started my next day's TO DO list by writing Hilda Chisholm's name on the topmost line. Then I retrieved my next message.

That one was from Lucille Enders down in La Jolla. "Detective Beaumont," she said, "I just left Anna Dorn's house. I've talked to her, told her that Don Wolf is dead and that her daughter may be as well. That way, in case something shows up on the news, at least she's been warned. She's taking the whole thing pretty hard. She requested that you not call back until tomorrow morning. I did ask her if she knew any other next of kin on her son-in-law, and she said she couldn't help us there. She told me that if he had any family, he never mentioned them to her."

*Bless you, Lucille,* I said to myself as I erased her message and wrote Captain Powell's name directly beneath Hilda Chisholm's. Being able to tell him that the next-of-kin notification was a fait accompli might help bail me out of the Larry Powell doghouse, as far as Grace Highsmith's public nonconfession was concerned.

Lucille Enders' message buoyed me up. The third one left me reeling.

"Hello, Beau," the voice said. "This is Dave—Dave Livingston, calling from Rancho Cucamonga."

My heart fell. I would have recognized Dave Livingston's voice even without the tagline introduction. Dave is my first wife's—Karen's—second husband. I could tell from the minute quaver in his voice—the slight hesitation between words—that this wouldn't be good news. Karen had been battling cancer for more than two years—most of that time without my knowing anything about it. I gripped the phone tightly and braced myself for whatever was coming.

"I had to take Karen back into the hospital early this morning," his disembodied voice continued. "I've been here all day. In fact, that's where I'm calling you from right now—a pay phone in the lobby. I've been in touch with the kids. Scott should be home within hours. Kelly will be coming with Jeremy and little Kayla. They'll be leaving Ashland sometime this evening and driving straight through. If you want to come down . . ."

Dave broke off. I could hear him struggling to regain his composure before he went on. "Sorry about that," he said finally. "I guess I got a little choked up. As I was saying, if you want to come down, too, it would probably be better if you did it sooner than later. Sometime in the next two or three days. I'm off work, so I can pick you up from the airport anytime. You're welcome to bunk in here with me if you like. It's a big house. Even with the kids, there'll be plenty of room. I'm leaving pretty much this same message on your machine at home in case you miss this one. I told Kelly I'd let you know, so she and Jeremy won't have to worry about getting in touch with you before they leave town. I probably won't be back at the house until fairly late tonight—sometime around midnight. Give me a call then. However late it is, I doubt I'll be asleep."

Then he hung up. I held the receiver away from my head, staring uncomprehendingly at it through tear-dimmed eyes. Faintly, very faintly, I heard the recorded voice mail reciting its familiar directions: "To replay this message, press four. To erase this message, press seven. To save it, press nine. To disconnect, press star."

But at that precise moment, I was incapable of pressing any number at all. The receiver simply tumbled out of my hand. For some inexplicable reason, it came to rest exactly where it belonged—in its cradle—automatically disconnecting the call.

Dave's chilling words sank in slowly. Karen was dying. The surgery, the chemo, the radiation had worked together and had bought her a little relief and a little time—enough for her to see her granddaughter born and to see her daughter, Kelly, happily married. But very little beyond that. Not enough. Not nearly enough.

And here was Dave—staunch old bighearted Dave—calling to see if I wanted to come down. Calling with the very generous offer of letting me decide whether or not I wanted to be included in the looming family crisis when there was no good reason for him to do so. When most people in his position would have said, "Screw you, buster. You blew your chances a long goddamned time ago."

I can't quite enumerate all the conflicting emotions that washed over me in the course of those next few awful minutes. Terrible sadness. Anger that life could be so unfair and that Karen would die so young. Regret that I had ever lost her in the first place. Thankfulness that, of all the guys out there in the world, the one she had chosen to marry had turned out to be as kind and caring as Dave Livingston inarguably was. Jealousy that Dave was there at her side instead of me. And last of all, the appalling realization that had our situations been reversed, I might not have been nearly as openhanded to him as he was being to me.

God help me, I didn't cry. Some kind of stupid pride stuck in my craw. I didn't let myself go, although it probably would have done me a world of good. Instead, I sat there stunned and empty and not moving for a very long time—ten minutes? Fifteen? Maybe longer. I have no idea.

Finally, almost like an electric shock, something else took over. Force of habit kicked in, and responsibility and maybe a kind of stiff-necked pride. Of course I'd go. I had to. I'd call Dave back and tell him I was coming, but not until after things were straightened out. After all, I was in the middle of a case. I couldn't just walk away and leave the job half done, could I?

The answer to that question should have been an unequivocal *yes*. The sensible thing would have been to pick up the phone right then. I should have called Paul Kramer, given him everything I had, and then caught the very next plane to southern California. But for some reason, I didn't do that. Couldn't do that.

When I glanced at my watch again, it was almost seven-thirty. That gave me four and a half hours before I could call Dave back. Opening my notebook, I thumbed through until I found the numbers Dave Riveira had given me for Virginia Marks. I tried the cellular number that was listed there. She answered almost immediately, "AIM Research."

"Hello," I said. "Is this Virginia Marks?"

"Yes. Who's this?"

"My name's Beaumont. Detective J. P. Beaumont with the Seattle P.D."

"I know who you are," she said. "What do you want?"

Her reaction wasn't exactly warm and fuzzy, but she didn't hang up on me, either. I hurried on. "I need to talk to you, Ms. Marks. I'd like to do it as soon as possible. Tonight, if it's convenient."

"Cut the 'convenient' crap, Detective Beaumont. I know what this is about, and I know I have to talk to you, so we might just as well get it over with. I'm already late for one meeting, but I'll probably be done with that by eight-thirty or so. How about nine o'clock?" she concluded.

"Where?" I asked.

"My place, I suppose."

"Where's that?"

"It's in Bellevue," Virginia answered. "It's a new condo at the corner of Bellevue Way and Northeast Twelfth. It's called The Grove on Twelfth. You'll have to park under the building and then call my unit from the security phone next to the elevator."

"Good enough," I said. "I'll be there right at nine."

Since I had to go back to Bellevue anyway, I decided to try to kill two birds with one stone. I dialed information and asked for Bellevue information. "Name, please," the information operator asked me.

"Gibson," I said. "Latty Gibson on Main Street."

"I have an S. L. Gibson on Main Street."

"That's the one."

She gave me the number and I dialed it immediately. It rang several times, but when there was no answer, I finally gave up on making any more calls, and devoted the next forty-five minutes to writing up a series of reports for Captain Powell. They detailed my day's worth of activities and clued him in on the unofficial ballistics information I'd picked up from Gabe Rios.

Flush with the illusion of having accomplished something, of having made some small progress, I left the office and headed home. There wasn't a lot of time between then and my appointment with Virginia Marks, but there was enough so I could spend a few minutes sitting in the recliner with my feet up.

In retrospect, I suppose I should have recognized that feeling of false euphoria for what it was, but I didn't. Instead, I took it at face value. I found some comfort in the idea that I was doing something constructive. That illusion kept me from thinking too much; kept me from contemplating the emotional quagmire that was lying in wait for me down in Rancho Cucamonga. Instead of seeing things for what they were, I blithely headed out into the night, convinced that I was perfectly capable of handling whatever was coming.

I suppose I shouldn't be too hard on myself about that. After all, when you've spent a lifetime stuffing your feelings, it isn't easy to change.

Down at Belltown Terrace, I didn't bother pulling into the garage. Instead, I parked on the street and then walked up to the lobby entrance so I could stop and pick up the mail before continuing on upstairs.

Kevin, Belltown Terrace's newest doorman, left his desk and hurried to meet me. "Good evening, Mr. Beaumont," he said, clearing his throat. "There's someone here who's been waiting to see you."

"Really?"

I glanced around the lobby. There, on one of Belltown Terrace's two handsome but highly uncomfortable lobby couches, sat a grim-faced middle-aged woman who looked as though she had just stepped out of a Grateful Dead concert. Her hair was a wild mane of unconstrained curls. She wore a tie-dyed ensemble—T-shirt and gathered skirt—that matched only insofar as the wild colored dies were of somewhat the same hue. Her small, gold-framed, round-lensed, glasses reminded me of the kind John Lennon used to wear. White socks under black socks completed her outfit. A well-used, grubby briefcase sat on the floor next to her feet.

My first thought was that maybe this was Grace Highsmith's niece. Whoever this woman was, no doubt she, too, had friends with one-word names. In fact, maybe *she* had a one-word name. "You're waiting for me?" I asked.

"If you're Mr. J. P. Beaumont," she said.

Rising from the couch and hefting the briefcase off the floor, she reached into the pocket of her skirt and pulled out a business card. She handed it over to me and waited, unsmiling, while I looked at it.

The name was definitely one with *two* words: *Hilda Chisholm*, the card read, *Investigator, Child Protective Services.*

"I left a message on your phone at work," she said.

"I know," I replied. "I was just down at my office and took your message, but I thought it was too late to call tonight."

"That's all right. I was here doing some interviews and I decided to do my paperwork here just in case you came home before I left. I would have called ahead, you see," she added, "but your telephone number is unlisted."

The accusatory way in which she said that single sentence made my hackles rise. She made it sound as though my having an unlisted telephone number was both suspect and antisocial, something I had done deliberately and for no other reason but to inconvenience her.

"I'm a homicide detective," I said, making an effort to speak in a civil fashion, more for Kevin's benefit than for hers. "I think, if you checked with some of my peers down at Seattle P.D., you'd find that most homicide cops have unlisted numbers. We all do the same thing, and for obvious reasons. What can I do for you?"

"I'm here to talk with you about Heather and Tracy Peters," she answered.

"Child Protective Services isn't wasting any time on this, are they?"

"Mr. Beaumont, as you are no doubt aware, my agency has been vilified far too often in the past for letting things go on and on without taking timely corrective measures. Where the safety and welfare of children are concerned, time is of the essence, don't you agree?"

"Oh, absolutely," I said.

There was no escape. I could see that even with my appointment with Virginia Marks looming at nine o'clock, I was going to be trapped into a conversation with Hilda Chisholm. My intention was to keep it short and sweet.

"I'll be happy to talk with you, Ms. Chisholm," I said, glancing pointedly at my watch. "You're welcome to come up to my apartment, but I do have a nine o'clock appointment."

"I don't expect this will take very long," she said with a chilly smile. "As a matter of fact, it shouldn't take long at all."

I pushed a button to open the elevator door and then waited—in the gentlemanly fashion my mother always insisted upon—for Hilda Chisholm to step aboard first. I stepped in after her and punched the button marked *PH* for penthouse. The doors swished shut quietly.

"You're right," I said. "It shouldn't take long at all, because what I have to say on the subject can be said in one minute or less: Amy and Ron Peters are excellent parents. It's ridiculous for anyone to imply otherwise."

"What makes you think I'm here to discuss Ron and Amy Peters?" Hilda Chisholm asked, eyeing me coldly.

That surprised me. "Aren't you?" I asked.

"Actually," she replied, "no, I am not."

"I see," I said, although that was a lie. I didn't see at all.

When we reached Belltown Terrace's top floor, once again the elevator doors swished open. "This way," I said, pointing her to the door of my apartment. Using my key, I unlocked the door, then held it open to allow Hilda Chisholm to enter.

My high-tech security system was on, which meant that as we entered the foyer, both lights and music came on automatically. I motioned Hilda into the living room. Again, alerted and directed by a sensor I carry on my key chain, both lights and music followed.

Hilda Chisholm stopped in the middle of the room and glanced around. "Very nice," she said.

"Thank you," I replied, although I didn't realize until much later that she never intended her comment as a compliment.

"Won't you sit down?" I invited.

Most people coming into my apartment for the first time are irresistibly drawn to the spectacular view to be seen from the window seat that lines the entire western exposure of the living room. Seated on the cushions under a long expanse of glass, my guests look out over the shipping lanes both in and out of Elliott Bay as well as farther out on Puget Sound. With the help of a mirrored corner column, nighttime visitors can also peer around the corner of the building to view the panorama of downtown city lights. In daylight, when the weather is clear and the Cascades aren't shrouded in clouds, that same mirror sometimes reflects back glimpses of a snowcapped Mount Rainier rising up above and beyond the downtown high-rises.

Hilda Chisholm made for the window seat, all right, but obviously, she was no connoisseur of views. Without even bothering to glance outside, she sat down with her back to the window, with her briefcase balanced on her lap, with her sock-clad legs clapped firmly and primly together and with her sour expression permanently etched on her face. Everything about her manner announced clearly that this wasn't a social visit. That being the case, I saw no reason to play host. Settling into my leather lounger, I pushed it back into a fully reclining position.

I was tired. I'd had one hell of a day. Still, I suppose dropping into the recliner that way showed a certain contempt for someone who, as an investigator for Child Protective Services, ought to have been a cosupporter of truth, justice, and the American way. In view of what was coming, however, a little healthy disrespect for my fellow public servant was definitely the order of the day.

"If you didn't come to talk to me about Ron and Amy's parenting skills, what are you doing here?" I asked.

"I came to talk about you," she said.

"Me?" I asked in surprise. "Why me?"

"Because you are a prime consideration in my investigation." Once again, she smiled her chilly smile, one that lowered the temperature in my living room by a full ten degrees. "What I'm most interested in knowing, Mr. Beaumont," she continued, "is why a man like you—a man with all the money in the world and with known transsexual contacts—would take such an unhealthy interest in those two little girls."

"Transsexual contacts?" I echoed.

"One of your fellow detectives mentioned to me that Johnny Bickford, one of Seattle's most infamous cross-dressers, is a special friend of yours."

"Special friend!" I choked. "Are you kidding? I barely know the man, but obviously, you've been chatting with Detective Kramer behind my back. That creep . . ."

"Naturally, I spoke with several of your coworkers," Hilda returned, unperturbed. "I'm conducting an investigation, you see."

Gradually, an understanding of the scope of her accusations was beginning to seep into my consciousness. "An investigation, or a kangaroo court?" I demanded, while my temper rose several degrees.

The room was quiet for several moments while Hilda Chisholm eyed my reaction with a disquieting, coolly speculative gaze.

"The girls' mother, Constance Peters, is very much concerned about that, especially now that she's learned—through a local television news broadcast, no less—that the girls are sometimes left alone in your care and under your control."

"Give me a break! Are we back to those stupid soapsuds again?" I sat up abruptly, letting the recliner's footrest slam down to the thickly carpeted floor with a resounding thump. "If so, you need to talk to Gail Richardson down on nineteen. Her mother's been visiting. It turns out *she's* the one whose attempt at cleaning turned into a mountain of suds."

"This has nothing whatever to do with soapsuds," Hilda interrupted, "although that incident is part of what brought this unfortunate situation to our attention. If the girls had been properly supervised at the time—"

"*What* unfortunate situation?" I interrupted.

"Your inappropriate involvement with the Peters girls."

"Inappropriate!" I exclaimed while the social worker's cold, unwavering stare sent a chill clear through me.

"Wait just a damn minute here! What exactly do you mean by *inappropriate*?"

She smiled. "You tell me."

"Are you suggesting that I'm some kind of dirty old man and that I'm interested in the girls for some kind of immoral purpose?"

Hilda Chisholm raised an eyebrow. "Aren't you?" she returned.

Calmly, she removed a notebook from her briefcase and thumbed it open. "For starters," she said, "let me ask you this, Mr. Beaumont. Did you or did you not pay money—your own personal money—to fund a good deal of the mission that sent Constance Peters to Central America three and a half years ago?"

"She was Roslyn Peters then," I told her. "And that was a contribution. A charitable contribution."

"I'm sure it was," Hilda smiled again. "Arranged by a man named Ralph Ames, I believe. Who exactly is he?"

"Ralph? He's my attorney."

"Your personal attorney?"

"Yes."

"And you keep him on retainer?"

"Yes."

"And why would an ordinary homicide detective need to have a personal attorney on retainer?"

"My reasons for having an attorney on retainer are none of your business, Ms. Chisholm. Although they could be. I'm sure Ralph would be more than happy to help me take you to court. Defamation of character is no joke, and I'm not going to take it lying down. And based on that, I think you'd better leave."

It took every bit of self-restraint I could muster to keep from leaping out of the recliner and simply throttling the woman on the spot.

Hilda Chisholm, however, made no move to leave. "But, Mr. Beaumont," she said, "I was sure you'd want to give me your side of the story."

"No," I returned, "I don't think so. I'm not going to dignify this ridiculous process by according it the benefit of two sides. In addition, as long as I have an attorney available to protect my interests, I don't intend to say another word to you until he is present."

"Your insisting on the presence of an attorney indicates a certain reluctance on your part, Mr. Beaumont. An unwillingness to cooperate. It makes it sound as though you have something to hide."

"I'm a police officer," I reminded her. "You're accusing me of a serious crime—a felony. Not having my attorney present at the time of questioning is a violation of my constitutional rights."

"This is simply an informal inquiry," she said.

"Like hell it is," I retorted. "Now get out of here."

"Very well, Mr. Beaumont," she said, carefully returning her notebook to the briefcase and closing the lock with a sharp snap. "But I will have to say in my report that you were uncooperative and abusive. Cursing is considered abusive, you know."

"You can put any damned thing you want to in your report, but only if you're out of my apartment within the next thirty seconds. Otherwise, you'll be writing that report with two broken arms."

"And I'll have to report that as a threat," she responded.

"No, Madame Chisholm," I said, "that was no threat. It's a goddamned promise!"

She retreated as far as the doorway before she paused long enough to deliver her parting shot.

"I suppose you know Captain Freeman?"

"Tony Freeman, of Internal Investigations?"

"Yes, that's the one. I have an appointment to discuss this matter with him tomorrow morning at nine o'clock. I expect he'll be taking some action pending the outcome of my investigation, of course."

Thankfully, she left then. And it's a good thing, too. If she had stayed one second longer, there's a good possibility I might have done something I would have regretted for the rest of my life.

# Fifteen

I brooded over Hilda Chisholm's visit all the way to Bellevue. Once there, I found my way to the Grove on Twelfth. Following Virginia Marks' directions, I parked beneath the building in a spot designated VISITOR. Then I locked the door to the Porsche and walked over to the elevator. There, almost on top of the elevator, sat the powder-blue Crown Victoria complete with its Braun Chair Topper. *At least she's here,* I thought.

After consulting the listing next to the door, I punched the proper number into the security phone and waited for her phone to ring. It did. Several times. On about the sixth ring, the same old voice mail recording I had heard before came on once again, inviting me to leave a message at the sound of the tone.

I didn't *want* to leave a message. I wanted to talk to this woman in person. And for good reason. Virginia Marks, a detective who certainly should have known better, had nonetheless conspired with Grace Highsmith to conceal evidence in a homicide investigation. To my way of thinking, not only did I have a reason to talk to Virginia Marks; I also had a scheduled appointment, so she, by God, owed me the common courtesy of answering her goddamned door. A glance at my watch told me I was five minutes early. Still, my old door-to-door-salesman instincts were already sending me the message that I was about to be stood up.

For a few minutes, I stayed where I was, standing next to the security phone and the elevator door. Three residents came by and let themselves into the locked elevator with keys. The last one, an elderly gentleman, gave me a particularly questioning look. "Can I help you with something?" he asked.

"It's all right," I said vaguely. "I'm just waiting for someone."

Rather than continue standing there looking like an idiot, I retreated to the Porsche. Five minutes passed; fifteen; then twenty. Every five minutes or so, I would climb out of the car, walk over to the phone, and dial her up again. Each time when there was no answer in Virginia Marks' apartment, I let it get to me that much more.

I say *it*, but I'm not talking about just one *it*. That *it* was all-encompassing—including everything and nothing. It was Virginia Marks for messing with the evidence and then standing me up when I knew damned good and well she was up in her apartment and simply not answering her phone. It was Karen Beaumont Livingston for having the bad manners to up and die on me. It was a pushy bureaucrat named Hilda Chisholm for accusing me of being a goddamned child molester. It was Grace Highsmith for being a dotty little old lady who carried a gun in her purse that turned out to be a damned murder weapon. And for Paul Kramer for being a gossipy, loose-mouthed son of a bitch.

All of those things taken together added up to quite a load.

Half an hour went by; thirty-five minutes; forty. I was still getting in and out of the car every five minutes to check on my appointment, and every five minutes, there still wasn't any answer. Finally, all those *its* became too much. Too damned much!

There were tools I could have used if I had wanted to avail myself of them. My cellular phone was right there in the car. My AA sponsor, Lars Jenssen, was literally only a phone call away. But I didn't care, and I didn't call.

Around ten or so, cold and disgusted, I decided to go somewhere and buy myself a cup of coffee, because by then, I had made up my mind that no matter how long it took, I was going to wait out Virginia Marks. I was far too stubborn to give up and go home. I had an appointment, by God, and I wasn't leaving before Virginia Marks shaped up and answered her phone. And since I was right there practically in the middle of downtown Bellevue, I decided to walk to wherever I was going to get that cup of coffee.

Bad decision.

There was a bank on the corner of Twelfth and Bellevue Way, and a strip shopping mall of some kind beyond that. But the very next place on the left-hand side of the street was a restaurant—one of those barbecued-rib joints. Drawn by the warm aroma of meat cooked over an open flame, I stepped inside.

Compared to outside, the restaurant was warm and inviting. A young, smiling hostess hurried to the front podium to inform me that the kitchen was just closing. "That's all right," I said, "all I want is a cup of coffee."

"In that case," she said, "would you mind sitting at the bar?"

"Not at all," I answered. "No problem."

I grabbed a stool at the near end of the bar, and there on the counter right in front of me, as if it were fate itself, I saw an old, dear friend of mine—a bottle of MacNaughton's.

"Did I hear you say *coffee*?" the bartender asked, hurrying toward me.

"No," I said, "I changed my mind. Give me a Mac and water."

And that was all there was to it. No drumrolls. No lightning flashes, just, *Give me a Mac and water.* The bartender who served it up to me was totally innocent of any wrongdoing. He had no way of knowing that this was my first drink in over two years.

In zoos you always see signs that say, DO NOT FEED THE ANIMALS. Maybe alcoholics should all be required to wear tattoos that say, NO BOOZE, PLEASE. I AM A DRUNK.

In Alcoholics Anonymous, I've often heard stories about people plotting out a game plan for falling off the wagon—planning the where, why, and when of it in great gory detail and well in advance of the actual event. For me, there was no planning. Until I saw the bottle of MacNaughton's sitting there on the counter staring back at me, I hadn't realized I wanted a drink— hadn't anticipated having one or even thought about it much. But when that first taste of booze touched my tongue—when that first long gulp of alcohol blasted into my long-sober system, it tasted great.

For the first half hour or so, I was on top of the world. Invincible. Nothing at all mattered. Nothing, including the fact that I hadn't had a bite to eat in more than ten hours.

"Ready for another?" the bartender asked sometime later.

That, of course, was the critical moment. If I could have walked away from the second drink, even more so than the first, I might have been all right. But it turns out that I'm an alcoholic. Saying *no* wasn't an option.

"Sure," I said, shoving my empty glass across the bar. "Why the hell not?"

By the end of the second drink, all the other things I had been worrying about and agonizing over disappeared off the face of the earth. They simply went away. I have no idea how many drinks I drank, because I don't remember much after I watched with grave interest while the bartender poured my third.

During most of my adult life, I prided myself on my tolerance for booze. When it came to drinking somebody under the table, I was usually the last man left standing in any given room. Maybe, without my noticing, that legendary tolerance may have been dropping some before I ever went into treatment. Inarguably, between then and the time I took that first drink in Bellevue, somebody pulled a dirty trick on me. It turns out that I couldn't hold my liquor anymore, not worth a tinker's damn.

From the time I took the first sip of the third drink to the time I woke up in what turned out to be the Silver Cloud Motel just up the street, I don't remember a thing—not a damned thing. And when I did wake up—when I finally came to my senses and opened my aching eyes—I wished I hadn't, because I was sick as a dog—more hung over than I've ever been in my whole life. Barely able to stand, I lurched into the bathroom and barfed my guts into the toilet.

Then, as I staggered back to bed, I realized that midnight had come and gone *without* my ever calling Dave Livingston down in Rancho Cucamonga the way he'd asked me to. Once again, I'd screwed up and let my family down. As usual.

Filled with revulsion and self-loathing, I looked at my watch. It said it was eight o'clock in the morning on Thursday, January 4. I was lying stark naked on the bed of a strange motel room with no knowledge of how or when I'd come to be there. The only thing I did know for sure was that since it was eight A.M., I was now late for work.

Slowly and shakily, feeling like an old man, I showered and managed to clamber back into my stinky clothing. Aware that I was checking out of the place without benefit of luggage, I felt like an errant schoolboy when I walked up to the desk in the lobby.

"Why, good morning, Mr. Beaumont," a cheery young female desk clerk said to me, looking at the number on my key and comparing it to the name on her computer screen. "I hope you slept well."

"Oh, yes," I stammered, hoping I sounded more convincing than I felt or looked. "It was fine." I glanced outside, but there was no sign of a parking lot in front of the motel.

"Can I help you with something?" the young woman behind the desk wanted to know.

Embarrassed, my ears turned red. "I seem to have misplaced the parking lot," I said.

She smiled tolerantly, as though having overnight guests lose the parking lot was a commonplace occurrence. "It's around back," she said.

"Thanks."

I found the lot with no further difficulty, but my Guards Red Porsche wasn't there, either. Not only had I misplaced the parking lot, I had also lost my car.

I walked back to the front of the motel. I was standing there looking blankly to the right and left, up and down Twelfth, trying to figure out what the hell to do next, when a Bellevue city cop came steaming by in a black-and-white, lights flashing and siren screeching. When he jammed on his brakes, skidded, and slowed, and then bounced into the parking garage underneath the Grove on Twelfth, I suddenly remembered very clearly exactly where I had left my missing 928.

About that time, a second cop car came screaming by and turned into the Grove's garage entrance, exactly the same way the first one had. As soon as the second patrol car disappeared into the building, I started getting a very bad feeling in the pit of my stomach—a feeling that had nothing whatever to do with the fact that I was as blindly hungover as I had ever been in my life.

I started toward the street just as a third squad car barreled down Bellevue Way and turned in on Twelfth, cutting across a double yellow line and through cars stopped in the left-turn lane. With a final squawk of the siren, that car, too, rocketed into the Grove's underground parking.

One cop car is bad. Two are worse. Three in a row means very bad news for someone. And somehow, I knew that one of those someones was going to be me.

Call it instinct, call it fate, or say that I've been in this business far too many years, but long before I jaywalked across the street at midblock, I knew that Virginia Marks was dead. Drunk or sober, there are some things longtime homicide detectives simply don't have to be told.

Walking into another guy's deal is always a tough call. That's especially true when you're not on your home turf, when you're hungover as hell, and when you're dragging around in yesterday's wrinkled, smelly clothing.

Halfway down the garage I could see the top of Virginia Marks' powder-blue wheelchair carrier towering over the roofs of other nearby vehicles. Just inside the garage entrance, a young, uniformed police officer headed me off at the pass.

"I'm sorry, sir," he said. "There's been a problem in the building. We're not letting anyone inside just now."

Shaking my head, I flipped open my I.D. "I'm a fellow police officer," I said. "Seattle P.D. I'm concerned that whatever has happened here may have something to do with a case I'm currently working on."

The young officer checked over my I.D., looked at me questioningly, shrugged, and then said, "Do you mind waiting here while I check with my sergeant?"

"Go right ahead."

A call on the officer's radio brought a sergeant on the double. He emerged from the same ele-

vator where I had spent so much time waiting for
Virginia Marks to answer her phone the night before. Looking anything but friendly, the sergeant
hustled across the floor of the garage to the entrance where his conscientious young patrol officer was still barring my way.

"Detective Beaumont?" he asked. I nodded.
"I'm Sergeant Orting. We're investigating a possible homicide. Officer Ryland here tells me you
think our case may have something to do with
one of yours?"

Orting hadn't stopped until he was almost on
top of me. When he did, he was close enough that
he evidently got a good whiff of my breath,
which must have still smelled like the dregs in
the bottom of a whiskey barrel. Frowning, he
stepped back out of harm's way while the expression on his face gave a whole new meaning
to the words *Give a guy some breathing room.*

I stepped back, too. "Two cases actually," I
said, "but it depends on who's dead."

Orting crossed his arms and looked even less
affable than he had before. "Supposing you tell
me."

"Virginia Marks?" I asked.

"How is it you'd just happen to know that?"

"Lucky guess?" I returned.

Orting shook his head. "Try again."

"I had an appointment to see Virginia Marks
last night, but she never showed."

"What time?"

"Nine o'clock. I waited around until almost

ten. When she still hadn't buzzed me in, I finally gave it up as a lost cause."

As we talked, Orting and I had started walking toward the elevator. We were almost there when the door opened and three men came out. Plainclothes or not, two of them had the unmistakable look of homicide detectives on the job. The third was the elderly gentleman who had questioned my presence in the garage the night before. Talking animatedly and waving his hands for emphasis, he was right in the middle of a sentence when he saw me and stopped short.

"That's him," he said, pointing directly at me. "That's the guy I was telling you about, the one who was hanging around down here in the garage right around nine o'clock."

"This is Detective Beaumont," Orting said, short-circuiting the necessity of an instant replay of his own set of questions. "He's with Seattle P.D. He claims he had an appointment with Virginia Marks last night regarding some cases he's working on, but that she stood him up. This is Detective Tim Blaine and Detective Dave Dawson."

While Orting answered the question, I pulled out a pair of business cards and gave one to each of the Bellevue detectives.

"But I'm telling you, this was the guy," the man was insisting, practically jumping up and down. "I knew from the way he was skulking around that he was trouble."

The guy was like a broken record, and he kept

right on, hammering away in that same vein. Meanwhile, one of the cops, after examining my card, reached out and shook my hand. "I'm Detective Blaine," he said. "What is it you're working on?"

"A double homicide," I said. "A man and a woman tentatively identified as his wife. Virginia Marks was a private investigator. She was working for the aunt of a woman who may very well end up being a prime suspect in one or both of those cases. I think we'll need to talk."

Tim Blaine, a bull-necked, weight-lifting type who looked far too young to be a homicide detective, nodded gravely. "I see," he said.

"You're certain the victim is Virginia Marks?"

"We've got a positive I.D.," Tim Blaine said. "From her bookkeeper—the woman who found the body."

"Cause of death?"

"This isn't official, of course," he said. "The M.E. isn't here yet, but I'm calling it a single bullet wound to the head."

"To the back of the head?" I asked.

Blaine's eyes bored into mine as he nodded. "You're right," he said. "We *will* need to talk. We have several interviews lined up to do in the next little while. If you have to go somewhere, leave a trail so I can find you later."

As he turned back to help his partner deal with the still-agitated resident, I used my keyless entry to unlock the 928 from across the garage. The taillights flashed once. As I walked away from the group by the elevator and headed for the car, I left behind a period of stunned silence and a not-so-subtle exchange of questioning glances. I've learned over time that homicide cops who drive brand-new Porsche 928s aren't exactly a dime a dozen. Nor are they always particularly welcome.

Once inside the Porsche, I reclined the seat, then lay back, and closed my eyes. My head was pounding. I had the shakes. My eyes hurt. Even so, I knew I had to call in and give Sergeant Watkins his shot at me.

"Why, Detective Beaumont," Watty said when he heard my voice on the phone, "how good of you to call. Did you finally decide to rise and shine?"

"I'm working," I said. "I'm over here in Bellevue, and I'm working. They've got a body over here that's most likely connected to the Wolf cases. I don't have any idea what time I'll be in."

"Maybe you'd like to pass that information on to Captain Powell and your fellow investigators? Detectives Kramer and Arnold are just now briefing the captain. I'll put you through to his office."

As soon as Captain Powell's tin-can voice came through the receiver, I knew he had switched on the speaker phone. "Nice of you to join us, Detective Beaumont," he said. "We were just talking about you. What's this about a murder over in Bellevue?"

"The woman who's dead is Virginia Marks. She was a private investigator who was working for Grace Highsmith on investigating Don Wolf."

"Grace Highsmith again," Powell said. "We were talking about her just now, too, and about her possible connection to the alleged murder weapon. Where did she say it came from?"

"I believe she said a gentleman friend of hers. Those may not be the exact words, but they're close. She refused to give me his name. She said she didn't want to drag him into all this."

"Oh, he's in all right," Captain Powell replied. "He's in regardless. Detective Arnold, maybe you'd like to tell Detective Beaumont here what you just found out about that little Seecamp auto."

"I called the factory," Sam Arnold said. Over the speaker phone he sounded tinny and distant, and more than a little nervous. "I gave them the serial number, and they gave me the name of the person who purchased it." He stopped dead and didn't continue.

"And . . ." I urged.

"His name's Foster. Darrell Foster," Arnold said.

Another astoundingly familiar name. My pounding headache was suddenly that much worse. "Not *Red* Foster?"

"The very one," Captain Larry Powell muttered. "However did you guess!"

Darrell Foster—Red Foster—was one of the good old boys who retired as the head of the Washington State Patrol years ago, sometime back in the mid-fifties, while I was still in grade school. Now in his eighties, he sometimes shows up at Police Guild events. For the last two years, he had tossed the coin for the Bacon Bowl, an annual fund-raising football game played by rival teams made up of police officers from Tacoma- and Seattle-area agencies.

"How did Red Foster get mixed up in all this?" I asked.

"Good question," Powell said. "Maybe you boys could get going and try to find out the answer, especially now that there's a possible connection to yet a third case. Where are you again?"

"In the garage of a place called the Grove on Twelfth at the corner of Northeast Twelfth and Bellevue Way in downtown Bellevue."

"Before we do anything else, we'd better get to the bottom of this gun stuff. What kind of transportation do you have?" Powell asked.

"My own," I said. "The nine twenty-eight."

"Detective Kramer, how about if you check out a car and go pick up Detective Beaumont. You and he can go pay a call on Grace Highsmith over there in Kirkland while Detective Arnold here tracks down Red Foster. I think he lives downtown here in one of the retirement homes."

"Ask him about the tapes," I heard Kramer say from the background.

"Oh, that's right. I understand from Detective Kramer that you've been given access to a security videotape that could show a clear motive for Don Wolf's murder on the part of Grace Highsmith's niece. Is that true?"

"The tape catches Don Wolf in the act of raping Latty Gibson," I answered.

"So you've actually seen it?" Powell asked.

"I have a copy of it," I answered.

"Where?"

"It's at home, still plugged into my VCR. I took the D.G.I. tapes there so I could watch them on a bigger screen, on a television set with better resolution than the one in the conference room."

"I'll just bet," I heard Kramer mutter in the background.

"But you haven't shared this material with either one of your fellow investigators on this case, with either Detective Kramer or Detective Arnold," Powell continued.

"No," I began. "There wasn't enough time to—"

Powell cut me off in midexcuse. "May I suggest, Detective Beaumont, that if there isn't enough time to share important evidence with your fellow detectives, then you'd better make it. Homicide detection is a team sport," he added. "You'd better either get on the team or off it. There is no middle ground."

# Sixteen

**I** knew it would take a minimum of fifteen minutes to half an hour for Phil Kramer to show up in Bellevue, so I used the time to make some of the calls I should have made the night before. The first one was to the house in Rancho Cucamonga. When no one answered, I was more relieved than anything else. For a change, I was more than happy to wimp out and leave a message.

"This is Beau, returning your call. Sorry I couldn't get back to you last night. I was out on a case." I swallowed a little after that last sentence. It wasn't exactly a lie, but it was certainly less than honest. "Thanks for letting me know what's happening. I'll keep trying."

After ending that call, I looked around the garage. There was no sign of either of the two detectives. The only officer visible was that same uniformed cop—an officer named Ryland—still standing guard at the garage entrance. With no potential interference on the horizon, I dialed in Lars Jenssen's number. Calling my AA sponsor then was a little late—like locking the barn door and all that crap—but it was better than not calling him at all.

The phone rang eight or nine times. I knew better than to hang up too soon. Lars is pushing eighty. If he doesn't rush to answer his phone, he has the perfect excuse.

"Hello," he bellowed into the mouthpiece when he finally lifted the receiver off the hook.

"Hello, Lars," I said. "It's Beau."

"What's that? You gotta speak up. I can't quite make you out."

I could hear him fumbling with buttons, most likely turning up the volume control on his telephone. "It's Beau," I repeated. "Is that better?"

"You bet. What can I do you for? Haven't seen you at too many meetings lately."

One of the things I've always liked about Lars Jenssen is his straightforward manner, the way he always comes right to the point.

"As a matter of fact," I returned sheepishly, "that's one of the reasons I'm calling right now. I had a little problem last night."

"How big a little problem?" Lars asked. "You in jail?"

"No, nothing like that . . ."

"Been in a meeting yet today?"

"Not yet. I'm at work right now, and—"

"Work?" Lars Jenssen sputtered. "Did you say *work*? If you know what's good for you, you'll haul your sorry ass off to a meeting and you'll do it now. Where are you?"

"I'm over here in Bellevue, and—"

"Bellevue? You hang on a minute. I'll be right back."

Lars slammed the phone down in my ear. I could hear him rummaging through papers, pulling drawers open and then shoving them shut, the whole while muttering under his breath. He's a widower who lives alone in a downtown high-rise retirement complex. His only son died in Vietnam, and his wife's been dead now for many years. When I first came back from treatment in Arizona and ventured into a neighborhood AA meeting down in the Denny Regrade, Lars Jenssen was the first person to come over to me and tell me how glad he was that I had come to the meeting.

"You keep coming back, now," he had told me as I headed for the door. "Just keep coming back."

In the last few months, I hadn't been back very often. I had let being busy get in the way of following that one very important piece of advice.

"Here it is," he said. "I knew I'd find it eventually. Hang on, let me find my damn magnifying glass. I swear, they make this gol-durned type smaller all the time. There it is. Okay, where are you?"

"Bellevue, but—"

"Hang on, hang on. Don't get your sweat hot. Now, what day is it again?"

"Thursday, I think. January fourth."

"Okay. Thursday. Let me see. It says here, there's a noontime meeting over there on Thursdays at a place called Angelo's. On a street called One hundred thirtieth. Think you can find it?"

"Lars, I swear, it was just a little slip," I began. "A one-time thing. I only called to talk for a couple of minutes. Like I said, I'm right in the middle of a case, and—"

"A case?" Lars repeated. "Baloney. And don't say it was a *little* slip. There's no such thing, and you know it. You let one of those go, and it'll turn into a whole damned train wreck right before your eyes. You get yourself to that meeting, Beau. Here's the address."

He was so insistent that I wrote down the restaurant's address when he gave it to me, but to be perfectly honest, I was just going through the motions. I was busy. I had my hands full with not one, not two, but three separate homicides. Detective Kramer was on his way to pick me up. I didn't really have any intention of taking off at noon to go wandering off to an AA meeting.

"You get that address all right?" Lars asked.

"Right, but—"

"No *buts*, and no time to talk," he interrupted. "I'll see you there."

"What do you mean, you'll see me there?" I asked.

"At the meeting. I'll be there, too. I haven't

been to a meeting so far today. It'll do me good."

"But Lars," I objected. "It's in *Bellevue*."

"So?" he returned. "What do you think, I was born yesterday? I'll catch a bus. Like I said. I'll see you there."

He hung up. End of argument. Shaking my head, I got out of the car and walked over to where Officer Ryland was waving one of the medical examiner's gray vans into the garage. I wasn't all that surprised when Audrey Cummings stepped out of the driver's seat.

"Not you again," she said, catching sight of me as she heaved a heavy leather satchel out of the back of the van and headed for the elevator. "Isn't this a little off your beat, Detective Beaumont?"

"Different beat; same case," I told her. "There's a woman dead upstairs. She happens to be a private eye who was hired to investigate Don Wolf's background."

"I see. What does it look like up there?"

I shrugged. "Like you said, it's not my beat. I haven't been invited upstairs. There are two Bellevue detectives up there, but if you see anything you think I ought to know, let me know."

She nodded. "Of course. By the way, did Detective Kramer tell you about the car?"

"What car?" I asked.

"Lizbeth Wolf's. It turned up in the visitor's parking place in the Lake View Condominiums. Detective Arnold found it. So we can be pretty sure that's who it is, although I'm still waiting for someone who knew Lizbeth Wolf to give me a positive I.D. Do you have anything for me there?"

"I've located Lizbeth Wolf's mother down in southern California. Her name's Anna Dorn. You should be hearing from her sometime today."

The elevator door opened. Sergeant Orting stood waiting inside, with one finger holding the DOOR OPEN button. "Good work, Beau," Audrey said as she stepped inside. The door started to close, but I pried it back open.

"Wait a minute. What about our deal?" I asked. "What's happening with those prints?"

"The ones we took off Don Wolf?" Audrey asked. The door had been held open too long, and the alarm began to howl. "I sent them over to the latent fingerprint lab. They asked me what they were supposed to do with them," she continued, raising her voice so she could be heard over the alarm. "I told them to run them through AFIS for an I.D. That is what you wanted, isn't it?"

"That's what I wanted all right," I answered, letting the door slide shut. "For whatever good that will do."

I walked the length of the garage and walked up the ramp into vivid midday sun. After the gloom inside the garage, the unexpected sunlight was almost blinding. The glare hurt my burning eyes and escalated the pounding between my ears. My mouth felt dry and cottony, and it tasted even worse. Standing with my hands in my pockets and waiting for Detective Kramer to show up,

I longed for a breath mint, for something that would combat the sour taste in my mouth. Kramer still hadn't arrived when I caught sight of a drugstore across the street.

"If anyone comes looking for me, tell them I'll be right back," I called over my shoulder to Ryland. "I'm going across the street for a minute."

I was back on the sidewalk and sucking on an Altoid when Kramer showed up in a full-size Chevy bulge-mobile a few minutes later. By then, though, I think excess MacNaughton's must have been leaking out through my pores. When I climbed into the car and shut the door, he wrinkled his nose in distaste and made a production of rolling down his window. "Where to?" he asked.

I looked up Grace Highsmith's address in my notebook and read it off to him.

"Where's that?" he demanded. "I'm from Seattle, remember? I don't know diddly-squat about Eastside."

"Is that so?" I returned. "I was under the impression you knew damned near everything. Since you don't, and neither do I, you might want to talk to Officer Ryland back there in the garage and see if he can give us directions."

Kramer put the bulky Caprice into a rubber-squealing U-turn and drove back to the garage entrance. While he was out of the car asking directions of Officer Ryland, I popped another relatively useless Altoid into my mouth. I briefly considered going back to the 928 to retrieve my

*Thomas Guide* to make it easier for us to stumble around in Bellevue and Kirkland. I decided against it, though. Why go out of my way to be helpful with good old Detective Kramer, my son of a bitch partner pro tem.

"I don't like being kept in the dark," Kramer fumed as he crawled back into the car and headed out of the garage. "You've been holding out on us."

"Holding out about what?" I asked.

"About your interview with Grace Highsmith, for starters. And then there's ballistics info, to say nothing of—"

*"Holding out* implies I had a chance to pass along information and didn't. After we all left the Lake View Condos yesterday morning, I never saw you again until just now. So don't give me that. And if you're interested in picking a fight, I'll be more than happy to oblige. You've been sitting on some info of your own, Kramer."

"For instance?"

"Finding Lizbeth Wolf's car, for one thing. And then, there's just being a general all-around asshole. Like spouting off your big mouth about my presumed sexual orientation to an investigator from Child Protective Services."

A flush crept up Detective Kramer's thick neck. "I didn't mean anything by that," he said. "It was nothing but a little joke. After all, it isn't every day some swish guy sashays around the fifth floor looking for autographs. I thought it was funny."

"It's funny, all right," I told him. "An absolute scream. Madame Hilda Chisholm of Child Protective Services seems to be under the impression that not only am I switch-hitter, I'm a pedophile as well. As a matter of fact, I'm considered such a serious threat as a child predator that Amy and Ron Peters may very well end up losing custody of his two kids by virtue of my being a friend of the family."

"I'm sorry," Kramer said. "I didn't mean to cause any trouble."

"Sure you didn't," I sneered, crossing my arms and staring out the window. "And when you went crying to Captain Powell about my holding on to the rape tape, I don't suppose you meant to do any harm with that, either."

For several minutes, we drove north through Bellevue and Kirkland, along Lake Washington Boulevard and Juanita Drive, in tight-lipped silence. Kramer was the first to speak.

"Look," he said, "Detective Arnold and I didn't ask to be put on this case with you. And if those rape tapes have something to do with our investigation, we should all have access to them. I thought Captain Powell ordered us to be a team."

"Kramer," I said, "Captain Powell ordered us to *work together*. He can't order us to be a *team*. Turning the two of us into a team would take an act of God!"

And that was pretty much where things stood when Kramer gave the wheel a sharp twist and sent us speeding down a steep, winding road through a forested ravine. I figured his temper tantrum was going to kill us both, but I was damned if I'd tell him to slow the hell down. When we finally reached the bottom of the hill, we turned north on Holmes Point Drive past a narrow band of high-priced, lakefront homes.

Remembering the almost reverential manner in which Suzanne Crenshaw, Grace Highsmith's attorney, had spoken of Grace's Lake Washington digs, and after seeing some of the nearby waterfront homes, I was prepared to be confronted by something downright palatial. I was surprised, then, when the numbered address in my notebook turned out to be attached to a ramshackle single-car garage that teetered on the edge of a steep cliff. The garage crouched between two massive houses that rose up in three-story splendor on either side. Like pricy waterfront properties everywhere, parking spaces in that neighborhood were at a premium. Grace Highsmith had evidently manufactured an extra, one-way-in-and-out space by leveling the ground above a retaining wall that was meant to keep her ancient garage from tumbling down the mountain. A berm at the end of the ledge was designed to keep cars from falling as well.

Kramer parked the Caprice with the front bumper grazing the berm. "Great view," he said, looking out over the lake, "but a hell of a bad place to have your brakes go out."

We got out of the car and walked forward to a

garage that came from an era of smaller, narrower vehicles. The door had been left open in order to accommodate the enormous tail fins of a hulking 1961 classic all-white Cadillac that didn't quite fit inside the four walls.

Next to the garage, a set of wooden plank steps, flanked by a two-inch pipe handrail, led down to a house tucked tidily into the side of the bluff some twenty-five steps below street level. Pausing at the top of the steep flight of stairs, we were almost even with the level of a rooftop chimney. A column of wood smoke spouted out of the chimney and curled out over the water.

"I guess some people have enough clout that they don't have to worry about burn bans," Kramer said sourly.

The Puget Sound area, always on the cutting edge of environmental activism, is one of the nation's first bastions of smoke police. During winter months—especially during periods of cold, clear weather—atmospheric inversions form, trapping dirty, polluted air near the ground. When the Cascades and Olympics disappear behind bands of reddish gray glop, the state of Washington imposes burning bans. During those bans, the use of woodstoves or fireplaces is prohibited except in homes where they provide the only source of heat. In order to enforce the bans, the state sends out smoke police whose job it is to warn and fine those poor misguided and mostly overly romantic folk who mistakenly try toasting their wintry toes in front of cozy fires.

For over a week, now, the weather around Seattle had been unseasonably clear. A burning ban
had been in effect for at least two days that I
knew of. It struck me as funny that Detective Kramer was so offended by Grace Highsmith's
breaking that particular rule.

"Look," I said, "if the lady doesn't worry about
concealed-weapons permits, why would she
bother with a burning ban?"

"Because rules should apply to everybody,"
Kramer said. "That's the way it's supposed to
work." At the top of the stairs, he stepped to one
side. "After you," he added.

The surprisingly steep stairway ended on a
landing that expanded into a bricked patio surrounded by raised flower beds that were thick
with hardy ferns and an array of bright purple
plants that looked for all the world like some
strange kind of overgrown cabbage. Part of the
patio was covered by a cord or more of cut and
stacked wood, stored under a blue tarp. I didn't
want to think about how much hard work it had
been to haul all that wood—one armload at a
time—down those stairs from street level.

The tiny house in front of us was divided from
its towering neighbors on either side by a tall
board fence that ran almost down to the water.
The fence was big, but the house itself looked
more like a shake-shingle dollhouse than a real
one—a miniature Victorian, complete with
steeply pitched roof, dormer windows, and real
shutters that may or may not have been operable.

Unlike the weather-beaten garage at street level, the house had a reasonably fresh coat of paint, and appeared to be in fairly good shape. Still, it was easy to see that the little cottage was nearing the end of its useful lifetime. Soon it, too, like all its now-vanished contemporaries, would be bulldozed into oblivion to make way for some new, oversized, million-dollar-plus showplace.

I stepped up onto a wooden porch that creaked in protest under my weight. The doorbell—an old-fashioned, push-button affair—sported a three-by-five card that said, in faded, almost invisible, inked letters, BELL'S BROKEN. PLEASE KNOCK.

I was raising my hand to do so when Kramer stopped me.

"Are you sure you have the right address?" he asked.

"Yes, I have the right address," I returned. "What makes you think I don't?"

"I thought you said Grace Highsmith is in her seventies or eighties. If so, how the hell does she get up and down all those stairs?"

While I turned back to look at Kramer, the door swung open on silent, well-oiled hinges. "One step at a time," Grace Highsmith answered before I could. "These days, it takes a little longer than it used to for me to get up and down. When I'm too old to make it under my own power, then I suppose it'll be time to check myself into an oldfolks' home, although I was rather hoping Detective Beaumont here would put me in jail so I wouldn't have to worry about that. Won't you come in?"

She held open the door, allowing Detective Kramer and me into a cozy living room that reeked of that peculiar old-house odor—a mixture of too many years of living, cooking, and burning. There was also more than a little dust and mold. A huge flagstone fireplace, far larger than the room called for, occupied most of one wall. A fire, fueled by the glowing remains of an eight-inch-thick log, crackled on the hearth.

At first glance, nothing in the room seemed to match. Inarguably authentic Navajo rugs—their colors long since faded to muddy browns and beiges—covered the floor, giving the place a warm, snug feel. The room was jam-packed with an odd collection of high-backed, old-fashioned chairs and couches—all of them sagging a bit here and there and all of them with upholstery that was more than a little threadbare. Frayed or not, what all the pieces had in common was an undeniable patina of age and quality and comfort as well. Their faded dignity seemed a worthy reflection of their spry but aging owner.

"Won't you sit down?" Grace invited. "I was just about to have a cup of tea. My mother was English, you know. I still much prefer tea to coffee. Will you have some?"

"No thanks, Miss Highsmith," I said. After introducing her to Detective Kramer, we both headed for opposite ends of the nearest couch. As I sat down, though, my elbow grazed something.

Cursing my clumsiness, I turned to examine what I had bumped. I found myself examining a three-foot-high bronze figurine of an emaciated Indian on an equally gaunt horse. The statue looked familiar.

Alexis Downey, that former girlfriend of mine, is up to her eyebrows in the arts. One of the reasons she's a "former" is that she was forever tweaking me about my general lack of artistic education, but even a complete Philistine like me can recognize a casting of *The End of the Trail* when he sees one.

On the floor next to the fireplace, tucked in behind a fifty-year-old leather ottoman, was a thoroughly modern fax machine. Its incoming message tray was half full of pages.

"Dusty didn't hurt you, did he?" Grace asked solicitously.

"Dusty?" I said.

She smiled. "The statue. Dusty isn't his real name, of course. I call him that because he gathers so much dust. I'm sure some of the artier types would choke if they heard me calling a James Earle Fraser Roman bronze casting by such an irreverent name. He's been in the family for years."

I gulped, grateful that in my infinite bumbling I hadn't knocked the damn thing over. With my luck, it would have bounced off the hearth and broken the horse's head off.

Grace smiled. "I had planned to give him to a museum someday, but not until I was good and ready. Now, what can I do for you?" she asked.

"Once again, this isn't really a social call. We've come with some rather bad news."

Grace's face paled slightly. She moved closer to a chair and grasped the back of it with her two frail and liver-spotted hands. "Not about Latty, I hope," she breathed.

"No," I agreed. "Not about Latty directly. We've just come from Virginia Marks' place down in Bellevue, Miss Highsmith. I'm sorry to have to tell you this, but she's dead."

One of Grace Highsmith's hands went to her throat while the other still gripped the back of the chair. "Virginia dead?" she repeated. "How can that be? How? When?"

"Someone shot her," I said. "It happened overnight, sometime between ten o'clock last night and eight o'clock this morning."

Slowly, Grace Highsmith made her way around the chair. When she sank into it, she seemed to shrink in size, like a balloon gradually losing its air. "Not Virginia, too," she murmured, covering her face with her hands. "This just can't be. What in the world is she thinking?"

At first I didn't quite follow her. "What's who thinking of?" I asked gently.

Grace shook her head. "I could understand with him," she said slowly. "I almost didn't blame her for that, and I don't think anyone else would, either. After all, the man was an animal. Whatever happened to him, he more than deserved it. The newspaper this morning said something about another body being found in

his apartment. And now this. Poor Virginia . . ."
Grace's voice trailed off in anguish. Her eyes
filled with tears.

"Miss Highsmith . . ." I began.

On an end table next to Grace Highsmith's
wing chair sat an old-fashioned dial telephone in
equally old-fashioned basic black. Without answering me directly, Grace took the receiver off
the hook and began dialing. Kramer and I waited
through the interminably long process while she
dialed a number from memory. I had forgotten
how long it took, after each separate number, for
the dial to return to its original position.

At last, someone must have answered the
phone. "Suzanne Crenshaw, please. Tell her it's
Grace Highsmith calling. Tell her it's urgent."

Again, there was a long pause. Kramer glowered at me but didn't speak. For some time, the
only noise in the room was the incongruously
cheerful snapping and popping of the blaze in the
fireplace. At last, Suzanne Crenshaw must have
picked up her line.

"Virginia Marks is dead," Grace Highsmith announced without preamble. "Detective Beaumont
and another detective just came by to tell me. No,
there's nothing you need to do at the moment,
but . . ." There was another pause, a shorter one.
"Why, yes. He's here right now. Do you want to
speak to him?"

Grace glanced in my direction and then held
out the phone for me. I hurried across the room
and took it. "Hello."

"Detective Beaumont, I'm on my way to an appointment. It's one I can't miss. I've instructed Grace not to say anything further to you until I can be present. That won't be until later this afternoon."

"But Ms. Crenshaw, surely you don't think Grace Highsmith—"

"It's possible Grace will be charged with some crime as well before this is all over. I don't want her speaking to you at all until she is properly represented. That goes for Latty, too. Will you be taking her into custody today?"

Clearly, both Grace Highsmith and Suzanne Crenshaw had leapt to the same immediate conclusion—that Latty Gibson was responsible for Virginia Marks' murder and maybe for the other two victims as well.

"Possibly," I hedged, although at that precise moment I knew we didn't have enough probable cause to arrest anyone, including Latty Gibson.

"When you have a warrant for her arrest or even if you just want to bring her in for questioning, let me know," Suzanne Crenshaw said. "Promise me that, Mr. Beaumont. Latty's very young and inexperienced. And she's in an emotionally precarious situation at this time. Give me your word that you won't take unfair advantage."

"You have my word, Ms. Crenshaw, but we will need to interview her. Could you meet with us at two this afternoon?"

"I suppose. Where?"

"The shop."

"All right," she said. "If for some reason I can't make it, how can I reach you?"

"Leave word with Latty," I said.

"Thank you," Suzanne Crenshaw said. "I'll see you then."

By the time I put down the phone, Kramer was looking daggers at me. I didn't bother to explain what had gone on. Obviously, he'd learned just enough to piss himself off by listening to my side of the conversation. In the meantime, Grace Highsmith had left her chair. She came over to my end of the couch. Taking a lace-edged hanky out of her pocket, she began dusting Dusty.

As her fingers absently polished the uneven planes of metal, there was an air of finality in the gesture—almost as though she were saying good-bye. When she finished, she put the scrap of handkerchief away and turned to me, her eyes bright with unshed tears.

"In the last few months, I had pretty well decided to leave this house and everything in it to Latty. I suppose that's all out the window now. I wonder how much of a criminal defense a signed and numbered Fraser will buy in this day and age? Defense attorneys don't come cheap these days, do they Detective Beaumont?"

"No, ma'am," I said. "They certainly don't."

"I'm forgetting my manners. I offered you both tea, and I still haven't—"

"No, thank you. Again, you don't need to bother with the tea. Detective Kramer and I were just leaving. Your attorney specifically requested that we not talk to you any further without her being present."

"And you're meeting Latty at the shop?" Grace asked.

I nodded.

"Would you like me to be there at the same time?" Miss Highsmith asked.

"No," I said. "We'll contact you later on."

"All right, then, Detective Beaumont," she agreed. "Whatever you think is best."

I caught a glimpse of Paul Kramer's face when she said that. He looked as though he was about ready to blow a gasket.

Grace led us to the door and held it open, shivering as the lake-dampened air chilled the room. "If it wouldn't be too much trouble, Detective Beaumont, would you mind bringing in another log? I can usually manage just fine, but right now . . ."

"Sure," I said. "I'd be glad to."

Hurrying out to the woodpile, I selected another ten-inch log, carried it back inside, and shoved it into the fire. As the new log dropped into place, the burning one disintegrated into a shower of sparks and glowing coals. A disapproving Kramer eyed this whole procedure from just inside the front door.

"I believe we're in the middle of a burning ban, Miss Highsmith?" he said, while I dusted crumbs of dirt from my hands. "Aren't you worried about that?"

"Oh, no," Grace answered at once, peering up at him through her tiny glasses. "Burn bans only apply if you have some other source of heat. I don't. My father was a very stubborn man, you see. When I was growing up, we had a dairy farm and orchard over where Magnolia Village is now. Mother and Father bought this place as a summer cabin when the only way to get here was to ride across the lake on the Kirkland Ferry. Coming here each year was a major expedition. Father insisted that a summerhouse shouldn't need central heat, and he refused to install a furnace. My parents argued about it for years, and my sister Florence and I continued that battle long after our parents were both gone. A few years back, when I decided to retire here, I made up my mind to leave the house just as it was. Now I'm glad I did. On a day like today, there's nothing quite as comforting as the flames from an open fire."

"No, ma'am," a suddenly subdued Detective Kramer agreed. "I don't suppose there is."

# Seventeen

I could see Kramer was fried as we huffed our way back up Grace Highsmith's stairs to the car. "Who the hell do you think you are?" he demanded. "Since when do we conduct police business based on the whims and schedule of the suspect's goddamned defense attorney?"

"Since I gave my word, that's since when," I responded. "And let me remind you, the suspect is entitled to representation. That's the law. Weren't you the guy who was telling me, just a little while ago, that rules are supposed to apply to everybody?"

I don't think Paul Kramer liked having his words spouted back at him. He yanked open the Caprice's driver's-side door, threw himself inside, and then slammed the door shut behind him. I climbed in on my side, matching slam for slam.

"You don't give a shit if we solve this mess or

not, do you?" he growled, starting the car and mashing it into gear. "It doesn't matter to you if Captain Powell is bent out of shape. It's no skin off your nose if we're up to our eyebrows in a case that involves a dozen high-profile folks from the mayor's main squeeze to some dotty old lady member of the Board of Regents to a murder-weapon-buying former head of the Washington State Patrol."

"What do you mean, it's no skin off my nose?"

By then, Paul Kramer's pot of seething resentment had come to a full boil. "It's all a game for you," he fumed. "You don't care if you ever get promoted or not. And whether or not we solve this case in a timely fashion is no big deal to you. For guys like Sam Arnold and me, though, it is. For us, it's real life. My getting a promotion means the difference between whether or not my wife can trade in her old station wagon for a newer car. It determines if we'll be able to put money aside for our kids to go to college. You can be a high-flying playboy all you want, Beaumont. Just stop pretending to be a cop to the detriment of everyone around you."

*Pretending to be a cop?* I could barely believe my ears.

"Wait a minute. Let me get this straight. You think I'm deliberately trying to blow this case? That I agreed to schedule Latty Gibson's interview around her attorney's availability out of some kind of spite? To keep you and Sam Arnold from getting credit and making the next promotion list?"

Kramer, driving hell-bent for election through downtown Kirkland, looked straight ahead and didn't reply, which, in itself, was answer enough. When we paused for a stoplight, I opened the door.

"Hey, what are you doing?" Kramer demanded, as I stepped out onto the sidewalk.

"What does it look like?" I growled back. "I'm getting the hell out of the car before I end up wrapping the steering wheel around your damned stiff neck. The interview with Latty Gibson is at two o'clock at Dorene's Fine China and Gifts on Main Street in Old Bellevue. See you around."

With that, I slammed the door shut and walked away. For a few seconds after the light changed, Kramer sat there in the Caprice, honking and gesturing for me to get back in the car. When frustrated drivers behind him started honking at him in turn, he finally gave up and drove off, shaking a fist at me as he went by.

Looking around, I found I was somewhere in downtown Kirkland. If you're a true Seattleite, that phrase sounds like an oxymoron. The buildings along the main drag of Western Washington's "little Sausalito" are low-rises—long on art galleries and trendy restaurants and short on much of anything else. I started to look for a phone, thinking I'd have to call for a cab, but surprisingly enough, when I reached the stoplight, a

Metro bus pulled up beside me. I dashed over to it and pounded on the door.

"Hey, in case you haven't noticed, this isn't a bus stop," the brown-and-gold-clad driver observed as he opened the door. "The next stop is two blocks down."

I flashed a badge in his direction.

"Where are you headed?" I asked.

"Bellevue Transit Center."

"Is that anywhere near downtown Bellevue?" I asked.

The driver shook his head, rolled his eyes, and motioned me aboard. "It's right in the middle of downtown Bellevue. Get in, will you? We're holding up traffic."

As the diesel-powered bus rumbled along, I sat there stewing over Kramer's totally unfounded accusations. What nerve, calling me a playboy cop! I was no such thing. Maybe I wasn't the world's best team player, but then again, neither was Kramer. I was absolutely offended by his thinking that I would deliberately undermine a case for any reason, whether to spite him or even just for the hell of it. I wanted closed cases every bit as much as he did. Maybe even more than he did.

I was so steamed that my hangover headache receded to a dull throb. What had seemed like possible hunger pangs in Grace Highsmith's living room faded into the background as well. Through some stroke of good fortune, the bus I had chosen at random traveled right down Bellevue Way, directly past the Grove on Twelfth, but I was so lost in thought that I missed it. I got off the bus two blocks later and walked back.

Bent on retrieving my Porsche, I headed straight for the parking garage only to be headed off at the garage door entrance by Maribeth George, the reporter from KIRO, packing her ever-ready microphone and trailed by her inevitable cameraman. As soon as I saw the devastated look on her face, I knew that she had made the connection. Maribeth's wheelchair lady from Pier 70 and the woman dead upstairs were most likely one and the same.

Maribeth ditched the cameraman and caught up with me before I made it to the elevator. "It's her, isn't it," she said.

"Probably," I agreed quietly, "although we don't know that for sure."

Maribeth closed her eyes and swayed on her feet. I caught her before she toppled over. "It's her, all right. I recognize the car. It's the same one. It's my fault," she said. "I know it is."

"How could that be?"

"I know you told me not to mention her, but I did. We weren't getting enough on the murders through official sources, and my editors wanted us to run everything we had on the two cases. You don't suppose the killer saw the tape and then went after her, do you?"

"No," I said quickly, wanting to comfort her. "I'm sure not." Although in actual fact, I wasn't nearly as certain as I tried to sound.

The cameraman showed up right then driving a van. He stopped directly beside us. "Come on, Maribeth," he said, rolling down the window. "If we're gonna make the five o'clock news, we've got to get this stuff back to the station."

Nodding wordlessly, Maribeth hurried around and climbed into the van. Glancing around the garage, I was relieved that Kramer's Seattle P.D. Caprice was nowhere in sight. If he had shown up right about then and climbed my frame about talking to a reporter, I'm not entirely sure what would have happened.

Officer Ryland of the Bellevue Police Department was still on duty in the Grove's underground garage. He nodded pleasantly as I came past.

"Any news?" I asked.

He shrugged. "Not much."

"Detective Blaine still around?"

Ryland nodded. "I think so. The victim's brother just showed up. I believe they're in the office. The crime scene techs are still working on the apartment."

"Which way?"

"Up this elevator to the first floor. If you turn right, I think it's at the far end of the hall."

On the first floor, the first door to the left of the elevator had been left ajar, but a festoon of yellow crime-scene tape had been strung across the entrance. I paused there long enough to peer inside, but I didn't try to enter. There was no sense in disturbing the techs as they went about their meticulous work. Instead, I continued on down the hallway to the office where a teary-eyed receptionist met me at the door.

"I'm sorry," she said. "There's been an emergency in the building. Our sales office is closed at the moment. If you'd like to see one of our units, could you please come back—"

"I'm a police officer," I interrupted, once again flashing my badge. "I'm looking for Detective Blaine."

"Oh, just a minute," she said. "He's meeting with someone in our conference room." She went to the closed door of an inner office and tapped timidly. Blaine himself answered her knock.

"I thought I said . . ." Catching sight of me, he let the rest of the sentence go. "Detective Beaumont, what's going on?"

"I've scheduled an interview this afternoon at two o'clock at Dorene's Fine China and Gifts on Main Street here in Bellevue. I think you'll want to be there."

"Why?"

"Because I'll be talking to someone named Latty Gibson, a young woman whose boyfriend-turned-rapist was being investigated by Virginia Marks."

Blaine opened his mouth as if to object, then shut it and nodded. "You're absolutely right. Two o'clock? One or the other or both of us will be there with bells on."

"Anything going on here that I should know about?" I asked.

"According to her brother, who just showed up, and to the part-time bookkeeper who found the body, the only thing missing that anybody can see so far is the laptop computer Virginia Marks used every waking minute of every day. She used it to take notes on her cases. Her calendar was in it, her database, as well as the information the bookkeeper used to do client billing. I guess when she wasn't working on the damned thing, she was using it to play solitaire."

"The computer's gone and nothing else is missing?"

"That's right," Blaine answered. "Including the jewelry in her dresser and the cash in her purse."

"I guess that lets out a random robbery or burglary, doesn't it."

Blaine nodded.

"And the computer's the only thing missing?"

"That's right."

"So maybe the computer contained some damaging piece of information, something so inflammatory that it's worth killing for."

"The same thought had occurred to me," Detective Blaine said. "All we have to do now is figure out what it was, right?"

"Right," I said. "See you at two."

"Where will you be between now and then?" Blaine asked. "Just in case something comes up."

I glanced at my watch. If I hurried, there was a slim chance I might still be on time for Lars Jenssen's AA meeting.

"Lunch," I said, without going into any more

detail than that. I handed Tim Blaine a card on which I had jotted my cellular phone number. "Call me at that number if anything comes up. It's a cell phone, and I may have to leave it off for a while," I told him. "If I don't answer, keep trying until you get me."

.  Back in my own car and armed with a new set of Eastside driving instructions courtesy of Officer Ryland, I headed for Angelo's, which turned out to be only a couple of miles away in the middle of a light-industry area north of Bel-Red Road. The meeting, already in progress when I arrived, was in a smoky back room, tucked in behind a packed and noisy lunchtime bar. The irony of the proximity of those two back-to-back and contraindicated meetings wasn't lost on me. And that day, if I'd had my druthers, I would have opted for the MacNaughton's side of the border.

I might have done it, too, but just inside the meeting room door, I caught sight of Lars Jenssen. Since he had gone to the trouble of coming all that way and of spending at least an hour on buses to do so, and since he also had managed to save me a chair, I could hardly not show up.

As AA meetings go, that noontime get-together certainly wasn't one of the best, but it wasn't the worst, either. And eating a hot roast beef sandwich washed down by several stiff cups of coffee made me start feeling almost human.

When it came time to talk, one guy mentioned that this was his twenty-fifth birthday of being sober. Everybody applauded and toasted him with coffee cups. "Hear, hear!" they cheered while I squirmed uncomfortably in my chair.

Twenty-five years! Damn. There's nothing like having someone bring you face-to-face with your own inadequacies. Later on in the meeting, when it was my turn to talk, I somewhat guiltily allowed as how I had something less than twelve hours of sobriety under my belt. The guy with the twenty-five years was the one who grinned at me and gave me some sympathetic encouragement.

"At least you're twelve hours to the good," he said. "Sometimes, a day at a time is asking too damned much. You have to go minute by minute and be thankful for that."

When the meeting was over, Lars hurried around the room, busily grabbing up extra rolls from the various bread baskets and greedily stuffing them into his pockets before the waitress had a chance to clear the leftovers off the tables. Meanwhile, I picked up both our lunch bills and headed for the cash register.

"Hey, wait a minute," Lars sputtered, limping out of the room after me. "You ain't gonna pay for my lunch now, are you?"

"Yes, I am," I told him. "You came all the way over here by bus. Not only am I buying your lunch, I'm also giving you a ride back home."

By then, the cashier—a good-looking, dark-haired woman with a bright smile, amazingly long fingernails, and a pair of bright green golftee dangling earrings—had already punched the totals of our two tickets into the cash register. I shoved a twenty across the counter.

"Keep the change," I told her.

Her smile broadened. "You keep coming back," she said.

"Sure thing," I said.

Once we were out in the parking lot, Lars nudged me in the rib and gave me a semitoothless grin. "You think that little lady back there is in the program, too?" he demanded.

"Could be," I answered, but I had a sneaking suspicion that the cashier's invitation for me to return was based less on the principles of Alcoholics Anonymous than it was on the generous size of my tip.

I had told Detective Blaine to call me, but it would have been rude to take my cellular phone into the meeting. As soon as we got in the car, I punched the recall button. Sure enough, someone had tried to call in my absence. As far as I knew, there was only one person in the world who would have been trying to reach me right then— Detective Tim Blaine. Heading out Highway 520 toward the Evergreen Point Bridge, I tried calling him back with no success.

When I put down the phone and glanced over at Lars, my passenger was sitting in the rider's seat with his arms crossed and a glum frown pasted on his face.

"Telephones got no place in automobiles," he

grumbled. "Don't see how people can drive and talk or dial at the same time."

"Sometimes, neither do I," I told him.

Three or four times on the way across Lake Washington I started to spill the beans to Lars about what was really going on with me—about Karen and Hilda Chisholm and the rest, but each time, I lost my nerve and kept quiet.

When Lars got out of the car, he turned and poked his head back in the window. "Think you'll need another meeting tonight?"

"I don't know," I answered. "Maybe. If I do, I'll call."

He walked away, shaking his head and muttering to himself. *Maybe* wasn't a good enough answer for Lars, which is part of what makes him a good sponsor.

Lars Jenssen's building is only a few blocks from my own. Looking down at yesterday's rumpled clothes, I decided a quick shower and change of clothing were both in order. I swung by Belltown Terrace, parked on P-1, and tossed the keys to Harold, a guy who owns and operates an auto detail shop on the first level of the Belltown Terrace parking garage.

"Do you want it washed today, Mr. Beaumont?" Harold asked.

"No, just hang on to the keys for a few minutes," I told him. "I'll be right back."

When I turned my key in the lock upstairs, I was surprised to hear classical music wafting through my apartment. *What day is this?* I wondered. At first, I thought maybe it was my cleaning lady, but she plays soft rock, never classical.

"Beau?" Ralph Ames called from the den. "Is that you?"

"Ralph!" I exclaimed. "When did you get here?"

He appeared in the doorway of the den looking tanned and fit, wearing a totally out-of-character tropical print shirt, and carrying a fanfold of papers. "One o'clock," he said.

I began stripping off my jacket and shoulder holster. "Just a few minutes ago?" I said.

"One o'clock this morning," he answered with an amused grin. "Our plane got in at midnight. You were supposed to come get us, remember?"

My heart sank. Ralph lives in Phoenix, but he had taken his Seattle-based girlfriend, Mary Greengo, to the Caribbean for an early winter cruise. I had taken Ralph Ames and Mary Greengo to the airport a week earlier when they had left on the cruise and had agreed to·come get them when they returned.

"Damn! I completely forgot."

"No kidding. By the time our luggage came off the plane, we'd pretty well figured that out, so we caught a cab. Don't worry. It's no big deal. I was talking to Mary on the phone a few minutes ago. Since it looked like you stayed out overnight, she's betting that maybe you've found a new girlfriend and maybe even got lucky."

A fog of guilt settled over me. Not only had I let my family down by not calling back Dave Liv-

ingston, I had completely blown a commitment
to my best friend.

"I can't believe I forgot," I said. "I had it written down on the calendar, but the last couple
days have been so hectic I haven't even
looked . . ."

Ralph followed me down the hall. When he's
in Seattle, he usually uses my den and guest bedroom as his center of operations. "Where are you
headed right now?" he asked.

"I want to grab a quick shower, then I'm on
my way back to Bellevue for an interview. I don't
have any idea how long it'll take."

"Your answering machine is on the fritz," he
said. "It started cutting people off in midmessage.
The one I heard was somebody named Harry. He
never finished what he started to say, and he
didn't leave a number. I've been answering the
phone ever since, and it's been ringing off the
hook. You have a whole stack of messages. Anna
Dorn called three different times, looking for you.
She says she's in town and staying at the Red
Lion out by the airport. The last time she called,
she said she'd try again after she goes to the medical examiner's office."

I turned on the water in the shower, giving it
a chance to heat up. "She's connected to a case
I'm working on," I explained. "Earlier this week,
somebody murdered her daughter. At least we
think the dead woman is Anna Dorn's daughter.
We need a positive identification. She probably
came to town for that."

Back in the bedroom, I sat down on the bed to take off my shoes, while Ralph continued sifting through a stack of messages. "Another woman called at twelve-thirty. She sounded upset. She said she needed to speak with you urgently, but she wouldn't leave a name or number. And then there's Captain Freeman."

"Tony Freeman called here?"

"That's right. Isn't he Ron Peters' boss, the guy who heads Internal Investigations? You don't suppose Ron is in some kind of hot water, do you?"

I went back in the bathroom and turned off the water. The hot roast beef sandwich that had tasted so good half an hour earlier suddenly solidified into a brick-size lump in my gut. If Anthony Freeman was calling looking for me, no doubt that meant Hilda Chisholm had made good on her threat to visit him. The head of I.I.S. was probably making a courtesy call to let me know I was under investigation.

"Ron isn't in any trouble," I said at last. "At least not directly. I am."

"You?" Ralph replied. "What have you done this time?"

All morning long, I had tried to keep my personal problems on a back burner, focusing instead on getting the cases I was working on cleared up ASAP. Even during the meeting—when I should have been dealing with what was really bothering me—I had held at arm's length both my missing phone call to Dave and my messy dealings with Hilda Chisholm over Heather and Tracy Peters. Now, though, with Ralph Ames standing there in the bedroom asking probing questions, all those suppressed personal issues rose up like a giant breaker and smashed over me.

"Mostly sins of omission," I said, attempting to joke about it. But my voice cracked on the last word.

"Such as?" he asked.

"I left Heather and Tracy alone for a while the other day. Now some hard-nosed bitch from Child Protective Services is investigating me as a possible child molester. She told me last night that she was going to notify Internal Investigations."

"*You* a child molester?" Ralph demanded. "That's the most ridiculous thing I've ever heard. Who the hell came up with that kind of fruitcake accusation?"

"It came from Ron's ex-wife."

"Roslyn Peters?" Ralph said derisively. "That figures. She *is* a fruitcake. When did she get back from Nicaragua?"

"Sometime recently, but long enough ago to make trouble. She's suing for full custody of the girls. She told the C.P.S. investigator that I'm a dirty old man and that I only funded the mission she went on to gain easy access to the girls."

At that, Ralph looked grave. "Roslyn Peters shouldn't have custody of a cocker spaniel. Who would be dumb enough to believe a word she says?"

"An aging hippie social worker, for one," I replied gloomily.

For a moment or two, there was dead silence between us. Finally, Ralph said, "Why didn't you call me about this?"

"It only came up last night," I answered. "Not the custody thing, but my part in it. I guess I was too upset to call. When Ron first told me about what was going on, it didn't seem that serious. Besides, you were on a cruise, Ralph. On vacation. It wouldn't have been fair to interrupt—"

"Not fair! Are you kidding? What the hell do you think friends are for, Mr. Jonas Piedmont Beaumont? Now what can I do to help?"

Everything seemed to be landing on me at once. Ralph's unconditional offer of help was just the last straw. "I don't know," I said, shaking my head. "I have no idea." Something in my voice must have given me away.

"What else is going on?" Ralph demanded.

When Ames puts on his no-nonsense, full-business mode, there's no point in trying to dodge the issue. I could maybe get away with it with Lars. I could maybe bullshit my way around a roomful of strangers in an AA meeting, but I couldn't skate out of harm's way with Ralph. He wasn't buying.

"It's Karen," I said finally, not trusting my voice any further than that. I couldn't breathe. It felt like I was suffocating. Or drowning.

"What about Karen?" he asked.

I took a deep breath before I answered. "Dave called me last night. She's back in the hospital and not doing very well."

"You mean she's not going to make it?"

"Yes, I guess that's what I mean," I managed. "Dave wants me to come down."

"When?"

"Right away. As soon as I can."

"So why aren't you on a plane right now?" Ralph asked. "What in God's name are you doing heading back to Bellevue?"

"It's this case," I began weakly. "I wanted to get it cleared up before—"

"Before you left town?" Ralph finished. "You mean you're messing around trying to finish a case when Karen is in a hospital dying?"

Ralph Ames is usually the most diplomatic person I know. When he let me have it full blast, I winced.

"Yes," I said. "It sounds stupid, but I guess I am."

There was another period of silence after that. Ralph was the one who broke it. "Stupid? It's completely asinine. Did anyone ever tell you, Beau, that at times you're a total jerk?"

"Yes," I said again, feeling enormously put-upon by the force of Ralph's righteous indignation. "I tell myself that all the time."

If I was looking for sympathy, I had come to the wrong place. Ralph Ames didn't cut me any slack.

"Well for God's sake," he said impatiently. "Get your butt in the shower and let me see what I can do."

While standing in the shower, a sudden mist of tears blurred my vision. One thing was certain. If Ralph Ames was going to see what he could do, it meant that I wasn't in the fight alone.

That realization made me feel infinitely worse. And better.

# Eighteen

**B**y the time I made it back to Old Bellevue, I had pretty well gotten a grip on things. Ralph was right, of course. If Karen was dying down in California, who was I to hang around Seattle finishing up a case? How much arrogance does it take to decide you're indispensable? Seattle P.D. wasn't that short of homicide detectives. Besides, it wasn't as though I *owned* the Don and Lizbeth Wolf cases. Captain Powell had already assigned both Paul Kramer and Sam Arnold to help out, and my opinion of their respective capabilities was much less telling in the scheme of things than the captain's was.

*In case you haven't noticed*, I lectured myself silently as I jockeyed the Guards Red Porsche into a particularly small parallel parking place directly across the street from Dorene's Fine China and Gifts, *the S.P.D. homicide squad was there long before you showed up, and it'll still be there long after you're gone.*

Glancing around the immediate neighborhood, I searched for a glimpse of Detective Kramer's ugly Caprice—to no avail. Tim Blaine's unmarked and empty Ford Taurus was parked across the street directly in front of the shop, but the Seattle P.D. Chevy was nowhere in sight.

By that time, it was ten to two. I settled back in my seat to wait. As the seconds and minutes ticked away, I found myself growing irritated. If I was the one who was such a lousy team player, if I was the one so damn uninterested in solving the case, why the hell was I present and accounted for when Paul Kramer wasn't? Where did he get off throwing stones?

A few minutes later, right at two, an enormous white Cadillac—one that suspiciously resembled the '61 I had seen overhanging the end of Grace Highsmith's garage—slowly nosed its way down Main Street. As the car drove past me, all I could see of the driver was a fringe of silver hair visible over the sill of the Caddy's left-hand window. I marveled that whoever was driving could see over the steering wheel, to say nothing of down that vast expanse of hood.

Maneuvering more by sound than sight, the Caddy's driver eventually wedged the car into a parking space, but only after a long sequence of backing and filling and after bumping both cars on either end of her chosen spot. As soon as the Cadillac came to rest, Suzanne Crenshaw appeared out of nowhere. She rushed up, opened the car door, and helped Grace Highsmith out onto the sidewalk. So much for my telling her not to show up for our interview with Latty.

Shaking my head at the old lady's stubbornness, I picked up the phone and dialed Watty. "Where's Detective Kramer?" I asked. "It's two o'clock. We're supposed to be interviewing a suspect over here in Bellevue right about now, and he's nowhere to be found."

"We had a call from Anna Dorn up at the medical examiner's office," Watty said. "She wanted to talk to you before she went back to her hotel out by the airport, but since Kramer is assigned to the case every bit as much as you are, and since he was here and you weren't, I decided to send him instead."

"What about Sam Arnold?" I asked.

"He's busy with Johnny Bickford," Watty replied. "I believe he left here to take her back home. She showed up on the fifth floor about an hour ago in a state of absolute panic."

"Not Johnny Bickford again. What does *he* want?"

"*He?*" Watty repeated dubiously. "I thought it was a she. According to Nell out front, she was pitching a fit all over the reception area."

"What about?"

"That dead woman over in Bellevue. The homicide Bellevue P.D. is currently investigating."

"Virginia Marks?"

"That's right," Watty answered. "That's the

one. Johnny Bickford saw a story about her on the noon news and recognized the picture. She says—"

"He," I corrected. "Johnny Bickford is a *he*."

"All right, all right. *He*, then," Watty agreed. "He said the woman on the news was the same woman he saw down on Pier Seventy about the same time he discovered Don Wolf's body and reported it. The woman was in a wheelchair. Bickford is convinced that since somebody went to the trouble of killing the Marks woman, that they'll come after him next. He's demanding police protection. He really wanted to talk to you, but I suggested—"

"When it comes to dealing with Johnny Bickford, better Sam Arnold than me," I said. "And if Kramer calls in anytime soon, tell him the interview in Bellevue is going on without him."

I got out of the Porsche and walked across the street. When the door to the shop opened, the bell overhead tinkled merrily just as it had the day before. The cheerful ringing of the bell was followed immediately by a series of raised voices.

"No, Aunt Grace. Absolutely not!"

"But, Latty, dear, you must listen to reason. . . ."

"No!" Sybil Latona Gibson repeated furiously, her voice rising in pitch. "I will not do it. I don't care what you say, I simply won't."

The door fell shut behind me and I found myself on the sidelines of a fierce family scrimmage. An uncomfortable Tim Blaine stood in front of the cash register holding a small, gift-wrapped package as gingerly as if it were a live grenade. Behind the cash wrap stood a highly incensed young woman—Latty Gibson, the Marilyn Monroe look-alike I had seen on Bill Whitten's security tape. Except the video recording hadn't done her justice. Even with her face flushed with anger and her blue eyes flashing outrage, she was lovely.

"How dare you bring people here in front of my customers to . . . to . . ."

She stopped, unable to continue, and glared at her aunt. Looking down at the two comparatively pint-size combatants, Tim Blaine shifted his massive weight uneasily from foot to foot. He looked as though he would have gladly been anywhere else on earth right about then.

Next to Detective Blaine, and with the crown of her head a full six inches short of his shoulder, stood Grace Highsmith. Backed by the solid presence of Suzanne Crenshaw, the old woman refused to give way to her niece's anger.

"Now, Latty," Grace crooned soothingly. "You really must understand. I couldn't possibly allow you to speak to any police investigators without your being properly represented by an attorney."

Latty Gibson spun around and turned the full force of her fury on me. "I suppose you're the detective?" she demanded.

Nodding, I eased myself one more step into the room. "One of them," I said. "My name is De-

tective Beaumont. J. P. Beaumont. I'm with the
Seattle Police Department."

Latty reached down and plucked something
out of a drawer under the counter, then she came
around the cash wrap carrying a purse. "You'll
have to watch the store for a while, Aunt Grace,"
she said. "I'll talk to him upstairs. In my apartment."

"That's fine," Aunt Grace said. "I'll be happy
to look after things for a while. Suzanne, you go
along with them, would you?"

"No!" Latty said again. "I don't want anyone
with me, not anyone at all. I'll talk to the detective
alone."

"But Latty . . ." Suzanne Crenshaw began, but
she gave up when Latty stormed past her without
a backward glance.

Clearing his throat, Tim Blaine sprang to the
door and held it open. "*Detectives*, actually," he
said apologetically. "I'm one, too, Miss Gibson.
Detective Tim Blaine with the Bellevue Police Department."

"You!" Latty exclaimed. "I thought you told
me you came in to buy your mother a birthday
present."

Now it was Detective Blaine's turn to flush
with embarrassment. "I was early," he mumbled.
"It seemed like a good idea at the time."

"You came into my store and talked to me under false pretenses."

"I'm sorry . . ." Blaine began, but Latty Gibson
didn't stay around to listen. Tossing her head, she

stalked out of the store with Detective Blaine and me trailing along behind.

"Detective Beaumont," Grace called behind me, catching the door before it had time to close. "Wait a minute. You can't do this. You know very well that Latty shouldn't talk to you alone like this, without Suzanne or someone else being present to advise her."

"It appears to me your niece has made up her own mind about that," I said. "I don't think she's likely to change it."

"But—"

"I'm sorry, Miss Highsmith. Latty has the right to make her own decisions."

"Even bad ones?"

"We all make bad decisions sometimes," I said.

Outside and around the side of the building, I found Detective Blaine waiting for me, holding an unmarked door that opened on a steep wooden stairway. "She went up there," he said.

By the time Tim Blaine and I made our way up the steep, creaking stairway, Latty Gibson had already disappeared through a doorway on the upper landing. After the gloomy darkness of the stairway, I was surprised when we stepped inside an airy but sparsely furnished apartment. Bright sunlight splashed into the room through sheer white curtains and from an overhead skylight. The living room was totally lined with fully laden bookshelves, but actual furniture in that room consisted of only a single couch, coffee table, and lamp. The dining room—with its small plastic

patio table and four matching chairs—wasn't
much better.

Several paperback books lay scattered on the
table—all of them of the bodice-ripper school of
literature. With a baleful glare in our direction,
Latty swept the books into a pile and banished
them from sight on one of the already overfull
bookshelves.

"Miss Gibson," Tim Blaine was saying. "I
didn't mean to mislead you, I—"

"I hope your mother enjoys her napkin rings,"
Latty said coldly. "You have excellent taste—for
a cop." She looked over at me. "I suppose the
only place we'll all be able to sit is at the dining
room table."

Tim Blaine hurriedly subsided into one of the
four chairs. I followed his lead. Latty Gibson
didn't sit. Instead, she walked over to a window,
pulled the dainty curtains aside, and looked out.

I cleared my throat. "As you are no doubt
aware by now, Miss Gibson, there has been a series of homicides in the Seattle/Bellevue area in
the last few days."

Still peering out the window, Latty nodded. "I
know," she said. "Aunt Grace told me."

"A number of different circumstances have led
us to the conclusion that you might possibly be a
suspect in one or more of them."

At that point, she turned to face me. "Why?"
she asked. "I haven't done anything."

"But we still need to talk to you," I said. "And

before we start, I'm required to read you your rights."

"Go ahead," she said. "I want to get this over with as soon as possible."

While I Mirandized her, Tim Blaine kept his mouth shut, and when it was time to start the questioning, he still didn't seem willing to say much. "I understand you knew Don Wolf?" I said for openers.

Latty took a deep breath. "Yes," she answered, almost in a whisper. "We had been going out, but we had broken up."

"Why was that?" I asked. I was reasonably sure I knew the answer to that question, but Tim Blaine didn't, and he needed to hear it.

Latty turned toward us from the window. "He raped me," she said.

Homicide cops aren't supposed to be taken unawares, but Tim Blaine was. His broad shoulders sagged under the weight of her words. The skin across his jawline tightened into a hard, grim line.

"But you shouldn't blame him," Latty was saying. "It wasn't his fault."

"Not his fault!" I responded. "How could that be?"

Latty shrugged. "We had both been drinking and dancing and having a good time that night. I don't remember a lot of what happened after we left the dance to go to his office." She looked at me with a momentary trace of defiance. When it melted away, she turned back to the window. "I guess I was ... well ... drunk. I was probably teasing him before it happened, flirting and leading him on. I don't know. I don't remember."

Latty may have forgotten, but the scene in Don Wolf's office was indelibly etched in my memory. Yes, they had both been obviously tipsy. But she was dead wrong about her leading him on. She had done everything possible to prevent the attack. When he had started trying to go further than she wanted, she had begged him to take her home.

"That's why this is all so silly, you see," Latty said.

"Silly?" I asked.

"Stupid, then," she returned. "Aunt Grace thinks I killed him because of it, because he hurt me. But since I don't really blame him for what happened, why would I kill him?" She turned from the window and focused her troubled eyes on me. "You do understand that, don't you?"

"Not exactly," I said, in a reply which was, in fact, a gross understatement. I didn't understand at all.

"It happened at his office downtown," Latty continued in an oddly dispassionate voice. "We went there late in the evening because he wanted to show me the lights. What I didn't know at the time was that Aunt Grace had me followed that the night. The detective was evidently parked right outside the building when we came downstairs after it happened. My dress was torn. I lost my coat. I had to wear his jacket home. The detective must have figured out what had happened. She reported it to Aunt Grace, and the next morning, Aunt Grace came after me.

"I wasn't going to tell her or anybody else anything about it, but she seemed to know everything anyway. My lip was cut. I'm sure I looked awful. I had barely slept, and I had cried most of the night. She wanted me to go straight to the police to turn him in, but I wouldn't. Aunt Grace and I had a big fight over it. She couldn't understand why I was mad at her for spying on me when I wasn't mad at Don for what he had done."

"Why weren't you?" Detective Blaine asked.

"Because I loved him," she said. "Or at least I thought I did. Even when she told me he was already married."

"Is that when you first found out about his wife?"

Latty nodded. "Aunt Grace gave me all the dirt that detective of hers—that Virginia Marks—had dug up. She warned me that a man like that was trouble and that I shouldn't see him again. I told her she was only my aunt, not my mother, and that if I wanted to keep on seeing him, nobody was going to stop me."

"And did you?" I asked. "Keep on seeing him?"

"Not right away," Latty answered. "I was hurt. I wanted to see if he'd call me first. When he didn't, I finally broke down and called him at work on New Year's Eve. I asked if I could see him later that night."

"New Year's Eve was Sunday, but he was working?"

"Yes."

"Doing what?"

"I don't know. We never talked much about what he did. It had something to do with finances, I guess. Something to do with raising investment capital for the company he worked for. He didn't seem to like his boss very much."

"So you arranged to meet him that night? On New Year's Eve?"

"Yes."

"What time?"

"He was busy earlier. Eleven o'clock was the earliest he could get away."

"Busy with what?"

"He didn't say, and I didn't ask."

"When you arranged this date, did you know his wife was in town?"

"No. I had no idea she was here."

"And what did the two of you talk about when you finally got together?" I asked.

The room grew suddenly quiet. In the stillness, I gradually became aware of the stark ticking of a hand-wound clock that sat on the kitchen counter. Latty turned back to the window. Her answer, when it came, was almost inaudible. "I asked him if he would marry me."

"You what?" Detective Blaine and I both demanded in unison.

"To marry me," she repeated. "I knew about his wife, but since he was up here without her, I thought maybe, if they weren't, you know, getting along, that he might divorce her and marry me."

There's a book that's supposed to be a very big asset to male/female communications, something like *Men Are from Mars, Women Are from Venus.* Or maybe it's the other way around. Since I haven't read it, I wouldn't know. But at that precise moment, it would have made more sense if the title had been *Women Are from Outer Space.* That would have been closer to the truth, at least as far as Latty Gibson was concerned.

"So you're saying you didn't go there armed and ready to kill him?"

"No," Latty said. "I never did. I can't imagine why Aunt Grace and that lawyer of hers would even think such a thing."

"And what did he say when you asked him?" Tim Blaine asked.

When she answered, Latty Gibson turned her fathomless blue eyes full on him. "He said he couldn't. That he and his wife had decided to get back together."

Tim's eyes widened slightly at that. He opened his mouth and then closed it again and waved for me to pick up the ball and run with it.

"How long had you known him before all this happened?"

"Three weeks is all. It was love at first sight, at least for me."

"What about him?"

"I thought he loved me," she answered.

"Did he fall in love with you before or after he knew about your Aunt Grace's little family home on the shores of Lake Washington?"

"Detective Beaumont," Latty said, "my aunt's home—wherever it is—has nothing to do with me. And it wouldn't have had anything to do with Don, either. I told him that. Aunt Grace is leaving everything to charity. And why shouldn't she? It's hers to do with as she likes."

I tried changing the subject. "Are you aware that yesterday at noon your aunt tried to confess to Don Wolf's murder? She wanted me to arrest her?"

"Yes. How could I help but? The phone rang here constantly yesterday afternoon and evening. I'm sure she was only doing it to protect me— because she thought I had done it. What I can't imagine, though, is how anyone could have believed she was serious."

"For one thing," I said quietly, "she just happened to have the murder weapon that killed Don Wolf in her purse."

Latty frowned. "What murder weapon?"

"It's a handgun," I answered. "A Seecamp thirty-two auto."

"Oh, no," Latty murmured. Leaving the window, Latty stumbled toward the table where Tim Blaine and I were seated. She dropped heavily into one of the two empty chairs. "Please, God. Not that one."

"Which one are you talking about?" I asked.

"Ours. The one we keep in the shop is a Seecamp. It must be the same one. I thought I had just misplaced it, along with my coat, but Aunt Grace must have had it all along," Latty breathed. "Maybe she did kill him, after all. What if she did?"

Since Grace Highsmith had no idea what kind of gunshot wound had killed Don Wolf, I was reasonably sure that wasn't the case. "What makes you say that?" I asked.

"If I didn't kill him, and if Aunt Grace's gun is the murder weapon, who else is there?"

"Tell us about the gun," I urged. "Where did it come from?"

"One of Aunt Grace's boyfriends got it for her when she asked him to. Most of the time, we keep it in a drawer under the counter downstairs, the same place where we store our purses."

"You keep the gun loaded?" I asked.

Latty nodded again. "Just before Aunt Grace bought the store, her friend Dorene Lowell, the lady who owned it before, was robbed on her way to the bank. It was dumb for anyone to bother, because—in a store like ours—very little cash changes hands. Most of our business is transacted either by check or credit card. Dorene wasn't in very good health to begin with, and that incident scared her to death. In fact, I think it's one of the reasons she sold out. So ever since we opened, Aunt Grace has insisted that I take the gun with me whenever I go to make a deposit, especially if it's after dark. I usually did, although sometimes I forget."

"I see," I said. "And when you took it along, where did you carry it?"

"Sometimes, just on the seat of my car. Sometimes, if I'm wearing a coat or a jacket with a pocket, I slip the gun into that. It isn't very heavy."

"I don't suppose *you* have a license to carry a concealed weapon, do you?" I asked wearily. The idea of having multitudes of untrained people walking around loose with loaded guns in their pockets is enough to make every cop in the country turn prematurely gray.

"Aunt Grace said that since the gun was just for protection, we probably didn't need one. She says it isn't ladylike for a woman to have to have a license for that kind of thing."

"Aunt Grace needs to have her head examined," I put in. "For your information, ladylike or not, having a permit to carry a concealed weapon happens to be a law around here. That goes for you as well as your aunt."

"I didn't know," Latty said.

"No, I'm sure you didn't. Go on."

"Last Saturday night, when I went to make the night deposit, the gun was missing from the drawer. I tore my car apart looking for it, but it wasn't there. I even went upstairs and checked in the pockets of all my clothes. That's when I found out my coat was missing as well."

"What coat?"

"My good winter coat."

"When's the last time you remember having it?" I asked.

"That night," Latty said.

"What night?"

She paused, her eyes clouding. "The night I went dancing with Don. I must have left it there somewhere." She stopped.

Again I recalled the scene on the tape. Latty hadn't been wearing a coat when she first appeared in Don Wolf's office, but she might have dropped it in the reception area before she entered camera range.

"So you think the gun might have been in the pocket of the coat?" I asked.

"That's the only place I can think of."

I felt a catch of excitement in my throat. If the coat had been left in the D.G.I. offices, then the guy who had called himself prime suspect number one also had access to the murder weapon. And if Bill Whitten had been screening Don Wolf's activities, he might have had inside knowledge of when and where Latty and Don had scheduled their New Year's Eve meeting. That would give him access and opportunity. By his own admission, Bill Whitten had plenty of motivation. Thinking about the Whitten connection, I dropped out of the interview for a while and let Tim Blaine ask questions about Latty's connection to and knowledge of Virginia Marks. Other than the fact that Latty knew Grace Highsmith had hired someone to investigate Don Wolf, Latty seemed to know very little about the dead detective. Finally, when we stood up to go, Latty started toward the door, then she stopped. "Wait a minute. I need to give it to someone," she said. "I could just as well give it to you."

"Give us what?" I asked.

"Don's coat," she answered. "The one I wore home that night. Ever since I heard he was dead, I've felt weird about having it here in the house—almost like I had stolen it or something. But I didn't know what to do about it."

She disappeared into what was evidently a bedroom and came back carrying a double-breasted wool blazer. I took it, thanked her, and headed toward the door. Blaine was behind me, but at the top of the stairway he stopped and turned back.

"By the way, Miss Gibson," he said, "if you decide to get a replacement for that Seecamp, I can probably help out with the permit process."

When he said that, I'm sure my jaw dropped. Dumbfounded, I looked first at him and then back to Latty. For the first time since I had been in their presence, Latty Gibson gave Tim Blaine the benefit of an actual smile.

"Thank you, Detective Blaine," she said. "I'll remember that."

"Are you crazy?" I demanded after the apartment door closed and as we continued down the stairs. "That woman's still an active suspect in at least one homicide case."

"She didn't do it," Blaine declared. "I'm convinced she didn't."

He stepped out onto the sidewalk carrying the gift Latty Gibson had wrapped for his mother as if it were the most precious cargo in the world.

"She's gorgeous, isn't she," he marveled. "She really does look just like Marilyn Monroe. I wonder if she's ever entered any of those Marilyn look-alike contests. She'd win, hands down."

Which only goes to prove, once and for all, that women aren't the only ones who come from outer space. Men do, too.

At least some of them do.

# Nineteen

When Tim Blaine and I came around the front of the building, I was eager to tell him where Latty's story about the missing coat might lead us, but Suzanne Crenshaw was waiting for us by the shop's front door.

"Miss Highsmith would like to see you before you go," she said.

That was fine with me, because I wanted to see her, too. And because group gropes are never a good idea in homicide investigations, I wanted to do it before Latty came back down to the shop from her apartment.

Folding Don Wolf's jacket over my arm, I stepped into the shop, with both Tim and Suzanne Crenshaw following behind. The door's bell gave three distinctly separate jangles. If I had been forced to listen to that thing day in and day out, I'm sure it would have driven me bonkers.

We found Grace Highsmith seated on a tall stool behind the counter. "Well?" she asked, assuming a certain regal air that implied we were lowly petitioners who had been admitted into her august presence to beg a royal favor, rather than police officers going about their sworn duties.

"Well what?" I returned.

"Are you going to arrest her or not?"

So we were off on the arrest tangent again. Yesterday, Grace had been focused on my arresting her. Today, her focal point was the probability of our arresting her niece.

"Miss Highsmith," I said patiently, "I think you have a slightly exaggerated idea of how we work. There's a lot more to our job than meets the eye—a lot of behind-the-scenes questioning—before an arrest ever takes place."

"I see," Grace said, but I wasn't at all sure she did.

"To that end, however, we do need to ask you a few questions about Virginia Marks, and about the work she was doing for you. Would that be all right?"

Grace glanced at her attorney, and Suzanne Crenshaw nodded her assent. "Of course," Grace said agreeably. "What do you want to know?"

"How did she come to work for you in the first place?"

Grace shrugged. "I've known Virginia since she was a child, but I had no idea what had happened to her or what she was doing until I saw her on television a few months ago."

"Television?"

"Yes, one of those television features they do from time to time on interesting or unusual people. They evidently chose Virginia because she was the only licensed private detective in Washington working out of a wheelchair. Later, when this thing with Latty and Don Wolf came up and I wanted someone to look into his background, Virginia was the one I called. There were things about Virginia that bothered me. I worried a little that she wasn't entirely honest with me from time to time, but still, she did a good enough job as far as Don Wolf was concerned. She's how I found out he was married."

"Did you know that before or after the night Latty was attacked?" .

"Before," Grace answered. "Virginia dug that up in just a matter of hours after she went to work on the case."

"But you didn't mention it to your niece?"

"I was hoping she'd come to her senses on her own, you see," Grace said. "That's how one learns things in the real world, through experience. And, I thought he'd probably do something to give himself away, although I certainly never anticipated that he would . . ." Her voice trailed off and didn't continue.

"Tell us about Virginia Marks' connection to what went on that night."

"Just as I asked, Virginia had placed Don Wolf under surveillance. She followed them, first to the night club and later to Don's office."

I had a clear memory of Virginia Marks' car pulling away from the curb just as the elevator door opened and Don Wolf and Latty reentered the lobby from the elevator. "How did she know about the rape?" I asked.

"How?" Grace repeated with a frown. "What do you mean?"

"Did she somehow see what happened?"

"Oh, no. She was waiting on the street. When they came back downstairs, she drove away. Not wanting them to see her, she waited around the block. When Latty left in a cab a few minutes later, Virginia followed. From the state Latty was in—she was crying, her clothes were in tatters—Virginia more or less assumed what had happened, and, of course, she was right."

"What about New Year's Eve?" I asked. "Did you know Latty was going to meet him that night?"

"Yes," Grace said.

"How did you know?"

Grace stole a sidelong glance at Suzanne Crenshaw, who was vigorously shaking her head. Grace looked back at me.

"Because I heard her on the phone. Virginia had fixed it, you see."

"Fixed it?"

"The phone. She made tapes so I could listen."

"In other words, she put a tap on the line?"

"Yes. I suppose that's what it's called."

"A legal tap?" I don't know why I even bothered to ask. As far as Grace Highsmith was concerned, I was a long way from being a virgin.

Suzanne Crenshaw was still shaking her head, but Grace Highsmith was not dissuaded. "I don't know what's *illegal* about it, Detective Beaumont. After all, it *is* my phone. It's in my name, and I write the check that pays the bill each month."

Great, I thought, another key piece of information gleaned from an illegal wiretap.

"So," I said, "you knew Latty planned to meet Don Wolf. Did you have any idea she was going to ask him to marry her?"

For the first time, Grace seemed indecisive. She hesitated. "I didn't *know*, but I was afraid she might. She's been reading all of Dorene's old romance novels, you see, the books Dorene couldn't take with her when she moved into smaller quarters. You know what they're like."

"No," I said, quite honestly. "I have no idea."

"They're the kind of story where no matter how awful the man seems to be at first glance— no matter how repulsive or obnoxious, or unreasonable—he always turns out to be all right in the end. True love triumphs. He and the heroine get married and live happily ever after and all that sort of thing. Very unrealistic, if you ask me."

"What does any of this have to do with Latty?"

"She's rebelling against her mother, you see," Grace answered. "Her mother is so impossibly unconventional—she never married, believes wholeheartedly in free sex, thinks marriage is the inevitable outcome of a patriarchal society, and all that other feminist nonsense. Naturally, Latty wants to do just the opposite—including wanting to marry the first man she became seriously involved with."

"She might have been rebelling against you, too, Miss Highsmith," I suggested.

"Heavens, no," Grace said immediately, underlining her objection with a definitive shake of her head. "Not against *me* certainly. I may not read all those books, but in my own way, I'm every bit as much of a hopeless romantic as Latty is or as her grandmother was. I'm sure I would have married and settled down myself, if I'd ever met just the right sort of man."

*Not bloody likely*, I thought. "Let's go back to New Year's Eve," I said, bringing the discussion back to the subject at hand.

"What about it?"

"Virginia Marks followed Latty to Myrtle Edwards Park?"

"No. Since we knew that's where they were meeting, I asked her to wait there for them."

"And what happened?"

"Don Wolf showed up first. When Latty got there, they walked off down by the water. A few minutes later, just after the fireworks started, Latty came running back alone. On the way to her car, she ran right past Virginia's. Virginia said she could see Latty was upset, that she was crying."

"And then what happened?"

"I had asked Virginia to speak to Don Wolf. She waited for a while for him to come back through the parking lot. When he didn't, she finally went to check, thinking he might have left the park somewhere north of where she was waiting. That's when she found the gun. It was right there just off the jogging path, near where Latty stood for a moment or two when she came back alone. Virginia picked up the gun, realized it had been fired, and assumed the worst."

"That Latty had shot him?"

Grace closed her eyes and nodded.

"What happened then?"

"She went back to her car, called me on her car phone, and asked me what I wanted her to do."

"Grace," Suzanne Crenshaw interjected urgently. "I really think . . ."

"Now, Suzanne," Grace Highsmith said, as stubborn in her own way as Latty Gibson was in hers. "Now that I've started, I'm going to finish. Damn the torpedoes, if you'll excuse the expression. As soon as Virginia told me what kind of gun it was, I knew it was ours—mine. At least I was afraid it was. I needed time to think, to decide what to do. I asked Virginia to hold on to the gun and to call me again as soon as she found out for sure whether or not Don Wolf was dead. She did just exactly what I asked. She was back there on the pier when the body was found the next morning."

"Miss Highsmith," I said, "willfully concealing evidence in a homicide investigation constitutes a felony."

"Oh, I know all that," she replied airily. "That's

what I have you for, isn't it, Suzanne?"

The attorney nodded grimly but said nothing.

"Wait a minute," Tim Blaine said, opening his mouth for the first time in the course of the interview. "When Latty left, why didn't Virginia Marks follow her?"

It was a good observation—one I wished I had made myself.

"I already told you. Because Virginia's assignment that night was to talk to Don Wolf, to conclude my negotiations with him."

"Negotiations for what?"

"To present him with my offer."

"What offer?"

"A payoff," Grace Highsmith said. "Or maybe it's called a bribe. I'm not sure which is which. Whatever you want to call it, I was prepared to give the man money if he would promise to get out of Latty's life and stay there."

"How much money?" Tim Blaine asked.

"One hundred g's," Grace Highsmith said. "I believe that's how the tough guys always say it in the movies. I've never been quite sure why they use that term. What does the letter *g* have to do with a thousand dollars?"

By then, I was a grizzled veteran of Grace Highsmith's little surprises. Tim Blaine wasn't. When she said that, the stunned look on his face probably wasn't all that different from the look on mine the day before when she had dumped the .32 auto out of her purse onto the linen tablecloth in Azalea's Fountain Court.

I could have told Grace that *g* refers to *grand* as in thousand, but I didn't feel like making any more contributions toward her growing criminal vocabulary.

"Back to Virginia Marks for a moment," I said. "Even after you knew Don Wolf was dead, Virginia kept working for you. Why was that?"

Grace shrugged. "By then, I assumed we needed to know everything we could about him in case Suzanne needed information on him to mount Latty's defense. Unfortunately, it doesn't seem as though there was much to find out."

"That's what Virginia's trip to California was all about?"

Grace nodded.

"Did she learn anything important?"

"Not really. I only talked to her briefly on the telephone. She said she had learned a few things, but that she'd get back to me later on today with the details. I wasn't all that excited about it because it sounded to me as though it was mostly more of the same."

"The same what?"

"The same old nothing," Grace answered. "At least, nothing much. She never did have any luck tracing his background prior to his going to work for D.G.I. last June. She said it was almost like he was dropped onto this planet, fully grown and fully educated, at age thirty-two. Virginia thought maybe he might be part of the federal witness protection program."

The slight discrepancy was so small that it almost sailed right past me without my noticing. "Wait a minute," I said, "did you say last June?"

Grace nodded, "Yes."

"But I thought..." The people in the shop stayed quiet while I thumbed through my notebook, looking for the notes from my interview with Bill Whitten. And once I found them, I spent more time searching through and deciphering my hasty scribbles until I found the exact reference.

"Here it is. According to what Bill Whitten told me, Don Wolf went to work for D.G.I. in early October."

"No," Grace said. "You're wrong about that. I'm sure Virginia told me he started working for D.G.I. much earlier than that, way back last summer sometime. Virginia didn't say exactly, but it sounded as though it was a consulting job of some kind. I'm sure she would have addressed that issue in her report if she'd ever had a chance to deliver it. She usually faxed me a written copy a little in advance of our face-to-face. That gave me a chance to think about it beforehand and to make note of any questions."

Tim and I exchanged glances. Most likely, he was thinking about Virginia Marks' missing computer. I know I was.

"But she didn't fax you anything last night after she got back to town?"

"No. Not as far as I know. She might have. There was a whole stack of paper in the tray this morning. It looked to me like it mostly had to do with shipments to and from the shop."

The bell over the door jangled noisily, and in walked Latty Gibson. She paused just inside the door and looked questioningly from face to face.

"Why are you still here?" she demanded, settling her gaze on me. "What's going on?"

"We were just talking to your Aunt Grace," I said. "We had to ask her some questions as well."

"Are you done now?"

Tim was already on his way to the door. "Yes," he said. "Now that you mention it, I think we are pretty much finished, aren't we, Detective Beaumont?"

"Evidently," I said dryly.

Nodding to each of the ladies in turn, I followed Detective Blaine out into the street. "Isn't she something!" Tim Blaine was saying as I caught up with him.

"I'll say," I agreed. "I've only known her for two days, but I can tell you that Grace Highsmith is full of surprises."

"I wasn't talking about Grace," he said. "I mean Latty. She's the most beautiful woman I've ever met. How could that son of a bitch do that to her! I swear, if he weren't dead already . . ."

As I said before, the late Don Wolf was amazingly unlamented. Even people who never met him were glad he was dead. It should have been enough to give the guy a complex. "You and everybody else," I said.

"I believe somebody's out to get her," Tim continued. "They're trying to frame her. Maybe Virginia Marks was even in on it. That business with her finding the gun is just too much of a coincidence.''

Cops aren't ever supposed to mix business with pleasure. With good reason. The people who turn up involved in homicide cases—suspects and witnesses alike—are supposed to be off limits, especially when it comes to romantic entanglements. The prohibition makes perfect sense. Once an investigator has a personal connection to someone involved in the case, his perspective and judgment both become clouded, and his impartiality flies right out the window.

Assuming the mantle of wise old man, I made a futile attempt to give Tim Blaine the benefit of my own hard-won experience. When I set out to pop his romantic bubble, I was speaking from the unenviable position of first-hand experience. Of being able to say, ''Do as I say, not as I do.'' After all, years ago, when I fell for one of my own prime suspects, that relationship had come within inches of being fatal—for both of us.

''Tim,'' I said, ''would you mind if I gave you a word of advice?''

''What's that?'' he asked.

''Forget about Latty Gibson, at least for the time being.''

''Forget about her? Are you kidding?''

''No,'' I said. ''I'm not kidding at all. I'm as serious as I can be. And I'm telling you this for your own good.''

Our eyes met for a moment as we stood there on that sunlit sidewalk. ''I'll take it under advisement," he agreed grudgingly. "But I'm not making any promises."

He turned toward his Ford, reached down, and wrenched open the door. "See you around," he added, before climbing in and slamming the door shut behind him.

In other words, "Screw you!" As I watched him drive away, I realized I had never told him about the real implications of Latty leaving her coat with the gun in it somewhere on the premises of D.G.I. That was all right, though. Blaine was a Bellevue police officer, and Bill Whitten was in Seattle.

The day before, Captain Powell had threatened to add more personnel to the case if, after twenty-four hours, Kramer, Arnold, and I weren't making measurable progress. As far as I could tell, we weren't. That meant that if Powell had carried through on his promise to increase the body count, we'd be able to draft someone to go to D.G.I. and collect the missing coat.

Tossing Don Wolf's jacket over my shoulder, I crossed the street to my own car. At three o'clock in the afternoon, there was already a traffic jam on Main Street in Old Bellevue. With the interview over, I reached down to check my pager. I wasn't particularly concerned when I realized it wasn't there on my belt where it belonged. I reasoned that I had probably left it on the bathroom counter earlier when I stripped out of my clothes for that quick shower. But that was no great loss. If people who knew me were trying to reach me, they were probably used to the idea that I didn't return calls instantly.

As I waited for my turn to go play in the grid-lock, I checked the recall button on my cell phone. Naturally, there was a call.

At first, I thought my caller might be Ralph, but when I tried reaching him at Belltown Terrace, there was no answer. Next, I checked in with the department.

"Sergeant Watkins here," Watty said, answering his phone.

"Did Kramer ever show up?" I asked.

"As a matter of fact, he did. But before I put him through to you, I've got a bone to pick with you, Detective Beaumont. Where's your pager?"

"Oops," I said, hoping this sounded like news to me. "It's not here. I must have misplaced it."

"Right," Watty answered. "You win the booby prize. And I just happen to know where you left it."

"Where?"

"A housekeeper found it at the Silver Cloud Motel over there in Bellevue. I told her to leave it at the desk, that you'd come by and pick it up. At least it was on. I checked with the person who called."

"Look, Watty," I said, hoping to mollify the man. "I'm just a couple of minutes from there right now. I'll go straight over and pick it up."

"And if I were you, in the future, I'd be a whole lot less careless with departmental equipment.

Now, do you still want to talk to Detective Kramer?"

"No, thanks," I said. "Not necessary. I'll see him when I get back down there. Tell him I'm on my way."

"Oh, one more thing," Watty said, before I could hang up. "Lori's looking for you."

"Lori?"

"You know, Lori Yamaguchi, who works in the latent fingerprint lab. She didn't say what she wanted, but she said to have you come see her as soon as you're back downtown."

"I'll go right away," I said.

"But not until after you retrieve your pager."

"I wouldn't think of it," I said.

I gave a generous tip to the desk clerk at the Silver Cloud who handed over the pager, and I left an equally hefty one for the housekeeper who had found it. Unwittingly, those two people had saved my life. If I had lost the pager for good, both Sergeant Watkins and Captain Powell would have had my ass.

Twenty-five minutes later, with Don Wolf's jacket still slung over my arm, I was standing leaning against the counter in the reception area of King County's Fingerprint Lab. When the receptionist told me Lori was on the phone, I told her I'd wait, and helped myself to a chair. Sitting there waiting and with nothing in particular to do, I picked up the jacket and started going through the pockets.

One pocket after another yielded nothing but

pocket lint. Until I reached the last one, the lower inside pocket. There, tucked into smooth lining, was a single tiny scrap of paper that had been folded once, twice, and yet again into a tiny square no bigger than a respectable spitwad. When I unfolded it, the resulting piece of paper was no bigger than an inch square. The printed message on the paper was equally tiny.

"Donnie," it said, "see you at the apartment at six." It was signed with the initials, "D.C." A heart had been drawn around the outside of the two letters and a whimsical pair of happy faces had been made of the insides of both letters.

I studied the note for sometime. *D.C.* Who's *D.C.?* I wondered. And then it hit me. D.C.— Deanna Compton. Bill Whitten's secretary!

"Detective Beaumont?"

I looked up. Lori Yamaguchi was smiling at me in a way that said she had spoken to me more than once without my hearing.

"Yes? Oh, hello, Lori. Sorry I didn't hear you. I was thinking about something else." Carefully, I refolded the piece of paper and dropped it inside my shirt pocket. "What's up?"

"We got a hit on those fingerprints of yours, the ones Audrey Cummings sent over."

I stood up and tried to seem less disorganized and distracted than I felt. "Really? That was just a shot in the dark. What kind of hit?" I asked.

"Not just one," Lori added. "There are seven in all."

"Seven," I echoed.

"That's right," she said. "It turns out, your dead guy is a probable serial rapist with a trail of unsolved attacks in jurisdictions all over California. Same M.O. each time. He'd make an appointment with a real estate agent to go look at houses, and then . . ."

"Rape them?"

"Right. There might very well be more than just the seven," Lori said. "It could be the same thing happened in other places and that one way or another they didn't end up in the data bank."

"But who is he?" I asked.

Lori looked at me blankly. "What do you mean, who is he?" she asked. "Don Wolf, of course. Since you were the detective on the case, I figured you already knew his name. Audrey Cummings said—"

"That's all you have on him then?" I interrupted. "No arrests, no prior convictions?"

Right that minute, I didn't attempt to explain to Lori Yamaguchi that as far as anyone else had been able to discover, the guy named Don Wolf had no known history prior to his sudden appearance in Lizbeth Dorn's life down in California some months earlier.

"Nothing. If there had been, I should have been able to find some record of it. I suppose it's possible that he fell through a crack somewhere along the line and his prints just didn't get entered into the AFIS computer. That automated fingerprints identification system is expensive and time-consuming, you know."

Lori was justifiably proud of her work, of having made the vital connection. No doubt she expected me to be either more grateful or else more impressed. Maybe both. But at the moment, that folded piece of paper with Deanna Compton's damning initials on it was burning a hole in my shirt pocket. Somebody else besides Latty Gibson had maybe been messing around with Don Wolf, and I wanted to pay her a visit.

"Look, Lori," I said. "Thanks a whole bunch. Don't think I'm not appreciative, because I am. I owe you lunch. No, more than that, I owe you dinner. But right now, I've got to go. Send me a detailed report on all this, would you?"

"You don't owe me anything, Detective Beaumont," she said, as I gathered up Don Wolf's jacket and headed for the door. "I was just doing my job."

With a quick wave over my shoulder, I darted out the door, realizing as I went that it's people like Lori Yamaguchi who, as opposed to the Hilda Chisholms of the world, give a whole different meaning to the word *bureaucrat*.

# Twenty

My mother always used to say, "A wise man changes his mind. A fool never does."

I had told Watty I was on my way back to the department. And I meant to go straight there. I even made it as far as the Third Avenue lobby of the Public Safety Building. But as I stood there waiting for a fully-loaded, rush-hour elevator to disgorge its mass of humanity, I was puzzling over what implications Deanna Compton's note might have for the cases I was investigating.

I kept remembering the Deanna Compton I had met two days earlier at Designer Genes International. She had seemed suitably startled when Bill Whitten delivered news of Don Wolf's death, but she had handled the resultant requests for information in a coolly efficient, businesslike fashion. I could recall nothing at all in her demeanor that would have indicated anything more than a business-colleague relationship with the dead man. That meant one of two things. Either Deanna Compton wasn't the D.C. in question, or, if she was, she had gone to extraordinary lengths to conceal any kind of inappropriate reaction to the news from me and from her boss, Bill Whitten.

What I needed to do was find some way to verify whether or not Deanna Compton and D.C. were one and the same. That was where my thought process stood when an elevator finally arrived and its door opened. And by the time the last of the passengers filed off and dodged past those of us waiting in the crowded lobby to get on, I realized that I had in my possession a tool that might make that verification possible: the videotapes—Bill Whitten's security tapes. If the surveillance camera switched on whenever someone had walked into Don Wolf's office, then Deanna Compton was bound to have made an appearance somewhere on the footage that was still in my den. If I could show a picture of Deanna Compton to Jack Braman, manager of the Lake View Condominiums . . .

In my eagerness to turn thought to action, I nearly collided with the people lined up behind me when I turned suddenly and dashed back out the lobby door. I sprinted down Yesler to the garage where I usually leave the 928. Naturally, it was already parked, but one of the attendants was more than eager to go fetch it.

In recent years, a good deal of Seattle's rush-hour bus traffic has disappeared into an underground transit tunnel. There were still buses moving up and down Third Avenue, but I was able to make fairly good time on my way uptown. And when I turned up Broad, not only was there an available parking space right there on the corner of Second and Broad, there was still time on the meter. After yesterday's all-time record low, things were starting to look up. A little.

I dashed into the apartment and went straight to the den without even pausing at the answering machine that was sitting there blinking like a crazed Christmas tree. I know the male gender is supposed to reign supreme in the world of television remotes. When it comes to clicker wars, however, I take a backseat to almost everyone— Heather and Tracy Peters included.

It took time to scroll backward through the D.G.I. tape. Characters came and went, walking in comic reverse overdrive back and forth across the screen. Don Wolf himself entered and exited the room several times. In between, there were long periods of time when he sat working at his desk. Once Bill Whitten came in and out. I was about to give up when my patience was rewarded with a view of Deanna Compton walking backward from the doorway to Don Wolf's desk.

Moving close to the set, I let the tape continue rewinding until I reached the point where she opened the door to enter, then I switched the V.C.R. to play once again.

"What's up, Mrs. Compton?" Don Wolf was asking. There was nothing in his greeting that was in any way suspect. If he was overjoyed to see her, if the two of them had anything going after hours, it was difficult to see that from their perfunctorily polite interaction on the screen.

Deanna put a stack of papers on Don Wolf's desk and then turned and walked away. "You lose, Beaumont," I said, getting ready to switch again into a backward scroll. Just then, Don Wolf reached out and plucked something off the stack of paper. It was a casual gesture that probably would have escaped notice under most circumstances. I switched to rewind and then ran the segment again. Sure enough. What he had picked up was tiny—barely as big as the top of his thumb. Moments later, smiling broadly, Wolf stood up, took his jacket from a hook on a hat rack in the corner, and left the office. As he was leaving, he put something in the lower inside pocket of his jacket—the same pocket in which I had found the note.

I rewound the tape, back to the point where Deanna Compton first entered the room. That was what I had wanted in the first place, a picture of Deanna Compton that I could show to Jack Braman at the Lake View Condos to find out whether or not she had been among the frequent guests at Don Wolf's apartment. About that time, the doorbell rang.

If anybody ever starts a Twelve Step Program for gizmo lovers, Ralph Ames ought to be one of the first to join. He's forever trying to update my technology quotient. He was the instigator be-

hind the high-tech electronic security/sound/
light system in my condo. Because of him, lights
and music faithfully follow me from room to
room. And if I happen to have the special pager
with me, I can open doors to allow arriving
guests into either the building or the apartment.

The telling detail here is having the pager actually in my possession when needed. And because I have an ingrained aversion to wearing
more than one pager at a time, the home pager
usually ends up parked on the bathroom counter.
Which was precisely where it was right then
when the doorbell summoned me away from the
VCR in the den.

Rushing to the door, I pulled it open to find
Ron Peters and his wheelchair parked outside in
the hallway. He was grinning from ear to ear. "In
case nobody's mentioned it, your answering
machine's broken," he said, rolling past me first
into the entryway and then on into the living
room.

His words of complaint about the answering
machine didn't nearly jibe with the jubilant expression on the man's face. For somebody whose
ex-wife was in the process of making life miser-
able for anyone within striking distance, he didn't
look the least bit concerned.

"What's got you so damned cheerful?" I grumbled, heading back toward the den to collect the
tape.

"I've got some good news and some bad
news."

"Come on, Ron. No games. I'm working on something."

He nodded. "You and me both."

"So what's the news? Give me the bad, first. We could just as well get it over with."

"We're both being investigated by Internal Investigations."

"That's hardly news, Ron. Hilda Chisholm paid me a little visit and dropped that bomb last night. So what's the good news?"

"Tony says I can't be working for I.I.S. at the same time I'm being investigated, so for the time being, they're shifting me back down to investigations. To Homicide. We're partners again, at least until Sue gets back from Ohio or until the I.I.S. investigation blows over, whichever comes first."

"I'll be damned," I said.

"As soon as I showed up on the fifth floor this afternoon, Captain Powell pounced on me and put me straight to work on this Wolf case. I can't tell you how good it feels to be back in the harness again, to be working on an investigation that counts for something out in the real world. I think I've come up with something important."

"What's that?"

"Detective Kramer—somebody needs to shove a corncob up that guy's ass, by the way—said that he thought I could be the most help by going to work on the financial considerations. He and Arnold had already interviewed the high-profile investors, so I went at it from the other end of the spectrum. Guess what? D.G.I. is in big trouble. The bank is within days of foreclosing on the building, and City Light is about to turn off the power. Same thing for trash collection and phone service. They've evidently been meeting payroll, but that's about all."

"Wait a minute. That doesn't make sense," I objected. "With all those big money investors, I thought D.G.I. would be rolling in cash by now."

"The cash may have come in, but they haven't been using it to pay bills."

"So where did it go?"

Ron shrugged. "Makes you wonder, doesn't it," he said with a grin.

Midwinter in Seattle means that it's dark by four-thirty. Somehow, the day seemed suddenly brighter. I found myself grinning back at him. "Aren't you off duty?"

"Depends on whether or not you have something for me to do."

"How about if we go pay a call on Bill Whitten?" I asked, switching off the VCR, ejecting the tape, and stuffing it into my pocket.

"Sounds good to me," Ron agreed. "We'll take my car, if you don't mind. When it comes to my chair, that Porsche of yours just doesn't cut it. I'll go get the car and meet you out on the street."

We had made it as far as the elevator lobby when a thought crossed my mind. "Hey, Ron, are you wearing a vest?"

Ron pressed the button. "You bet I am," he returned, "although I'm not sure why. Who would go around trying to kill a crippled cop?"

"You'd be surprised," I said. "Sitting in a wheelchair sure as hell didn't keep somebody from shooting a freelance detective named Virginia Marks over in Bellevue last night. My guess is that whoever killed Don Wolf also killed the private eye who was investigating him."

I bailed out in the lobby and went to the street to collect my cellular phone from the 928. By the time Ron came around to where I was standing on the curb, I was attempting to take messages off my broken machine upstairs. It was frustrating going. There must have been nine calls in all. Most of them were hang ups, but the messages that were there weren't really messages at all. They were more like message fragments.

"This is Tony Freeman. There's been a little difficulty..." One was from Gail Richardson, the woman downstairs: "My mother went home today. Want to go out and..."

Midway through the messages, I heard the one Ralph Ames had mentioned to me earlier. "Detective Beaumont, this is Harry..." And that was it.

The last partial message, left after several abortive tries, was from Ron Peters. "This damned thing's obviously not working. Call when you get home."

As Peters' Buick came around the corner of First Avenue onto Broad I was just erasing the last message. He stopped on the street to pick me up. "Next stop D.G.I.," he said, as he drove around the block to head north on First. "Do you think they'll still be open? It's almost five o'clock."

"Somebody is bound to be there."

"By the way, on my way down to the garage, I remembered another call that came into the office earlier this afternoon, from Harry Moore down in La Jolla. He wants to talk to you in the worst way."

Sighing, I shifted the seat belt away from my chest and groped for my notebook. Ron beat me to the punch by handing me a Post-it with a California number jotted on it.

"Here's the number," he said. "I didn't think you'd want to look it up."

"Thanks," I said, keying Harry Moore's direct number into the phone. "After being stuck with Kramer and Arnold for a day or two, it's nice to have a real partner again."

"No lie," Ron said.

Moore answered almost immediately. "Detective Beaumont here," I said. "What can I do for you, Mr. Moore?"

"When I first got the fax, I couldn't believe my luck, but now, with her dead . . ."

"Whoa, not so fast. What fax are you talking about?"

"The one from Virginia Marks. I left a message on your machine—"

"My machine ate your message, so let's start over from the beginning. What fax did Virginia Marks send you?"

"She sent it last night, after I went home, so I didn't actually see it until I came in this morning around ten. But when I tried calling back Virginia this afternoon, somebody told me that she's dead. Is that true?"

"Unfortunately, yes."

"Damn!" Moore muttered. "I suppose that means I'm screwed then anyway."

"I still don't know what we're talking about."

"Virginia Marks told me she had some critical information for me. She said she could prove that Bill Whitten is using my research—Alpha-Cyte research—to attract investors for D.G.I. And she offered to sell me that information—for a fee, of course. Her asking price was astronomical, but if what she was telling me was true, I could have taken Bill Whitten to the cleaners."

It sounded to me as though someone else had already wiped out Bill Whitten's finances, but I didn't mention that to Harry Moore. He didn't give me a chance.

"So first I sat here and tried to figure out how Bill Whitten could end up with Alpha-Cyte proprietary information, and finally, it dawned on me. Lizbeth!"

"You think Lizbeth Wolf gave it to him?"

"No, don't you see? That worthless bastard stole it. Don Wolf stole it, probably right out of Lizbeth's computer, and handed it over to Whitten. That's got to be it."

By the time Harry Moore finally stopped long enough to draw breath, Ron had already parked the Buick in front of the curb at D.G.I. and was waiting for directions.

I looked over at the door to the building where the five o'clock exodus was already in full swing. "Look, Mr. Moore. I've got to go to an appointment right now. Can we get back to you on this a little later?"

"Sure," he said. "Don't worry about how late it is. I'll be here."

By then, Ron had already lowered the wheelchair and was waiting for me on the curb. "What's going on?" Ron asked. "It sounded bad."

"Come on," I said. "I'll tell you on the way."

But then I glanced up and saw the security camera stationed over the door. It reminded me of the ones inside.

"Come to think of it," I said, "I'll tell you the rest of it when we come back outside. If I tell you in there, Bill Whitten will have it all recorded on his personal *Candid Camera*. From what Harry Moore is telling me, that's probably a real bad idea."

We went on upstairs, but when the elevator opened onto the sixth-floor reception area, it was like entering a deserted village. Deanna Compton wasn't at her desk. Bill Whitten wasn't at his, either.

"Looks like everybody took off early," Ron said, glancing around.

But it didn't feel right to me. Most CEOs I've ever heard of don't punch time clocks. Neither do their private secretaries. Trying to understand what my instincts were telling me, I walked all the way around Deanna Compton's desk. Everything was in order. When I had been there before, the top of her desk had been covered with papers and files. In the upper right-hand corner had sat an oversized, leather-bound appointment book. But now, at two minutes after five, none of those things were in evidence.

I was about to suggest that we head back to the elevator, when I glanced down at the three separate trash containers stowed next to the wall. Leaning down, I pulled out the mixed paper recycling box. One of the top items was an envelope from one of Seattle's downtown, bicycle-dependent messenger services. And inside that was a second empty envelope. The return address said The Travel Guys with an address in a high-rise on Pike.

I started adding things up. The investment money the mayor's boyfriend and his friends had dropped into D.G.I. was among the missing. Harry Moore didn't know all the details about who had stolen what from Alpha-Cyte, but if Virginia Marks had been able to figure it out, someone else would be able to uncover that information, too, now that they knew what to look for. Three people connected to Bill Whitten's dying D.G.I. were dead, and there was a good chance we were coming close to finding out how come and who had killed them.

And if Bill Whitten was our man, there was an

excellent possibility that he was about to blow town.

Sometimes, you just have to go for it. I picked up Deanna Compton's phone and dialed the number listed on the outside of the envelope.

"This is Jason," an overly sibilant male voice answered. Jason of The Travel Guys sounded as though he and Johnny Bickford might frequent some of the same hangouts. "May I help you?"

"This is Bill Whitten!" I grumbled into the phone. "There's been a mistake. The tickets you sent me have somebody else's name on them. Where are mine?"

When he heard me say that, I'm surprised Ron Peters didn't tumble out of his chair.

"Oh, I'm so sorry," Jason said quickly. "I can't understand how that happened. Christopher is already gone for the day, but let me check your records, Mr. Whitten. Just a moment."

"What the hell are you doing?" Ron demanded.

Silently, I shushed him with a finger over my lips. And it was a good thing, too, because just then Jason came back on the line. "Here it is. Those must be the tickets to Puerto Vallarta at ten thirty-five tomorrow morning. If you'll just tell me whose tickets were sent to you, I'll have someone come pick them up, and we'll get this whole thing—"

Jason was still talking when I put down the phone.

My mother would have been ashamed of me. I didn't even say thanks.

# Twenty-one

"I guess I'd forgotten how you do things sometimes," Ron said in the elevator. I didn't remember whether or not I had told him about the surveillance cameras in the elevator. But if Bill Whitten was on his way out of town, maybe that didn't matter.

"It worked," I said.

Ron just shook his head. "Where to next?"

"Next, we find out where Bill Whitten lives, and we go there."

"And what kind of subterfuge are you planning to use to do that?"

"No subterfuge," I answered. "How about if we try directory assistance?"

It probably would have worked, but we never had a chance to use it. My pager was going off as we headed to the car. While he loaded his chair into the carrier, I dialed Watty's number. Kent

Reeves, the night-shift homicide sergeant, answered the phone.

"Hey, Detective Beaumont," Kent said, "you just missed her."

"Missed who?"

"A lady named Grace Highsmith. She said if you called in to tell you that your answering machine at home isn't working."

"I know."

"And that if you want to drop by her house, she has some information for you. Something to the effect that she knows who Don Wolf really is. Does that make sense? Her message was a little hard to understand."

"Grace Highsmith is like that," I said. "Did she leave a number?"

"She said you had it."

"I do, but I'll have to look it up."

"Sorry, Beau."

"What's going on now?" Ron asked, as I started fumbling my notebook out of its pocket. One of the advantages of two-way radio communications is that both partners hear the communication without unnecessary repetition. "And where are we headed?" he added.

"Kirkland," I said. "We've been summoned to Grace Highsmith's house," I said. "She's got some kind of—" I stopped cold.

"Some kind of what?" Ron asked. "What's wrong?"

"Information. All of a sudden she has information about Don Wolf, about who he really is."

"So?"

"And she didn't have it earlier today, when we were talking to her at the shop this afternoon."

"Beau," Ron said impatiently. "You're talking in circles. What the hell are you blithering about?"

"If it came from Virginia Marks, then it was probably sent the same way Harry Moore's was—by fax before she died. And if she sent it with that little computer of hers, then there'd be the full text of the fax as well as a complete record of where it was sent. That information would have been in Virginia Marks' computer which, as far as anyone can tell, was the only thing missing from her condo when her body was found there this morning. And if whatever it was made it worthwhile to kill Virginia Marks . . ."

Ron didn't need any further urging. "Whereabouts in Kirkland?" he asked.

"Down along the water, below Juanita Drive. On Holmes Point Drive, just below Denny Park."

"There's a bubble light in the glove compartment," Ron said. "Drag it out, turn it on, and give it to me."

We were at the north end of the Regrade. The shortest way to the north end of Kirkland would have been across the Evergreen Floating Bridge on Highway 520. But by now, at five-fifteen, we were smack in the middle of rush hour, and the floating bridge would be a parking lot. Even with lights and siren, it would be slow going. Ron made the entirely sensible decision of going south to head north. It may have added another sixteen miles to the trip, but we both knew it would save time.

We were headed down Fifth Avenue when Peters asked the tough question. "Are you going to call Kramer?"

At that juncture, calling Detective Kramer was the last thing on my mind. "Why would I do that?" I returned.

"Because you need to," Ron answered. "Look, you told me yourself that Grace Highsmith's house is halfway down a cliff."

"That's right. What's the point?"

"Think about it," Peters said with a glower. "If I were you, and if my partner had turned out to be some kind of gimp, I sure as hell would call for backup. You should, too."

Ron and I are good friends. We go back a long way. He was the one, who on that disastrous day when I married Anne Corley, had done me the incredible kindness of stuffing the remains of that damned wedding cake down the garbage disposal. Most of the time, his physical infirmity is a taboo subject between us—one of those unmentionable but understood issues that hover in the background of our friendship. We didn't sit around discussing the permanent injuries that long-ago car wreck had done to Ron's body any more than we did the indelible damage Anne had inflicted on my heart.

"You're worth three or four Paul Kramers any day of the week," I said at once.

He glared at me again. In the glow of the head-lights from oncoming vehicles, I could see the stubborn set of his jaw.

"That's bullshit and you know it," he returned. "Now shape up and dial the damned phone. I don't want anything to happen to you because I'm physically incapable of bailing you out if your tail ends up in a sling."

After Ron's accident, it had taken a long time for him to reach an accommodation with his new and permanently rearranged physical reality. Other people, those of the bleeding-heart persuasion, might pretend his handicaps didn't exist or else meant nothing. Peters himself, viewing those limits from the inside out, had no patience for phony sentimentality. Not from anyone. Including from me, his best friend.

"All right," I said.

Without another word, I shut up and dialed Paul Kramer. He didn't answer, but that didn't get me off the hook. "Call Sergeant Reeves back," Peters said. "Have dispatch find him."

"Boy, you guys are really racking up the over-time," Kent said. "I think he's on his way back from the Eastside right now."

"Patch me through to him, if you can," I said. "I need to have him turn around and go back."

By the time Kramer came on the line, Ron and I were driving through the International District. "How soon can you and Sam Arnold meet us at Grace Highsmith's house in Kirkland?" I asked.

Putting it that way, without any polite preamble, clearly raised Paul Kramer's hackles. "Why should I?" he asked. "It's after hours. I'm on my way home."

"What if I told you Bill Whitten may be our man?" I said.

"How'd you happen to come to that brilliant conclusion?"

At least the instant antagonism between us was a two-way thing. With Ron hanging on my every word, however, I knew better than to let myself be sucked into an argument.

I took a deep breath. "Look, Kramer, cut the crap. Grace Highsmith claims she has some important new information about Don Wolf, information that was probably faxed to her by Virginia Marks before her death."

"So?"

"Three people are dead so far. You want to try for four, or are you going to get your butt over there so we can check it out?"

"I'll go, I'll go," Kramer grumbled. "Because of the traffic, I was heading home by way of Lynnwood. So I'm only a few minutes out. How soon will you be there?"

"Twenty minutes, maybe? We're in the express lanes heading for the I-Ninety bridge."

"If this turns out to be a wild-goose chase, Beaumont . . ."

I punched END on my phone and cut Detective Kramer off in midthreat. "Satisfied?" I asked.

"For the time being," Ron Peters said.

Back when he was married the first time, Ron

and his family used to live in Kirkland. So when
we ventured off I-405 at Totem Lake, he didn't
need either a copilot or a map. Within minutes of
leaving the freeway, we were careening along the
steep, winding road that led down the bluff to
Grace Highsmith's cliff-side cottage.

"You're a hell of a lot better at getting here than
I am," I told him.

"I ought to be," he answered. "When we lived
on this side of the lake, the girls and I came to
Denny Park about once a week."

Heading north along the water, we were just
passing Grace Highsmith's neighbors to the south
when I caught sight of Kramer's car. "Pull over,"
I said. "He must have gotten here ahead of us."

We pulled up alongside the unmarked Caprice.
Empty, it was double-parked, half on and half off
the roadway. It sat at an angle partly behind and
partly alongside a second vehicle that was
stopped on Grace Highsmith's parking ledge. The
positioning of the Caprice effectively blocked the
other vehicle, a Lexus, from being able to return
to traffic.

The Lexus had Washington plates. Using the
cell phone once again, I called through to records
to check ownership of the parked vehicle.

"Where do you think Kramer went?" Peters
asked as we waited for the clerk to give us an
answer. "I heard you tell him to meet us. He
wouldn't have gone down there by himself,
would he?"

"Somebody who's as much of a fan of teamwork as Detective Kramer? Surely you jest. Of course he went down by himself. Why wait for the rest of the troops when you have a chance to play hero?"

The records clerk came back on the phone. "The Lexus is owned by a company named D.G.I.," she said.

"Bingo," I told Peters, tossing him my cell phone. "Get on the horn to Kirkland Police and tell them we need help here. Fast."

"You're going down, too?" Peters asked, picking up the phone.

I nodded. "One fool makes twenty."

Just then, a pair of bright headlights appeared in the northbound lane behind us. The driver flashed his brights impatiently and laid on his horn, trying to move us the hell out of his way. He was probably some big-wheel executive, pissed off because we were holding up cocktails and dinner in his lakeside mansion. He certainly didn't give a damn that his rude honking horn would effectively squelch any hope of our arriving on Grace Highsmith's doorstep unannounced.

Ignoring the guy behind us, Ron waved me out of the Buick. "Go on ahead," he said. "I'll pull up beyond the garage so the cops from Kirkland can in-fill behind us."

Nodding, I pushed open the car door and jumped out, wrestling my nine-millimeter Beretta out of my shoulder holster as I did so. By the time I hit the pavement, the weapon was in my hand.

As the creep behind us—an asshole driving an Infiniti Q45—pulled even with me, he couldn't resist flipping me off. In the process, he must have caught a glimpse of the weapon. He floored it. The Infiniti shot forward, barely missing Ron's rear bumper.

I was left there standing night blind in the sudden silence. And that's when I heard a moan coming from somewhere I couldn't see. The moan was followed by a single word, a very faint *Help*.

The hair stood up on the back of my neck.

"Kramer?" I whispered. "Is that you?"

"Beaumont . . . down here."

Following the voice as best I could, I crept over to the edge of the retaining wall and peered down. Paul Kramer lay sprawled on the rocks ten feet below. One leg was folded under him, bent backward in a way ordinary human anatomy never intended.

"Are you all right?" I asked.

"Be careful," Kramer warned. "He took my guns."

Not only was Kramer injured, he was also disarmed. "What happened?" I asked.

"I got out to check—"

Farther down the hillside, a door slammed shut. Footsteps on the wooden porch and voices wafted up from below. "Shhh," I whispered. "Someone's coming."

With my heart pounding in my chest, I looked around for cover, choosing at last to fall in behind the back tire of the Caprice. Just then, a car door

opened. I heard the distinctive whir of the lift
mechanism as Ron lowered his chair to the roadway.

While I ducked into the shadow behind the car,
a motion-sensing fixture shot a beam of light
down the stairway. Seeing it, I uttered a silent
prayer of gratitude. If I had headed for the stairway right then instead of toward Kramer, the
light would have flashed a vivid warning to
everyone below that someone was coming. Had
I been caught in that blinding shaft of light, I
would have been a sitting duck.

"Come on, come on," Bill Whitten urged. "Get
a move on."

"I'm moving as fast as I can," Grace Highsmith
returned crisply. "I'm no spring chicken, you
know."

Bad as the situation was, I couldn't help smiling. Faced with the very real possibility of her
own death, naturally Grace Highsmith was arguing with her self-appointed executioner, lectur-
ing this man who was most likely a multiple
murderer as though he were nothing but an errant schoolboy.

Long seconds passed before she finally came
into view, pulling herself along the handrail, her
purse dangling from one forearm. Seeing that
purse, I couldn't help wishing that the .32 auto
was still concealed in Grace Highsmith's pocketbook rather than languishing in the safety of the
Firearms Section of Washington State Patrol.
Latty had said her aunt had wanted the gun for

protection. If ever that stubborn old woman needed protection, it was now.

I had hoped for an opportunity to get off a clean shot, but there was no chance of that. Bill Whitten was walking directly behind Grace. If he had killed three times already, there was no reason to think he would hesitate to do so again. In fact, what I couldn't understand was why he was bringing Grace along.

"Mr. Whitten," Ron Peters called, rolling into sight around the garage. "Let the woman go."

Everything stopped. No one moved. For several seconds, no one said a word.

Then Bill Whitten grabbed Grace Highsmith and pulled her back against him. I saw the gun then as he pressed it against her head.

"Who are you?" he demanded. "What do you want?"

"I'm a police officer," Ron said, raising his hands in the air. "I'm unarmed. Let her go. Just because your life is falling apart is no reason to go around killing people."

"Shoot him," Grace shrieked. "Don't worry about me. Get him. He's a killer. He tried to frame my niece. He—"

One-handed, Bill Whitten lifted Grace Highsmith off the ground and shook her. "Shut up!" he ordered.

I understood at once what Ron was doing. By keeping Whitten's focus on him, he was hoping to give me an opportunity to fire off a shot. But I was too far away. There was no way I could hit

Whitten without running the risk of hitting Grace as well.

"Get out of the way," Whitten said, as the two of them gained street level. "We're going to get in the car, and we're going to drive away. Otherwise, she dies."

"Don't listen to him," Grace said, finding her voice. "I don't matter. This man is evil. Don't let him get away with anything more."

Ron moved his chair back, as if clearing a path for them to come up the stairs and walk past him. Just then, another car came up the street. This one wove around the haphazardly parked cars, momentarily leaving me fully exposed as a Mercedes station wagon loaded to the gills with a mother and several kids made its way past our little tableau.

And at just that moment, when any kind of change in the dynamics of the situation could have been most damaging to a carload of innocent children, Grace Highsmith took decisive action. At first, she seemed to slump over, as though she had fainted. Then, when Whitten looked down at her to see what was happening, she twisted around in his arms and kneed him in the groin.

With a startled gasp, he stumbled and seemed to fall forward, landing on Grace, who had dropped to her hands and knees in front of him. In the flurry of arms and legs, I realized that the gun had been knocked from his hand. At that point, Whitten was unarmed, but again, there was no chance of getting off a clear shot or even any shot at all. Whitten leaned back and reached for the gun while Grace scuttled away from him. Meanwhile, Ron rolled forward with one hand outstretched and reaching to help. He caught Grace by the arm and somehow pulled her clear, dragging her with him by one hand while rolling backward with the other.

By then, Whitten had retrieved the gun. Before he had time enough to raise it or aim, I squeezed off a single shot. The bullet caught him in the left shoulder. It turned him around and sent him tumbling backward down the stairs. As I raced forward, hoping to fire again, Ron dragged Grace to relative safety behind the garage.

"Stop," I yelled. "Stop or I'll shoot!"

Whitten's answer came in the form of a sharp report of gunfire. Suddenly, the light over the stairway was snuffed out, leveling the playing field, momentarily blinding everybody.

Dropping down on all fours, I wiggled up to the edge of the stairway and peered down. By the time my eyes had adjusted to the dark, Whitten had disappeared. When another shot rang out and sent a bullet whizzing over my head, it didn't come from the landing at the bottom of the stairs, from behind the woodpile, or even from the cover of the house. The report came from off to one side of the stairs, from a rocky, brush-covered bank ten feet or so from the shoulder of the road—from much the same area where Paul Kramer lay wounded.

"Get away from me," Bill Whitten ordered. "You shoot me, Detective Beaumont, and this officer friend of yours is a dead man."

Off in the distance, I could hear the sound of sirens. Ron Peters had done his job—both his jobs. Not only had he dragged Grace Highsmith to safety, he had also summoned help—the Kirkland cops. But from the sound of it, our backup patrol cars were just then starting down the ravine.

In a world where vest-piercing bullets can end a life in a heartbeat, Paul Kramer could be dead long before help arrived. In hostage situations, the idea, of course, is somehow to open up the lines of communication, to keep them talking.

"What do you want?" I asked.

Another bullet pinged off the top of the stairway, inches from my face. It wasn't the kind of answer I wanted, but it was, by God, an answer.

# Twenty-two

In those few brief moments, personalities disappeared. Kramer stopped being the jackass who had always rubbed me the wrong way. He was a cop in trouble. Like it or not, that gave him a claim on me—the responsibility of trying to save his damned hide.

The next thing I knew, someone was tapping me on the shoulder. I turned around to find Peters lying on the cold ground next to me. Using his powerful arms and dragging his legs, he had belly-crawled up beside me.

"Grace is okay," he whispered.

Armed with his nine-millimeter Glock, Ron gestured for me to move off to the left. The unspoken plan was that while he created yet another diversion, I should try to get the drop on Whitten from some unexpected angle. Nodding,

I slipped away, leaving Ron Peters to be our mouthpiece.

"Look, Whitten," he called down the bluff. "You're not going to get away with any of this. Listen to the sirens. More cops are on their way. Give up while you still can, before somebody else gets hurt."

Ron's attempt at communication, like mine, was immediately met by a similar answer—another gunshot. The inevitable conclusion had to be that time for talking to Bill Whitten had ended some time ago.

Meanwhile, I scooted away, back toward the parking ledge with its two parked cars. Staying low, I crept along the shoulder of the road, following the edge of the bank. I tried to keep the noise to a minimum, but each time my feet scraped over a loose piece of gravel, the resulting crackle in my cringing ear sounded almost as loud as a clap of thunder.

Several days into a Pacific Northwest January, the early nighttime chill was cold as blue blazes. The pavement wasn't yet icy, but it would be by morning. With every move, sharp frigid edges of rocks and pieces of gravel bit painfully into my skin. My teeth chattered. The hand that held my gun shook convulsively, as much from cold as from fear. The Beretta in my frozen fingers felt as though it weighed ten pounds.

The first patrol car pulled up behind me. Its siren squawked and fell silent. Headlights and flashers illuminated the whole world around me. The arrival of any kind of reinforcements should have been met with wild relief. That wasn't the case, not when I realized that I was stuck in the middle, in no-man's land. With armed cops on one side and with an armed crook on the other, I wondered how the newly arriving cops would ever manage to sort good guys from bad guys. How would they know who to help and who to shoot without someone—namely me—ending up hurt or dead?

I shouldn't have worried. Just then, another gunshot blasted away, kicking up a shower of gravel and sending the one newly arrived patrol officer scurrying back to his vehicle for cover. I was grateful when, a moment later, he doused the lights. In the dark again, I uttered another quick prayer—this time, thanking God that, whatever else Bill Whitten might be, he wasn't a very good shot.

A second patrol car arrived. The officer in it must have received some kind of radio transmission from the first one describing who was who and what was what. Getting out of his vehicle and staying low, he headed straight for Ron Peters. They talked for what seemed like several minutes, then the two Kirkland officers took up defensive positions. One settled in between Ron and the garage. The other one hunkered down in the shadows at the end of the garage.

"Did you hear that, Mr. Whitten?" Peters called, once our reinforcements were safely in place. "More cops arrived just a minute ago and more are on their way. The police boat will be here soon as well. You're surrounded. There's not a chance in hell that you'll get away. Leave the officer alone, Mr. Whitten. Move away from him. Come up the stairs with your hands up. We'll see to it that you don't get hurt."

By then, I had made my way as far as the berm at the end of the retaining wall. Slowly, ever so slowly, expecting another incoming shot at any moment, I raised myself up and peered over the side. Kramer was still there, lying in the same exact position as the last time I saw him. Bill Whitten, on the other hand, was nowhere in sight.

"Kramer," I called. "Are you okay? Are you awake?"

"I'm awake. Whitten just went down to the house. You've got to get me out of here quick," Kramer said in a hoarse whisper, "before that crazy bastard comes back."

"Why did he do that?" I asked, peering down the hill where Grace Highsmith's house was shrouded in darkness.

"How the hell should I know? Just get me out of here."

Kramer was right, of course. Moving him out of harm's way had to be the first priority. "Hey, somebody," I yelled up to the others. "Over here. Ron, cover us. You other two guys, come help me. My partner's injured. I can't lift him by myself."

Grasping the edge of the retaining wall, I lowered myself over the side. Even when I was fully extended, the bottoms of my feet were still a good four feet from the surface of the ledge. Dreading the price that four-foot drop would exact from the bone spurs on my heels, I dangled there for a moment before fear of being shot made me let go. I dropped down beside Kramer in a low crouch. Within seconds, the two uniformed Kirkland officers joined me.

"That leg looks real bad," one of them observed. "Shouldn't we wait for the EMTs?"

"No, damn it!" Kramer grunted through gritted teeth. "He might come back. Get me out of here now! Just do what you have to do and get it over with."

The thought was daunting. With the prospect of bullets flying at any moment, it wasn't simply a matter of moving a man with a broken leg. There were other injuries as well. Later, we would discover that in his tumble off the ten-foot ledge, Detective Kramer had broken six ribs in addition to damaging his leg. And at the time we were considering moving him, it seemed likely that he might have suffered neck or spinal injuries as well. With those, there's always the possibility that any kind of jarring or unprotected movement may lead to further injury—to paralysis even.

Moving him by hand, especially over such rough terrain, flew in the face of every grain of first-aid training I'd ever had drummed into my thick skull. Yet, there was no choice. Cop instinct warned me that an armed standoff was coming. We couldn't very well leave Kramer lying exposed right in the middle of it. Besides, with the extent of his injuries in that terrible cold, it seemed likely that if a stray gunshot didn't get him, shock sure as hell would.

One of the patrol officers looked up at me. "What do we do?" he asked.

"We carry him out. From the sounds of those sirens, we don't have long. I'll take this side. You take the other," I told the cop who had asked the question. "That leaves the legs for you," I told the other.

Kramer's a big guy. With only three of us, lifting him was no easy task. He gasped when we first raised him off the ground, and he groaned again when we finally put him down. Other than that, he didn't make a sound. While we were carrying him up the steep stairs, I thought—hoped—that maybe he had passed out, but when we reached the far side of Grace Highsmith's garage and laid him down on the ground, I saw that wasn't the case. He was wide awake. His jaw was clenched shut while tears streamed down his face.

"Sorry about that," I apologized. "I know it was rough."

"It's okay," he managed. "Thanks."

Grace Highsmith appeared out of nowhere carrying a blanket. She covered the injured man, then she disappeared into her garage. She emerged carrying a walking stick.

"We can use this to splint his leg," she announced, moving purposefully toward Kramer. I could tell from the look of her that she was fully prepared to put word to action.

"No, Miss Highsmith," I told her. "That won't be necessary. An aid car will be here soon."

"An aid car," she sniffed disapprovingly. "I've splinted legs before, you know. I'm perfectly capable, and I know how to do it."

"I'm sure you do," I told her. "And so do I, but how about if we leave that job to the professionals? Come on. We need to get you out of here."

Grace shot me a withering glance. "I'm not going anywhere, Detective Beaumont. This man was injured on my property because he was trying to help me," she said determinedly. "I'm not leaving until he does."

By then, the street in both directions was rapidly filling with arriving emergency vehicles, although to the north there was still one lane open to allow vehicles to leave as needed. Giving up on the futile idea of arguing with Grace Highsmith, I walked over to where Ron was huddled with a group of uniformed Kirkland officers. When I arrived, he was briefing them on the situation—giving them the information they would need to pass along to the commander of the Emergency Response Team, who was due to arrive at any moment. The department's chief hostage negotiator had also been summoned.

"How many people do you think are down there besides the bad guy?" one of the Kirkland cops asked me.

"Just him as far as we know," I answered, "but I'll go check."

Getting up, I hurried back to where Grace Highsmith still hovered over Detective Kramer. "Is he alone?" I asked.

"Yes," Grace answered, but Kramer shook his head.

"There must be two of them," he said. "I was approaching the Lexus when the lights over the stairway switched on. I remember seeing Whitten on the stairs, and that's when something hit me from behind."

I looked at Grace. "What did he want? Why did he come here in the first place?"

"My fax," she said. "He came looking for the information Virginia Marks sent me. But I was smarter than that. I had hidden it, but I told him I didn't have it, that I had sent it somewhere for safekeeping. I asked him if he planned to kill me, too."

"You asked him that?"

"Of course. He's a dangerous man, Detective Beaumont. Very unstable. Like a vicious dog. Father always taught us that you can't afford to back down with one of those. You should never show any fear, either. I believe, from something he said, that Virginia may have tried to blackmail him. That may have pushed him over the edge."

"Blackmail? With what?"

"Detective Beaumont," someone called from behind me. "The captain wants us to clear this area."

Looking around, I realized that the unit commander of the Kirkland Emergency Response Team had taken control of the situation and was busily deploying personnel and weapons in what he viewed as the most strategic positions. Kramer, sheltered behind the garage, would need to stay where he was. Grace Highsmith wouldn't.

"Look, Miss Highsmith, you heard the officer. We've got to get out of here," I warned her.

"No," she replied. "I already told you I'm staying until the ambulance gets here and that's final. I'm eighty-three years old. If I get hit by a stray bullet, it's my choice. I'd much rather do that than shrivel away in some old people's home."

"I give up," I told her. "Suit yourself." I turned back to the officer. "Leave her be," I said. "She's waiting for the ambulance."

"Okay," he said dubiously. "But the captain isn't going to like it."

"Have him come talk to her then."

Just then, an arriving ambulance came threading its way toward us through the bottleneck of parked cars. Ron Peters and I, benched by the arrival of the locals, watched from the sidelines while the emergency medical technicians splinted Kramer's leg and loaded him onto a backboard. I think they also must have slipped him some kind of medication. By the time they were ready to load him into the ambulance, he seemed to be in far less pain. When he saw me hanging around in the background, he grinned faintly and held out his hand.

"Don't think this makes us best buddies, Beaumont," he said. "But thanks. Thanks a whole hell of a lot."

"You're welcome, asshole," I replied, squeezing his hand. "You'd do the same for me."

Moments later, they loaded the gurney into the ambulance. When one of the EMTs turned away from the aid car after closing the two back doors, she was holding Grace Highsmith's blanket.

"We use our own blankets on the way to the hospital," she explained. "Do you have any idea whose this is?"

"It belongs to Grace Highsmith," I said. "She's around here somewhere. I'll see that it's returned to its proper owner."

Taking the folded blanket, I looked around for Grace some more, but still didn't see her. Assuming that one of the local officers had finally succeeded in convincing her to move out of harm's way, I unfolded the blanket and draped it over my own chilled shoulders, then I walked up to the Buick where Ron Peters was in the process of loading his wheelchair.

"Come on, Chief Sitting Bull," he said, glancing at me and my blanket. "The captain wants all nonessential people out of the immediate area. That includes you and me."

"Did Grace Highsmith come up this way?" I asked.

"If she did, I didn't see her," Peters replied. "But one of the uniformed officers just herded a whole group of people into the house next door. Maybe that's where she disappeared to."

"You're probably right," I said. But just then, something drew my eyes to the open door of Grace Highsmith's garage. I was startled to see a fat cloud of exhaust steam suddenly stream out of the back of Grace Highsmith's Cadillac and rise in the cold night air. At the same moment, a set of taillights flashed on.

"What the hell . . . ?" I began.

Then the backup lights flashed on as well and the Caddy, belching clouds of steamy exhaust vapor, began backing out of the garage. I immediately assumed that Grace was at the wheel. My expectation was that she would back out to the right and then leave to the left, driving away in the single northbound lane that was still open to traffic—the one that ran past Ron and the Buick.

Instead, the Cadillac turned in exactly the opposite direction. Rather than driving *away* from the danger, the Caddy headed directly into it.

Turning his attention from the Chair Topper, Ron stared at the Cadillac. "That can't be Grace Highsmith, can it?" he asked.

"Who else?" I returned.

*Who else, indeed!*

Walking after her, intent on turning her around, I wasn't in any particular hurry. After all, the road where Grace was headed was chock full of official police vehicles. Not only was she not going anywhere, she also wasn't going anywhere fast.

That was the thought that crossed my mind at the time, anyway. Which shows how much I know.

As the Cadillac lumbered toward the command-post van, a uniformed officer broke away from the group. Waving his arms and gesturing madly, his message to the Cadillac's driver should have been perfectly clear: *Go back!* To my absolute astonishment, the Caddy stopped at once, exactly as directed.

Grace Highsmith would never do that, I thought. Somebody else must be driving her car.

I was curious to see what the driver would do next. At that point, what would have been sensible and easy would have been to reverse course, return to the garage, and repeat the whole process over from scratch, turning into the opposite lane. Instead, with the squeal of a fluid-starved power-steering pump, the Cadillac's wheels turned sharply to the right. She began to turn around on the spot right where it was, in a place just beyond the top landing of the stairs, where there was almost no shoulder on either side of the road.

That's when I realized for sure that Grace Highsmith was at the wheel.

Instantly, I flashed back to the parking ordeal on Main Street a few hours earlier. I remembered the whole series of bumper-bashing backing and filling maneuvers it had taken for Grace to wedge the Cadillac into a regular parking space. Compared to this, that was simple. Here, if she misjudged the distance, it wasn't a matter of creasing somebody else's chrome. There was no bumper to stop her if she went too far. Only a straight drop, with nothing at all to break the fall—other than the possibility of tumbling into the arms of the gun-toting maniac who was waiting in the house at the bottom of the cliff.

The other cop—the one who was officially charged with stopping her—and I reached opposite sides of the Cadillac at pretty much the same time. By then, Grace had wrenched the car around so she had it perpendicular to the roadway, sitting squarely astraddle both lanes of traffic. The Kirkland officer pounded on the driver's window with his flashlight, then aimed the beam into the vehicle.

"Lady!" he yelled. "Turn off the engine and get out of the car."

There was no sign from the driver that she so much as heard him, so I took a crack at it. "Grace," I called, bending down and peering in the window. "You've got to—"

That was as far as I went. Suddenly, the Cadillac's powerful engine surged from a simple idle to a full roar. In the beam of the flashlight I caught a glimpse of the car's interior. As she shifted the car out of reverse and into high, both Grace Highsmith's feet were planted on the pedals—one on the brake and one on the gas. There was only a split second to react. The other cop and I both dodged back while the Cadillac shot forward in a spray of gravel.

The first casualties of the speeding car were the handrails at the top of the stairs. The Caddy plowed through the one-inch pipes as if they were made out of so many straws. And then, in the best tradition of Evel Knievel, the vehicle sailed out into space. For several slow-motion moments it seemed to stay level, as though a ribbon of invisible pavement were still holding it up. Then, ever so slowly, it began to arc downward.

The other cop and I stood paralyzed with only the suddenly empty width of the Cadillac between us, then we turned as one and headed for the stairway. We arrived just in time to see Grace Highsmith's Cadillac plunge nose-first onto the steep roof, directly between the two dormers.

The blow sent a storm of glass shards and flying wood splashing out from the windows. For a moment, the car stood poised on its nose. It seemed for a second or two that the roof might actually hold, but then the whole house trembled. The air came alive with the screams of twisting nails, shattering glass, and breaking wood. Ever so slowly, with a cloud of debris mushrooming up around it, a hole opened up in the roof, and the car disappeared inside.

The house quivered again, almost as if it were made of Jell-O, then as the car crashed through from the second floor to the first—taking a bearing wall with it—the front of the house seemed to pucker and wrinkle as the upper rafters fell over into one another. It reminded me of the collapse of a house of cards.

The other cop and I stood transfixed. When the dust cleared, I think I expected the whole house to be flat, but it wasn't. It was crooked and out of focus, but the outer walls were still standing while smoke curled from the tilting fireplace.

I was still standing there dumbstruck when the other cop found his voice. "I'll tell you what," he said wonderingly, "they don't build 'em like that anymore!"

His words and the sudden wailing of a car horn functioned like a pistol shot at the beginning of a race. We both headed for the stairs. I must have looked like a brown-caped superman with Grace Highsmith's blanket billowing out behind me as I started down. On the second step, I lost my balance when I tripped over a tangle of twisted pipe from a demolished section of handrail. If the guy pounding down the stairs behind me hadn't managed to grab me by one flailing arm, I might have broken my neck.

The only reality for me, right then, was the honking horn—the hauntingly god-awful wail of it. Anyone who has ever witnessed an auto accident and heard that terrible sound knows all too well what it means. Those old horn rings don't work unless something is pressing on them. In the aftermath of a serious accident, that *something* is usually someone's body—someone's *broken* body.

When we reached the bottom of the stairs, I looked around for a way to get into the house. Head-high debris spilled out the ground-floor windows and doors.

For a moment, we stood indecisively on what was left of the wraparound front porch and looked at one another. The cop, who had managed to remain focused on the armed standoff part of the problem, was still carrying his drawn gun. Mine was put away.

"Let's try the other side," he suggested. "I'll cover you."

Until that moment, my only thoughts had been of Grace Highsmith and the infernal horn. Now, as we picked our way along the uneven, broken porch, I, too, remembered Bill Whitten. Was it hours earlier or only minutes when Grace Highsmith had referred to him as a vicious dog? What had made her decide to take the law into her own hands and attempt to put him out of his misery herself?

For some reason, the window over the kitchen sink was relatively clear. I climbed in.

"What if something blows up?" the other guy asked me, as I reached back and helped pull him in. For the first time, I caught a glimpse of his name tag—Officer Smith. Hell of a name for a hero.

"Good point," I said. "The living room's that way. There's a fire in the fireplace. We'd better try to put it out, especially if there's gasoline leaking from that Cadillac."

There was no sense in thinking about it any further. We were already in the house. Backing down then would have been unthinkable, especially with the horn still honking.

"You look for the woman," Officer Smith said. "I'll handle the fire. Here's a flashlight."

"Grace!" I shouted, pointing the frail beam off into the dark and dusty interior of the house. "Grace Highsmith! Can you hear me?"

Tripping and stumbling, we fought our way through the darkened kitchen. We scrambled up and over a huge pile of unidentifiable crap that reached almost to a nonexistent ceiling. And just on the other side of the mountain of debris, nose-down into the floor of what had once been the front entry, sat the remains of Grace Highsmith's Cadillac. With Grace still belted inside.

"Grace?" I shouted again. I braced myself against the crumpled flank of the car and climbed the jumbled wreckage of shattered plaster, lath, shingle, and demolished furniture. "Grace?"

I landed on something soft, a mattress or some kind of cushion, and aimed the flashlight in through the destroyed driver's-side window. I saw Grace Highsmith then, bloodied and broken. Her glasses were gone and so were her teeth. Until that very moment, I don't think I had realized that she wore false teeth.

The force of the crash had pushed the whole engine block back through the fire wall and into

the passenger compartment. Grace sat there up-
right, crushed into a tiny corner of what had once
been a spacious front seat. Small as she was, I
knew that corner of the car was far too small to
hold a human body; too small for that body to
come out alive.

The horn was still screeching. Guided by some
kind of higher power, I reached into the incredible tangle of metal and wire and pulled for all I
was worth. It was a miracle. My first yank shut
down that infernal noise.

In the eerie silence that followed, I became
aware of the steady drip of leaking gas, but by
then, Officer Smith had found water somewhere
and was already dousing the remains of the
flames which, amazingly, were still confined to
the fireplace.

"Grace," I said, "can you hear me?"

She opened her eyes at once and squinted at
me. "Detective Beaumont," she said, more lucidly
than seemed possible. "Thank you . . . for thut-
ting off . . . that awful racket."

Without teeth, she was hard to understand. "Be
quiet," I said. "Don't waste your strength."

But this was Grace Highsmith I was talking to.
Even on the point of death, why would she
bother to listen to anyone else, most especially
me?

"Did . . . I get . . . him?" she asked. Her voice
was fainter now.

I looked around. There were other cops and
other flashlights scrambling into the wreckage

now. I could see no sign of Bill Whitten, but that didn't mean he was dead. I didn't want to tell Grace that, though.

"Yes," I said. "You got him."

"Good." When she smiled a toothless smile, an ugly streak of bloody spittle dribbled out of the corner of her mouth. I took out my handkerchief and did my best to wipe it away.

"Tell Latty . . ." Grace paused. For a moment, I didn't think she'd be able to go on.

"Tell her what?" I urged. "Tell Latty what?"

"To take . . ."

She said something unintelligible then.

"Take what?"

"Duthty," she repeated. "Duthty, Duthty, Duthty."

"Oh, you mean *Dusty*. The statue."

Relieved, she nodded. "And tell her that my foot . . ."

Again she stopped. I waited to see if she would speak again.

"What about your foot?"

"It mutht have thlipped."

And that was it. She was gone. I reached for something to cover her with, but of course, the blanket had long since disappeared. All I had to offer was my own ragged jacket.

Some minutes later—I don't have any idea how many—I was still crouched there beside her with tears streaming down my face when Officer Smith came to get me.

"Come on, fella," he said. "There's nothing more you can do for her here."

# Twenty-three

The aftermath of something like that is almost as nightmarish as the event itself. Officer Smith—everybody else called him Smitty—along with another flashlight-wielding Kirkland cop, found Bill Whitten, what was left of him, sticking out from under what had once been the front door. He had evidently been hiding in the entryway. Without knowing it, I had told Grace Highsmith the truth. Her chosen trajectory through the middle of the house had scored a direct hit.

Smitty and I were up by the van, debriefing the unit commander when another uniformed young patrol officer came hurrying up to us. "The canine unit just found a woman, hiding down along the beach. They're bringing her up through a neighbor's yard."

Moments later, a scratched, bleeding, and handcuffed Deanna Compton was led into the command-post circle. "Mrs. Compton!" I said.

Captain Miller, the emergency response team commander, looked at me sharply. "You know this woman?"

"She was Bill Whitten's secretary."

"For a secretary, she put up a hell of a fight," the officer with her said. "If we hadn't had the dog, she might have gotten away."

"What do you have to do with all this?" Captain Miller asked.

"I want an attorney," Deanna Compton said.

"We'll see if we can't get you one," the captain replied. "Just as soon as we finish cleaning up some of the mess. Lock her in a patrol car until we're ready to deal with the paperwork."

"Sir?" another officer said, speaking from outside the tight little circle.

Captain Miller turned to face him. "What now?"

"There's a Bellevue cop just up the road. He wants to come down. He has a woman with him. He says she's the dead woman's niece."

"That's most likely Detective Blaine," I said quickly. "The niece is Latty Gibson."

"You know them?" Miller asked me.

"Blaine's been working this case with me. It's a joint operation."

Miller shook his head. "Sounds like everybody and his uncle knew what was going on," he grumbled. "Everyone but us, that is. Let 'em through."

A few minutes later, Latty Gibson came stumbling into the light, followed by Tim Blaine. She came straight to me. "Aunt Grace?" she asked.

I shook my head. "I'm sorry."

Without another word, Latty collapsed sobbing in Tim Blaine's willing arms. And as he stood there, holding her and patting her shoulder in that useless way men do when they don't know what the hell else to do with their hands, I had a sudden flash of insight.

Latty didn't know it yet, because she had no idea Grace Highsmith had revised her will. And Tim Blaine didn't know it yet, because the men involved are always the last ones to figure it out. But I had a very strong suspicion that the number of independently wealthy homicide detectives in King County was about to increase 100 percent.

I turned to Captain Miller. "There's an important piece of artwork down in the house," I said. "A statue. We've got to move it out tonight."

"The hell we do. It can stay there until morning."

"No," I said. "This is a very valuable piece. I don't think you want to be legally responsible for it. Grace was talking about it just before she died."

Miller glowered at me. "Is the damned thing even still there?"

"Yes," I said. "I saw it while we were looking for Bill Whitten's body."

"Well, take somebody with you and go get it then."

I ended up taking Smitty and another Kirkland

cop. Armed with flashlights, we made our way
back into the building. Dusty was heavy enough
that it took both of them to lift it. As soon as they
did, several pieces of paper, taped to the base of
the statue, waved like flags in the wind.

The papers turned out to be Virginia Marks' fax
to Grace Highsmith. I tore them loose and read
the first few sentences by flashlight, standing in
the wreckage of Grace's demolished home.

Daniel James Wilkes, aka Donald R.
Wolf, was a disbarred patent attorney
who used to specialize in biotech prod-
ucts. Until May of this year, Dan Wilkes
was living in a pay-by-the-week motel in
Las Vegas, Nevada. Early in April, there
was an international biotech convention
in Las Vegas. Bill Whitten was in atten-
dance at that meeting. Wilkes disappeared from Vegas two weeks later and
resurfaced in San Diego, California,
early in June. When he reappeared, he
had a new name, a new car, and a new
wardrobe. With more digging, I believe
we'll be able to verify that Wilkes and
Whitten had an employee/employer relationship as early as the beginning of
June.

"Hey, Beaumont," Smitty growled. "Bring that
flashlight and come on. This thing is heavy as all
hell."

Folding the papers, I stuffed them in my pocket. Virginia Marks had been one hell of a detective after all. This was information we would all need as we unraveled the strings of our several interconnected cases—starting with Captain Miller of the Kirkland police and working our way back across Lake Washington.

"I'm coming," I said.

I followed Dusty's slow progress as the two laboring officers carried the heavy bronze up the debris-littered stairs. When they reached the top, they set *The End of the Trail* down. "Where to now?" one of them asked.

"I'll take it," Tim Blaine said, lifting it single-handedly and looking to Latty to see where she wanted him to carry it. "It belongs to the little lady here."

*And so do you, you dimwit*, I thought. *And so do you.*

# Twenty-four

It was six o'clock the next morning by the time Peters and I finally dragged our weary butts back home. My Rollaboard suitcase was already packed and sitting by the door.

"Your plane's at nine o'clock," Ralph Ames said. "You could maybe even grab two winks."

"I can sleep on the plane. What I can't get in the air is a decent breakfast."

"You hit the shower," Ralph told me. "By the time you're dressed, breakfast will be ready."

When I finished dressing and came back out to the kitchen, coffee was made and two matching waffle irons sat warming on my counter. With a phone to his ear and evidently waiting on hold, Ralph was mixing up waffle batter.

"Where did those come from?" I asked, indicating the waffle irons as I poured myself a cup of coffee. "I don't own any waffle irons."

Ralph grinned. "You do now," he said. "It's a bread-and-butter gift. I suppose I should say a waffle-and-butter gift."

I started to say something else, but whoever had put him on hold must have come back on the line. "I'm here," he said. "Go ahead."

Leaving him a little privacy, I went into the living room and sat down on the recliner. I was dog-assed tired. I fell sound asleep and Ralph had to wake me when the waffles were ready. Over breakfast—the waffles were delicious—I gave him the highlights of the previous night's activities. Telling him about Ron's part in the proceedings reminded me of something else.

"What about Hilda Chisholm?" I asked him.

"Oh, that," he said. "That's who I was on the phone about when you came out of the shower. Do you remember someone by the name of Arnold Duckworth?"

"Not that I know of. Should I?"

"You evidently sent him to the slammer a few years back. He and his partner had a lucrative business growing pot in the basement of a house over in the University District. They got into some kind of beef and Arnold beat the other guy to death with a shovel. You nailed him for second-degree murder. He's still in prison up in Monroe."

"What does Arnold Duckworth have to do with Hilda Chisholm?"

"He's Hilda's brother, her baby brother."

I choked on a tiny sip of coffee. "Are you kidding?"

"Not at all. What you told me this woman was doing was so far off the charts that there had to be something to it. I did some behind-the-scenes checking. We're not altogether out of the woods on this thing. There'll still be an investigation, of course, but you can be reasonably certain that Hilda Chisholm won't be running the show. I shouldn't have any difficulty convincing Child Protective Services that she has a serious conflict of interest here. You go on down to California and let me worry about it."

For a minute or so after he finished talking, I just sat there staring at him.

"Is something wrong?" he asked finally.

"Nothing's wrong," I returned. "Not a damned thing."

# Epilogue

With Hilda Chisholm off my back, I headed for California. As the plane left Sea-Tac Airport, I was wondering if Sam Arnold and Ron Peters would be able to finish nailing Deanna Compton without either Detective Kramer's and my totally indispensable help. Hard as it is for me to admit it, Seattle P.D. did just fine. Arnold, Ron, and several others eventually uncovered the fact that all the while Wolf had been bringing in the investment money, expecting to end up with part ownership of an important company as his reward, Bill Whitten and Deanna Compton had been gathering the monies into a separate fund.

When Don Wolf figured that out and was preparing to take that information to the D.G.I. board of directors, Whitten and Compton decided to get rid of him and his proof as well. Lizbeth Wolf, sick with pneumonia and sound asleep in her husband's apartment, was an accidental victim—somebody who died for no other reason than being in the wrong place at the wrong time.

In the days after the murders of both Don and Lizbeth Wolf, Whitten and his lady love Deanna had been transferring funds out of the country—to Colombia. Their airplane tickets, had they ever had a chance to use them, would have transferred them there as well. And with Latty Gibson as a likely suspect to take the murder rap, they might have gotten away with it, had it not been for Virginia Marks and Grace Highsmith.

The private detective's investigation had come far too close to the truth, necessitating her death as well. And Grace, by virtue of having access to Virginia's findings, had also been targeted. I had to give Grace Highsmith credit for her single-minded determination to protect Latty from all comers, cops and killers alike.

By the time somebody finally got around to charging Deanna Compton for her part in the three murders; by the time they charged her with the theft of Lizbeth Wolf's engagement ring, which Deanna Compton was still wearing at the time of her arrest; by the time they finally located Don Wolf/Daniel James Wilkes' real family who, even after all those years, still lived in Tulsa, Oklahoma—I had long since stopped thinking about the case. By then, I had been in California for a week and a half and was far too preoccupied with more important things.

Hospitals are for people who are sick and plan

to get better. Hospices are for people who are sick and plan to die. You'd expect that the latter would be very depressing places, but for some strange reason, they aren't. Once somebody's sick enough to be in a hospice, most of the masks come off. People are free to be who and what they really are, at least that's how it seemed to work with Karen.

Her room was sunny and warm. It overlooked an immaculately kept expanse of lawn dotted with graceful palm trees. There were brilliantly colored flower beds all around. Patio doors opened out on a vividly vital world where a perpetually filled bird feeder brought a never-ending parade of feathered visitors. Sometimes, when I was sitting there in that dazzlingly bright room during my allotted visiting hours, we would go for thirty minutes at a time without saying a word.

"Birds are fascinating," I said one day. "I wonder why I've never noticed them before."

"Because you never took the time," Karen said.

My experience with my mother's final illness had been so appallingly awful, that coming into it, I didn't know if I'd be able to handle being around Karen at all. Cancer is a ruthless opponent, no matter what, but I learned that the philosophy of treatment has come a long way since my mother's time. Maybe it doesn't work exactly the same way everywhere, but in the hospice facility in Rancho Cucamonga, Karen got to call the shots. Literally. I think there were times when she chose to decrease her medication dosages, opting for lucidity over pain control. I'm not sure that given the same circumstances, I would have been tough enough to make the same choices myself, but I blessed her for it. It gave us a chance to talk, to say things that had needed saying. For years.

"Time," she murmured thoughtfully a long time later. "That's why I divorced you, you know."

It was simply a statement of fact. There was no anger or accusation, no acrimony, and no self-pity, either. What goes on in hospices leaves no strength or energy to drag around any unnecessary emotional baggage.

"I know," I said. "With the job and all there was never enough of that."

Karen smiled. "With the job and the booze there was never enough time for me," she corrected.

But this wasn't a fight. It was a conversation. I didn't bother to say I was sorry, because we both knew I was.

"Did you know I fell off the wagon a couple of days ago?" I asked a few minutes later.

"No, but you got back on, didn't you?"

"Yes."

"Good."

More time passed. An hour, maybe. I believe she slept for a while, but when she woke up again, she resumed the conversation, almost in midthought. "When I found Dave, Beau, I couldn't believe my luck. From the moment we met, he always put me first."

"He's a good guy," I acknowledged without rancor. "A real good guy."

"But I'm worried about him," Karen said.

"Worried? Why?"

"Because I'm afraid he'll be lost without me. I'm afraid he'll fall apart."

"He'll be fine, Karen," I reassured her. "He's a smart man, a solid man."

"But you'll look out for him, won't you?"

"Yes," I said. "I'll do my best."

Dave showed up a little while later. It was his time. We had divided up the days so that one or the other of the kids was there in the mornings, I took the afternoon shift, and Dave did the evenings.

That was the last time I talked to her. By noon the next day, Karen Beaumont Livingston had drifted into a coma. I stayed away after that. From then on, Dave and Kelly and Scott were at her side around the clock, and rightfully so. Three nights later, Dave came home at eleven o'clock—early for him. His eyes were red; his hair was standing on end.

"It's over," he said. "Mind if I have a drink?"

"Go ahead," I said. "Help yourself."

"I knew it was coming," he said a few minutes later. "I thought I was prepared. But I'm not. I feel so lost. What am I going to do?" Unchecked tears streamed down his face as he turned away from me.

"You'll be all right, Dave," I told him. "That's what families are for. And friends."